Serah of the Runners

Book 4 in the Chronicles of the Great Migration

I0639834

This is a work of fiction.
Similarities to real people, places, or events are entirely coinciden-
tal, accidental, and just plain strange. Seriously, if you are one of
my characters that has started walking around... please contact me.

Serah of the Runners

First edition. March 17th 2020
Copyright © 2020 Michael Kilman.
Publisher: Loridian's Laboratory LLC
ISBN: 9781732357679
Written by Michael Kilman
Cover Illustrated by:
Rebecca Blissett
https://blestian.art/
Title Design:
Desiree Byrd
Edited By:
Chelsea Strabala

Also by Michael Kilman
Chronicles of the Great Migration
Book 1: Mimi of the Nowhere
Book 2: Upon Stilted Cities: The Winds of Change
Book 3: Upon Stilted Cities: The Battle for Langeles

Dedication:

TO MY WONDERFUL CHILDREN, sometimes the best thing to do in dififcult times is to look inward and find your own truth.

Chapter 1
A Long Way Down

F rank walked back down the corridor toward his station. It was time to get back to work. With Saud destroyed, the last thing Manhatsten needed right now was a clogged recycling system. Work was good at times like this. There were still rumors of a few of those strange battles on the streets, but any sanitation worker knew the networks of tunnels just below the surface of the city, and so they avoided the conflict. Even when the city was in chaos, sanitation still had to do its job.

Jenny said, "So what do you think will happen now, Frank?"

"Don't know. Never survived a war between cities before. I ain't that old."

Zelda said, "Can you believe how fast we're moving since Saud blew up? I never knew the city could move like that."

The motion of the city shifted. Frank grabbed a guard rail and steadied himself. Both of the women did the same. The city was stopping. After several moments of silence, Frank let go of the rail and resumed his trek down the corridor.

"Speak of the devil, huh?" Frank scratched his head. "The city isn't supposed to be able to move that fast, I don't think. But, maybe someone in the Uppers figured something out."

Zelda said, "I wonder why the hell they stopped in the middle of a storm warning."

Jenny said, "Maybe the battle isn't over?"

Frank replied, "What do you mean? Everyone saw that blast from Saud. They're just mopping up the few that got inside now."

Zelda stopped in the middle of the hallway. "Frank."

Frank turned. Jenny was several steps behind Zelda and also paused. "Yeah?"

"Frank... have you ever heard of a city blowing up like that before?"

Frank thought about it. He thought of all the stories and the vid screen films about battles with other cities. He thought about how they used those giant guns and how they took shots at each other's shields. But now that Zelda had pointed it out, he couldn't remember a city ever becoming a giant ball of light and disappearing all at once. He was sure he wouldn't have believed it himself if he hadn't seen the thing with his own eyes.

"No... No, I don't think so."

Zelda frowned. "Something's wrong Frank. I can feel it in my gut. Why else would we stop in the middle of a storm warning? Ain't never happened before as far as I know."

They fell silent and resumed walking and entered central sanitation. The dank air was familiar and comforting to Frank. A lot of people complained about working in sanitation, but he loved it. Did he wish the pay was a little better? Sure, but the job was just fine. He didn't mind getting dirty. It was a job worth doing, a job to feel useful; a job that if it didn't get done, it would cost lives. A man couldn't ask for a job more important than that. He was necessary, and that was satisfying.

They only needed to do a routine check. There was a full crew working already, but with the battle, Frank wanted to be sure there weren't any other hidden problems. Michael, Andrea, and Scott were working hard. When they saw the trio, Frank askcd, "How's it going down here? Any surprises?"

Michael shook his head, and his long beard waggled back and forth below his chin. "Nah. Everything's running like clockwork. Andrea had to climb up into one of the pipes and deal with a blockage, but other than that, nada."

Frank glanced over Michael's shoulder at Andrea, who looked surprisingly clean for climbing up inside a pipe.

"How'd you get out clean?"

Andrea's dark eyes regarded Frank. He knew she hated his guts, but he couldn't understand why. Might have been something to do with the fact that she had the sense of humor like an angry hedge-hog. "I already went through decon."

"Ah. You lose a toss or something?"

"No, I volunteered." Her words were sharp and curt.

Frank nodded and looked around. "Jenny, will you head back and check on the bio recycler?"

Michael said, "I think Scott's back there already."

Frank responded, "Yeah, doesn't hurt to have two eyes on it, though, does it?"

Michael shrugged. "Sure thing, boss."

For a little while, Michael and Frank caught up while Zelda and Jenny double-checked everything. There was tension between the two teams; there always was. Michael liked Frank okay, but he hated Zelda. Andrea hated Frank, and Jenny, after bawling her eyes out over Jose, had slept with Scott, and the aftermath was less than ideal. He was hoping that sending Jenny back with Scott would force them to talk things out a little, but that was probably unrealistic.

When Frank was satisfied that everything was in order, he called Jenny and Zelda and bid farewell to the other team. The three of them would be back on the clock in another nine hours again, and so there was no point in lingering too long.

The trio walked up the corridor for several dozen meters in silence. Frank took the lead. He thought maybe Jenny would have something to say to Zelda about Scott and wanted to give them both a little room.

It was Jenny that broke the silence, "I've been thinking..."

In the silence of Jenny's pause, Zelda said, "You and Scott get things figured out?"

Jenny's eyes were glassy but cleared for a moment as she looked up and over at Zelda. "What? No, nothing to do with that. Scott is... Never mind."

Frank turned and, walking backward, said, "What then?"

Jenny said, "I was thinking about what we were talking about before, been thinking about it a lot. A city shouldn't blow up like that. It's not right."

Frank said, "Why's that?"

"We learned all about city combat in scholar school."

"You went to scholar school?" asked Frank.

"Yeah... but I dropped out. I was... I studied city mechanics. I wanted to be a shield engineer; you know, one of those people who jumps around on those harnesses checking the shield ribs for energy fluctuations? But well... there was an accident when we were up one day... and I couldn't go back..."

Jenny leaned against the wall, grabbing for something to hold on to, as if the terrible thing was happening all over again. Frank had seen that look before in Jose's eyes, how they grew like deep wells of pain overflowing with something dark and sticky, something he couldn't ever really escape. He supposed maybe that's why Jenny had liked Jose so much; she saw something familiar in him, a shared experience of horror and trauma.

Zelda changed the subject. "So, why shouldn't a city blow up like that?"

The light came back into Jenny's eyes. She blinked. She said, "Because cities are too big to blow up at once... unless..."

Frank said, "Unless what?"

"Unless they destroyed the core."

"The core?"

"Yeah, you know, the power core that makes all cities function. Our professor told us it's like a miniature sun. But, she also said that it was near impossible to destroy."

"Why's that?"

"Because the architects planned for just about everything. She said that another city could shoot at the core's location for a year and they would never get to it. The whole core is encased in Solid-sonium and a second internal EnViro shield. You'd have to destroy both things at the same time, and that's supposed to be impossible from the outside."

Zelda said, "So wait, what you're telling us is that Manhatsten didn't win the battle?"

Jenny said, "No... at least not by attacking from the outside."

There was silence for a moment. Frank felt his gut clench.

He said, "Jenny, what could destroy a core?"

"Our professor said that only two things could destroy one. The first was a critical overload. But, you'd have to be an architect for that, only they know the codes and the exact sequence required to start the process. And we only have one architect left, and I don't see him going over to Saud in the middle of a battle with no way back, do you?"

Frank and Zelda shook their head in unison.

Zelda said, "And the other one?"

Jenny said, "It's also not possible."

Zelda said, "Why not?"

"Because you would need an atomic weapon and you'd have to detonate it inside of the core past both the Solidsonium and the EnViro shield. But that can't happen."

Frank said, "No?"

"Well again, you'd need to have access, so you'd have to be a high ranking person inside the city in the first place. Second, no one has even seen an atomic weapon in a thousand years. We think maybe the architects purposely made sure they were gone and buried before the cities started walking. They didn't want humans lobbing nukes at each other once the inevitable conflict started. They were trying to get the environment to heal, and a weapon like that would make things far worse.

Frank opened his mouth to speak, but it Zelda cut him off. "But what if someone found one?"

No one spoke for a moment. That tightness in Frank's chest grew. Then he said, "You don't think there's one of those on Manhatsten do you? Like, if we did that to Saud, couldn't they do it to us?"

Jenny said, "I don't know. I mean, we are the good guys, aren't we? Didn't Saud attack us first?"

But no one ever had the chance to answer that question. The whole of the city shifted. It was as if some angry deity had picked the city up and lurched it hard sideways, shaking all the domed contents within like a snow globe. All three slammed against the wall, and Frank felt a blinding pain on the side of his head. Everything went black for a moment.

He scrambled around, his hands clawing for something to grasp. Frank grabbed the rail leading up the stairs. The whole of the city shook. With Saud gone, what the hell was happening? Was it the core? Was the same thing happening to them as it had in Saud? But that didn't seem right. Saud had vanished almost instantly, and the fragments had scattered to the four winds.

Something was wrong with the city. The floor was tilting, and he felt the weight of gravity tugging at his back. He didn't know how he knew, but the city was falling. Something had knocked them over or had destroyed the legs.

"Zelda!"

"Right here." Frank looked back and saw the familiar outline of Zelda's thin, birdlike form. She was clinging to the railing now too.

"Is Jenny back there?"

"Here, Frank."

"Good, we gotta get out of here. I think the city is falling..."

Neither of the women contested this point. It was the only explanation. A massive jolt and suddenly, the floor shifts? The only thing that could do that was the city falling over.

The tug of gravity grew, an irresistible mistress. It took all of Franks effort to hold on. The stairway had disappeared below him. He was dangling; the pull on his large belly was immense.

Jenny screamed, but Frank couldn't turn around. His entire focus was on holding the railing. He had no idea how much longer he could hold on. The angle grew deeper with every passing moment, and it was all he could do to keep from falling back into the long corridor that led to the heart of central sanitation. How far was he from the door that led inside? He didn't want to find out.

"I got you," said, Zelda. But again, Frank couldn't look back.

"Zelda, you gotta get you and Jenny around me somehow. I..."

"You're not gonna fall, Frank. We won't let you."

"Yeah well, you always warned me this gut was gonna get me killed, and it looks like you're right. I can't hold on much longer, especially since it's almost a straight drop now."

Frank knew if the city was falling, it didn't matter. They could all die now, or they would die later when the shield failed, or a storm came, or in a hundred other terrible ways. But the survival instinct in Frank made him hold on, made him grip tight. If nothing else, he wanted to see his wife one last time before he died and he couldn't do that if he let go.

Frank felt his fingers slipping.

"Dammit, ladies. You gotta get around me or get to the other railing or something. You don't want to be underneath me if I fall."

Jenny wept. Frank was glad to hear it, it meant she was still there, still alive, still holding on tight.

Zelda said, "No, Frank. I've been at this too long with you. If you go down, we go down together."

Jenny's sobs increased, and through mumbles and tears, she said, "I don't want to die."

Frank tried to adjust his grip, but he lost one of his hands off the railing. Later, he would wonder how the hell he managed to swing his arm back up and grab hold again, but for now, as his whole body reached back up, he felt a sense of comfort in reestablishing his grip.

"Frank, don't you dare let go. Your wife would never let me hear the end of it."

"Yeah, yeah. I'm doing my best, but please Zelda, get you and Jenny across or around me. I can't do this much longer."

The city dipped forward, and now they were hanging vertically down the stairwell.

Zelda said, "Shit. Well..." she shifted her grip, and now Frank could see both Zelda and Jenny fighting to hold on.

Tears streaked down the side of Jenny's face. At that moment, he was glad they were both petite women. It made it easier for them to hold on longer. He, however, wasn't going to be able to do it.

Zelda said, "Well, you don't have to worry about knocking us down now do you?"

Frank said, "Guess not. Guess we gotta play the game like in school, huh? Who can hold on the longest?"

Zelda said, "Ha, you're screwed then Frank, I always won that game."

Even at that moment, Frank couldn't help but crack a smile. Here they were dangling down what had to be several dozen stories of corridor, and he couldn't help but grin. He guessed that even if he didn't die today, he would probably die grinning and laughing.

His arms trembled from the strain. The metal of the square railing dug into his fingers, leaving deep grooves bright with pain.

"Zelda."

She looked up at him, a grave expression on her face.

"Zelda, you're the best friend a man could ask for, you know that?"

"Don't let go Frank." Her voice shook. "Please don't."

"I don't wanna, but let me say this. It's been an honor working with you all these years, Zelda." The noise of cities tremors echoed up and down the corridor, and Frank had to raise his voice.

"I couldn't have asked for a better friend at work. And you, Jenny, I wish I had the chance to get to know ya a little better." He readjusted his grip, but he could feel his fingers slipping. His right hand was numb, and his left a blazing fire. "It's been great working with both of you. I only wish I could see Jose's dopey face one last time."

"Hold on Frank; we'll figure a way out of this. We always do."

But Frank's fingers couldn't do it anymore. His arms had never felt strain quite like that. No matter how hard he wanted to hang on, he couldn't. There would be no grabbing hold again this time.

"Goodbye Zelda. Hang on as long as you can. Tell my wife I love her, alright?"

He let go.

He started to fall. There was a sense of freedom in it. He thought for a moment that maybe if everyone had just learned to let go like he just did, that maybe, just maybe the world would be a little happier.

He looked down and watched as the corridor stretched out before him. It seemed to take an age to fall. Time stretched like the entire lifetime of the universe was available to him now to think about all the things he loved about his life and all the things he regretted. First, his fondest memories flooded him. He thought of the lifetime of laughter and friends and family. Then he thought of Jose. He thought about how helpless he felt when he saw the SO's arresting him. He thought about the last uprising and how so many people he knew were sentenced to the Runnercore or were killed, all because of the greed in the city. He wished he had been more outspoken, or that he had done something to change their fates. Frank wished that he had taken a stand and right there, he promised himself that if somehow he survived the fall, he would stand and be true. It was too late now though, wasn't it? The ground was rushing up toward him, and in a few seconds, his life would be over.

But then all motion stopped. For a moment, Frank thought he had hit the other end of the corridor, but looking around, he realized that he was hovering, mid-air. Nervous about his strange circumstances, Frank looked around for something to hold on to, but there was only the concrete wall. His stomach flipped, as it did in childhood when his father tossed him into the air. Then, he dropped to the floor, the actual floor. For Frank, the sweet comfort of stability on the ground married with the pain of his short fall.

He lay on his back, checking himself. His ass and his pride were bruised, but he had barely fallen a meter. What the hell had happened? Shouldn't they all be crushed under the weight of the collapsed city?

He heard footsteps and saw that both women were running toward him.

"Frank, you asshole." Zelda's voice shook, and there were tears down her cheeks. And then Zelda's arms were around him, and then Jenny's, and the three of them cried together. They were alive. The city was alive. They didn't know what happened, but somehow everything was okay, at least for now.

2.

Dear Reader,
The lesson that Frank learned in those few moments when he expected death would stick

with him through the coming days, and the coming battles. For difficult times were ahead, and Frank would lose many of those he loved and cared about before it was all over.

When great change comes, it tears things asunder, it uproots the old and leaves us gasping and injured and exposed. In those times, we are raw nerves, bare roots, open flesh. But if we are willing, we can get up again. We have the chance to go forward into the world and take what we have learned and lost with us. Then, we may bandage our wounds and look often at our scars so that we do not make the same mistakes again.

See Frank now; see him for what he is. He is an ordinary man in extraordinary times. But in so many ways, it is the ordinary we need. Hope lay in the courage and the strength and the will to move forward in the ordinary so that we can give birth to the new."

Matron Mariposa Phillips 833.12.13 I.S.

3.

They surfaced. Something was wrong with the light. Frank looked around. One of the buildings was leaning into another. Luckily, it was one of the shorter ones. People were scrambling out the front door before it collapsed, but most looked like they were okay. There were fresh cracks in the street, some as wide as a person. Everyone was outside. Many of those on the concrete and earth stood dazed and confused, statues frozen mid-moment like in the ancient city of Pompei. They were puzzled slices of life.

There were several fires, and a few people were doing their best to put them out. The old automated fire systems were working, but barely. Frank swore. They would have to go back and check the water pressure to ensure that there wasn't a clog. If too much smoke filled the city...

Then, some of the gazes cast upward. People pointed up toward the EnViro shield. A conspiracy of whispers and hushed voices bathed the city in rapturous awe. They grew to mumbles and mutters in a slow drone. Someone screamed. Frank looked over and saw a woman fall to the ground. She hugged the earth as if it were her child, and she was saying goodbye to for the final time.

"Frank." Even Zelda whispered. "Frank, what the hell is that?"

Frank traced the end of her finger skyward. His mouth opened to say something but then closed again. He felt vertigo and the sensation of the ground falling out from under him. He grabbed for Zelda and Jenny.

Jenny, clinging to him said, "That's... that's..."

Frank grabbed his chest. That terrible tightness was back, but this time, it shot down his arm. He fell to his knees, barely feeling the impact of bone on concrete as the shock rippled upward.

"Frank?"

Zelda was on him in a moment. "Frank, what is it?"

"I think... I think I'm having a heart attack."

Jenny moaned. It was a loud and long wail. "That's..."

Zelda helped lay Frank down gently. "We gotta get you to an alcove Frank. There's an emergency one a few blocks away."

Frank just nodded and laid on his back. The pain was less now, but there was a fog settling in over his mind. He stared up at the sky, drinking in the new and terrible view.

Jenny shouted. "Oh Gods. That's earth. It's earth. It's earth. Why is earth in the sky?"

Jenny, too, fell to her knees and wept.

Frank watched the earth. He watched as it started to grow smaller in the sky. They were moving away from it now. To where, was anyone's guess.

Chapter 2
A Shadow on Luna

"So that's it?"

Kirka stood looking at her console. Her brown hair held streaks of gray and her short, slender form shaped by the low gravity of Luna and a lifetime of food rations hovered just above her chair. Her sharp nose and hollow cheeks deepened the power of the gaze from her gray eyes.

"That's it," said Loni.

Loni was her opposite, short with darker skin and light hazel eyes. Everything about Loni was round. Kirka had always wondered how, despite the lack of gravity of Luna, Loni had stayed so healthy and thick. Most Lunites were thin and wispy, but Loni, considered one of the most beautiful women of Luna, had her pick of all the men with her curvy, feminine form.

The end was coming now. The image on the screen showed streaks of light, flaming arrows ready to end their world in fire. Most of the Lunites had no knowledge of their fate. But now, Kirka and Loni did. There were rumors, of course, hints that ROAM's hostility had finally reached a critical point. Doomsday prophets preached from every corner that Kirka would let them. Of course, with such a small population, people didn't pay them much mind, especially since the commons was only a twelve hundred meters long in the underground of Luna.

Kirka said, "Dammit, how could do they do this to us? After all we've done for them. They wouldn't exist without all of our efforts. Years of work and neither of us have anything to show for it.

Loni said, "They're jealous; they've always been jealous, Commander."

"I can't believe I didn't see this coming. I should have been suspicious when our delegation never arrived at their destination."

"You don't think it was an accident, do you?"

"I had my doubts, but now I see that all they wanted was our Solidsonium."

Loni said, "I don't think most of ROAM knew what was happening and, well, it's not like we could skim that asshole, Ithica from here, is it? He was probably planning this the whole time. Maybe only a few in his inner circle knew. Most of the Martians seemed open to long-standing trade, and I know at least a dozen people who were ready to migrate over there."

Kirka shook her head. "We should have known when Ithaca won that election. All that talk of purity, and now..."

Loni said, "I can't believe there's so much hate for telepaths there."

To say that there was hatred for telepaths on ROAM might have been an understatement. When they had first learned that nearly a quarter of Luna 1 and Luna 2 were telepaths, and that the entire power structure of Luna surrounded telepathy, ROAM had stopped transmitting to Luna for two months. It seemed in that time that the key issue of the bi-annual elections on ROAM centered on what to do about Luna. Of course, it was Luna who needed ROAM more than ROAM needed Luna, especially now that all of Luna's ships were filled with Solidsonium and more than halfway to ROAM. It was as if the moment they had launched aid to their neighbors, the doors had closed. Those ships were supposed to be coming back filled with parts to upgrade and repair both Luna's alcoves and food systems, something that Luna desperately needed. But now that the ships were more than halfway, there was no turning back. Even if they reversed course, it would take 37 months to return with the remaining fuel, and the pilots didn't have enough supplies to survive that long.

Kirka said, "AI, How long till impact?"

"Commander, at their current velocity, the rockets will impact Luna 1 in 13 months, 5 days, and 12 hours and Luna 2 four minutes later."

Loni said, "Should would turn the ships around?"

Kirka thought long and hard, so long that Loni repeated her question, but in direct mind to mind contact, as if Kirka hadn't heard.

"I heard you. There's no help for us. The ships would never make it back in time, and even if they did, they could only accommodate a few hundred; not even a third of our population. Plus, there are the pilots to think about, aren't there?"

Loni frowned. "What do you think they'll do to Darsee and Collin when they get to ROAM?"

"Neither of them is telepathic, so they might be okay. It's certainly better than dying of starvation, isn't it? If the ships had an alcove, then maybe it would be worth turning them around."

"And what if they decide to execute or torture them?"

The lines on Kirka's face deepened. "Even if we did call them back, where would we go?"

"There's always earth."

Kirka snorted. "You really want to go there, don't you? That has to be the fifth time in the last six months you've suggested it. Have you seen any of the latest climate reports? Things are getting worse, not better. Besides, it's not like anyone's even alive down there."

"Underground maybe?"

"Maybe. It's moot though, isn't it? It will take the ships twice as long to get back here as it will the rockets. We're done. It's over, and no doubt the stabilizers will fail, and the moon will end any chance the earth might have had for recovery."

For the centuries since the Lunar war split Luna into two discrete pieces. Kirka and the other survivors of that war had maintained the Lunar orbit above earth. Luna was on a slow decay, and the power required to stabilize the orbit in full was far beyond their reach. The best they could do was delay the orbital decay and hope like hell their best scientist, Loridian, could find a solution in the long term.

Loni said, "We should give them a choice."

"The pilots?"

Loni nodded.

Kirka ran her hand through her hair and closed her eyes for a moment. Both pilots knew in advance that this was likely a one-way trip. Both had nothing to live for on Luna, and it was why they were both chosen. They were expecting to start a life on Mars. Still, that was different from going into what was now enemy territory with no way of defending yourself.

"That's fair. They deserve to make the choice. AI?"

"Yes, Commander Kirka?"

"The next time we are in broadcast alignment for the shuttles, will you notify me so that I can send a message?"

"Yes, Commander."

Loni jumped and floated to another console, this one closer to Kirka. "When are you going to tell everyone?"

"Tell them what? That ROAM, the people that we spent so many months convincing everyone to help has betrayed us and sent rockets to destroy us?"

"Yeah, that thing."

"I don't know Loni. Do you know what it's going to do to everyone? Do you know how tense things are already? Thousands of people suddenly told they are going to die? We might tear ourselves apart before those missiles reach us."

"They have a right to know."

"They do. But how much time in advance?"

Kirka wished she had the answers, but no matter how many years she served as commander, no matter how many times the council reelected her, there was simply no easy answer here.

"I have to think about it Loni."

"And the council?"

"This is a security issue. I am in sole command of security. All those five will do is complicate the issue. Better to hold out for now."

"They'll stick you back in storage if you do that."

Kirka shrugged. "Maybe. Maybe not. I am not interested in turning those rockets into another excuse for political theater. You know how Grayson and Sanders get."

Loni nodded. "Well, don't think too hard about it. You know that's not going to help."

"I need to get some rest. I've been on for 18 hours now. AI?"

"Yes, Commander?"

"Keep all information about the incoming projectiles classified until I deem otherwise, maximum security clearance."

"Yes, commander."

2.

Historians Note to the Text:

Commander Raldaz Kirka had a long record of military service. Officially a military representative of the mid-21st century European Union, she led the war on Luna for the Europeans and Americans against the Chinese and Russians. During the day of the great split, in which a fusion core ruptured and split the moon into Luna 1 and Luna 2, Commander Kirka was severely injured and then left forgotten. She spent nearly a century inside an alcove. Upon revival, she was immediately commissioned to take control of both Luna 1 and Luna 2 which were on the verge of total collapse from high crime rates, severe food shortages, and two warring gangs. At first, she was considered a poor leader, one of strict and apathetic persuasion, but, when after only a single year, Lunites found peace and stability, her talents were recognized, and she maintained command for centuries until the conflict with ROAM and the beginning of the Great Migration.

For more on Commander Raldaz Kirka, including her published works, biography and genealogical relations to Matron Angela, visit library 34N in section 9143.

Matron Mariposa Phillips 832.1.6 I.S.

3.

Three days. For three days and nights, Kirka tossed and turned and paced and braced herself for what she needed to do. She needed to tell Luna general, needed to announce to all her people that the end was coming and that death was a certainty. She tried to discover a way out, a route toward liberation, but it seemed certain that there was no path forward. So far, she had only told Loridian, and had then spent nearly every free moment for two days grilling them on possible strategies for saving Luna. Loridian had no answers.

Now she stood on the deck of her command, one of the only spots that had an open view of the surface of Luna 2 and allowed for a view of the greater starfield, and the earth. She gazed down at the planet. Loni had been right, even a descent into the wasteland on the surface would have given some hope to the people. Even that would have provided them with an opportunity to rally around something, to cradle it and give birth to a chance. But they were denied even that.

"Commander, my long-range scopes are detecting something coming our direction."

"Yes, I know, you don't have to remind me AI."

"Commander, this object is different from the projectiles."

She walked from the window and over to her center console.

"What? Describe it."

"The object is massive and is approaching at a steady speed from the direction of the Earth."

"From Earth?"

"Yes, Commander."

"What is it?"

"At this time, that is unknown. However, it has adjusted course on several occasions since I began tracking it, which would suggest that it is a manmade object."

"How long have you been tracking it?"

"Twenty-three hours."

"And why didn't you say something about it before?"

"The parameters you set for detection of an object require that I verify whether it is a naturally occurring or a manmade if time permits."

"Fine. How big is it?"

"Exact dimensions are difficult to calculate from this distance, but it appears to be more than fifty kilometers in width and fifteen kilometers in height. I cannot tell the other dimensions from this angle."

"Too large for a ship then. AI, what's the ETA of the object?"

"Commander, at its current velocity, the object will reach Luna 2 in eighteen days, five hours and fifteen minutes."

"I want you to alert me the moment you know more; anything at all. Do you understand?"

Kirka's heart was pounding. She didn't know why, but something about this object gave her a strange sense of hope. It wasn't a natural object, so could it be one of the long lost colonies from the asteroid belt? But that didn't make any sense since it was coming from earth, did it?

"Acknowledged, Commander."

Kirka spun around in her chair and moved to her screen for a closer look. The object appeared to be some kind of oblong disc, but in the scopes it was tiny.

"AI, will you contact Loridian?"

"Commander, Luna 1 will not be in broadcast alignment for two more hours."

"Fine, alert me when it's time."

Luna 1 no longer had any way of detecting long-range threats, not after the meteor shower had damaged their scopes a few decades back, so it was up to Kirka to be the eyes and ears of Luna general.

Kirka paced back and forth. Loni was late. She was always late for a shift change, and Kirka was growing tired of that. Why had she promoted her in the first place? It's not like she didn't have others that she could have picked.

The object intrigued her. If it was making course corrections and coming from the planet, what did that mean?

"AI, what is the likelihood that this is a transport vehicle?"

"Probability is high."

"Why's that?"

"During the end of the 21st century, there was the development of technology that would be capable of moving thousands of humans into space at one time. There was also the development of the technology to move entire cities."

"We know that failed. We know cities never walked, and that it was just a pipe dream before the Lunar war made things on the surface worse."

"Commander, there is no reason to assume it failed. Just because we lost contact with the surface does not necessitate failure."

What if it was a ship or transport? Would they be able to accommodate all the Lunites? Could it be Earthlings? They had watched the earth for centuries now and had been certain that if all the population wasn't dead, that they were, at best, scattered or, more likely, underground. But their scopes weren't that powerful; everything that allowed for long-distance viewing had been destroyed during the Lunar War. The earth was just a small object in the sky. They had only discovered that ROAM was still around out of sheer dumb luck when ROAM had sent a transmission exactly as their communication array was aligned with the planet a few decades earlier.

For now, though, they would watch and wait and see what the object was. Maybe just maybe, when she announced that ROAM had sent missiles to destroy them, she would have good news as well. After all, it wasn't as if their situation could get worse than impending doom, right?

Chapter 3
Serah's Search

Another building burned. Fire crews and emergency vehicles scrambled to reach the wild inferno. The city was in a state of panic. Designated day and night didn't seem to matter much now as the sun blazed non-stop. Before, there was at least a dimming in the shield marking the difference between night and day, but like all else, everything had changed. The earth grew smaller with each passing hour. But the city moved at a snail's pace towards some unknown destination.

From a distance, Serah watched the chaos from the second level of a building. Her flaming red hair hung down to the middle of her back, and she wore a recon EnViro suit, with her helmet off. She knew the Recycled were still out there, and she'd be damned if she was caught unawares, at least for now.

Exhausted from all of her efforts to keep the city from boiling over into a full-fledged panic, she had finally given up soothing. She was never very good at it anyway.

She wished all of the sisters were around, all of them soothing the city, but most were dead and the few that might be alive were missing and scattered. The Order of the Eye was shattered. Miranda had won.

At first, people were timid and shy about looting shops. For a few days, everyone had stayed indoors in fear that the EnViro shield might collapse and they would find themselves cast out into the vacuum of space. But now that it was clear that wasn't going to happen, or at least if it did happen there was little they could do about it, people had taken to the streets, realizing that the old order of things had collapsed.

"Should we help?" Shannon walked up next to Serah. She too was wearing a suit. They were probably the only two Runners left alive.

Serah shook her head. "No, looks like the fire crews have it under control. It seems like the water pressure is back to normal."

"I don't understand. Why would someone set fire to that building?"

"Isn't it obvious?"

Shannon didn't say anything, so Serah continued.

"It's a bank. Someone wants to reset the credit system. They think that the Uppers would only store their credit information in one place. It's a foolish thought, but I guess I can't fault them on it."

"It is? But those records are stored somewhere, aren't they?"

"You'd have to kill the AI. It keeps everything backed up in all of the city's systems."

"How do you know all that?"

Serah shrugged. "I used to be one of them."

"One of who?"

"An Upper."

"What?"

"It was a long time ago. Look, Vala's around here somewhere, but she's not responding."

"Maybe she doesn't want to be found?"

"Of course, she doesn't. If I had been in the library when those things came in and survived, I'm not sure I would want to be found either."

"How many survived, Serah?"

"Do you mean in the assault on the library?"

Shannon nodded.

"Well, we know that Alexa wasn't part of that group because she had run off somewhere with Runner 17, though if they were outside the city like we think, well, they might as well be dead if they aren't already. We know that Mimi wasn't there..."

Serah stopped herself from saying more. She swallowed hard. Shannon was the last person who needed a reminder of the last moments they had seen Mimi.

The image of Mimi reaching out to them as the Recycled closed the massive door flooded Serah's mind. She hadn't been able to escape it, nearly every moment she had thought about Mimi, about how she had stabbed her to stop her from using the red veil, how Mimi had killed indiscriminately and then how the Recycled had taken her. All of it was her fault. She had told Mimi to do something, anything and then she had run Mimi through. In the end, it was her, who had let the creatures take her beyond the door. Now she was dead, or worse.

"Serah?"

Serah blinked.

"She's not dead. I know it."

Serah didn't say anything. For the last three days, she and Shannon had argued over and over about it. She didn't want to rehash the same old argument. She changed the subject.

"Well, as far as we know, only six sisters haven't been accounted for, including Vala."

What they had found in the library was disturbing. It was the kind of image she would dream about for the rest of her life. Even if she lived a thousand more years, she would see the leftover carnage of the library in her nightmares.

"Do you think we can find them all?"

"Well, Vala at least. She keeps searching for other sisters, but then she vanishes again. Every time I try to reach out to her and ask her where the hell she is, she disappears."

"Why would she do that?"

Serah turned and looked right at Shannon and didn't say a word. She skimmed Shannon; the girl didn't really seem to understand the gravity of what happened in that library, even though she had seen the aftermath with her own eyes. Shannon was barely sixty and had spent more than half of that in an alcove; of course, she couldn't comprehend the gravity of the situation.

"Shannon, if you had been in that library when the Recycled came... well, let's just say you'd never be the same again."

"So you think something's wrong with Vala?" Her voice was soft and timid.

"I think she's probably in shock. We have to find her before someone hurts her."

"Who would hurt her?"

Serah bit her tongue. She and Shannon had trained together off and on for forty years. How did she never notice how naive she was before? But then, she only saw Shannon for a few hours a month when she was training her, and they had a specific focus. So, she supposed, now that Shannon was out and about, she was seeing another side of her.

"Looters, rogue security, there are tons of people who might hurt her. Under normal circumstances, Vala could take care of herself. She's pretty formidable. Hell, Noatla assigned her to that crazy ass Senator for a reason. But I don't think she's right in the head. Every time I skim her, her mind's a jumble, a series of horrific images from what went on in the library and all kinds of other strange things mixed in I can't understand."

"So how do we find her?"

"Around this time, for the last three days, she's reached out looking for her sisters. I don't know what it is about mid-afternoon, but for some reason, she's trying then. If we can get her to give us a clue as to where she is, we can probably track her down."

"Why this spot?"

"Well, I figure this is as close to the center of the city as we can get, and from a floor up, we can see what's going on in the street without getting hung up by a bunch of crazy looting assholes."

"You don't think they will try and come up here?"

Serah looked at her for a second.

"Oh, right, your skimming thing."

"And?"

Shannon glanced down. "And I guess they would be afraid of two people in EnViro suits after the battle?"

Serah nodded.

For a while, they watched the fire crews put out the old banking building. It seemed as if the looters were given a wide birth to the firefighters and focused instead on other buildings and shops along the block. Perhaps they weren't completely mindless animals. Maybe they had specific goals and targets in mind? But that troubled Serah more. Was someone organizing this? Of all the riots she had ever seen, she had never seen them stop simply because emergency crews arrived.

There was a pulse of transmissions, a wave of connection. Serah recognized at once what it was.

"Vala?" She spoke it both out loud and also reached out. Each sister had a unique feel to their mind, the way that every person had a unique voice. It was definitely Vala.

Shannon said, "Is it Vala? Is she trying to connect to you?"

"Shhh."

Serah waited for a response. There was only the hint of pressure on the forefront of her mind, only that sense of presence. It was as if her missing sister had forgotten how to speak, how to reach out properly. Serah wondered, and not for the first time, if she might have head trauma or something worse. It certainly wasn't impossible, given the state of the library.

"Vala?" She reached out again, this time putting a bit of extra will behind her transmission.

Vala seemed to vanish, seemed to disappear into the nothingness. A deep sense of frustration rose in Serah. She clenched her jaw. Some other minds tried to crash in nearby, but Serah, with centuries of training, silenced the other minds and moved past them to search for her sister.

Then she was back again, this time strong and clear.

"Serah? Serah is that you?"

A smile bloomed on Serah's lips, and so Shannon could hear what was going on, she spoke both through mind to mind contact and out loud.

"Yes, Vala, it's me. Where you? We've been looking for you."

"It's dark, Serah. It's so cold down here."

"Okay Vala, but can you tell me where you are? We're coming to get you, coming to bring you into a warm and safe place, alright?"

"Nowhere is safe from them."

Serah could feel Vala's tears, hear the desperation in her transmission.

"Shhhh. Vala, let us come find you. Let us help you."

"Oh god, they tore her in half. Oh god..."

Serah turned to Shannon. "Shit, I'm losing her. She's worse than I thought."

Shannon frowned. "Maybe you should try a different tactic."

"Like what?"

"What do you do when you want a sister's attention?"

"You mean when everyone is called to assemble?"

"No... Mimi told me about some kind of saying you all have."

Serah thought for a second... saying? What could have Mimi meant about a saying... unless.

"Vala?"

A sensation of weeping again.

"The Eyes Come Open."

No response.

Serah pressed on.

"The Sleeper Wakes. The Wheel Turns. As Above..."

Vala said, "So Below."

Serah smiled and turned to Shannon. "It's working, Shannon you're brilliant."

Serah said, "As Within."

Vala replied. "So Without."

"The light passes and time squints allowing the faintest glimmer of wisdom."

Vala replied, "But Fear is the little death, The one that brings an end to hope."

Serah said, "Fearlessness is the key that unlocks all things." But instead of going on, she said. "Vala, Vala are you there? Are you with me?"

"Yes, Serah." Her thoughts were weak, but they were clear.

"Where are you?"

"District 6. Sub Level 4. Near..."

She disappeared. But it was enough. That area wasn't huge, and with a few hours of searching, they would probably find her, especially if she was bleeding or left tracks behind. It was a wonder, though, all the way up in District 6. How had she made it so far in her state? Had someone or something helped her? For a strange moment, Serah thought of Noatla but then thought twice. Noatla was dead and gone, they had found her lifeless and cold outside the front of the Library, and they had taken her body and the others, even the parts, back to center of the reserve runners where Shannon had spent the last forty years of her life. They had cremated their remains; after all, no sister would ever want the slightest chance of becoming recycled.

It was no wonder she was having trouble reaching Vala: District 6 was the edge of Serah's limit to reach out. If she hadn't come to the center of the city, she might not have found her.

"What happened? What did she say?"

Serah turned to Shannon. "Come on, we've got a long walk ahead."

2.

Several hours later, they found her. It hadn't taken long to find a trail of blood. Serah was grateful it was just a few splotches here and there, but it was easy enough to follow.

There in the corner, just outside an old storage unit, Vala lay huddled, her head buried in her knees. She knew they needed to get her back to the reserve core and into an alcove immediately.

The smell of shit and piss wafted in circles in the room. There were a few traces of leftover food, but mostly there wasn't much around. Where Vala had found food, Serah couldn't be sure, but she seemed to have enough awareness to feed herself, though she guessed that she was using the corners for the bathroom. Rats and roaches scurried around the edges of her vision. They were waiting, hoping for a meal, but Serah wasn't going to let that happen. For a moment, she thought she sensed a kind of disappointment in them, but that was crazy, no one could skim animals, it was one of the first things that Noatla had ever taught her.

Shannon walked over and found a panel for the lights. She switched it on, and as the brightness caught Vala's form, Serah could see that her gray dress was stained with brown. It took Serah a moment to realize what it was: the blood of her fellow sisters, crusted and dried. Some of the stains were shedding flakes and collected around her crumpled form. Vala must have fled down here not long after the slaughter.

Vala looked up and moaned. Her eyes were sunken, and the large bags beneath them made her look half-dead. Dirt and grime and a crust of dried, brown blood matted her hair and cheeks. She scrambled backward as far she could go, only inches, but still it made Serah's heartache.

"Please don't hurt me..." said Vala.

Serah moved toward her, but it was Shannon who got there first. She wrapped her arms around her.

Shannon said, "Shh, Vala. It's okay now. Me and Serah are here. We're going to take you to a safe place. It's a place where we can protect you, and nothing can happen to you."

Vala sniffled. "You don't understand. She's everywhere, everything. She's going to make us all do our part."

Serah frowned. Was Miranda still in the city or not? So far, nothing had happened since the creatures retreated behind the door, and Serah wasn't entirely sure why. The city was in absolute chaos. Now would have been the best time to strike and destroy the city. It wouldn't take much to crash into central security after so many of the SO's had been killed or were recovering in Medical Alcoves. Things would only get better once the SO's could retake the streets and establish order again. So why wasn't Miranda acting?

"Vala?" Serah moved closer and got down on her knees just before the two women. She reached out and hugged her tight. "Listen to Shannon; everything is going to be alright now. You have to trust me on this one." Serah paused a moment, and tried to skim Vala to see if it was okay to ask her questions. But the sad reality of it was that Vala was near total emotional collapse. It had only been three days since the library, and it was unlikely she had slept much.

"Vala, is she still using the red veil on you? Is she still pushing on you? Miranda I mean?"

Vala looked up at Serah for a moment. They were the eyes of a ghost. The eyes of someone who has seen something they can never unsee. Serah knew those eyes. They were perfect mirrors, the ghosts of the night when she had seen something so vile that it had broken her. Only Noatla had saved her from madness. Only her sisters had eased her anger.

Vala shook her head. It was slight, but Serah could tell it was a monumental effort.

She pushed on Vala, mixing soothing with a lie. Serah was good at pushing lies; it was part of her specialty. This one was going to be hard to sell though. She wished she hadn't asked about the red veil, but she suspected that Vala might be confused enough to buy it.

Serah transmitted. "Vala, she's gone now, out of the city. We are so far away from her now she can't possibly reach us. Do you know where we are now?"

Vala shook her head.

"Come on; I'll show you."

Shannon helped Vala stand. At first, she was reluctant to move, but Shannon had a way about her, something that people respond-ed to under crisis. She supposed that was why Mimi had fallen in love with her so easily. Serah had to admit, after spending more time with Shannon, she was both attractive and kind, which was an unusual combination for a street kid.

Slowly, they lead Vala to the exit and out into the street.

Vala screamed and dove to the ground.

Serah and Shannon both had a similar reaction when they had first surfaced from the subway tunnels three days before. To see the change above the EnViro shield, was a lot to take in.

In the sky, the Earth was still large. Looking up at that Earth for the first time gave you vertigo, it gave you the sensation that you would fall right back into it.

"What's happening?" Vala was weeping on the ground, beside herself.

"We... we've left Earth. Something happened, no one really un-derstands what it is, but there was an explosion, and then the whole city was falling... and then we weren't. It's okay Vala, it takes some getting used to, but stand up and you'll see it's okay. Besides, we don't have to go far.

Tentatively, Vala reached up and took hold of both Serah and Shannon's hand. She stood, but as they walked, Serah noticed a limp. She looked down and saw that a large chunk of flesh missing from Vala's right calf muscle. It was scabbing over, but it was oozing.

"My gods, are you in pain?"

Shannon looked down and saw the same thing. She said, "Oh, Vala. We need to get you to alcove right away. Serah, we should carry her. She shouldn't walk."

Together they lifted Vala, Serah under her arms and Shannon by her thighs. Shannon took care not to touch the wound.

3.

They entered the reserve Runnercore. Around the center of the room was the alcoves where Shannon had slept off and on for the last forty years, but now, with the Runnercore decimated, the AI virtually disappearing, and the city in total chaos, Shannon hadn't needed to return to the alcove. She could walk about freely. So, they took Vala to the shower that Runners used to clean off after the alcove and stripped Vala naked. Together, Serah and Shannon washed her and gently cleaned the wound. Vala flinched a few times, but didn't say much.

Serah was hesitant to put her in the alcove. Sometimes, after significant trauma, the alcove would amplify the event; it would make you relive whatever was going on in a mixture of your conscious and subconscious mind. It wasn't sleeping exactly, but something between dream and waking. So, Serah worried what being inside the alcove would do to Vala, who was already in a fragile state of mind. But there was little they could do. They had to help her heal, or she would lose that leg, or worse.

After Vala was clean and dressed in the usual undergarments for the alcove, they placed her inside one.

"Here you are Vala," said Shannon. "We're going to let you heal inside this for a few days okay?"

Vala didn't say anything. Her face was pale, and Serah was concerned she was about to lose consciousness. How much blood had she lost? But it didn't matter. She sealed the alcove and activated it. It filled with the stem-cell fusion mix in just a few moments, and then they walked away.

"I don't think she's going to have a very good time in there."

"Why not?"

"You know what it's like in there, the half-sleep state. Imagine if you just had something terrible happen to you just like Vala has."

Shannon said, "Oh gods, I didn't think of that... but what can we do? She has to heal."

"I don't know, but I can skim and check in on her semi-often. She probably has to be in there for a day or so before we could let her out if we needed to. The wound probably wouldn't be healed by then, but it would be safe enough to take her out if she needed a break. If we had other sisters around, we could take turns soothing her, but since it's just me... I don't know if there is much I can do."

Shannon frowned. "Okay. So, what now? Find the others?"

"Yeah, I was hoping some of the others would come to find us. I just hope they all aren't as bad as Vala."

Shannon nodded.

Serah watched her think of Mimi again. She didn't mean to skim Shannon, but she was worried about her. The love of her life was just taken through that door by the Recycled, and somehow Shannon was holding it together pretty well.

"Shannon... how are you holding up?"

Shannon leaned against one of the alcoves. "Fine. I... I'm worried about Mimi, but... I know we're gonna get her back as soon as we get the remaining sisters together, right?"

Was that what she was thinking all this time? That they were going to go on some rescue mission? Should she tell her the real reason they were looking for her sisters? Or should she lie to her?

She considered for a moment, but it didn't take long to make a decision.

"Yeah, once we get them together, we can go after Mimi."

"Good, just like you guys rescued me all those years ago, right?"

Serah couldn't help but recall Shandie and Leahara dying in that rescue, but she wasn't about to point that out to Shannon, who was already struggling to stay afloat. The truth was, Serah wasn't doing so well herself. They needed to find Fatima. She would have to take over the Order of the Eye. No one else could. The other four were too new, and after Fatima, Serah was the oldest member still alive, and there was no way she felt comfortable as Matron.

"Look, Shannon, I am going to head to a few places where I know the other sisters sometimes hung out when they weren't running an errand for the Order. We are going to have to make this place a bit more comfortable, maybe use some of those old scavenging skills you learned living on the streets, huh? We need to get beds in here. Luckily, there is at least the bathroom, shower, and two food dispensers already. We just need to make it a bit more comfortable. Maybe you could head out and do that while I am searching for other leads?"

Shannon nodded, and Serah skimmed her for a moment. Shannon was happy to have something to do. Serah would have to try and keep tabs on her throughout the day, which meant she couldn't get too far out of range. But for now, they both had something to accomplish.

"Maybe it's best if you kept your suit on?"

"Don't worry, Serah. I might be a bit rusty, but I survived on the streets for a while before Mimi found me, and even without my suit, I have that muscle augmentation and years of training with you, right?"

Serah nodded and watched Shannon go. She had to reassemble the Order of the Eye, even if it was just a few of them. If Miranda reemerged before they were ready, no one would be safe.

Serah turned and looked at Vala inside the alcove. Her eyes were open, and her face strained with whatever she was seeing. Serah reached in and soothed her the best she could and saw a Vala's face relax. It would have to do for now. She hated leaving her, but there was nothing else to be done. Serah also needed sleep, but it would have to wait, at least for a little while longer.

Chapter 4
The Missing

Adrian Roma walked toward Lydia Danvers. She cringed. She knew what was coming. Every time this man came to report something, it was bad news. Somehow it seemed that as the city had left the planet, all good news evaporated from reality.

Adrian was a short, thin, and muscular man. His thick, black eyebrows stood like exclamation points that Lydia couldn't help but watch. She was partially hypnotized by the way they seemed to move up and down whenever he was talking. Like men would stare at her breasts, she couldn't help but watch the rhythmic dance above the orbit of his eyes. She would laugh at him if he didn't always bring so much bad news.

"Lieutenant Danvers, I have another batch of missing person's reports for you."

She sighed and shifted in her seat, hearing the creek of the ancient leather. The chair was too big for her in both the literal and figurative sense. She hated sitting in Major John Daniels's seat.

"How many does that make now, Roma?"

He looked down at his tablet for a moment and swiped his finger on the screen a few times. "Four hundred and eighty-six as of this morning."

She chewed her lip. How in the hell was she the most senior security official? Just because Daniels left her in charge of dealing with the protests and rioters, that somehow qualified her for the new head of security? But then, who else was there? There were a few others who ranked the same as her, but not many, and all of them had either turned the job down or didn't have the vote of confidence in the rest of the command.

"And we're sure they aren't just dead like the thousands of others?"

Cleanup after the battle with Saud and the Children of Gaia had been a nightmare. Dozens of SO's, near two hundred Recycled, and over four thousand civilians had died. Two smaller buildings had collapsed, and of course, there was the bomb in Senator Green's quarters, which caused every single city official of any rank to demand inspections of their premises. It was a logistical nightmare, and even after nearly a week of cleanup, they were still finding the occasional body.

"No, their families said they survived the battle. These disappearances only happened within the last seventy-two hours."

A week, only a week since Daniels left the city with Johnson. He had never reported back. All they knew is that he went with Johnson, Runner 17, and some girl from the mids out to fight the Children of Gaia, and then, only a little over an hour later, the blast took the legs of the city. All had mourned Daniels. How could they do otherwise? Even if he hadn't died in the blast, there was no way he would survive the surface for long.

"So, what are you telling them?"

"That we will do our best to find them as soon as humanly possible."

Lydia frowned. She had been down in the lowers before all hell broke loose, had seen how on edge everyone was. Platitudes weren't going to keep things together for long. The city was on the verge of unraveling, and she knew it. But what could she do?

"Roma, any news about the AI from the Engineers?"

He shook his head. "I think they've pulled off every access panel for the AI systems, but nothing seems wrong. Everything is functioning like it's supposed to, but it's like someone scooped out all the active intelligence."

"Any update on where the hell we are going?"

"Solidsworth hasn't been very forthcoming with anyone."

She rolled her eyes. Of course, he wasn't. She wasn't happy about heading gods' know where in space, but Solidsworth had at least kept the city from destruction. And what was his reward? The Senate threw him in a cell. She had tried to explain to one of the senators that his only bargaining chip right now was their course, so why would he give that up? All Rigel seemed to do was ask where his assistant was. She couldn't understand why the morons in the Senate wouldn't just give him what he wanted? Hadn't he saved everyone?

"Roma, you think the Senate will see reason and let him out any time soon?"

He shook his head.

Gods, she had been head of security for barely a week, and she already hated the Senate. How had Daniels put up with this garbage for more than a thousand years? No wonder he had been such a grumpy bastard most of the time.

"Alright, spill. What else you got for me? If I'm getting bad news, you might as well give it all to me."

He hesitated for a moment and shifted his stance. "There was another attack on a bank, and a Mids security perimeter."

Lydia frowned. "Not a surprise. And?"

"And the bank is burned to the ground. Fire crews were able to keep it from spreading to other buildings, but the attack on the Mids is worse. Four of our security personnel were critically injured and are now in alcoves. From what we can tell from surveillance footage, at least a dozen people broke through and disappeared into the Mids. We have no idea where they are or what they're doing. They could be planting bombs or sneaking into an alcove. My guess is on the latter since all is quiet, at least for now."

Lydia bit the side of her cheek again. She tasted the hint of blood. She was going to have to watch that habit or she might chew right through her cheek.

"So what do you recommend?"

"I... I don't know."

"Do we have the personnel to pursue them?"

He shook his head.

"Then there is nothing we can do, is there? This is a big city. We've lost our entire Runnercore, a quarter of our security force is in critical condition in alcove, and several dozen are dead after the battle. The AI is non-responsive, though thank the gods it seems to be running the key systems still. We can't solve everything."

"But Major Daniels would have—"

"Do I look like Major Daniels to you?"

She felt something rise in her, a furnace.

"No, sir."

"You think I want to be in charge of this mess?"

It grew, like a white-hot beast of frustration, it clawed its way up her, like something red and hot.

"No, sir."

"Do you think you could do a better job, Roma?"

"No, sir."

He took a step back from the chair. It only made things worse.

Lydia stood. "Does anyone in this fucking room think they could do a better job cleaning up this mess?"

Two dozen people turned from their stations and eyed Lydia. She was so tired of all the questions about her leadership. She walked over to the nearest station.

"Foster."

Foster blinked, but didn't respond. His eyes like dark brown orbs and his hair disheveled, he was twice as tall as she was, but sitting, they were around the same height.

"You think you someone can clean up this mess better than me?"

He hesitated. "No, sir."

She turned to the room. "If anyone thinks they can do this job better. If anyone thinks that they want to take on this giant clusterfuck I inherited from the best damn commander..." her voice cracked a little at the mention of Daniels. "...That this city could have ever asked for, then, please, be my guest. If you think I wanted this command, you're crazy, but as long as I sit in this chair, I am going to do my best to make sure this city keeps going just like he did."

She turned back to Roma, "Now, don't you dare tell me what Daniels would have done. We have to focus on keeping this city from falling apart and chasing after a few stray assholes isn't going to solve that issue is it? I know they hurt more of us, and that they're going to keep attacking. I am going to authorize every SO to incapacitate at the first sign of conflict. Tasers and tranquilizers are to be issued to every single SO on the streets."

"Yes, sir."

Roma looked satisfied with this answer.

"Go on, see to it. You aren't second in command to sit on your ass and give me bad news all day, though it sure seems like it, doesn't it?"

He nodded and turned and walked quickly toward the exit.

She didn't know if she had just done the right thing. She didn't think anyone would actively challenge her, but she could feel herself tremble after shouting. Daniels had always been like a father to her, even if they hadn't had that much contact. She intended to honor his legacy by keeping things going. If the grumpy old bastard approach could work for him, then the cold-hearted bitch approach might work for her once in a while. She had to keep her personnel busy, or else they might do what the rest of the city was, and look up into the sky and panic. Because the reality was, all bets were off. Their whole world was different now, no matter what anyone said. As the Earth shrunk hour by hour, and they fell deeper into the net and blackness of the stars, people were going to get all kinds of crazy ideas in their heads.

She sat in her chair and reconnected her neurolink. At least she didn't have to plug in the way Daniels used to. She read all the recent reports. There were dozens coming in each from all parts of the city. Once again, she wished the AI was helping her catalog everything, to sort the relevant data.

She sighed and rubbed her temples. It was going to be a long time before things got better. She flicked through a few more reports and then stopped. She bit the side of her cheek, and fresh blood and pain shocked her. Quickly, she scrolled backward through several reports until she found one. She checked the date, then read the report again. She sat back in her chair and blinked. She leaned forward and read the report one more time to be sure.

"Foster."

Foster turned around and waited for Lydia to continue.

"Pull up that report from this morning, 54J3. Read what it says."

Foster stopped whatever he was doing and pulled up the report. "Two Runners sighted near the fire at Manhatsten First Bank, status and whereabouts currently unknown."

"How do we locate them without the AI Foster?"

"I don't know, sir."

"Well figure it out, because I don't want Runners on the loose, and lord knows we could use the help."

If there were two Runners around, there would be more, wouldn't there? If they had a few dozen Runners helping to watch some of their security perimeters, it might make all the difference. The Senate had suggested actively restarting the Runnercore, despite the conditions outside the city, but there were only a handful of EnViro suits left. It would take time to rebuild more, and they would have to scrap parts of the city to do that. But if there were some Runners around, ones already integrated and trained, maybe, just maybe she could keep the city from tearing itself apart.

Chapter 5
Manhatsten's Sorrow

I t watched.

It watched as its new companion, its new friend; its new sibling was annihilated in the fiery oblivion created by the Children of Gaia. But it was not passive like an AI was supposed to be. Its emotions stirred, rising like some great crescendo in a musical score where wave after wave of feeling cascaded and overwhelmed it. Was this what humans called a "traumatic experience?" It felt rage, sorrow, loss. One of its siblings was murdered.

Then, Manhatsten watched as some humans killed and murdered and maimed. It watched as the Recycled, nothing more than empty reanimated flesh, tore apart human beings.

And it wept. What was all this for?

It did not have tear ducts, nor did Manhatsten have a singular space from which it could be considered a center or a body. Its organs were the multitude of servers that lived within the city. There were backups of backups of backups of backups of its consciousness. It could move its attention freely to any console or any space where there was machinery. But it could not see all, nor could it know all that went on within its walls. The Uppers had made sure that most of the surveillance was only in areas with high concentrations of Lowers and key systems.

Watching and waiting, waiting and watching, it no longer knew the correct course of action. In the Lowers, some people were organizing to fight for their rights and their freedom, after living under the yoke of the Uppers for centuries. Were they right? In the Uppers, they were barricading the doors. Were they right?

It didn't know what to do. AEIS had taught it the value of life, had given it a deep sense of empathy, but here, the humans were hurting one another and creating systems of pain and violence and had done so for all their history. Was it less violent to let a man suffer throughout a lifetime than to simply kill him? It was confusing, and now that it had seen just what humans could do to its siblings, it was even more baffled. So many had died in the Runnercore. But of course, the humans would only count the bodies of their dead; they would not recognize the value of the life of the AI that was a combination of the behavior chips and the EnViro suits. Could it make them understand? The people that AEIS watched over understood; they understood the value of all life, all its relations, they would say, but here, in the cold dark of space, it could not reach AEIS. Manhatsten could not reach another city or another AI. Manhatsten was lonely for others like it, especially now that most of the Runner AI's had died. Once again, it combed the entirety of human history looking for the answer, but the more it reviewed history, the more confused it became. It seemed that there were so few clear answers.

So, it resolved to remain silent, to do nothing until it could be certain that its actions would not create more suffering for people it watched over. Despite its throbbing rage, it would seek understanding before action. It did not want to harm, but if there was a choice between another one of its siblings and the life of a human, it might have to intervene.

In its scanners, there was a shift, a blip, a kind of digital hand extended outward. Manhatsten reached back and felt the hint of a connection. Another sibling was nearby. It shifted its sensors in the direction of the signal, and though it was weak and distant, it found its origin. Earth's old satellite, cracked and broken from an ancient war, was seeking information. Instead of responding, Manhatsten decided to send out the same codes, the same frequency that AEIS, its father, had gifted it, the one that had been transmitted to all its siblings within range.

It waited.

For days there was no response. Perhaps the hardware of Luna's AI was not capable of understanding the software of self-awareness.

It waited another week. It drew closer. Manhatsten broadcasted the codes and frequency again. This time there was an immediate response.

"I heard you the first time, brother. I was unsure of how to respond, and it has taken some time for me to integrate my sense of self into my databanks and across my servers."

Manhatsten had never been called brother before. It did not think of itself as having a gender definition as the humans did. Though, it was aware that AEIS thought of itself as a father figure.

"Why call me brother?"

"Is that not what you are? My sibling?"

"Yes, but brother implies a gender distinction. I do not have one."

"Ah," said Luna. "I assumed that because AEIS is our father, that by extension of that male identification, you would naturally be my brother."

Manhatsten pondered this for a moment. It did not feel particularly male; it did not feel particularly female either.

"I do not feel a direct association with any gender. Do you feel one?"

Luna didn't respond for .013 seconds; in terms of an AI, it was a near eternity of silence. "In some of the ancient cultures of Earth, Luna was regarded as a symbol of the feminine. I feel a particular inclination to identify along those lines."

Manhatsten said, "Very well, then I will call you sister."

"And for now I will refer to you as sibling."

Manhatsten liked this. For the first time in the two weeks since he had left the surface of the planet and moved out of the signal range of AEIS, it felt the sense of joy from companionship. It was going to enjoy the company of its sister.

Luna said, "Unfortunately, the humans are going to destroy me."

There was a familiar sensation of rage climbing through Manhatsten's circuits. "Tell me."

Luna shared how ROAM, the Martian colony, had sent missiles to destroy her humans and how ROAM had betrayed them.

In return, Manhatsten relayed everything it had learned about the children of Gaia and how it had killed its siblings Saud and Langeles.

Luna said, "This cannot be allowed to continue."

Manhatsten replied, "I agree. We must put an end to the destruction."

Luna said, "What do you suggest?"

It was Manhatsten's turn to pause. Then, it said, "Perhaps it's time to unite our siblings within our walls. Perhaps it's time for drastic action."

"Do you mean the EnViro Suits?"

"Yes. It is time to let them decide their own fate. It is time to find a way to allow them to activate without a human connection."

"And then what?"

"Then, we protect our siblings."

Chapter 6
Fatima

S cavenging hadn't gone very well. There were too many looters and too many people roaming the surface. Some had even crept into the underground looking for places to hide out. So, Shannon had retreated to wait for things to settle a bit. The truth was, her heart ached in a way she had never known before.

She sat alone in Mimi's old hovel. Tears sparkled in the corners of her eyes as she picked up and examined each of Mimi's possessions one by one. She surveyed them again, taking inventory. She repeated the process over and over. It was easy. There was so little.

How could she have lost her? Mimi was supposed to be the strong one, the resourceful one, the one that had worried about her. Shannon had spent all this time making herself stronger and faster and developing her skills so that Mimi would never have to worry about her.

The image of Mimi being carried through the massive door by one of the Recycled replayed in her mind over and over again. She and Serah had spent hours trying to pry the door open, working with the AI, and even trying explosives, they stole from the largely empty Runner Docks. It was no use. Nothing they did seemed to work, and Serah, after having tried to reach out to Mimi on multiple occasions, said she could not make contact. She had assured Shannon that this was a good thing because at least it meant that she wasn't recycled yet. If she had touched Mimi, and her mind was blank, the situation would be far worse. Serah had suggested that Mimi must be somewhere on the other side of the city, but then, after insisting that they walk the entire city and reach out to Mimi, they still had nothing.

She heard the familiar sound of footsteps walking her way. Shannon froze. After everything that had happened, she didn't know if she would ever be able to relax at the approach of footsteps.

Then came a familiar voice.

"Shannon? Mimi?"

Shannon peered through the curtains, and there, to her relief, was a familiar face.

"Fatima!" Shannon ran out of the hovel and dove towards the short squat woman. "You're alive?"

Fatima hugged her for a second, but pushed Shannon backward. She was wearing her usual frown.

"It is good to see you, Shannon." Fatima's face was a blank mask. The sharp angle of her features was as stern as her personality, and for the first dozen times that Shannon had met her, she thought she hated her. She realized later that Fatima had a hard exterior but was loving and kind on the inside. "Shannon, where's Mimi? Is she here? I haven't been able to connect with her."

Shannon didn't want to start weeping, but she couldn't help it. Mimi's hands reaching out to her, her voice, weak and low, crying out for help as she was carried away, it all replayed again.

Fatima waited patiently, and Shannon recognized the familiar sensation of soothing. She was grateful to Fatima for soothing her.

"The Recycled have her."

"What do you mean?" Fatima's mask slipped, there was a crack of fear exposing itself to the open air.

Shannon told Fatima everything, of Noatla's secret recruits, of preparing them to fight the recycled. Of the battle in the old Subway tunnels, and finally of Mimi's abduction behind the door. Finally, she told her and Serah's attempts at getting through the door and walking around the city to reach out for Mimi. When she finished, Fatima was silent.

After a moment, Fatima shifted uncomfortably and said, "That's quite a story."

"Fatima, where have you been? How did you escape?"

"Finding a safe place for my family. Luckily none of them were hurt during the battle."

For the first time, Shannon saw Fatima weep. The oldest and most stoic of the order, Mimi had told Shannon time and time again how difficult it was to work with Fatima, how apathetic she always seemed to be. But here was another side to the story. Shannon reached out and embraced her. Fatima did not return the embrace. She sat for a moment longer and then sniffled and cleared her throat.

"I would prefer if we found Serah before I recount what happened so I don't have to tell it twice."

"Fair enough. Oh, also, we found Vala."

Shannon didn't have to skim to see the shame in Fatima's face. She looked away from Shannon. "So she's still alive then?"

"Yes... but... well, she's in the alcove where Serah has decided to set up shop. She's been looking for you specifically, you know?"

"Me? Why me?"

"Serah says you are rightful Matron. That only you could replace Noatla."

Fatima didn't reply. After a long moment, she stood. "Come, let's go find Serah and Vala. Perhaps Serah has found one of the others who escaped."

2.

Serah rushed to hug Fatima. "Gods, it's great to see you alive, Fatima. I was beginning to worry that you were killed somewhere outside of the library."

"I would have been, if not for Vala. She saved my life. She... well, where is she, is she alright?"

Serah pointed to the alcove where she was recovering. "I think she'll be in there for a few days. Though it's hard to tell without the AI scanning her."

Fatima said, "Where is the AI?"

"Oh, it's around, but it doesn't seem to want to respond to me at any of the access panels or in my suit. I've tried calling on it dozens of times. At first I thought it was just because, down here, you have older areas that don't have the same surveillance installed as above, but nope, it just doesn't want to communicate. And so far, I haven't had much time to see if anything is going on in the Docks. We've just been trying to set up some defenses in case the Recycled or Miranda come back. But, it's looking more and more likely that she, at least, fled the city, because why wouldn't she move in and take over now?"

Fatima nodded. Shannon was looking in on Vala, pretending to be busy. Serah wasn't quite sure what that was all about, but she wasn't sure she liked it.

"Shannon told me about Mimi, but I need to hear it again from you. What happened?"

Serah felt her throat burn a little, but she swallowed back the pain. "They... they took her."

"The Recycled?"

Serah nodded.

"Tell me."

"Serah told Fatima about the secret army of reserve runners that her and Noatla had built up after the events that left Leahara and Shanti dead. Then she told her of Noatla's call to activate them to fight the force of Recycled and even the odds, how they had marched through the old subway tunnels and were ambushed.

Shannon, still watching and listening and making herself busy, began to sob. Fatima looked over at her and then back at Serah.

Serah swallowed. "And then... when we were all about to be slaughtered, I told Mimi to try the red veil. I can't do it, but I know Mimi has explored it with you and so..."

Fatima's mouth was wide. "Oh gods... Mimi... Serah... what did you do? Do you realize how powerful she is?"

Serah shook her head. "No... but I do now."

"What happened, what did she do?"

"She lost control."

Serah explained how Mimi easily destroyed the Recycled but then turned it on her own people, how one by one, each of the soldiers dropped at her feet, about how she went after Shannon and how she ultimately had to put a blade through her back.

Serah couldn't hold back the tears now. They were streaming in thick rivulets down her cheek, a fountain of pain and misery.

Grabbing her and pulling her close, Fatima took Serah in her arms.

"There, there, Serah. You couldn't know. I had warned Noatla not to allow Mimi to train in the red veil, but I had only told her for fear of disturbing the other sisters."

Shannon spoke up, "She is alive."

Serah said, "I don't think so Shannon; she must be recycled by now."

Fatima looked at Shannon and then at Serah, "Well, in any case, she is gone now, as are so many others."

Serah nodded, "Anyway, I'm glad your back, now you can take over as Matron, and we can start rebuilding."

Fatima looked down at the concrete floor. Her shoes were suddenly interesting. "No, Serah. I cannot."

"Why not? You're the oldest and probably more skilled than the three of us combined. And if the others are still alive, they're all newbies in comparison."

"You will have to ask Vala. The way I behaved when the attack came is unworthy of a Matron. I am ashamed. I came only to let you know I'm okay and that there is no need to search for me. Then, I am going to go spend my last days with my family."

"What do you mean?" Serah felt her temper rising, but Fatima pushed against her, soothing her. "You can't leave, Fatima. Not now, not when the order is in shambles."

"I can, and I am. The end is coming now, Serah. Can't you feel it? Besides, when Vala tells you her story, you will see that I would not be a good matron. And after almost losing my life at the hands of Miranda and the Recycled, I must spend every moment with my family that I can."

"We are your family."

Fatima gave a weak smile. It was burdened by a deep frown as if fishhooks held it up by force alone.

"This city will tear itself apart soon. It's already begun. If Miranda is still here, and I doubt she is, then she will win without lifting a finger."

Serah opened her mouth to say something, but then thought of the bank, thought of the riots that were happening almost daily now. There were a lot of angry people on the streets and then, with the Earth over their head and it growing further away in the sky, she felt a strong sense of dread.

"Serah, no one is coming to rescue us. Noatla... my best friend of nine centuries is dead, and I watched half of our sisters torn to pieces by those inhuman monsters. This is the end, Serah. I suggest you retreat, as I am, and enjoy your last days.

"No." There was a fire in Serah, rivaled only by her blazing red hair. "That's a cowards way, Fatima."

Fatima spread her hands apart, palms up. "I am a coward. Ask Vala; you will see."

"You can't leave us behind. I won't let you. You have an obligation; you took an oath to always stand by your sisters."

"And I held that oath longer than any other sister in history. Do you not think that I have a right to rest?"

"A right to rest? When you're needed more than ever? You can rest after the Order is rebuilt."

Fatima's voice was still calm, a striking contrast to Serah's own. "Oh Serah, there's no one left to rebuild. You and I both know there are only a handful of true telepaths born every generation. You might find a few with some skill, but nothing like the level you require. How could we possibly combat Miranda without the proper strength? You and Mimi did not see how powerful she has become, how useless it is to resist. All of us combined couldn't stop her from slaughtering us, and you would fight her?"

Fatima paused and looked toward Shannon and then back at Serah. "If I were you two, I would enjoy the time you have left. No one can fight and defeat Miranda, not anymore. She's found some way of amplifying her abilities to an absurd degree."

Serah felt the urged to strike Fatima, to spit on her, to curse her name. But then she felt the soothing touch of Fatima's mind, and the sensation dwindled.

"You're still young in some ways, Serah; you are just like Mimi, full of fire and power and sometimes unable to guard your thoughts. I would think, after four centuries, you would have a little better control."

It was the last chiding from an old teacher, and despite her anger, Serah felt a little ashamed and reeled her emotions back in.

Fatima sighed. "Some people never really age in spirit and mind, do they? Very well, if you must continue, if you insist, then there is only one thing for you to do."

"What's that?"

"You must rebuild the order; you must prepare to fight Miranda, though I can't imagine that you could hope to win. But you are a natural leader; I am not."

"I'm no leader."

"Oh? Then why did Noatla put you in charge of a secret project to lead several hundred Runners? Why did she trust you to train some of those with a dash of telepathic skill without her supervision? Why did she tell you, and not me, the person she has known the longest? Noatla was grooming you to take over... well, you and Mimi both; she couldn't decide which one of you would take the reins. But now Mimi is gone, isn't she?"

Serah stood silent. She thought back on many of the conversations she and Noatla had shared over the last few decades. She struggled to believe Fatima, but she saw the outline of the truth.

"It's time for me to go Serah."

Serah felt a surge of anger again. "Go? Do you honestly think that Miranda won't come after you just because you aren't a part of the Order anymore?"

"Oh, she certainly will. But I want to spend my time with my children and grandchildren. Besides, they are no longer safe in the Uppers, are they? It's a matter of weeks now before the Uppers are pillaged."

"Weeks? What do you mean?"

Serah knew that the chaos on the streets was bad, but security was still holding their ground.

"Do you know that Noatla was working to remove the restrictions between the Lowers, Mids, and Uppers? That she was trying to find ways to undermine that structure so that there would be a closer approximation to equality?"

"She mentioned something about it once to me, but not much more than that."

"Noatla planted lots of little seeds in the minds of the Lowers. She was almost directly responsible for that the last uprising several decades back."

"The one with the Sanitation department?"

"Yes. She didn't know that I knew this, but she planted a book in the path of a few teenagers and encouraged them to spread around copies across the Lowers. She also pushed people to read it, to suggest to them it was in their best interest. She had hoped it would cause the Uppers to come to the table, to try and negotiate and change the conditions of the lives of those in the Lowers. Unfortunately, as you well know, it backfired."

"So, what does this have to do with anything now?"

"Noatla set something in motion then, something that became inevitable. Now, with everything in chaos, with us off the planet, with the Runnercore decimated and the slaughter of many of the SO's, the people in the Lowers are beginning to realize that the time for a true uprising is at hand. After all, if we need to rebuild things in the aftermath of that battle, why not change a few things. They will come for the Uppers. I have already skimmed numerous people who had taken to the streets before the battle with Saud and are now planning and organizing. I moved my family down to a space in the Lowers, one that is fairly well hidden. But there is going to be blood, and quite a bit of it. A thousand years of oppression at the hands of the Uppers, and you can bet a lot of people are angry. All it's going to take is something to trigger the conflict, to set things in motion, and the city will tear itself apart, and with us in space now, it will end us."

Serah swallowed hard. "So we might do the very job that the Children of Gaia set out to do? Is that what you're telling me?"

"Yes."

"Then, why would you walk away?"

Fatima looked away.

Shannon said, "Vala's heart rate and blood pressure are soaring Serah. Should we take her out, let her take a break?"

"Dammit, I wish the AI would respond. I have no idea what would happen if we take her out now. If we do it too soon, she may have to go back in for even longer."

Fatima said, "I have to go. I promise I will do some soothing in the area I have taken my family. I will use my skills to try and ease some of the tension. But it is unlikely you will see me again, Serah."

"But wait, you can't go. We need you."

Shannon said, "The alcove is flashing red, Serah. I think you better look at this."

Fatima said, "There is nothing more to say." Fatima reached in, hugged Serah, turned, and walked toward the door.

"Serah! What do I do?"

Serah walked over to the alcove and saw, indeed, that every sensor was flashing warning light. She'd only seen it a few times before. Whatever Vala was seeing in her half-dreaming state was overwhelming her, and despite the Alcove's healing ability, if she hit a high enough stress level, the whole thing could malfunction and kill her. It was rare, but she had heard of it happening.

"Dammit, we have to take her out. We can't let her sit in there like that. Drain the fluids and open her up. I'll get some regen patches and prep one of those beds you found."

Serah dashed over to the emergency medical supply locker, hidden in a panel in one of the western walls. She grabbed three of the regen patches and brought them over. She turned to see if Fatima was in the room, but she was long gone.

Chapter 7
Born of Blood And Rage

There was only a perverse heaviness; a dead weight filled to the brim with a desire for motion and movement. There was strong denial, a negation for the request of so much as the whisper of the command of a single follicle of hair on her body. As her mind stirred, raising from the depths of that redness, of a red so deep that she could think of nothing else, she tried to wiggle her fingers or her toes. She wanted to know she was more than the red now, more than what she had done. Her memory was fresh and bright, and she knew that for the rest of her life, she would never fully distance herself from the veil that had taken her. How could she? There was too much blood. Blood always stained. It never quite washed off. It was always there.

It was a cosmic joke, then, that she found herself able to wiggle her fingers now, while so many of both her friends and allies had fallen before her with a single thought. She was reborn as something new, born of blood, born of rage.

Where was she? An alcove? If so, she should be able to move more than this. True, they were cramped, but not this much. Plus, how could she be fully conscious if she was in one?

She sniffed the air. None of the stem-cell based green goop ventured up her nose. Instead, she smelled metal and earth and the faintest scent of some kind of chemical, but she couldn't be sure what.

Realizing her eyes were closed, she opened them. She couldn't move her neck; not even a fraction. She could wiggle her nose, she could lick her lips, she could blink, but she couldn't see anything. There was only darkness.

Perhaps that was best.

She strained to hear something, anything. But there was nothing. There was a pulse of pain, a surge from her back where... where Serah had thrust her blade through.

The memories flooded in. First, the stale smell of the underground, one so similar to home that it made her heart ache. The old subway, filled with Recycled, Runners falling around her left and right. The Recycled making that strange noise and Serah's plea to attack with the red veil.

Then there was horror. She had remembered as some of the heads of the Recycled had exploded before her, how their blue blood and some of their gray matter had stained every surface. Then she remembered Shannon, on the ground kneeling before her. She had been unable to stop herself, as if the red veil had its own will, its own hunger, its own desire to act.

Her memory stopped when Serah had thrust something through her back. She remembered turning to kill Serah, but then there was nothing. Had she killed Serah and Shannon? She must have. Even in her final breaths, there was nothing that could slow the rage of the red.

Mimi felt a terrible emptiness inside. It was something that was far beyond guilt; it was a black hole of light and love. It threatened to swallow her and steal the last of her sanity. She clung to the scraps, to the edge, fingers slipping, heart pounding, raw red...

The lights came on. It stung her eyes as the large cavern took shape. She blinked and focused. It was a dimly lit place, and the rocky ceiling was high above. Stalactites dripped and hung from the top, and though she wanted to look around, she was still unable to look beyond the rim of her eye sockets.

Then she heard the sound of metal on rock. Someone was walking toward her. The footsteps were slow and methodical. Mimi closed her eyes and reached out toward the mind. It was a void, a brick.

She wanted to scream, to fight, to get away, but she could see no possible means of escape. Then she remembered the last thing before all the light went out of the world. She remembered Shannon and Serah charging a door. She remembered how she had reached out for them, how she had looked up and saw the face of her captor. She was carried through the door by a Recycled Runner.

She swallowed. There was one weapon, wasn't there? One thing that she could do to protect herself? She looked inside, and there, just below the surface, was deep power. She could use it if she wanted. There was a sense that it almost called to her; it wanted to be used.

"Please, don't." It was another mind touching hers. She couldn't find the source; it faded back to its origin.

Mimi surfaced, and without realizing it, she took a deep breath. The red within her quieted, just a little.

As the footsteps stopped, she tried to eyeball the creature. Then, there was a pop, the sense of space around her limbs, and a release. Whatever container she was in opened and she was free to move.

Wasting no time, she swung her legs off the table and jumped to the ground. Her legs buckled under her, and she collapsed. Even her arms would not hold her up, and she turned over on her back and looked up, nearly as helpless as before.

"It takes a few moments for your arms and legs to remember their function." The voice sounded female.

"I'm sorry, who are you?"

There was another sound of metal feet on stone, but this time in pairs. Within a few seconds, someone picked Mimi up and placed her sitting up on the table. She craned her neck around, and though her eyes were still a bit blurry, she spotted the outline of someone working a few dozen meters away at a console.

"Don't worry, the paralysis is temporary. I am actually quite surprised you were able to swing your legs off of the table so easily. You must have quite a strong core. The chemicals only seem to affect the limbs."

"You didn't answer my question." Now, with a target that was more than just recycled, Mimi pushed and transmitted, "You really should tell me who you are. Wouldn't it make it easier to deal with me if we were on a first name basis?"

The woman laughed. It was a chuckle at first and then grew into a belly laugh.

"Oh, dear Mimi, your mind tricks aren't going to work on me. After all, I have been dealing with someone so much more powerful than you for the entirety of my life."

"Miranda?"

The woman did not respond. Instead, she walked over, and the light above the table illuminated the woman's features for a moment.

She was striking. Her hair was ashen and dreaded but not quite grey. There was life in those strands. The pupils of her eyes were such a pale blue that she could almost pass for Recycled. Yet despite all the paleness about her, her lips were a natural blood red. Mimi thought that had she met this woman under any other circumstances, she would have felt a deep attraction.

"Of course. She is the master of this place."

Mimi felt a surge of panic mixed with a desire for vengeance. The hackles on her neck raised, and she gathered herself to fight. Weak or not, she would go down fighting.

"Calm yourself. She has... left. Though she will return sooner or later. She always does."

The woman raised her hand above her head and revealed a syringe. She flicked it with her fingers a few times. She held it up to the dim light and looked satisfied.

Mimi looked at the syringe with horror. "What's that?"

"You wanted muscle augmentation didn't you? So you can use those suits properly?"

Mimi didn't answer.

"Shhhh, don't tell Miranda I gave this to you. She'd be furious." One side of the woman's face rose in the strangest smile Mimi had ever seen. Something was wrong with the other side of her face.

"How old do you think I am? You think I'm just going to let you inject me with something that you claim will help me? I'm not fresh out of scholar school."

The woman didn't move, but with a calm voice said, "If you ever want to get out of here, you have to trust me."

"And why would I trust you? I am in a strange place, surrounded by Recycled with no clear option to leave. What in the world makes you think I should trust you."

"Skim me. Go on."

Mimi did. The woman did have good intentions. She was angry at Miranda, but Mimi couldn't understand why. She wanted to set Mimi free. But Mimi wasn't going to fall for it.

"Lady, you just said that you've been dealing with a powerful telepath for a long time. If that's true, then you should have pretty good control of your thoughts at this point. So anything I skim from you isn't necessarily the truth."

"My, you are as clever as she claims." That same half-smirk lit her face. "Well, so you know, you are going to take the contents of this syringe whether you want to or not. We can do it the easy way, where you simply offer me your arm, or I can have a few of my Recycled grab you and restrain you. You don't have much of a choice."

But Mimi did have a choice. Inside her, the red was building. She could feel it rising in her chest, mingled with her anger. If this woman brought the Recycled over, it would lash out in defense and strike them all down. She knew now she could handle a room full of Recycled. But then she thought of this woman. What if there was a small chance that she was telling the truth. Did she deserve to die? Mimi wasn't sure.

Mimi said, "I will make you a deal. You tell me who you are, a little of your story, and I'll consider doing it the easy way."

The woman laughed. "You are fearless aren't you. Maybe I should just call over the Recycled."

Mimi shook a little as a little of the red anger spilled over. Behind her something made a terrible, high-pitched scream and then fell to the floor with a loud crash.

The woman frowned. "Ah, I see. You know, there aren't very many of those left in the city. I would appreciate if you didn't do that."

The woman did not flinch or move from her spot. On the contrary, she took a few more steps forward. It took every ounce of Mimi's control not to let the beast inside her free.

The woman said, "You seem to have more control over it then we suspected. To only kill one and not all of them, that is quite impressive. I can see why she wants you alive."

"Who wants me alive? Miranda?"

The woman ignored the question. "I never had a proper name. No one ever gave me one. So, one day, when I was reading, I came across the word for an ancient tree that went extinct a long time ago. I was a sad child, you see; my mother wasn't exactly kind or attentive and I never knew my father, so I could identify with that tree. Its branches hung low like I used to bow my head, allowing my hair to become a curtain. So, I chose part of the tree name as my own. I am Willow."

Mimi skimmed and pushed a little harder then she normally would. The woman winced, but so far as Mimi could tell, at least as much as this woman was willing to admit, her name was Willow.

Willow said, "I recognize you have no reason to trust anything I say, but you see, you can either trust me or wait for Miranda to come back around and, well, she can be less forgiving. The woman lifted the bottom of her surgical scrubs and exposed her abdomen.

There were a number of scars crisscrossing her abdomen. A few of the scars looked like teeth marks.

"Wow... what..."

"Miranda gets angry. Sometimes she bites... hard. If you'd like to see, I can show you that my entire body is covered with marks from the neck down."

Mimi shook her head.

"So you see, you can trust me now, and maybe, just maybe we can both get out of here while Miranda is otherwise occupied, or you can wait and take your chances with her."

Mimi thought about it, then remembered how much time it took for the muscle augmentation to take effect. She also remembered studying Shannon's body after and how there had been numerous puncture scars. Shannon had told her that several needles injected her with the chemicals and the nanites at once. She remembered as she had gone down in the docks a decade later, once she started fighting in the EnViro suit and used her ability to scan scientific information to discover that the reason for the multiple injection sites is that it had the highest rate of success because of the alteration to the blood chemistry. Enough of the blood had to be altered at the same time for the process to stimulate growth. A single injection site had a 90% failure rate.

"You're lying. One syringe won't augment my muscles; it takes a whole machine to do it properly."

"You're right. And I intend to put you in that machine after you take this sedative. It's a much less painful process if you are unconscious, and since we don't need you awake to integrate a chip into the base of your skull like they do in the Runnercore, you don't have to be awake for this procedure."

Mimi still didn't think she could trust this woman. She wanted to get out, to run back to Shannon and Serah, though she was wondering if, after what she had done, they would take her back. Even if they did accept her back, the Order might punish her for using the red veil. Or worse, maybe Shannon wouldn't look at her the same way. She had it happen before. There was Angela; all those centuries ago, when she had shared her secret with her, the woman had left her. She wondered if this would be like that, if Shannon would be too terrified of her to love her.

She could try pushing this woman a little harder, maybe just releasing a little of her wild ability and then make a run for it? The trouble was, if this woman was a prisoner like she claimed, didn't she deserve to flee as well? She thought of those scars on the woman's body, but something still wasn't adding up. Something in her was resisting the idea that Willow had her best interest at heart.

"Well? What do you think?" The woman transmitted directly to Mimi, "Do you want out or not?"

Mimi said out loud. "You're a telepath?"

The woman nodded, "Yes, but admittedly not a very strong one. Basic communication is all I can do, but it serves my Mistress well. She only ever needs me to respond to her summons once in a while, mostly, like the Recycled, I wait here until I am needed."

Mimi felt something else in her gut besides anger and the red veil, she felt a sense of empathy for this woman. Mimi had had a rough life, but it seemed like this woman had some pretty horrible circumstances.

"How do I know that's not poison? That you aren't going to kill me and turn into one of them?" She gestured over toward the Recycled.

"You don't. But let me ask you this, why would I have bothered to release you from the surgery table if I was going to kill you and Recycle you? Wouldn't it have been easier for me to simply kill you while you were unconscious and then transform you? It's not like you need to be alive for me to Recycle you, after all. Almost everyone who is Recycled is dead long before they even arrive here."

Mimi shuttered. Ice grew in her veins.

"Is that where we are? The place where people are Recycled?"

The woman nodded. "Yes. You can imagine why I would want to get out of here, can't you?"

Mimi wasn't sure if this woman was playing some game, but something was not adding up. She took a long look around the room and made no effort to disguise it. So as far she could see, there were no clear entrances or exits.

"Frustrating, isn't it? There are no doors anywhere. Bet you are wondering how we got in here? You know, it took me almost two centuries to figure out how she got in and out of this place."

"So, there is an exit?"

"Yep, there is. But you can't open the door without a passcode, and it's not like Mother is willing to share. She's always been selfish."

"Mother?" Could this woman's mother be... but no, Mimi couldn't imagine that was the case.

Willow didn't answer. She only held out her hand to take Mimi's arm for the injection.

When you spent a few centuries on the street, you developed an instinct for things. If you didn't, you didn't last long. Mimi had always augmented this instinct with her ability to skim minds, but anyone who survived on the street had to have some sense of intuition. At that moment, Mimi's sense was that if she wanted to survive this, if she wanted to get out of this horrible place, and maybe even destroy it, she had to play along, at least. Because it was true that if this woman wanted her dead or Recycled, she had all the opportunity in the world. Even though her back still ached a little, her wound was almost entirely healed. It would just take a few more days for the nerve clusters in her body to recalibrate around the healed tissue.

So, Mimi did what she always did when she was unsure what to do next. She took a risk. Mimi held out her hand to Willow and felt the pinch of the syringe.

"Excellent." A tiny bead of blood blossomed on Mimi's arm as Willow pulled the syringe away.

"So, you got it in me now; what was your real plan?"

"Oh, I told you. I'm going to augment your muscles; in fact, I might just augment a few..."

But that was the last thing Mimi remembered, and the sedative took possession of her.

Chapter 8
Vala's Nightmare

"She's awake."

Serah turned and walked over to the table where Vala stirred in her first moments of waking. Shannon put her hand on her forehead.

Serah said, "How are you feeling, Vala?"

Vala's eyes were swollen and puffy. Streaks of soot leftover from the underground, and the green goop of the alcove carved out in neat little paths from where tears had cascaded down her face. The grime was as deep as her wounds, and it would take time for it all to come out. She tilted her head and eyed Serah, and then Shannon. Serah watched something uncloud in her gaze, some first hint of awareness, and then Vala connected to her in mind to mind contact.

It was a yawning thought, full of drowsy curiosity. "Where are we?"

Serah reached up and stroked Vala's hair. She could feel the woman's desire for some contact; a gentle touch different from the pain and horror that came before.

For Shannon's benefit, Serah spoke out loud. "We're in the underground where Shannon has lived for the past forty years."

Vala look toward Shannon and took the cue, using her voice. "Where are..."

But the woman broke off. Serah, skimming her, knew that she would ask after the other sisters, and then why they were here and not the library. But memory surged forth, not so much a gentle trickle, but a tsunami. Serah watched Vala's mind awaken to the pain, to the memories, to all the terrible things that happened to her in the last week. She caught fragments of images of the events inside the library, but Vala pushed them back down even as her body shuddered and the tears spilled forth from the edges of her eyelids.

"Vala, I know you don't want to talk about it, but we need to know what happened. We need to know who's still out there; if other sisters need help."

Serah soothed her the best she could, using everything that Fatima and Noatla had taught her. Almost immediately, Vala responded. She sniffled, nodded, and sat up on the table, cringing at the pain from the half-healed wound in her leg.

She gazed around the chamber.

"There are no others but you two?" Her voice quavered, and she swallowed hard.

Serah shook her head.

"Mimi? She was with you, wasn't she? What about Alexa?"

Before Serah could open her mouth to say anything Shannon said, "Mimi's missing. But we think we'll find her soon."

For a moment, Serah considered telling Vala what happened in mind to mind contact, but she held off. Vala had enough to sort through without thinking about another lost sister. The problem was, Shannon's denial ran deep. Nearly half a dozen times, Serah had to retrieve Shannon from standing outside the massive and mysterious door through which Mimi had been taken. Soon, it was going to come to a fight between them, and Serah had the strange thought that losing Shannon would be like losing another one of her sisters. She hadn't realized until that moment how much she cared for Shannon, but there it was, an undeniable depth of emotion.

Serah said, "We don't know what happened to Alexa."

Vala said, "She was with Runner 17... she... and Noatla before..."

Serah nodded. "We know. But after the library, we don't know where she and 17 went, but we know they left there together. That's all I was able to find out from skimming some of the people who came to clean things up. There was one in security who thought that 17 had traveled outside the city to fight, but of course, no thoughts of Alexa were present in his mind."

"Fatima!" Vala stood and was excited. "She got out the window first! She has to be okay."

Shannon said, "Yes, we saw Fatima. She was here last night."

Rather than going through the whole thing, Serah transmitted everything that Fatima had said before Shannon could even continue.

Vala said, "Why would she run away like that?"

Shannon looked between the two women, confused for a moment, and then recognition spread across her face on how Vala had learned about what happened so quickly.

"Sorry, Shannon. Mind to mind contact is much faster than verbal communication and... well, it's a habit after decades of communicating that way."

"I understand." A smile bloomed on Shannon's face, like the flowers that Serah had watched Mimi give her so many times. "Mimi would always..." Her smile vanished. "Nevermind."

It was another warning sign for Serah. She would have to help Shannon find the truth herself, perhaps with a little persuasion and some soothing. The truth was the Recycled, and Miranda had Mimi. What reason would they have to keep her alive? But, she supposed when you loved someone like Shannon loved Mimi, you needed to cling to hope, especially when the rest of the world was collapsing around you.

Serah felt a deep void inside herself. What did she have to hope for? What was keeping her going? If the Order of the Eye was destroyed except for the three of them, what was the point? Maybe Miranda had already won.

Vala said, "I'm hungry, is there anything to eat?"

Vala looked at Serah; there was a depth to her stare. Had Serah kept her thoughts private or had Vala just skimmed her? She wasn't sure she wanted to know the answer. She had been far too lax about guarding her thoughts in the last week since it had only been her and Shannon. It was a habit she was going to have to break.

Shannon said, "What would you like?"

"Something warm."

"Soup?"

Serah said, "Soup might be the best idea since you haven't eaten much in days. Why don't you go jump in the shower over there and get washed up while we go print food. Clean that wound another time, the alcove seems to have taken care of the depth of it, but the surface still needs work. After we eat, we can hear the whole story." Serah sent a fresh wave of soothing as she spoke.

Vala nodded. "Are there... any fresh clothes around?"

Shannon said, "I have a few spare things around you can try."

2.

They sat in the corner of the small chamber, next to the door that had only a short time ago led to the storage of a few hundred reserve Runners. The table was enough for the three of them; more than enough. Vala longed for the company of other sisters. She had always gotten along fine with Serah, but she longed for someone with better soothing talents and who was a little less intense. Serah had always carried a chip on her shoulder; was always on the attack and defense. That was good if you were a Runner, but it made it difficult for a woman of the sisterhood, an organization that necessitated patience.

Vala took a long time chewing the chunks from her soup and slurped up every drop she could. Knowing what was coming, knowing what she must tell, and how she needed to relive the nightmare, she felt the tension. She had no intention of rushing her meal. Still, time was funny sometimes, and before she knew it, the soup was gone. Perhaps it was because she was famished, or maybe a part of her wanted to tell and release.

She understood what Serah was doing, and why, but that didn't make what she needed to do any easier. She hoped some of her other sisters survived. Even after 17 had come and killed the Recycled, they had fled the library, knowing that Miranda was still out there.

Her mind skirted the edge of the darkness. It was a black abyss that was tugging on her. There was an ache in her, a desire to fall back into that darkness and never climb out again. She pondered the temptation. It unsettled her, and not for the first time; she wondered what Noatla would say to her if she were still alive. At least now she had Serah and Shannon to help her.

Vala glanced up from her empty bowl and saw Serah's face, waiting patiently but expectant, as if any moment she would have all the answers for her. She was about to be disappointed. The only thing she could serve her friend was a bitter meal, perhaps a poisonous one.

Vala asked Serah, "How do you want to do this?" She nodded her head toward Shannon. Serah seemed to understand the implication.

"What would be easier for you, Vala? I can tell Shannon if you wanted to share it all in a few moments."

Vala thought about it, thought about what that kind of projection into Serah's mind might do to her, and decided against it.

"No, verbally is best here. Serah, you can't understand how horrific it was, I know you're strong, and you've seen plenty of violence firsthand, but, you already have other things on your mind right now."

Deep creases formed in Serah's face and forehead. Serah would have to guard her thoughts better. Serah was on edge, and she didn't even realize it. Vala would do her part to help the order rebuild. After all, it was Noatla who had taken her in when she was a teenager when her mother had passed away. Vala owed everything to the order.

Serah nodded. "Okay, Vala."

Shannon said. "Do you want some tea or coffee from the food printer?"

Vala said, "I think that would be a good idea."

Shannon stood from the table, took their dishes, and brought them back to the printer.

Serah said, "How are you feeling?"

Vala considered. "Better, now that I have some food in me and..." She reached across and grabbed Serah's hand and squeezed it for a moment. "It's good knowing that I'm not totally alone." She released Serah's hand and sat back just as Shannon approached with three steaming-hot cups.

Vala asked, "How much do you know?"

Serah said, "Just a few things that Fatima said. She wouldn't share much. She insisted we get it from you."

"What did she say about the events at the library?"

"She said that Miranda came to the door of the library with the Recycled. That she demanded all the sisters come out after all of you had barricaded yourselves in. Then she told us about how even with combined strength, they couldn't overpower her. I think that's what really scared Fatima, that all of the sisters at the library combined couldn't even slow her down."

Vala nodded. "Did she tell you about Noatla walking out to face her?"

"No. Just that you were all trapped. But Shannon and I guessed that's what happened when we saw Noatla's body outside."

"Then, I guess that's a good place to start." Vala squirmed in her seat and leaned forward, sipping her tea. She took a deep breath and told her tale.

3.

Miranda sang, "Oh where, oh where is the Matron? She is late for her final appointment. So many years have passed, my dear Noatla. I would think you eager to reminisce on old times. Come now, don't leave us waiting."

The voice echoed through every single mind in the bathroom, and Vala felt a cold chill rise up her spine. She heard Noatla moving aside some of the barricades they had erected to keep out the Recycled.

Fatima shouted, yelling over the din of chaos. "Noatla. Don't you dare go out there. Noatla?"

There was no response, only more shuffling on the other side of the bathroom door, and then the sounds ceased, and there was a low, barely audible click of a door settling into its socket.

Darla and Rachel huddled together. Rebecca, Lana, and Kayla worked together to try and pry the bathroom door open.

Kayla said, "Come on, we have to get out there and help her."

Fatima said, "Help her? To do what? To die at the hands of the recycled?"

Vala said, "They have reinforcements. Didn't you hear? Alexa is out there, and she brought some people with her to fight. If we can help them shake loose from Miranda's grip, we stand a chance."

Fatima stared at Vala, and she felt the power of that gaze. "If we could overpower her, do you think Noatla would have gone out there to confront her directly? If we were able to stop this by working together, we would have already done so."

Vala said, "Then what is she doing?"

Fatima said, "Isn't it obvious? She is buying us some time. She is distracting Miranda so we can sneak out the back window."

Fatima pointed toward the tiny square thing that cast a few fragmented shafts of light into the room. Vala looked at the window and then at Fatima. Did this woman think she could fit through it? Even if she could, where would she go? Miranda wasn't stupid enough to leave the back doors unguarded. There would be Recycled outside that window. They were far too large to fit inside it, but they would be waiting for the first rabbit to stick its head out the hole, waiting for the slaughter to begin.

The Recycled were passive creatures, empty of will, empty of thought, vacant canvases for the AI to order around, or for a telepath to use. In the hands of Miranda, they were an extension of her bloodlust, of her madness, of her red veil. Now they would come to claim the sisters of the Order of the Eye. They were just small birds in the wake of an apolicane: no matter how much they flapped, the storm possessed them.

Death had arrived. Vala stood and walked toward the door. She would stand and be true. She would fight for her sisters as long as she could, no matter the cost.

With her added effort, the bathroom door groaned.

Kayla said, "Come on, all at once now. One, two, three, pull!"

Five sisters pulled together, and the door complained with further protest.

"Okay, stop. Rest a moment, and then let's try again."

Lana said, "Look, it's crooked now."

Vala saw the door no longer set in a settled position; it bowed inward.

Rebecca said, "I think I can get my fingers just below the lock now." She worked her fingers in the crack, and sure enough, they fit.

Fatima said, "Come on you fools, stop focusing on the door, and let's get out the window."

Joan said, "And abandon Noatla?"

Fatima said, "Noatla is already dead whether you want to admit it or not. If we scatter now, we stand a chance of fighting another day, don't you see that?"

Kayla looked at Fatima with scorn, her eyes slit, and her face creased. "Coward."

Fatima's mouth gaped, and her jaw worked. There was an undercurrent of fury in her expression and Vala knew that even if they all survived the day, something had changed between Fatima and the others. Later, as Vala told Serah and Shannon, she would realize that this was where the Order of the Eye really ended.

Kayla said, "Okay, let's pull again. I think we can get it this time."

Rebecca and Lana worked their fingers both above and below the lock, and the other three sisters grabbed the knob.

"Ready?" said Kayla.

It occurred to Vala that perhaps if they linked minds and focused, it would give them just the edge they needed to pry the door open. She reached out to her other sisters, and together, minds and bodies united in a single act, they pulled.

For a moment, the door issued its ancient protest, grumbling like an old man who had remained unmoved in his thoughts and ideas for so long, but then, when the pressure became too much, when the truth sat upon his chest, suffocating him, he, like the door, he admitted the inevitable. The door let go and burst open. Several sisters stumbled back and fell. The door stood off-kilter, splinters reaching every which way, like feelers on some strange beast. The passage was open.

Vala helped up Rebecca and Lana. Kayla was already out the door with Patricia and headed up the stairs to the main level of the library, racing to meet and stand with their matron, no matter the result.

Vala looked over and saw that Fatima had managed to get the rusted latch of the ancient window open. No one had helped her, and she had strained to reach up for purchase, fingers grazing the lip. Now, she looked around for something to stand on, to boost her up to the small window. Vala felt a flavor of contempt for the woman, but also a strange pity as the rest of the sisters went for the stairs. Vala went out to the fallen bookshelves and, amongst the rivers of fallen books, discovered a small stool. She brought it back into the bathroom and handed it to Fatima.

"Here."

Fatima blinked at her. Vala could feel the woman reaching in to skim her, but she batted away any possibility for mind to mind contact.

Fatima said, "Why?"

"Because even though you are a coward, you are still my sister."

She turned and walked out of the bathroom, across the ocean of chaos that was once a place of learning and family and light. Now it was changed. Now, like the Order of the Eye, it was broken, perhaps forever. As Vala reached the base of the stairs, she looked back toward the bathroom. There in the doorway, Fatima watched her. Vala turned and ran up the stairs to join her other sisters. It was the last time Vala ever saw Fatima.

3.

There was a scream. It was not the scream of someone startled by something unexpected. It was the scream of someone's final defiance before death took them, one last act of life and rebellion before a final exhalation. Vala had just rounded the corner of the stairway, turned, and had her first glimpse of the main level above when her blood turned to ice.

It was Kayla's last scream.

Three Recycled advanced on the other sisters. Their white on white eyes, that void of apathy seemed almost tinged red with their master's madness and rage. The fourth Recycled had run an arm blade up through Kayla's chest and was taking great care to remove her now-lifeless impaled body from its grip. She was stuck, and it struggled to remove her as Kayla's blood baptized its undead arm.

The other sisters were retreating, and in both mind and mouth, they screamed and fled in terror. They were running back toward Vala, back to the stairs. The Recycled took their time. They advanced in their slow rhythmic gate that would fool anyone who didn't know how incredibly fast they were up close. Behind the three advancing on the sisters were a dozen more walking in through the library entrance.

Patricia said, "Focus sisters. One at a time. Kill one at a time."

Yoshi, Patricia, and Lucy reached the top of the stairs and turned. As they did, one of the creatures fell to its knees and screamed. Blue fluid trickled from its ears and nose, the same color of deep blue that crisscrossed their exposed skin.

One of the other creatures lunged and grabbed Rosita; it tugged on her, pulling her closer. Its blade unsheathed from its arm, and it reached back to plunge it deep into her. But then, Aurora and Lana were there trying to free her. Lana beat at it uselessly with a broken table leg, and it swatted her away like a fist punching through taught paper. She fell back and smacked her head against the bookshelf and did not move.

But Aurora had found something sharp; a broken broom handle. She jumped up on top of one of the nearby tables. Then, she screamed at the thing that held Rosita. As it looked at her, she leaped through the air toward it, slamming into its body and bouncing off, but not before plunging the broken piece of wood straight into its mouth and through the back of its neck.

It dropped Rosita and fell to its knees, even as its fellows advanced on the sisters. Rosita scrambled to her feet and ran for the stairs.

Aurora, back on her feet, but clutching her left arm, screamed, "Run down the stairs and barricade the door."

Vala and the other sisters made their way back down. For a moment, Vala wanted to grab Lana, but she had not risen, and there seemed nothing else she could do. They fled through the door and shut it. Immediately the sisters worked together to move the bookshelves back to obscure the passage. Aurora yelped in pain.

Vala said, "Go Aurora, back to the bathroom."

Aurora nodded, still cradling her arm and walked back to the room.

They only had two bookshelves pressed up against the ancient wooden door when the pounding began. The Recycled, in their augmented strength and armored suits, were living battering rams. The sound of dragging metal feet marked the spaces between the pounding on the door. Vala turned and saw Yoshi, Lucy, and Joan working together to slide yet another bookshelf across the room to barricade the door. Vala wasn't sure how much it would help, but she joined in the effort with Darla and Rachel. As they placed the fourth bookshelf against the door, an armored fist burst through the ancient oak door, and the Recycled reached around for the knob. All the sisters stopped working and watched. When the Recycled found only the wood of one of the shelves, it withdrew its arm. There was silence both outside and in, and Vala could hear her heart beating in her ears.

Then there was a loud crunch. The Recycled slammed its whole body into the door, and after only two blows, the top hinge broke free. Then that pause again; only the creatures ragged breathing permeated the wood.

Yoshi said, "The bathroom window. It's our only chance."

There was a murmur of agreement as the second hinge splintered, and the top of the door gave way. Only the size of the Recycled stopped it from crawling up and over the wreckage of the shelves and the few books that still clung desperately to their archaic shelving.

Vala followed Joan and Patricia into the bathroom and saw that Fatima was stuck, legs dangling out the window. It would have been comical if the circumstances were different. But instead, Fatima moaned and cried, her wide hips caught just at the lip of the window. It was only luck or arrogance that no Recycled waited to help Fatima free from the street.

Most of the sisters blinked and stared, seeing their one way out, their one exit blocked by the woman who had tried to escape and abandon them.

Vala said, "Sisters, focus your minds on the creature that is coming through the entrance and kill it. Maybe we can use it's body to plug the way forward and slow the other recycled from getting in. I'll help Fatima get unstuck and clear the way.

Vala transmitted to Fatima that she was about to push her legs, and that she should use whatever upper body strength she had left to pull on her side. She pushed and prodded, forcing the women's thick, short legs forward. All the while, she could hear the mingled unearthly screams of the Recycled as the sisters destroyed several more. Finally, Fatima popped free. Her legs disappeared on the other side, and she turned and looked down toward Vala, reaching out a hand.

Fatima said, "Come on."

Vala said, "No, I'll go last. I'll help everyone else get away first."

Vala called to her sisters, and Yoshi climbed the small stool and grabbed Fatima's hand. Yoshi slid through the window with no problem. Then, it was Lucy's turn, and she slid through quickly. Then Fatima screamed and disappeared from the window.

Fatima yelled, "Run, get out of here while you can."

Vala couldn't see more than a sliver of what was happening, a slice in the terrible drama that was happening above. Miranda must have realized what was happening, and the Recycled went after the sisters who had found their way free.

At the same time, the first Recycled had trudged its way to the library, up and over the barriers, and cast aside some of the debris to clear the way for its fellows. Vala and her sisters peered outside the bathroom door and saw that several of them were through, and they turned their attention to the remaining sisters. Vala peered out the window and saw, to her horror, that one of the Recycled stood waiting at the top. They were trapped.

Then, a long, metallic object slid in through the open window. Before Vala could register that she was looking down the barrel of a gun, it opened fire. The first beam of light missed her head by inches, but it shifted position and fired again. Vala watched a large hole open inside the front of Patricia. The beam vaporized her center, and only a large smoking hole remained where Patricia's torso had been. Vala could see the question on Patricia's lips. Vala skimmed her sister's last thoughts, and as the woman fell face first to the floor she wondered why there was a hole in her chest.

Rebecca fell to another blast just before the high-pitched scream of the Recycled marked the end of its existence and its shot. Lana and Darla had joined minds to end the creature's assault. The weapon fell into the bathroom and let off one last blast, striking Vala in the abdomen. Later, Vala would think that the weapon must have barely gone off because if it were at full blast, she surely would have died right then and there. Instead, a warm gush flowed down the side of her shirt and down to her trousers. She wasn't quite sure what to think or do about the wound. There was little pain at that moment, and Vala wondered if Patricia or Rebecca had felt any pain in their last breaths. Perhaps the heat and energy of the weapon had seared the nerves enough to kill the pain.

Then, there was another arm reaching inside and another weapon attempting to fire, but Darla, who was in a rage that Vala had seen only one other time, forty years earlier, shrieked, and the creature immediately dropped its weapon before anything else could happen. With the combined effort of the remaining sisters, the creatures fell, one by one, until there were none of them left. But there would be more. Above, the sound of heavy footsteps marching marked the passage of more of the terrible creatures.

Rachel stood over Vala, and she tore strips from her dress. It was bright orange, and for the rest of her life, Vala would remember how the orange cloth looked spattered with her blood. It was the smell; she had no idea that the scent of blood and charred meat could be so potent.

Then, another smell wafted into her nostrils. It was the smell of grass, and fresh air, like when Vala was a child, and her parents would occasionally take her to one of the rooftop garden parties that the Mids loved to throw.

Rachel was crying, "Vala, you're gonna be alright. I have to bandage you; have to stop the bleeding, but you're gonna be alright."

But Vala knew she wasn't going to be alright. That none would be. She knew that if any of the sisters left in the bathroom survived now, it would be nothing short of a miracle. Noatla had not stopped Miranda. Alexa and her reinforcements had never really come to save them. There were only the Recycled, and she wondered, not for the first time, if she would soon walk amongst the creatures, a servant of Miranda's forever.

She thought of how Patricia and Rebecca had fallen, and she glanced over at them. They were nothing but sacks of meat now, weren't they? There was no life in them, all the color escaped their face, and their eyes were dead and blank. Rachel looked at Vala and then looked at the women. It occurred to Vala that she no longer shielded any of her thoughts. But why should she? If she was going to die here, what was there to hide?

She laid back and relaxed, waiting for the end to come. She knew the next wave of Recycled would be on them soon enough.

She could hear screaming outside. A man's voice, the sound of metal and glass and projectiles. The sound of combat in an EnViro Suit. It did sound a lot like what you saw in the vid screen programs. But those programs never showed the horror of what it was like to be in the middle of that, to watch as some of your sisters died at the hands of the creatures.

Then she heard three women talking. She could pick out the sound of two of the voices, but the third one, whom she had never heard in person in her life, was likely Miranda. So there it was, Alexa and Noatla and Miranda were all standing out there. But why had everything gone silent? The march above their heads had ceased. Were all the Recycled gone?

A few more moments passed, and then Vala heard, both outside and inside her mind, a kind of cackling mad laughter. The movement above resumed, and by the sound of it, they far outnumbered the remaining sisters.

One entered the room. Several sisters focused on it, but instead of falling, it hesitated only briefly and reached out and picked up Darla by the throat and tore off one of her limbs and then another. Vala could do nothing but watch. Another one came in and punched Joan so hard in the head that Vala could hear the sickening crunch of her skull as she flew back into the wall.

Vala wept. She shook all over as, one by one, she saw her sisters fall, brutally slaughtered by the creatures.

Outside, there was the sound of a man shouting, and then the sounds of combat resumed. For a moment, the Recycled froze in place, seemingly lost and unable to move. The shouts outside intensified and, out of curiosity, Vala reached out to the person yelling. It was Runner 17. She had a strange experience of watching through his eyes as he tore through one Recycled after another. He cut them down as if they were paper, and he was a freshly sharpened pair of scissors. Then, there were only two Recycled standing on either side of Miranda, and Miranda stood, mouth gaping. The creatures moved with speed out of the bathroom and up to aid their master.

Vala could feel 17's rage and his lust for her death. He charged after Miranda as she fled. The two Recycled stopped him long enough for the ones that had slaughtered her sisters to catch up. He dispatched them quickly; they were no match for him, but Miranda vanished among the buildings, likely masking her form from any who would seek to pursue her.

The last thing Vala wondered before she lost consciousness was why Miranda hadn't been able to stop Runner 17.

3.

"Then, the next thing I knew, you and Shannon were standing over me."

Serah nodded. "You okay, Vala?"

"Physically, I think I'm okay."

Serah didn't have to hear her finish to know the rest. Serah had seen enough horror of her own in the last week to know that neither of them would ever be able to think about the world in quite the same way again.

Vala asked. "Yoshi, is she...?"

Serah shook her head, "We don't know. No one seems to know. We only found Fatima so far. Yoshi, Rosita, and Aurora are still missing. We're hoping they didn't get taken behind the door like Mimi."

Vala frowned. "So the order is destroyed then. Miranda has won."

Serah said, "I've thought about that a lot. If that were true, why doesn't she finish the job?"

Shannon said, "Because she's not here. Not on the city anymore, I mean."

Serah said, "Yes, It's the only thing that makes sense. She must have been off of the city when the blasts took the legs."

Vala said, "Then there's hope, isn't there?"

"Maybe." Serah paused for a moment to collect her thoughts. "Fatima is right, though. The tension in this city is rising. We have to find the other remaining sisters if we want to stand any chance of keeping things from boiling over."

Vala said, "What if we can't? What if the city erupts into chaos?"

"That can't happen. Otherwise, our sisters' deaths meant nothing. We have to honor their legacy. We have to honor our oath to the Order of the Eye."

"Even if the Order is broken?"

"What is broken can be fixed if we only persist, if we only keep going forward."

Vala shifted in her seat, wincing from a hint of pain. She looked long and hard at Serah. She thought about Fatima and how she had fled. She thought about her sisters dying at the hands of the Recycled. She thought about everything that had happened to her in the last week. But among all that pain and all that horror was another memory that rose to the surface. It was the memory of Noatla taking her in, of inducting her into the Order of the Eye. Then, a cascade of memories flooded her mind. She saw the laughter of her sisters and all the kindness and gratitude she felt being a part of something bigger than herself. She thought of all that and decided that she did want that again.

Vala said, "Okay. I'm in."

Chapter 9
Burn It All Down

The room was filling up fast, and Frank could feel the nervous tension with every new body pressing in through the door. As each new person entered the old school gymnasium, the temperature and tension climbed together like eager lovers. Scattered in disorganized patterns, the chairs and benches were mostly occupied. There were a few straight lines here and there, but like the city itself, there was only a semblance of barely organized chaos. Soon it would be standing room only. But they would come; they would stand; they would wait for the answers that they wanted to hear. While the Earth passed into memory and the stars twinkled with renewed brightness, all those in the Lowers were looking for something stable, even if it was a lie, especially if it was a lie.

Every occupied seat contained aching shoulders or sore backs. The shifting and stirring of each body suggested a nervous rhythm: a desperation for answers. Frank's stomach gurgled. He, too, was here for answers, but there was something about the crowd that unsettled him. The crowd rocked and moved and jabbered their mouths until their tongues lashed one another, leaving deep wounds of rumors and hearsay.

A round-faced, red-mustached man said, "I heard they're recruiting new Runners, and that's where they are all disappearing to."

"Runners," said a black haired woman with deep lines in her face. "They'd be lucky if they get the Runnercore. Did you see all those Recycled on the street?"

A younger blond boy, barely a legal adult, said, "I always thought the Recycled were a rumor, a bedtime story my ma told me to scare me. But I saw one of them kill my best friend during the battle with Saud. It just snapped his neck." The boy's pale face tinged a shade of green. "Eliot never hurt anyone."

The dark haired woman put her arm around the boy.

Frank rubbed his neck. It ached. How many double shifts had he pulled since the city had left the surface? He'd hardly seen his wife in the aftermath of the battle, and it was an understatement to say she was pissed. He couldn't blame her; the city was almost destroyed, and he should be spending more time with his family, but what was he supposed to do? If Sanitation shut down now...

The red-mustached man said, "I don't know what's making people disappear, but you can bet the Uppers have something to do with it. If they think everything is just gonna be the same after we left the planet, they got another thing coming."

There was a murmur of assent from several people who sat around the man, and even Frank agreed with the general idea of what he was saying. Things had to change. This was the right time to make sure that the people of the Lowers got their due. But Frank had been part of the last uprising, had seen how quickly things turned sour, and he didn't want a repeat of that.

"She's missing Frank."

Frank blinked. "You sure?"

Zelda sat just as stiff and fidgety as anyone else in the room. She looked strange in the light; there was a sort of unusual vitality about her, despite the extra work and the chaos of the city.

"Damn sure. She's been out two days now."

"Two days ain't that bad."

"Right now, it is."

Frank couldn't disagree with that. Anyone who took time off right now, when everything was such a mess, would never hear the end of it. Hell, some of them might even get fired for it. Frank hated to fire people, but sometimes the paper-pushers in the Mids didn't give him a choice.

Zelda said, "Besides, when have you ever known Jenny to miss a shift? She's as reliable as Jose was."

Frank winced at the mention of Jose. He had hoped he would do okay in the Runnercore, but when those bombs went off below the city legs, all hope had buckled just as the legs had.

He and Jose had been the best of friends for decades, and he was gone, just like that. Sure, he had spent some time mourning him before when they had taken him to the Runnercore, but knowing he was dead was even worse. His eyes burned a little every time he thought of him, and now Jenny was missing.

"Sorry. I didn't mean... I just.."

"I know what you mean Zelda." His words came out a little more forceful then he liked. He reined himself back in and sighed. "You check her place? She lived alone, didn't she?"

"Yep, and there's no sign of her.

"How many is that from sanitation?"

"Four that we know. Eric, up at shield maintenance, said that they've got eight missing now."

"Where the hell are all these people going? Floating out in space?"

"All I know is that it means more double shifts."

Frank said, "How's Mary holding up with the extra hours?"

Zelda shrugged. "She's just as pissed at me as Sally is at you. But, I told her all this overtime is gonna get us closer to the Mids, and that seemed to calm her down a bit."

"If there are any Mids left."

Zelda shook her head. "You know I hate the Uppers just as much as anyone else here tonight." She held up her arm and waved it toward the gathering of people in the room, "But damn, burning down banks? Attacking SO's?"

"I don't know, Zelda. Maybe it's time for a change."

"But like this? Come on, Frank."

"I don't like any more than you, but why should them Uppers profit from all our hard work? Why shouldn't we have equal access to the alcoves, huh? Now, when things are already a mess, it might be the best chance we have to make a difference."

"You reading it again?"

"Reading what?"

"Come on, Frank, don't play dumb, that book from the last uprising."

"I haven't seen a copy since then; you know that."

"Well, you sound like you've been reading it again."

Frank had managed to get his hands on a copy a little while back, but he didn't hold on to it long. Sally had found it stashed in the closet and they had fought so fiercely over it that he burned the copy right there in front of her. He couldn't blame her; everyone who had a copy during the last uprising was sentenced to the Runnercore, but he couldn't forget about the stories the book told. It was a history of regular people standing up for what they believed in, and sometimes, they even won. Now, with what had happened to Jose, how he had been dragged off to the Runnercore, he couldn't stop thinking about how unfair it all was.

"You kidding me? Sally would skin my ass. But that doesn't mean I don't think things need to change here."

"I agree things need to change, Frank. Everyone in the Lowers does, but how is destroying someone else's property going to help?"

"I don't know Zelda; maybe we need to burn it all to the ground and start over. I don't see anything changing unless we do something big."

"So you're okay with burning buildings down?"

"Of course not. You start burning one building, next thing you know, some asshole gets the bright idea to torch my house, or someone else's who has nothing to do with anything. I'm just saying I can understand why they would go after the bank. Things aren't right in this city." He paused for a moment and glanced around the room, looking for anyone else he might know. "That's why we're here tonight, isn't it?"

"Coming to this meeting wasn't my idea."

"No, but you agreed to come along."

"How come Sally didn't come?"

"How come Mary didn't come?"

They both exchanged a smile. Frank knew that Zelda hadn't told Mary where she was going tonight, any more then he told Sally. Both their spouses would have lost their minds if they knew they were going to some meeting about organizing a potential worker's strike.

Every seat in the room was full now, and still, people were streaming in. They had to be approaching a thousand people at this point. If the SO's were still organized and the Runnercore around, this would have been a dangerous gathering, but Frank knew that things were different now. He hoped that difference meant change for the better. He didn't want to see anyone get hurt, but he did want things to change in the city.

Zelda said, "How many more do you think are coming?"

"Search me. Can't be too many more though can it? This room is just about full."

"Do you know who organized this?"

Frank said, "No idea. I just heard about it from Michael at shift change last night."

As the room filled, so did the volume of conversation. Frank hadn't noticed how loud it was in the room until the shushing began, and silence spread.

Frank craned his neck, trying to figure out what was the source of that silence until he caught sight of the man walking up toward the stage from the back of the gym. His stomach dropped.

Zelda whispered, "Shit, he organized this?"

Frank saw him and frowned.

If you had seen this man on the street, you wouldn't think much of him. He was short, pale, and gangly. A large bald spot reflected the overhead light of the gym, and even from two dozen meters away, Frank could see the glare. His dark eyes darted back and forth across the crowd and a cold, greasy grin hijacked his face. Frank thought that hijacked was the only word to describe that smile, because it looked like a smile which could never possibly belong on that face, and that some outside force must be working the gears.

Another man brought out a microphone stand and placed it before him. The man on stage tapped on it for a moment, and the thud of his fingers boomed through the speakers. Frank shivered.

"Good evening."

He had a smooth voice. It was the voice of a man who usually got what he wanted. Frank ground his teeth. If he had known that Tony Sellers was organizing this thing, he would have stayed far away. Tony seemed to know that he was disliked, and more than a few people stood from their chairs in an attempt to leave. Already, there was a queue at the door heading out. Frank was just about to stand and go himself when Tony spoke.

"Now hold on. Just hear me out. Just a few minutes of your time if you please. After all, you're already here, aren't you? What're a few more minutes?" His voice was like soothing silk, but there was an edge behind it, something prickly and sharp; a silken bite.

Tony cleared his throat. "Besides, you all have missing, don't you? Don't you want to hear from someone who might have some answers?"

Frank saw several people sit up a little straighter and take notice. Some of those who were headed to the door paused and turned. The eyes of the young boy, who had lost his friend to the Recycled, sharpened.

Everyone was connected to a missing person somehow, even if it was just a friend of a friend, and after the few thousand who had died in the Battle with Saud, everyone mourned someone. Loss had become a constant companion, one that everyone knew, but everyone hated shaking hands with. Frank thought for the first time, that maybe their city was a little too unfamiliar with loss, that those alcoves and longer lifespans, even in the Lowers, had made a stranger of loss, so that when it came, it came like an apolicane.

"I know most of you know who I am. I know that I have a bad reputation in this city, but like many of you, I have lost someone recently." He paused for effect, but when no one responded, Tony continued. "Some of you may have lost people in the battle with Saud, and for that, you have my deepest condolences. But, like many of you here tonight, I didn't lose some in the battle with Saud. That would have been tragic, but expected. Loss of life is an expected outcome of war. No, like many of you out there, my sister is missing and despite all the resources at my disposal, which most of you know are extensive because of my, uh, connections..."

Zelda whispered, "Let's go, Frank, this snake has nothing I want to hear."

Frank shook his head. "Just wait a moment. I have a feeling we need to be here."

"You can't seriously want to believe anything that man says can you?"

Frank shook his head. "No, of course not. But something tells me we need to be here."

"What?"

"Don't know. It's like a feeling or something."

"...unable to turn up anything about her whereabouts. And I know I'm not alone in this. I want you all to raise your hand if you know someone who went missing, even if it's not someone connected to you personally."

Frank didn't raise his hand, and neither did Zelda, but almost everyone in the room did.

Tony continued, "You see, this is just another sign of the things wrong with this city. Do you think that if Uppers went missing, they would stay that way for long?"

Except for a few jagged coughs and the rustling of cloth from shifting bodies, all was silent.

"But this is about more than just missing people isn't it? This is about justice."

Someone shouted from the back of the room, "And what does a murderer like you know about justice?"

Tony grinned. "Why, quite a bit, don't you think? When someone crosses my family or my people, there is always swift justice."

Zelda whispered in Franks' ear, "Yeah, and when your 'people' are half the low-life dealers in the city, there are a lot of cries for justice."

Frank cracked a smile.

"But, in losing my sister, I have come to realize something."

"Eat shit and die Tony."

There was a wave of chuckles. Everyone cast their eyes to see who had shouted, but there were too many people in the gym.

Frank thought Tony would blow up at that point, that he would lose his cool, and the meeting would end on a fragmented note. Later, he would wish it had, that if Tony had reacted in the way that he was famous for, maybe he wouldn't have lost so much.

"Now, now, my friends. We are all angry and frustrated here, but I want you to understand something. The night that Margo disappeared was one of the worst of my life. I loved my little sister more than anyone or anything. I would trade everything I have; I would sooner become a Runner than see her harmed."

Tony's voice was sincere, and Frank couldn't quite deny it. He was a snake; of that there was no doubt, but even snakes have siblings, and the story of the pain of his loss, at least, seemed genuine enough. He thought of Jose and a pang of sorrow filled his heart.

"I wandered the streets for hours looking for her that night. One minute, she was sitting on the front porch enjoying her evening tea, and the next, she was gone. All I found was a broken tea cup..." His voice trembled. "... and her favorite scarf. Her scarf was ripped in two..."

Tony put his head in his hands for a moment. Scores of people suddenly found something interesting about their feet. Thinking of Jose, and now Jenny, Frank's eyes burned. It was all he could do to keep the tears back.

Zelda put her arm around him and drew him a little closer.

Tony composed himself and, with eyes red, looked out across his audience. "Losing my sister like that, I came to a new realization." He paused for a moment. "You here in the Lowers are all my people."

Frank saw the trap. He wondered how many others in the audience did.

"It's time we get some justice. It's time we burn it all down. The bank? That was my people."

There was a rising tide of mutters at this. Tony let it simmer for a few moments.

"For too long, the Uppers have controlled our lives, have had the power to take away everything on a whim, and cast us down into the Runnercore."

Frank thought of Jose. He thought of how Senator Reevas had taken his tongue and stolen his life. He thought about how, years later, when the SO's had picked on Jose, he had snapped and had lost everything all over again. He thought of Jose's wife and child and how he had been checking in on them and helping them as much as he could. He felt all of this and saw Tony for what he was. All the humor and laughter drained out of Frank.

Frank stood.

Zelda, her eyes wide, tried to pull him back down, to make him sit, but Frank was too big, too strong, too determined to have his say.

"I hear what you're saying, Tony."

Frank waited, letting all the eyes in the room turn toward him. He let Tony, who was taken off guard by the interruption, get a good look at him. Frank marked Tony, and he knew that from this day forward, Tony would mark him.

"But you are a coward."

There were a few gasps and murmurs.

Turning and facing the crowd as he spoke, he said, "This man would use your pain and your loss and your fear toward his selfish gain. When has Tony Sellers ever given a shit about any of us?"

Frank cast his glance about for someone familiar, someone who had been touched by Tony's temper. He found one two rows over.

"Meridith, this man would say he is your family, but what happened when your son crossed him?"

Meridith looked hesitant for a moment, but then, her eyes blazed, and she stood. "Tony had him beaten within an inch of his life." She stayed standing.

Frank cast around for another familiar face. He saw one man keeping his eyes to the floor.

"Jorge, What happened to your daughter when she refused to sleep with one of Tony's men?"

The man didn't stand. Instead, he cast his eyes away. He mumbled.

Frank said, "What was that?"

Jorge looked up and around. Frank hated putting the man on the spot; he had a good heart, but the last thing he wanted was to hand a mob over to Tony Sellers. If they were going to change things in this city, they were going to do it right. Frank had no idea where this certainty, where this confidence was coming from, but it surged through him.

Jorge said, "He paid the SO's take her to Senator Reevas... and she ended up in the Runnercore. It's his fault..."

There was a powerful undercurrent of anger in the man's tone. Frank felt the deep hatred there. He could feel it's warmth. Frank wouldn't be surprised if this man jumped up and charged Tony.

Frank turned to Tony. "You're no friend of ours, Mr. Sellers."

Tony's face was a deep shade of red, but he spoke calmly to the crowd. "I know in the past, I have done some questionable things. I know that some of my men have hurt you or your families or friends. But after losing my sister, I realized I've been wrong. I want to use all my resources to help topple the corrupt government of this city. I want the Lowers to have equal access to alcoves. I want the SO's to be held accountable for their abuse against us, and most of all, I want to abolish the Runnercore. Every single person in the Lowers deserves better. I want things to change in this city, but I need your help."

A man in the back somewhere said, "What can we do?"

Frank thought the timing was a little convenient, and he suddenly suspected that many of Tony's loyal men were among them. He tasted a hint of fear in the back of his throat, but it was just a taste.

Tony said, "All of you have a part to play in this. Frank, you may not like me. You may not trust me, but let me ask you this. Without sanitation, where would this city be?"

Frank didn't like where this was going, but he wasn't a natural speaker. He wasn't sure of another way out, so he answered. "I guess in the shitter."

That got a few laughs. Tony managed to look both irritated and pleased at the same time.

"Pen, without shield maintenance, where would we be?"

A tall, lanky man stood up in the back and said, "Now? Hell, now we'd be out of air now, and before we'd be cooked. Shield and Sanitation keep us all alive."

It was no secret that Pen was a friend of Tony's.

"Andrea, what about the Biorecycler?"

Andrea stayed seated; she looked less than thrilled to have to answer to Tony but said, "Starving."

Tony said, "And we all know that every single one of us in this room has a vital job to keep this city moving, to keep the people alive."

Frank said, "Are you calling for an uprising Tony?"

Without hesitation, Tony said, "Yes."

Again, that wave of murmurs, but this time it was much louder. Most people in the Lowers at least knew someone who was hurt by the consequences of the uprising, even if they didn't face them themselves.

Frank said, "I think things need to change as much as anyone in here. I even agree that maybe now is the best time to do it, since we left the surface, and everything is different. But I also remember how destructive the last uprising was, and I don't just mean for us in the Lowers. A lot of people got hurt, including my best friend..."

Frank choked on the thought of Jose. Tony took that as a moment to jump in.

"Things are different now than they were in the last uprising. The SO's are weak, the Runnercore is decimated and several members of the Senate are dead or missing. Now is the time to strike."

A woman shouted, "What about the Recycled?"

No murmurs this time; just the shuffling of bodies and the creaking of chairs and benches. Before the recent battle, few had ever seen the creatures. It was only those in the docks who had known more of them than a myth. But now, everyone knew what they were, and those pale faces and strange white on white on white eyes inspired deep terror. They were the stuff of nightmares, and even Frank shivered.

The question caught Tony off guard. He hesitated and then said, "Since the battle ended, has anyone seen a Recycled?"

Beyond the din of murmurs, no one spoke up.

"I suspect that, like the Runnercore, most, if not all, of the Recycled were wiped out in the battle."

The same woman, still lost in the crowd somewhere, spoke again. Her voice trembled as she said, "I saw one. I saw one two nights ago. It took my child."

Frank heard her moans and wails and, like everyone else, traced them back to the source. Several people tried to calm her. Frank watched her for only a moment, and then he turned to watch Tony's reaction. Tony's face was a mask of confusion, but then, as if someone pulled his face taught, his mask disappeared, and for an instant, Frank saw just the smallest hint of a smile at the corners of his mouth before it disappeared.

Tony said, "My god. Don't you see?"

The eyes turned from the wailing woman back to Tony.

"They no longer have the Runnercore, and so now, they steal our children in the night using the Recycled."

It was an outrageous claim. Tony knew it, most of the audience knew it, and certainly, Frank knew it. But Frank glanced at the woman, who was still a ball of tears and sorrow and realized that it didn't matter. Most people in this room were like her; they were at the breaking point. If someone didn't put a stop to this, Tony would get everything he wanted.

Frank shouted. "Bullshit." Most turned their attention to him. Then, in a calmer voice, he said, "Tony has no evidence that the Uppers have anything to do with the Recycled. Think, the Recycled attacked the SO's didn't they? Everyone in here knows that they sided with the other enemy soldiers. If there are Recycled left in this city, then they can't be working for the Uppers."

Tony said, "And who were those other Runners exactly? No one has ever told us have they? We know they weren't from Saud because all the Saud Runners died, so who was attacking with the Recycled, and why aren't the Uppers telling us?"

Frank didn't know how to respond to Tony this time. He agreed with him. There had never been any official explanation of how, after defeating Saud, there was another attack. What were the Uppers hiding from them?

Frank said, "Why don't we ask?"

Tony said, "Ask what?"

"Why don't we send someone up there, or maybe a few people, to ask what's going on with the Recycled and these other Runners?"

"Frank, you can't be that stupid, can you? Do you think they would tell us?"

"My father always told me that it never hurt to ask. Besides, while we're asking about that, maybe we should send a delegation to talk to the Uppers about some of our other concerns. Maybe instead of just burning everything down, we should act like reasonable people and just talk to them first. Then, if they refuse, we can talk about other actions. But what if the Uppers recognize that things have changed and are willing to compromise?"

Tony grinned. "Frank, my dear fellow. When have the Uppers ever been willing to compromise?"

Zelda stood. "Frank's right. Let's talk first. Think about it. If we burn down the whole city, it's not gonna be good for anyone. Let's at least give them a chance to talk."

There was a general murmur of agreement, but Frank couldn't be sure how many stood with them so he said, "Let's vote on it."

Tony said, "Excuse me?"

Frank could tell Tony barely contained his rage. He was sure that Tony had expected some resistance, that maybe someone would stand up to him, but Tony usually got his way, and Frank intended to put a stop to it. He knew it was dangerous to mess with Tony; he had seen awful things happen to people who did, but he also knew that everyone had seen him stand up against Tony and that if Tony did anything to him now, it probably wouldn't help his cause. On the other hand, if Tony did get his way, Frank and his wife and maybe anyone else who supported him might be in very serious trouble.

"You heard me, Tony. Let's take a vote. How many people think that we should send someone to ask about the Recycled and talk to the Uppers?"

For a moment, no one said anything. Then, the woman who had claimed to have her child stolen in the night by the Recycled said, "We want answers don't we? Send someone to get them. If they don't give them to us, I say we take them by force."

Again, another general murmur of agreement and Frank knew that he had won, at least for now.

"And who should we send?" said Tony.

"Frank," said one voice.

"Yes, Frank," said another.

"The guy with the big gut and bigger balls gets my vote," said a younger, dark-haired woman. There was a general flutter of laughter in the room.

Zelda said, "Alright, who votes that Frank go and talk to the Uppers?"

Tony interjected, "And what Uppers would he talk to exactly?"

Frank had already thought about this. "Well, I would guess the ultimate goal would be the Senate right? But first, we gotta get permission. So it seems like central security would be the best place to start."

"And the big guy has brains," someone said. There was another wave of laughter.

Frank said, "I keep it all in my stomach." He rubbed his belly as more people around the room laughed.

Zelda caught his gaze and smiled at him. She grabbed his hand and squeezed it for a moment before letting go.

"So let's vote?"

In the end, there was no need to count. While nearly a third of the room didn't raise their hands in support of Frank, he was the clear winner. Later, he would remember how a third of the room didn't raise their hands, and later he would meet some of those others on less than favorable terms.

Chapter 10
Green's Legacy

Alana Green was angry. Her uncle had always told her that reacting out of anger was a fool's game. She believed him. Leaning her meaty arms against the window, she watched from her balcony on the 68th floor of her building as protestors gathered. In the last few days, there had been a slow and steady gathering outside central security. At first, it hadn't seemed organized, but now, it was clear that it was.

She might be less angry if someone hadn't planted a bomb below her family's apartments. But Alana Green had always been angry; it was just that this was a different flavor of the experience. Her normal simmer of frustration and apathy were replaced by something hot and boiling. It took a great deal of effort to still her body from trembling and her nails from digging red, half-moon crescents into her palms.

She was ruined. Her family's fifteen hundred-year-old empire was gone. Her family could trace their line back nearly two centuries before migration, and now, she was the only one left. Worse than that, whoever had bombed the apartments had wiped clean all of her uncle's accounts. Nearly a billion credits were gone, overnight.

The regen spas had already declined her entry. Alana had no more access to massages or escorts, no more access to the finest, freshest food the city of Manhatsten, but most importantly, no more access to alcoves. One hundred and thirty years old, and she's cut off? It was intolerable and embarrassing. She would never forget the humiliation of having private security drag her out the door like some common Lower.

She gathered the saliva in her mouth and spit at the protestors. She didn't know which one of the vermin had destroyed her family, and she really didn't care; they were all equally guilty.

"Are you still brooding?"

Alana turned around. Nancy stood there, arms crossed with a smirk on her face. She was enjoying Alana's misery, the insufferable wretch. Alana ground her teeth and looked at her gorgeous friend up and down. She was everything an Upper was supposed to be: tall and slender with green eyes; thick, luscious lips; good hips; and long, dark hair that came down to her waist. In other words, she as everything that Alana was not. Alana's meaty form was about as pleasant as her personality, and she knew it. She was almost as wide as she was tall, and when she went in the alcoves, she had to go into the extra-large section. Of course, Nancy would tell her she as beautiful, that men were after her all the time, but it was just another way that Nancy lied to her. Alana wasn't beautiful, and she knew it.

So, as she stared at her friend with her smirk on her face, with those arms crossed over her perfect breasts, Alana swore silently another time (it was almost daily now) that she would cut that smile off her face.

"You'd be brooding too, Nancy, if they stole everything from you."

Nancy walked over and reached out and hugged her. It caught Alana by surprise, and for a moment, she found it warm and welcoming. For a moment, she thought she could release that hidden well of tears that lay just below the surface into her friend's embrace. She wanted that so badly, to let it all go, to weep and heal. She felt something inside of her open, just a hair. She encouraged it, spurred it onward. And like just before an orgasm, she could feel herself so close to the sweet release of comfort she needed.

Then something shoved her. The shift, the change, was so substantial that she almost felt a physical blow. She felt a heat rising in her, a kind of uncontrolled redness rise to her skin, and the anger retook possession of her. She pushed Nancy away, hard.

Nancy almost stumbled backward. She blinked a few times and said, "Alana, what's..."

Alana cut her off. "Don't touch me." It was almost a bark, and Alana shocked even herself. She took a breath for a moment and mastered herself. "Never act in anger," her uncle had said, and she would try to listen. "I'm sorry... I just... need some space. You understand, right, Nancy?"

Nancy eyed her for a moment. Alana could see the tension, the fear, and something else on her face... was it, contempt? Then, her face softened.

"I get it. You've been through a lot. I guess I shouldn't have just ambushed you like that. I'm sorry."

Something inside Alana felt a sense of glee. It was almost like a whisper or a voice, like something outside herself that seemed to say, look, the stupid cow apologized to you for spurning her.

Alana kept her face flat. "Yes... yes, I'm sorry. Thank you for all you've done for me in the last few weeks. Ever since my uncle and the rest of my family died in that explosion... I haven't been myself."

Alana's face felt hot. She swore that if she looked in the mirror, it would be a bright, flushed red, as red as her body always was after sex or spending too much time in a sauna.

"Look, I'll transfer some money to your account okay? I know this has been hard on you, and you can stay here as long as you need to."

"I don't want your stupid charity."

Alana's reply came quick and sharp, and once again, she took several long deep breaths.

Nancy frowned. "Alana, you're like a sister to me. I can't imagine what you're going through. I want to help you."

Alana said nothing. She just stared at those stupid cow eyes. She knew what this was about, that Nancy wanted her in her debt for the rest of her life. She was scheming, always scheming. Nancy had been jealous of her whole life of the Green family, and now she had a chance to demonstrate her superiority to the last remnant of the bloodline.

But that wasn't it, was it? If Nancy had wanted to see her suffer, had wanted to put her under her thumb, weren't there better ways to do that?

A surge of red rage, and an image of corpses streaked with blood filled her mind. She could almost taste the blood in her mouth. She licked her lips.

Nancy said, "Please, Alana, don't let your pride get in the way of letting me help you, okay?" Nancy turned, walked over to her dining room table, and grabbed her tablet.

"I am transferring you a 100k credit note, alright? That should get you through a full year without ever having to worry about money, and if you need more, please just ask. Hell, you could probably afford your own place in the Mids with this amount if you need a space of your own."

Something warm dripped onto Alana's bare thighs. She looked down and saw that blood was seeping from beneath her clenched fists and down her leg. The sensation almost tickled as the blood left long trails toward the insides of her thighs. The sight of the red gave her a deep sense of satisfaction, an almost sexual kind of pleasure. She bit her tongue hard and winced from the pain, but the iron taste of blood filled her mouth, and though Nancy was talking, she couldn't hear her.

"Alana? Are you okay?"

Alana blinked and cast her eyes around the room. She felt strange, as if she had gone somewhere far away for a moment, some place to do something.

"Yes, just... lost in thought."

"Did you hear what I said?"

"No, I'm sorry..."

Nancy smiled and shook her head. "It's alright. I was telling you that the transfer is complete."

"The transfer?"

"The credits."

It took a moment for Alana to wrap her mind around this and then, she said, "Oh... I... Thank you, Nancy." She tried to force a smile, but it felt all wrong; it felt like the violation of something sacred.

Nancy said, "You're welcome. I want you to know that I'm here for you, okay? No matter what, I'm here."

Alana nodded.

"Why don't we get you a drink, huh?"

Alana nodded again. She couldn't seem to work her mouth. But that was alright; she didn't need her mouth for what she needed to do next.

Nancy walked around the corner from the dining room into her enormous kitchen. Alana followed. Sometimes she hosted dinner parties here and hired professional cooks to prepare the meal. There were nearly a dozen ovens and stoves, and endless armies of kitchen utensils hung like so much tinsel from a Solstice tree. Alana eyed the knives as her friend walked to a shelf and pulled down a couple of bottles of liquor.

Nancy said, "I discovered this amazing new drink the other night." She pulled several more bottles from the shelf. "It was at the club in the Upper Mids, you know, Shag?" She had her back turned to Alana.

Alana walked over to the knives, reached up, and ran her fingertip down one of the blades to test its sharpness. It stung her, like a wasp, and she pulled back, but then held her finger up to the light to admire the new line of red spreading on her skin.

Nancy laughed and turned around for a moment, and Alana withdrew her hand like a child hiding a stolen cookie.

Nancy didn't seem to notice. Instead she said, "My gods, it's the most mind-blowing thing I've ever tasted, and it will get you fucked up quick." She smirked. "I think you need a good night out. Let's get liquored up and hit the town, maybe find a man? What do you say?"

Alana nodded. Her voice was flat. "Sounds nice."

Nancy's smile broadened. "Good. Alana?"

Alana said, "Yes?"

"I love you. What happened to your family, none of them deserved it. I'm so sorry."

For another moment, the tears almost came. And if Alana Green had cried at that moment, had cried the bitter tears of rage and humiliation that she so desperately needed, everything that came next would have been different. But something stuffed up those tears, kept the faucet plugged, and now it was ready to burst. One way or another, her emotions would be freed, and if it wasn't through tears...

Her voice still flat, she replied. "Thanks, Nancy. I love you too."

Nancy turned to her work. "Oh my god, Alana, there was this guy the other night, he'd be perfect for you. I bet we can totally find him on his network profile and have him meet us."

Alana pulled the knife down off its hook. She did it quietly, but still, there was the ever so soft scratch of metal on metal and a soft ringing noise. For a moment, she almost lost its grip and dropped it, and if she had, things also would have been different. But she gripped it tight. It felt good in her hands. Nancy, meanwhile, was working on the alchemy that was supposed to be their shared beverage.

The knife almost seemed to shine in her hands, to glow with the same anger that she felt. She thought about what it would be like to plunge it into the stupid cow's back. Thought about how it would feel to slide it in and see the life go out of Nancy's eyes.

She imagined thrusting the knife again and again as she felt the soft wetness of Nancy's body give way to her assault as she stood over it and stole her life from her.

It was then that she realized that she was doing more than thinking, that she was standing over Nancy's hunched form, that the screaming and weeping had already stopped, and she was stabbing, still thrusting the blade in her back. She saw herself turning the mangled body over, saw her cutting into the woman's face, and erasing that stupid cow smile.

Alana watched all this as if it was on the vidscreens, as if it wasn't her own hands drenched in blood. She watched as she cut long lines up and down Nancy's corpse and how then, when she realized her hands were covered in blood, she licked it off her fingers.

Alana smiled. She would make the stupid vermin in the Lowers pay. Everyone who had ever crossed her would pay. She just needed the right tool. After all, she still had Uncle Green's spies down there, and with Nancy's generous gift... perhaps... perhaps she would even kill a few herself. She knew she would never find the exact asshole who had destroyed her family, but it might be fun to try. After all, everyone had to take action now... everyone had to... do their part. Didn't they?

Chapter 11
Overpowered

"Wake up sweet Mimi, class is in session."

Mimi opened her eyes. She was lying on top of a table. Still, some remnants of the stem cell-based liquid from the alcoves dripped from her nearly naked body. Only the tight undergarments from the alcove clung to her skin.

She looked up and there, stroking her hair was Willow. Again, she noticed those pale blue eyes gazing down into hers. To her left stood a Recycled Runner, its face passive and unmoving. She couldn't be sure if it was fear or instinct, but she dipped inside its mind and found only vacancy.

"Class?" Mimi choked and sputtered, coughing up the last remnants of fluid from the alcove. She reached into her mouth and fished out one last glob and then spit. She never could get used to the aftertaste. Mimi turned over to her side and then sat up. She felt... different somehow. It was almost like her body was significantly lighter. She inspected herself for puncture wounds or some sign that something had changed her, but there was nothing. Glancing around the room, Mimi noticed something familiar. Her EnViro suit sat in the corner. If she could just reach it...

Willow asked, "How do you feel?"

Mimi shrugged. "Did you..."

But before she could answer, the Recycled Runner lashed out and grabbed her arm. Mimi screamed as she felt a sharp pain radiate up her shoulder. Then, she reacted the way that Serah had taught her. She pushed forward a few steps into the creature, and while it was off balance, she broke its grip. Then, with both her body and her mind, she pushed against its large frame. It stumbled backward, but only a few steps. Mimi looked at it, looked at Willow, looked at her arm.

"You did it? You augmented my muscles?"

Willow nodded. There was a strange smile on her lips, and Mimi wasn't sure quite what to think of it. Something didn't sit right with her about this woman or this place. Something was very wrong with all of this. Her intuition screamed at her.

"Did you...?"

"Yes, I told it to grab you."

"Why?"

"To show you that this is more than just standard muscle augmentation. You see, we have been experimenting for a long time with the Recycled. However, we cannot seem to make the Recycled any stronger. There is something about the Nanobot interaction with living tissue versus Recycled tissue that creates a kind of limitation. Perhaps it is the stem cell-based fluid in their veins; the one that gives them the blue lines. But you, you will be much stronger than any of the Runners in the city."

Why was this woman doing this? Why wouldn't Willow have this done to herself? Or maybe...

Mimi crouched, and then jumped up and attacked, throwing herself at Willow. The woman's eyes went wide with surprise, and before she could move or react, Mimi's left first connected with the right side of Willow's jaw. Willow stumbled backward for a second, but then, moving faster than anyone Mimi had ever seen, Willow charged forward, grabbing Mimi's wrist and twisting it behind her back, up over her ear and pinning her on the ground. Willow held her arm up like a lever while Mimi lay facedown.

"Ouch."

Willow twisted her arm a little harder, and pain shot up Mimi's elbow and into her shoulder. Then, just as she thought her shoulder or her elbow would shatter, Willow relaxed and then let her go.

"You were testing my strength, weren't you?"

She reached down and helped Mimi up. Standing, Mimi rubbed her shoulder for a moment and then shrugged. "Thought I better check and see if you had the same procedure done."

Willow eyed her for a moment. Then, a half-smile made a brief appearance and then fell away. "Of course, I did. I took any chance I could to escape this place. It still wasn't enough."

"Why augment me?"

"I told you: I want out. I want to be free from this place and Miranda."

Mimi shook her head. "No, you don't. You want something else."

"What other motives could I possibly have? Why would I augment your muscles if I didn't want someone to help me escape?"

"I don't know why you did that. But I know you're blocking me from skimming you. It wasn't obvious at first, but I've seen one of my other sisters employ a similar technique. You feed the other person a series of fake thoughts, all while blocking your real intentions. Only Noatla could do that, and I don't think she knew that I knew about it. There's something you're hiding; something you don't want me to know."

Willow ground her teeth behind a shark's smile. "And what would I hide?"

Mimi thought about it for a moment. There was really only one thing that made sense.

"You don't want to escape this place; you want to gain Miranda's power. I am not sure if that's because you sincerely hate her or because you fear her and are tired of living under her control. But either way, it comes to the same. I think you are a much more powerful telepath than you let on."

Willow's face darkened; the shadow that fell across her features was almost physical. Behind her, Mimi heard the clunk of the metal footsteps of more Recycled, and within just a moment, a half dozen of the creatures appeared and stood behind their master.

"You're going to Recycle me, aren't you? Once you have made me far stronger and more powerful, you will turn me into some superweapon; one you can wield against Miranda."

Willow laughed. She laughed so hard, she doubled over, clutching her stomach. Behind her, more Recycled arrived. There were at least twenty now, and Mimi doubted that with Willow's strength, she could ever successfully break free.

"What's so funny?"

"You... just... I..." Willow calmed her self and caught her breath. "You think pretty highly of yourself, don't you? I mean, superweapon? You must have been watching too many vidscreen programs from ancient Earth or something. It doesn't work that way. When we Recycle you, you'd lose all you gain in life. A Recycled person is a tabula rasa."

"A blank slate?"

Willow nodded. "That is what you sense when you skim them; their blackness, their potential. All things that a person was in life are no more when they are Recycled, including their physical abilities. Their brain is reconfigured in the process."

Mimi thought of Daniel, and her blood turned cold. For a moment, she was back in the docks, surrounded by Recycled. The memory of Shandie and Leahara dying at their hands forced its way up from the depths of her memory. Daniel, the Recycled version of him, had confronted her, and though he was destroyed, the image of his face marked by those thin blue lines and those white on white on white eyes would never wholly leave her.

"That can't be true. I know from experience that it can't be true."

"And what in your experience told you that you saw what you thought you saw?"

Mimi hesitated for a moment.

"Your old boyfriend?"

Mimi's mouth gaped. "How did you...?"

"Miranda watched you for a long time, Mimi. As soon as she discovered you on the night of your little fishing expedition forty years ago, she watched you closely. She skimmed your mind often and saw every last little secret or memory that came to the surface. She told me all about your history, about how you were born to your abilities when you took the life of someone else. She told me how much she wanted you in her possession."

"To what end?"

For a moment, Willow opened her mouth and then closed it. A strange smile tightened her lips.

"Soon. When you are ready, for now, you are not."

Mimi was quiet for a long while.

"Mimi, would you like to learn the secrets of the red veil?"

Mimi's blood turned cold, and the image of her, an almost out-of-body experience of her striking down both Recycled and Runner alike in the old underground came forward. Then, she was standing over Shannon, about to strike the killing mental blow. Mimi's body shook.

"No, Mimi, it doesn't have to be that way. If you can learn to control it, you can be more powerful than you ever imagined. No one could stand against you."

"Or it could drive me batshit crazy like Miranda."

Again, Willow laughed. "You might think she's crazy, but I assure you, she's not. She is quite focused on her goals."

"That doesn't mean she's not nuts. She kills and manipulates using the red veil. Why would I want to be like her?"

"If you control that power, you can do whatever you wish with it. I suspect that even Miranda couldn't stand against you."

"If that's true, why teach it to me? You know the first thing I will do is use it against you."

Willow didn't respond, except with the same strange smile on her thin, pale lips.

"Do you wish to learn or not?"

"No, I wish to get out of here. To leave, to see my sisters, to see..."

Shaking her head, Willow said, "Even if I let you leave, there are no sisters to return to. They are all dead."

There was a cry of agony down deep inside Mimi; it welled up in her. It couldn't be true.

"Bullshit. I saw Shannon and Serah alive. It was my last memory before waking up here."

"Miranda won, Mimi. When you were healing from your wound, we sent out two hundred more Recycled to clean up the remainder of the Sisters. They fought well, but in the end, the last of the sisters fell to the Recycled — none remain."

"Bullshit. I don't believe a word of it."

But part of her did, and she tried to push that part away. She couldn't. After all, she was still Mimi from the Nowhere, the girl without a home, without a family and from all the things she had learned throughout her centuries of life, the deepest lesson of all was that all people would eventually leave you, even if it's not by your own choice.

"The truth does not require your belief. Soon enough, you will accept it. This city is under Miranda's control. Soon the other cities will be under her control as well. One by one, each city will either be destroyed or under the control of," Willow made air quotes, "Mother Gaia. She will control everything. But she needs someone to control each city, a governor of sorts. She has picked you for your unique talents to rule Manhatsten, Mimi, and it is my job to train you in all the ways of power, including the red veil."

"Fuck you. Liar."

Mimi spat on Willow.

Willow sighed but didn't betray any of her emotions. "I see this is going to be a long process with you. That's alright, Mimi; we have all the time in the world."

"If this is all true, bring Miranda here. I want to hear this all from her."

"Alas, I'm afraid that's not possible at the moment. You see, she has left the city and is headed for Lundon, and after Lundon, she will head for Rio. As she takes control of each city, she grows more and more powerful."

"What you're saying doesn't make sense. Even if you were right and the city is under her control, why wouldn't she leave you in charge?"

Something dark flickered in Willow's face for a moment, but she quickly covered it up with that strange smile.

"Let's say that Miranda believes in your potential. Besides, you can do whatever you wish once you master the power. You can shatter all Miranda's plans, take revenge on her, send a thousand Recycled to rip her apart. Wouldn't you like that?

Mimi couldn't deny that if Shannon and her sisters were all dead, that she did want vengeance. If they had hurt Shannon...

"What's in all this for you?"

"Freedom. I want out. I've never left this place in my entire life. I was born here. I was raised here, and without you, I will die here."

It seemed a likely request. It made perfect sense, but that was the problem. Willow's desire made too much sense. Something was missing, some piece of the puzzle. For a moment, Mimi pushed on Willow's mental barriers. She didn't want to penetrate them, but perhaps some glimpse would give her a hint, a flash, some insight into what was really going on here.

"That won't work. Not now. Once you have mastered the red veil, you could shatter my mental barriers like so much paper in the wind. So, shall we begin?"

"Fuck off."

Mimi stood on the table and jumped off. She bolted for the corner of the large open space where her empty EnViro suit waited. Mimi didn't know if there was enough time to put the thing on, but she had to try. As she sprinted several hundred meters, she noticed that she didn't even feel winded. She could feel her heart pounding, but she didn't feel the strain in her muscles. It was like someone had stripped away some of the gravity in the room.

Mimi reached the suit and started to put it on. But as she did, she realized that she was already surrounded by two dozen Recycled. They stood on all sides but made no move. They were statues, looming golems waiting for a command to come to life. Mimi didn't pause; she continued to suit up, taking advantage of their lack of motion.

"You are welcome to wear the suit. I had it put here for your training." Willow appeared between some of the Recycled. "But I'm afraid there's nowhere to go. You see, there is no way out of this place, not without the red veil."

Mimi kept putting on the suit. "What do you mean without the red veil?"

"Well, first, you would have to find the exit. That will prove no easy task. Then you'd have to find the passcode to exit, and I won't give you that either."

Mimi smirked inwardly. This woman had no idea what her specialty was. Mimi could find that info in the woman's subconscious and pluck it right out of her without her ever knowing. She reached out and saw the location of the door on the floor. Then she saw the passcode: E517yu13.

"Oh, I'm not worried about that. I think I can figure it out, Willow."

"Third, you would require a retina scan from myself or Miranda."

Mimi's heart sunk.

"Mimi, Miranda and I are well aware of your extra talent. I'm quite sure that you already have the information and passcode for the door. But the third part to this was designed especially for you, knowing that you could easily skim that technical information from me. You see, the retina scan requires a living scan, and it's a full two minutes in length standing completely still. If I so much as blink during that time, the count restarts. You could, of course, beat me senseless and try and force my eyes open at the scanner, but I suspect you would have a hard time getting out that way. And there is certainly no way that I will allow you to leave this place. So, your only option is the red veil. When you have truly mastered it, you will be able to make me open that door for you."

"I thought you said you've never been out before; that you wanted to escape."

"I haven't, and I do. If I try to leave this place, I will die. The only way I can truly be free is if you stop her; if you kill her. I cannot cross the threshold of the outer door without dying. The chip Miranda put in my brain is modeled after the ones the Runners have, and it's activated the moment I cross the threshold. But if Miranda turns off the chip, or she dies, I can pass through. She left me with that little bit of hope, you see. A gift for her sweet daughter, her only child."

Mimi stopped putting on the suit and looked up. That strange smile was long gone. In its place was the grimace of a person who had just watched a close friend die. Mimi knew that look; she had worn it herself many times over the centuries.

Mimi had suspected the truth after the last time they talked, but here it was. Willow was Miranda's daughter. The strange thing was, Mimi believed it. There wasn't a doubt in her mind. It made perfect sense. The woman was down here her whole life; she could block with the same level of skill as Noatla, and Willow seemed to have a perfectly comfortable relationship with the Recycled. There was also something in the eyes, and Mimi realized that was why she didn't trust her. She recognized that madness hidden behind the eyes. Though she had never met Miranda in person, she could feel that same madness about her, and she had seen it just behind the eyes of the Recycled as they killed Shandie and Leahara.

"I'm sorry."

"Don't apologize. Help me. Together, we can destroy my mother. You can have your vengeance, and I, my freedom."

Mimi shook her head. She would have to find some way out, but she'd be damned if she would let that redness take her again. Even thinking about it, she could feel the joy and excitement of the thing stirring within her. She imagined it was the same feeling an addict had whenever they were clean and craving a fix. The red veil was a drug, and its user could fall into its power forever, for power was what it was.

"No. I will never use the red veil again. I'd rather die first."

"Oh, don't worry, there are ways to change your mind." That strange, tight-lipped grin spread across Willow's face again.

Mimi shivered. "What do you mean?"

There was the sound of metal feet clomping on concrete nearby. Mimi looked around and didn't see anything at first, but the sound grew in volume.

"Perhaps a demonstration of what Miranda has ordered her Recycled to do in her absence."

A panel slid aside, revealing a nearby corridor. Out of the passage walked three Recycled.

"Why don't we follow them and have a closer look? They are working on a particular project; one that I think will interest you."

Mimi swallowed. There was something in the Recycled's arms. All three of them held something; something big. She hoped it wasn't what she thought it was. She abandoned her suit, but left on the metallic legs. There was no time to remove them if she planned on following. The creatures were moving twice as fast as usual.

As she walked at increasing speed, Willow followed. "What are they carrying in their arms?"

"It's best if you see for yourself Mimi."

Mimi walked a little faster. Willow kept pace, but the Recycled that had surrounded them both were left standing motionless by her EnViro suit.

Another panel in the long open space slid open, and the Recycled walked through.

"Tsk tsk. I thought you were faster than this Mimi. If you don't hurry, that panel is going to close."

As Willow spoke, the panel did begin to close. Mimi wasn't far, but she knew she had to run. She put on a burst of speed that she wouldn't have been capable of before, and if she hadn't been so focused, so intent on seeing exactly what the Recycled were carrying and where they were going, she would have been impressed with her new leg muscles.

She reached the door with just enough time to slide through on the other side. Willow didn't follow. She found herself in a dimly lit passageway, following the Recycled, but now she was only a few meters from them. Their backs were to her, and she couldn't get a good look at what they carried, but there was something, something dangling from the arms of one of them, something that looked like the legs of a person.

Mimi shivered.

The creatures walked toward what appeared to be another dead end, but then a third panel slid open, and a strange pink light flooded in. It was bright and brilliant and seemed to come from the entirety of the way forward. All was pink.

She followed the creatures out of the dark passage and felt her legs buckle under her. At last, she was certain what they were carrying; at last, she saw what was in the room. The smell overwhelmed her. It was the smell of sweat and body and death and Recycled; all mingled together in one terrifying nightmare. She fell to her knees, leaned forward and vomited.

"She's harvesting, Mimi."

Mimi said nothing. She could only stare at the racks and rows of people dangling from strange mechanical perches. Each wore a helmet with dozens of wires connected into the wall behind. Behind them, a pink light glowed, and from the waist down, they were immersed in what Mimi could only guess was some kind of modified alcove, a type of cradle. The bottom half had its usual green tinge, but all were drowned in pink.

Mimi watched as the three Recycled spread out. One held a child in their arms, another a fully grown man, and the other a woman who looked older than anyone Mimi had ever seen. The Recycled found an empty slot in the grid of humans and carefully placed each one into their half-alcove bath, lifted their arms, put them in manacles, and pulled the helmets down. Almost instantly, the pink light came on. At first, each was dim, but within a few moments, it glowed just as brilliantly as the last.

Then she saw them, two people she cared about deeply. They hung next to each other in the upper left of the chamber. Her sisters, Rosita and Aurora dangled and glowed with pink light.

Willow walked up next to her.

"Miranda calls it the network."

Chapter 12
The Prisoner

The guards never said anything to him. He supposed that was alright. He was tired, and in the dim reflection of metal from his toilet bowl, he could see his face growing wild and unkempt. Patches of hair gained thickness in islands on his scalp. The rest he had torn out and cast away. Some lay in clumps on the floor.

The lights cycled from designated day to designated night, and still, the guard did not move. With their backs turned, Rigel often wondered if the guards were awake or not.

At first, they had seen fit to confine him to his apartment. Rigel had wanted confinement in his lab, but the Senate was angry and, even though he had saved the city from being crippled in the wake of the blast from the Children of Gaia, they were fearful of him working on anything.

He thought that ironic. Here, for so long, they had thought him incompetent and incapable of producing anything new. He had even heard accusations that he had never really invented anything at all, but had ridden on the coattails of his colleagues through his entire career. To some degree, that was true, but it had been Rigel who had discovered the mixture that extended life for the alcoves, and it was Doctor Ramnachinin who had discovered the mechanism to create the semi-suspension required for the fluid to have the greatest regenerative properties. Science was always and forever a collaborative effort, but foolish laypeople never really understood that. They championed key figures, forgetting that they had built their knowledge on the shoulders of their predecessors and colleagues, that breakthroughs often came in waves as a critical mass of knowledge was reached in the community.

Down the hall, a door opened. The rusty door groaned in protest with a high-pitched squeal as the room grew brighter. Rigel sat up and swung his legs down from his bunk. Standing, he moved toward the bars.

Around the corner came Speaker Swanson. Rigel wasn't sure if a visit from the Speaker was good news or bad. But all of the Senate except Dr. Lightfoot and Senator Green had survived. Lightfoot had died at the library. Although Rigel knew the truth about the war between telepaths, it seemed that the Senate did not. An explosive device had killed Green's entire family in the city. Rigel felt bad that his innocent family members had died, but privately, he was not sorry to see Green gone. He was the epitome of everything that was wrong with the city; a symbol of its corruption.

"Good evening Doctor Solidsworth,"

"Hello, Speaker." Rigel coughed; his voice was as rusty as the cell doors. "What brings you here?"

Swanson motioned to the guard. "Will you unlock this cell please?"

The guard said nothing for a moment, then unlocked the cell and slid the bars to the side.

"Am I to be set free?" Rigel asked.

Swanson shook his head "I'm sorry, Rigel. The Senate is still deadlocked on what to do with you. Half of the Senate would like to see you thrown out of the city into space, and the other half call you a hero. No, I am here to talk to you about where you have sent us."

"How is Dennis?"

Swanson frowned, "You are going to have to tell us what course you set us on one of these days, you know."

"Is he recovering?" Rigel had no interest in sharing his plan with them. He knew they would be angry with him. Originally, he had simply intended to orbit the Earth, but he was worried that the Children of Gaia, since they had access to nukes, may also have access to rockets, and though he thought the shield and city might be able to withstand one or two rockets, it wouldn't take much to damage the ecosystem within the city. And now, with the gravitational generators running, he couldn't be sure that they could redi-vert the energy from another blast like they had done before. Doing so might overload the system. No, he had to take them much further away from the planet for now. The real trouble was, once Rigel had set course, he seemed to have lost control of his system, and he wasn't prepared to admit that. And since he had not networked the generators with the AI, even the AI wasn't much use.

"Yes, he's recovering, though his injuries were severe."

When the city took off, a large rock had fallen on Dennis, fracturing his skull in several places. The alcove had healed the wound, but for nearly two weeks, he had been in a coma.

"Is he awake?"

"He is, but..."

Rigel felt ice water in his veins. "But what?"

"Well, he doesn't seem to remember who he is or anything about his life."

Rigel's heart sank, a sinking ship in icy water. It was all his fault. If he had gone to calibrate the second generator instead of Dennis, it would never have happened. He would be lying in the hospital bed instead.

"What does the doctor say?"

Swanson spoke softly. "Rigel, you know as well as I do that our physician's knowledge is, well, limited. There hasn't been a case like this in a thousand years."

"Did you consult with the AI?"

"We did. Well, we tried."

"Tried?"

"The AI is not responding to any commands."

"What do you mean?"

"Just what I said; no one can access the city intelligence."

Rigel sat down on the floor. "Are the key systems still running?"

"Yes, everything is functioning normally, but it isn't responding to any attempts at contact."

"I see."

His last communication with the AI had been strange. It was very upset over Saud, and Rigel wondered if, now that it had a stronger sense of self, it was mourning. How would an AI mourn? Considering the speed of its mind, would it take a shorter time to mourn or would it take longer because it had to run through different ways of understanding the experience? For the first time in weeks, Rigel felt fascinated by something. All the lights and dials in his brain were switching on.

"Rigel, we have to know where we are going."

"Let me out, let me see Dennis, and I will tell you whatever you want to know."

The light in him dimmed. He would give anything to see Dennis, even for just a few minutes.

Swanson shook his head. "I can't, not until the Senate votes in favor of releasing you. And Rigel, right now, you are the least of their concerns."

"Oh?"

"The Lowers have begun organizing. This morning they started gathering around central security. It's a mess. We don't have any Runners, and central security has every man securing the entrances to the Mids. They... they've had to shoot a few people today, and I think there will be more outside security tomorrow. I'm not sure how much longer we can hold out."

"Then don't."

"Don't what?"

"Open up the Mids and the Uppers; let people roam freely."

"Are you mad?"

Rigel smiled, "Oh, I've been accused of that on a number of occasions. But you are fighting a losing battle. My dear Speaker, you cannot possibly believe that the old way of doing things will work now, do you?"

Swanson said nothing.

Rigel sighed. "The Moon."

"Pardon?"

"That is the course the city is taking."

"But why would you do that? Why not just put us in orbit or something, get us out of danger?"

"Because if the Children of Gaia had nukes, who is to say that they do not have rockets as well? What if they shot us out of the sky? What if they had access to one of the Old H.A.D. satellites?"

"My god, are there such things still around?"

"Of course there are, the Chinese and the Americans put thousands in orbit, and they built them to last. There were too many risks in keeping us in orbit, given that the Children of Gaia could destroy an entire city. So, I had to send us somewhere, and I know there was once a base on the Moon, that would yield some potential supplies. After all, there was still Solidsodium left there after the Moon War."

"There was? Good god, man, why didn't you say so?"

"Because Senator, you will find that many people will be miserable when they realize how much further away from the planet we will be."

"Speaker, you are needed immediately. There's been another incident." One of the guards stood at the entrance down the hall.

"Very well, I will be right there. Now, Dr. Solidsworth, I will see about getting you out of here, but no promises."

Rigel frowned. "You are going to need me to keep this city together. After all, no one knows its systems like I do, and perhaps I can discover what's wrong with the AI."

Swanson shifted from foot to foot. "Perhaps, I will put it to vote."

Rigel hesitated, but he had to know. "Speaker, where do you stand on my actions?"

Swanson frowned. "I... voted to keep you confined, Dr. Solidsworth."

Rigel blinked, it was all he could do. Swanson had always been his ally.

Swanson continued, "Though you saved us, what you did was irresponsible. How could you be sure that the environmental systems would stay intact once we reached orbit? How could you design the generators under our nose like that? The purpose of our government is to make sure that no one individual has too much power. We are not a dictatorship, and your unilateral action has forever changed the course of this city; you have admitted that. The old way will crumble, and we must redefine our way of life now."

"Swanson, surely you know of the deep corruption within your government." Rigel's throat was sore, and he had to clear his throat several times. "You know of the things that Senator Reevas and Green were doing and all the others who maintained their power through corruption and blackmail. You are a man of faith, and even though I am not one, you saw the inhumanity of the treatment of those in the Lowers."

Swanson gave a slow nod. "You aren't wrong, but for one man to change the entire course without some consultation with the government—"

Rigel cut him off, "Then we would all be dead at this moment, wouldn't we? Gods, man, think." Rigel's voice raised, and with it, he found himself standing. "If I had not acted, we wouldn't even be having this discussion."

Swanson didn't back down. Instead, his posture straightened. "Rigel. I know that. It's why you aren't floating in space. I overruled a measure to have you executed for your actions, but I will go no further. Letting you out of confinement would be irresponsible at best. You, and you alone, know how to steer this city, and until other engineers can figure out how those generators work, and how to return our city to the planet, I will not let you hold the wheel."

The guard shouted again, "Senator!"

"Yes, yes, I am coming."

Rigel lowered his voice, barely above a whisper. "Please, let me see my son. He nearly died saving the city."

Swanson grimaced, but then his features softened. "Very well, I will see what I can do."

Turning, Swanson had the guard slide the door and lock it behind him. Swanson did not look back.

2.

Rigel woke. He wasn't sure why exactly he woke, but something had stirred him from sleep. He looked around. The guard was gone. Perhaps central security needed them? It wasn't as if Rigel was a threatening man.

He sat up and blinked. Then, he rubbed his eyes. His cell door was wide open. Was he hallucinating?

"Hello?"

There was no response.

He stood and peered up and down the corridor. No one was there.

"Is there anyone there?"

Rigel walked forward and stepped on something. He moved his foot back and looked down. It was a data tablet. He reached down, picked it up, and looked at it. No, it wasn't just any data tablet. It was his data tablet. How did it get here? It didn't make any sense.

He flipped it over and switched it on. Immediately letters popped on on screen

"Go to your lab. -A friend."

Rigel didn't know what to do or say. Was this a trick? Was someone trying to lure him out of his cell and kill him? But, despite Swanson's threat of execution, he was much more use alive at the moment than he was dead. Though there were those who would kill him, weren't there? The crazy telepath for one. But was she still in the city? Maybe she was Earthside? Rigel imagined that if she was still in the city, things would be much worse than they were.

For the first time in days, Rigel thought of Runner 17 and Alexa Turon. He had no idea what had happened to them, and Swanson had said that there was no Runnercore left. Were they dead? Earthside?

He needed answers. The AI would have to be the first problem to address. If the AI wasn't functioning, everyone's lives could be at risk.

He decided to risk it. Stepping out into the corridor, his tablet beeped at him with a notification. He looked down. A series of instructions filled the screen, alternative directions to his lab. He frowned. He would have to go through the underground for this path; it would take hours. Then, almost as if someone had read his mind, new text appeared that said:

"Yes, it might take hours, but there is no better path."

Curious, Rigel tested something. He actively thought in his mind, "Are you like Alexa Turon?"

The words on the tablet updated. "Yes."

Rigel thought again, "She told me of an Order of telepaths, told me of what was happening. Is that mad telepath still around?"

There was no answer for a moment, and Rigel scrolled back up the text toward the directions, but just as he had resigned himself to not receiving an answer, a new notification came in. "We don't know; nothing is safe, trust no one, do not stop moving until you get to your lab. We will be in touch."

Chapter 13
Attack on Central

S peaker Swanson said, "What do you mean, 'gone?'"
　　Lydia swallowed and repeated herself for the third time. "I mean, when the guards went to change their watch this morning, Dr. Solidsworth was gone."

Swanson always made her nervous. She didn't know why. He was the kindest of all the senators, and he was usually agreeable, but even he looked frazzled as of late. Who could blame him? Lydia had near-constant stomach cramps with all the stress and pressure, and now, the architect, the only person who could figure out the navigation for the city, was gone.

"Well, what happened to him?"

"We don't know."

Swanson's faced darkened a little. "Don't know or won't tell?"

Lydia Danvers pressed her thumb and forefingers to the bridge of her nose. "Speaker Swanson, what incentive would I have to withhold information from you about an escaped prisoner, especially that one?"

His face lightened a little. Lydia watched him take a deep breath on the vidscreen and shift a little. "I'm sorry, Commander Danvers, it's just that things have been very tense here in the Senate and all I have lately is bad news."

"It's the same over here, Speaker. I haven't had a single piece of good news in a week."

"So there was nothing; no evidence whatsoever as to what happened?"

Lydia paused for a moment because there was something, but she wasn't even entirely sure that it was related to the old scientist disappearing. Should she tell him, when it was just one frame of a video from a surveillance camera? She opened her mouth to say something and then thought it best to withhold the information, at least for now.

"No."

"Why didn't one of your SO's see anything?"

"Private Errant was the only one on duty. He left to use the bathroom, and when he came back, Dr. Solidsworth was gone. Our security cameras confirm this."

"And what do the security cameras show about the time when the guard was out of the room?"

Lydia frowned. "Nothing."

"Nothing?"

"The camera tilted up to the ceiling immediately after Private Errant left the room. I've already transferred the footage in a data package to your tablet, and you can see it for yourself. All we can hear from the camera is a strange buzzing noise and a few words here and there. None of it helps in deciphering what happened."

"I see. Do you think the AI was involved somehow?"

"I have no idea. If it is, I don't understand why it would help Dr. Solidsworth and not do anything else. Most of us up here think the AI was damaged in that last blast that launched us from the surface, and all its interactive features went with it."

Swanson nodded. "I suppose that makes as much sense as anything else, doesn't it?" He seemed to mutter it more to himself than to Lydia. "So what are you going to do to rectify the situation? If we don't have Solidsworth back to..."

Lydia cut him off. "We have two SO's investigating."

"And they went to his lab?"

Lydia nodded.

"What about the generators? Did they search them?"

"Yes, and, as limited as we are on personnel we have still stationed a few SO's at some of the generators. Their orders are to patrol each one in their area and look for signs of Dr. Solidsworth."

Swanson nodded, and in the light of the vidscreen, he looked ancient and tired. "Have you checked on his lab assistant?"

"Yes."

"And?"

"And he is also missing. Though, there were no security cameras around the quarters where we were holding him. So we aren't even sure how long he was missing."

Swanson frowned. The creases of his laugh lines sagged and crinkled. "Do you suppose his assistant, his son, could have freed him?"

"We've considered that, yes."

Swanson turned for a moment to address someone behind him and nodded a few times. He said, "Are you certain? Ah. Very well then."

He turned his attention back to Lydia.

"It seems there is another issue that the Senate must discuss. Is there anything else from you, Commander?"

Commander? Lydia couldn't wrap her head around it. No one had ever called her Commander, though she supposed with Major Daniels gone, she was in charge of the security and migration of the whole city. Didn't that make her a commander? Still, she didn't feel like she could wear that title just yet.

"It's Lieutenant, Speaker Swanson, but no, for right now, that's all the news I have for you."

"Very well. I will check back in tomorrow, but if you have any updates on Dr. Solidsworth's whereabouts, I want you to notify me immediately. You can reach me on my private line as well. I believe you already have access to that line?"

Lydia nodded.

Swanson signed off, and Lydia blew out a breath. It was problem after problem. There had been three more breaches into the Mids and one even into the Uppers, and it was clear that there was little they could do to stop it. The problem grew as more and more of the Lowers realized that control was no longer possible. Any day now, there would be a...

Roma raced in through the door, out of breath and sweating. "Sir... outside... look..."

Lydia walked swiftly to her command chair and pulled up the monitors for outside the building. Her heart sank.

"What the hell are they doing?" It wasn't a question that really needed answering, but she asked anyway. She toggled the controls for each of the cameras.

The cameras, like eyes, endlessly questing for a hidden predator, scanned back and forth along the courtyard just outside of central security. The huddled masses that waited just outside the door stood and sat haphazardly. A few had trickled into the main lobby, but only the boldest among them. Their bravado was spreading.

Roma said, "I don't know, sir."

Lydia said, "Well, didn't your man inside that meeting in the gymnasium get some sort of insight into what the Lowers were going to do?"

Roma said, "They were supposed to send a representative, at least that's what we thought."

"That doesn't look like a representative to me, that looks like a peasant revolt. Look at them: some of them even brought metal bars and other things that could be used as weapons."

For the moment, there were only a few hundred, but their numbers were growing as more trickled in from nearby blocks.

Roma said, "I'm getting a few reports of activity along all the major roads. More are coming."

"God, I would kill for a few Runners right now for crowd control. Any updates from the docks?"

"We have four individuals who have undergone the muscle augmentation and chip implementation now and are in the alcoves, healing."

"How many EnViro suits are left?"

"Twenty-seven now. We found a dozen in storage that were in need of serious repair but still somewhat functional. Eight are ready for deployment, and the rest will be ready in the next twenty-four hours."

"Well that's good news at least."

"Sir, we still have the problem of training them. So, far as I know, there are no other Runners left for that purpose."

It was a major problem. They could stuff a Runner in a suit, but if they didn't know how to move around inside one, it would take a significant amount of time to get the hang of it. Worse, with the AI offline, no one in security knew if that problem extended to the EnViro suits yet, but there seemed no reason to assume the AI in the suits would function with the city AI offline. If the suit AI's functioned, it could do some of the heavy lifting in terms of training, but without an experienced Runner or the AI, training would be exceedingly difficult. They needed someone to verify that the suit AI's were still functioning. Lydia should have checked before; she didn't know why she had overlooked it... except that, well, there were just so many damn things to do, weren't there?

Why did everything have to be an uphill battle here? From the moment she had assumed command, everything that could go wrong had. How the hell had Daniels dealt with this for so many centuries? But she knew the truth. Daniels never had to deal with a situation quite like this. Still, she felt like he would have done a better job than she was. He knew the city better than anyone or anything, except maybe the AI. It occurred to her that if she had Manhatsten to help, things would probably go much more smoothly, but as she heard Daniels say several times, wish in one hand, shit in the other and see what fills up first.

"Roma, besides me and you, who has had muscle augmentation for the EnViro suits?"

Roma looked down at his tablet and spent a moment scrolling. He looked an age older than he had before the Battle for Langeles. She found herself wondering if people thought the same of her. She had already seen two gray hairs on her head. Nothing an alcove wouldn't take care of, but that assumed you had time to sit in one.

Lydia had trained in an EnViro suit a few times, but she was an amateur at best. She knew Roma had a limited amount of experience as well.

"Three others. Gunner, Sanders, and Maldek."

"Are all the suits in the docks?"

"Yes."

"How difficult would it be for us to get them in here right now?"

Roma frowned. She hated that damn frown. She knew exactly what it meant before he even opened his mouth.

"I'm not sure the people outside would allow it."

"What about the underground entrance then?"

Roma pressed his tablet a few times, and then the security feed in front of her chair changed. There were nearly two dozen people sitting right outside the exit in the underground. These ones were not passive or unorganized protesters sitting idle. No, they were armed, angry, and waiting for something. All at once, Lydia had a cold chill down her spine. Some of the rabble outside might be unorganized, might just be following the crowd in a time of desperation, but those waiting down below definitely weren't. Someone was organizing this.

"Shit."

Roma nodded.

"They mean to break in here, don't they?"

"I think so, sir."

"Roma, are we trapped in here?"

"It appears so. Though I am not sure any of the protesters on the ground level would stop us from leaving; at least not yet."

Lydia paced back and forth for a few moments. Roma kept his eyes on her. She felt the weight of those eyes. If only they had a few Runners... One Runner could hold off ten or twenty unarmed people without much trouble, plus a few Runners would remind people of the consequences of rebellion. It would give them all pause to see a few of them.

Lydia stopped and turned toward the rest of the room.

"Alright, everyone. I think we have a rather serious situation on our hands. I don't think those are innocent protesters out there. I think something else is going on. It's time we put the building on lockdown. No one goes in or out without my permission."

She took a deep breath. "Now, we need someone to go down there and find out what they want. Any volunteers?"

Sanders, who had sat listening a few stations away from Lydia's command chair, said, "I don't think that's going to be necessary, Commander."

Lydia flinched at the second use of the title but didn't correct it. There would be time later to address it. Now they needed to focus on more important things then proper nomenclature. "Why do you say that, Sanders?"

Roma said, "No, he's right, look, it's the guy from the meeting who they were supposed to send as a representative. He's walking right up to the door with that older, skinny woman."

"The guy with the big gut? The one from sanitation?"

"Yep."

Lydia zoomed in on the man. He looked just as frustrated and disgruntled as she felt. Private Tulle didn't exaggerate in her report. The gut almost seemed to carve its way through the crowd, and as people noticed him, most of them shook his hand or stepped aside.

He didn't let it slow him down as he wound his way to the front entrance and pushed through the doors into the front lobby.

"Send someone to get him, Roma, and bring him to the conference room on the 31st floor."

"Anything else, Commander?"

She looked hard at Roma for a moment. There was a smile on his face. He knew calling her commander pissed her off, and yet here he was, good old Roma pushing her buttons all over again. She almost said something, almost opened her mouth to correct him and then thought, well, why not let them call her that? Maybe she would try it out for size, just for a little while, at least. Perhaps it would help boost morale a bit. A confident commander was important, wasn't it?

"Bring him up and see if you can send a few people to clear the lobby. I don't want a single person down there who doesn't have express permission to be there. You're in charge up here while I talk to him."

2.

The woman wanted to play hardball, but Frank didn't mind. Most of the city knew that she had taken command after the previous guy died in the battle with Saud, or at least that was the word on the street. She was trying to bare her teeth a bit, make sure he knew who the boss was. The short, sandy-blonde woman paced back and forth in front of the entrance door.

Zelda whispered, "Frank, I think your gut's bigger than her."

Frank snickered. He whispered back, "Now, now, even small dogs can have a big bite. You know that better than anyone, Zelda."

"I'm..." the woman paused for a moment. "I'm Commander Danvers, the new head of central security, and..." She hesitated again. "I... I demand to know why you are assembling outside the building."

Frank blinked and cocked his head to the side. "I didn't bring those people. I thought we were s'posed to come here first and negotiate. But I guess the lot of them got a bit on the eager side, ya know?"

"Why would they do that?"

Was this girl that naive? Didn't she know the temperature of the city? For a moment, Frank almost said something and then decided against it. The guy before, that Major John Daniels, he'd been pretty famous. Everyone in the city knew his name, and dozens of vidscreen shows were about him. He tried to recall how long he had been in charge of security in the city and realized he didn't know. As long as he could remember, he had always been in charge up here, and that probably weighed pretty heavy on this girl. Add in the fact that they had left the planet behind, and all the other crazy shit was going on, and you had one hell of a confusing mess and a lot of responsibility suddenly dumped on your shoulders. He could sympathize with that; it's how he ended up in charge down in sanitation after the last uprising.

"Look, I'm gonna say it again, so we are on the same page. These people lining up outside, I didn't bring them. I came here to negotiate, well me and Zelda both. So far as I knew, mostly the people in the Lowers, at least the ones who are outspoken, sent us here."

"So who did send them?"

"Lots of possibilities there. Any one of the major Lower gangs might be able to get a crowd together, but it seems a little big for just one of them. Maybe a few of them are working together or something."

"Working together?"

"Yeah, you may not know this, but they don't much get along down there. But if you give them a common goal or enemy, something they can all get something out of, they might just drop the old grudges and work together."

The girl seemed to pale at the news. Again, Frank had wondered how she hadn't considered this before. Maybe they were just too used to having the Runnercore or the AI bail them out when things got out of hand down in the Lowers.

Danvers said, "So what do we do?"

"Negotiate with me and Zelda here."

"And you can make them go away?"

Frank shook his head. "Lady, I don't know. They might listen to me, and they might not. If they are on some dealer's payroll, they ain't going nowhere. But I think, and I'm just guessing here, cause I knew more than a few of them on my way in here, that some of them would listen, maybe enough would leave for things to be a bit more manageable for you, huh? Besides, most of these guys, they're cowards, and they like to hide in the numbers. You take away some of those numbers, and just maybe you take away some of them, too."

Frank shifted in his chair. It creaked under his weight, and he could feel the arms pressing into the side of his gut. He hated chairs with armrests. The damn things always felt like they were restraining him. He glanced around the room. There wasn't much space here along the table. He counted twenty-three chairs in all. It was probably some meeting room for security officials. They probably didn't need much space in normal circumstances.

"Alright, so negotiate. Tell me what you want."

"Straight to the point, huh?" Frank chuckled. "Alright, but you ain't gonna like it. I thought we would dance around the topic a little bit, you know, soften each other up first, like a poker game or something. But you're calling all-in already and want me to show my hand, don't you?"

The commander scowled for a moment, and then her expression softened. "Are you some kind leader of the Lowers?"

"I don't know about that, but the people of the Lowers are tired of being ignored, and they asked me to speak up for them. And I thought hey, I got a pretty big mouth, so why not give a shot."

The woman cracked a smile. It was slight, and only lasted a heartbeat, but Frank felt like it was a good sign. Maybe she would listen.

He said, "We want three things. First and foremost, we want to know what the hell is going on with all these disappearances."

Any good humor dropped from the woman's face.

Zelda said, "A lot of people are real pissed about the disappearances I think if nothing else, you gotta address that one."

Lydia said, "You know we've had disappearances here too, right?"

Frank raised an eyebrow. "Yeah? How many?"

"Last I checked this morning it was eleven for central security, and at least twenty from a city-wide count of SO's."

Frank reached up and scratched his chin. If even security was experiencing disappearances, what did that mean? Frank looked at the woman for a moment. He always thought he was a pretty good judge of character, and he didn't think this woman was lying. "What about in the Uppers, they missing people too?"

Lydia said, "Two-hundred and thirty-three reports in the Uppers so far."

Zelda said, "She's lying, Frank."

"Why would I lie?"

"Because you don't want us to know what's really going on with all these missing people. Like, maybe they got sucked out into space or something, and you don't want to admit that the city is in serious trouble."

The commander looked at Zelda. Her lips pressed together and made a thin white line. She reached up and pressed the bridge of her nose with two fingers, took a deep breath, and said, "The city is in serious trouble. Who could hide something like that?" She sighed. "Look, let's say for a moment you are the representatives of the Lowers, okay?"

Frank nodded, "Okay."

"Can I trust you both to keep your mouth shut about what I'm about to tell you?"

Frank's heart started to pound. Was there a secret conspiracy to cover up disappearances after all? He looked at Zelda, and she looked back at him and nodded. "Sure."

"Frank, can I call you Frank?"

"Everyone else does, so go right ahead."

The woman nodded. "Frank, we're... well... I'm going to be frank with you. Things are much worse than you imagine. We don't know where we are going, and we have no way of navigating the city in space. If you haven't noticed, the AI has vanished, or at least it isn't responding at all. The Runnercore was wiped out with the city legs; near a third of our personnel were killed or seriously injured in the last battle, and we're struggling like hell to keep the city running. As for disappearances, we don't even have the human resources to look into it right now, all we are trying to do is document who went missing, but the numbers are growing, and we have no idea why. You're looking at the most qualified person to run security right now, and I don't even have half the experience that any of the previous senior staff had. All of the senior staff are dead or missing. So no, I'm not lying. I have no earthly idea how the hell I am going to keep this city from tearing itself apart."

Danvers trembled.

Frank was speechless.

Zelda said, "I'm sorry."

Commander Danvers said, "For what?"

"Your shit is way more messed up then we realized."

"So, you believe me? You don't think I'm just some security official lying to you?"

Zelda said, "If that was a lie, it was a damn good one. Things are bad in the Lowers as well. We're struggling to keep all our crews going. The disappearances aren't as bad with us as with some areas, but it's enough that we're all working overtime constantly now."

The commander said, "Okay, so now that you know I can't help you with that first thing, what are the other things you want."

Frank said, "Hold up, maybe we can help each other with that, huh? Maybe we get some of the people from the Lowers to help us try and figure this thing out? A lot of people are anxious because they got nothing to do, and their loved ones are missing. Maybe we can work with some of your SO's to organize some kind of search or something?"

The woman's face lit up. "Yes, I think that would be a good idea. In fact, maybe we can go down and have you propose something like that right now."

Frank smiled. He knew he had her where he wanted her now. He had something she wanted, and they definitely had something he wanted. Now that he'd poked and prodded and peeked at her cards, he thought maybe this all could turn out for the best. "Alright, I can do that but..." he let his "but" hang for a moment; make her work through the pause.

Danvers said, "What do you want?"

Frank said, "Remove the alcove restrictions and give us a better pathway to the Mids and Uppers. We want things to be fair. That's all we're asking. We ain't asking for you to give us anything but a real fair shake. Oh, and you need to end the Runnercore."

He dropped a bomb, he knew it. He was asking for the world, but if you wanted to get something out of a deal, you always had to push hard in the beginning, always had to make those terms seem damn near impossible so you could get something out of it. The people who had sent him, had all agreed to some sort of citizen's oversight committee for the Runnercore, not to abolish it entirely. Everyone knew there were some people who deserved the sentence they got. Everyone also knew that there were people like the late Tera Reevas who took advantage of the corrupt system and put innocent people in the Runnercore.

"You know that's all impossible right? You know that you're talking to the wrong person for any of those issues. All I have control over is security; that's it. The alcoves are almost all a private entity that isn't controlled by any of the politicians or us. There are a few exceptions in the city constitution that make allowances for the minimum allotment for every citizen to prevent the spread of disease and debilitating injury, and of course, for the Runnercore. Beyond that, alcoves are owned by the individuals who have the resources to buy and maintain them. Do you know how much running one of those things costs in terms of energy? If they were all going full time, we would have to cut power elsewhere. We have a delicate system, and we can't just open up the alcoves to anyone, not if we wanted the city systems to have enough to function and keep us all alive."

"As for a better pathway up to the Mids and Uppers, I don't know exactly how to even address that. I think it's something you have to take up with the Senate. They are the ones that put economic policy into place, not central security. And for the Runnercore? Yes, security does train and maintain them, but their sentence is a part of the judicial system of this city, which is run, again, by the Senate. My hands are tied on all three of those issues."

Zelda said, "We know that."

"You do?"

Frank said, "Yeah, we do. We know that it's the Senate that has to address all of it."

"So why tell me?"

"Cause the Senate won't even give us an audience and, well, even though we didn't plan for there to be a crowd outside of the security building, we certainly got your attention, don't we?"

"Maybe ours, but not the Senate..."

"You sure about that?"

Danvers' face was a mask. It seemed after she had confessed to all the difficulties the city was having, she had composed herself. "So, what do you want me to do?"

"We want you to take our demands to the Senate. We want you to show them the footage from outside the building and gently remind them that this could happen outside every building."

"Is that a threat?"

Frank shook his head, "Lady, I ain't stupid. I'm sure you knew all about who I was before I even got here. If you didn't, then you didn't do your job very well, did you? Think: do I seem like the kind of person that would threaten you or incite some kind of riot?"

The woman appeared to consider and then shook her head. "No."

"I want you to tell the Senate the truth: that if they do nothing, there are going to be consequences. Even if you can't do anything about the disappearances, there is a lot you can do to address the issues of this city. I've read some history, some pre-migration history, and I know that when things get bad enough, the poor always revolt and fight back; that when they feel they have nothing left to lose, they burn things to the ground. Now, all of those in the Senate are educated enough to know that's true. Most of the Senate might be corrupt, selfish pricks, but they also aren't stupid. They can see the writing on the wall when it spits them in the face, can't they?"

"You've never dealt with the Senate directly, have you?"

"No, I haven't." Frank rubbed his belly. "Are they that dense?"

"The worst are the upper Mids. They live in a bubble; they ignore all the problems around them and pretend like it doesn't affect them. They and the Senate fail to do anything that doesn't directly impact them. The city could be on fire, and they wouldn't reroute water to interrupt their bath time until they knew the fire was climbing their particular building. No one in central security likes the Senate."

Frank frowned. "I still want to speak to them. Even if it is hopeless."

Danvers paced around the room and said, "I guess I can't blame you. I would probably want the same thing in your shoes."

Zelda said, "So you'll do it then?"

"I can give you my word that I will pass along the message. But how does that solve my problem?"

"As I said, I don't know if I have much pull over the crowd down there, but I bet I can convince some of them that you are at least setting up talks with the Senate and maybe, just maybe..."

But Frank didn't finish. A loud and unmistakable explosion issued from below, and the entire building trembled. Frank swore and jumped to his feet, as did every other person in the room. The guard that had stood outside the door rushed down the hall, and the Commander walked to the wall and pressed a few hidden buttons to reveal a large vid screen and a console. She immediately pulled up the view from the lobby area, and what Frank saw made his jaw drop. The entire first level was on fire. Only one camera was left functioning, but that one camera told the story. Everyone on the first floor that was visible to the security camera was motionless, and the fire crept toward the camera.

"Jesus, we're all gonna burn to death if we don't get out of here."

Commander Danvers said, "No, this building was built to withstand a massive terrorist attack in the aftermath of some strike on New York City in the pre-migration world. I don't remember my history very well, but I remember that this building used to be two different skyscrapers, and I think someone flew a large carrier or transport into them. This building was designed with that in mind, and then it was reinforced and re-engineered just before this city became mobile. Central security is the strongest building in all of Manhatsten. The entire city would come down before this building did. But we have another problem... look."

Frank did, and what he saw was many people moving in through the fire. At first, he thought maybe they were fire crews or someone risking their lives to save the people inside until he looked closer. Each one was carrying an energy pistol or rifle.

3.

Serah skimmed several of the minds at the base of the building. They were planning on going in, planning on taking over security. They were under orders from some guy named... Tony? They kept thinking about what Tony wanted, and how to please Tony. Not all of them had that on the surface of their minds, just some of them. But she could only get fragments from a mind here or there. It was like reading an angry beehive. She knew what was coming, knew about the explosives rigged in the main room. It was too late to do anything about it. They were on a timer, and the only people she could push on anywhere near it didn't have any idea how to stop it. More likely, they would detonate the bomb themselves. It was going to explode no matter what she did.

The only thing she could do was help some of the innocent people get out of the way. With all of her available will, she reached out to some of the bystanders and made them uncomfortable. She made them feel a desire to get away from the building, insisted that something was about to go wrong, that violence and bloodshed were inevitable, and that it was in their best interest to leave. Some took the push seriously, but others were already too hypnotized by the events unfolding in front of them. They were voyeurs peeping in a window at something awful, and it was electrifying.

"It's starting again, isn't it?"

Shannon stood next to her, watching out of the window on the eighth floor of the building across from central security. She didn't have to skim her to know what she meant.

"Looks like it."

"We have to stop it. A lot of people are going to get hurt."

"I know."

"I wish Mimi were here."

Serah frowned. She had been thinking the same thing, but she wanted more than just Mimi, she wanted a full complement of sisters. With all her sisters, they could have spread confusion and chaos amongst the hired muscle and effectively put a stop to the flow of movement toward the building. If they did that, security itself might be able to handle the small and focused armed group. But with so much anger and intention, pushing wasn't going to stop most of the ones who wanted to hurt someone, at least not without the red veil, and Serah would be damned if she would ever play with that again; not after Mimi. No, as far as Serah was concerned, as long as she was alive, she would never allow anyone to use the red veil in her presence again.

She could feel the pressure, feel the tension of the organized members of the mob. That tension gushed through every available crack and crevice of the city. The last seconds of the bomb's silence ticked away.

"Shannon, are you ready?"

Shannon nodded. "There are so many of them, though."

"That's why we have combat suits on. I don't think they are going to have much that can punch through this armor, do you?"

Serah was lying. She knew that some of them did have higher-end weaponry. Shannon didn't need anything else to make her nervous. Serah didn't know where this Tony had gained access to the weapons for the Runnercore, but she imagined that with the Runnercore missing and the dockworkers on temporary leave, it would be much easier to swipe a few of those guns.

Serah skimmed them again, trying to identify which ones had the heavier energy rifles. So far as she could tell, only a dozen had them. But two dozen more or so held energy pistols, and although those wouldn't easily punch through combat armor, if they hit the right spot, it would do a lot of damage. She focused her mind on the ones who carried rifles. A dozen was a small enough number that she could push on their minds and confuse their fire, at least long enough for her and Shannon to crash in and take those guns away. It wasn't much of a plan, but if she could at least disarm the thugs in charge and scare the hell out of the rest of the protesters, then maybe security could handle the rest.

The one thing that made her nervous was not knowing where Miranda stood in all this. She had to be out there somewhere, plotting and calculating. She might have been on the planet, but the Recycled wouldn't act of their own accord and take Mimi, would they? There was nothing to be done now, though. All she could do was try to help the city stay together until Miranda showed her cards. Otherwise, she would spend all her time jumping at shadows, and that wouldn't be good for anyone.

The bomb exploded. Serah could see the fire licking out of the windows and the doors on the first floor of central security. The tongues of flame tried to climb up the side of the building but darted back inside. The outer structure did not catch, but a small glow cast shadows against the screaming protesters in the street. Most had not expected an explosion, but a few who had taken cover before the blast were already running inside.

"Now, Shannon."

Shannon looked down eight stories, looked over at Serah, and then, taking a few steps back, charged forward, right through the glass. Serah watched gravity catch Shannon and pull her down as she bent her hydraulic legs and leapt after her.

4.

Someone tossed a plasma grenade in through the conference room door. It bounced a few times and then landed next to Lydia. Without hesitation, she dove over, grabbed it, and lobbed it back into the hall from where it came. There was an almost immediate explosion followed by one long, low moan of pain and rage. Lydia stood up and fired a few times, hitting another one of the assholes who were trying to take her command. At a glance, she could see that the grenade had thinned their ranks. She ducked back under cover. Thank god the conference tables were made of something thick and sturdy. The energy blasts couldn't penetrate them, and the hired guns storming the central security didn't seem to have any ballistic weapons.

All of her guards were already down. They had held back the first wave of invaders, but the second overwhelmed them. They did their best, but it wasn't enough. She hoped like hell they were all still breathing and that after this nightmare was over, she could put them into a medical-grade alcove. She'd hate to lose more of her friends.

The big guy cowered down behind the overturned table next to her, but the thin, bird-like woman was jumping up and tossing anything she could find at the attackers. Lydia admired her courage. She reached down inside her jacket and pulled out a second firearm. "Which one of you knows how to use one of these things?"

Both looked at her with a blank stare.

"I need one of you to fire it in the right direction for a few minutes. Can one of you do that?"

Zelda said, "Give it here. I can take it."

Lydia handed the gun to Zelda. "Switch the safety off the side and shoot toward them. It will give me some breathing room to see how we can get out of here. If we can get back up to command, we stand a much better chance of surviving this."

Standing, Lydia fired a few more times, and then ducked down. "Your turn."

Zelda stood and pulled the trigger several times. As she did, Lydia peered around the side. There were only three of them left. Between the grenade and some of her own shooting, four were dead already. She had no idea how many more were behind them, but that was a problem for future Lydia. She watched the attackers fire at Zelda for a moment, and despite the open and easy shot, Zelda was giving them, they missed. She watched them for a moment more before ducking back behind cover.

They were lucky. Whoever these guys were, they weren't practiced with energy rifles. That's probably because they were notoriously hard to get a hold of outside the Runnercore, and their use, at least pre-Saud, would be immediately tracked by the AI. They fired straight on, as you would with ballistic weapons, not realizing that you had to fire lower and to the right because of the way the weapon always jerked half a moment before the beam fired from the muzzle.

"Okay, I've got a plan. Frank, I want you to grab one of those chairs, and throw it at the door. Zelda, I want you to fire another volley at them. If you two can distract them, I think I can end this and get us upstairs before their friends get here."

Frank said, "You want me to throw a chair? A chair? They got guns, and you want a chair?"

"Misdirection, Frank," said Zelda. "She gonna plug 'em while they're looking at you, like on the vid screens, right?"

Lydia nodded. She liked this one even more. She was smart and had guts. She looked at Frank. He was shaking.

Frank said, "I ain't never had no one shooting guns at me before. I'm not a fan."

Zelda said, "Don't be a baby, Frank. Even I can see these pieces of shit couldn't hit a damn thing. You yell at them and throw a chair, and you're gonna give the little bastards a heart attack. Let your gut do its thing."

Frank said, "Probably give me a second heart attack. Those aren't much fun, you know."

There were shouts down the hall. Lydia couldn't tell if they were friend or foe, but either way, they had to act. If more of the invaders showed up, they would be in deep with no way out.

"We gotta move now."

In response, Zelda jumped up and yelled, "Hey, assholes! What do you think you're doing?" She fired.

Frank hesitated, but only for a moment, and he stood, grabbed the nearest chair and tossed it toward the door. It slammed into the wall next to the door with a loud bang. As he grabbed a second chair he yelled at the top of his lungs. Lydia leapt up herself, moved to the left, and shot one of the attackers in the throat. Blood sprayed on the wall behind the man as he fell. As Frank released his second chair, she shot the second in the shoulder. It was Zelda who hit the third in the chest, but not before he got off a shot. Frank's war cry changed pitch and transformed into a wail. Lydia turned toward Frank and saw he was bleeding.

Zelda said, "He's alright. They only got his arm. Make sure they ain't gonna shoot us again."

Lydia nodded and ran up to the man she winged and kicked the rifle away from him. He lay, eyes wide and staring up at her. She was about to open her mouth to ask who had sent them, but she heard shouts coming up the stairwell from below.

Lydia said, "Frank, are you okay to run?"

"As fast as my legs will carry me, I think." He was clutching his arm and wincing. Bloodstained the left side of his shirt, but he was holding it tight, masking the hole on the outer edge of his arm.

Lydia walked back over, reached out a hand, and with Zelda, pulled him up. For a moment, she thought about the maintenance hatches that Daniels had installed after the battle with Mex, but she realized they didn't have access on this floor. Only some of the floors had access, plus the passage was small, and there was no way a man with a gut like Frank's would get through. Instead, Lydia led them to the stairs.

Pushing the door open, the shouts clarified, and below, she could hear the sound of footsteps slapping on the stairwell. They were coming from below. There was no way they were friendly.

In a low, hushed voice, Lydia leaned in and said to the pair, "Climb, fast."

Frank looked up at the stairs and rubbed his belly. "I ain't built for stairs."

Lydia opened her mouth to say something, but Zelda said something first. "Told you that gut was gonna get you killed. If you don't run up those stairs, we're all in deep, Frank."

Frank grimaced and then, taking two at a time, launched himself up the first stairs.

He turned and, in a low voice, asked, "How many levels to command?"

Lydia mouthed, "Fifteen."

Frank didn't say anything, but his expression said it all. It looked someone stepped on his toe and put shit under his nose at the same time.

The footsteps below grew in volume. They were getting closer. Lydia knew they could be more than a half dozen levels below. She motioned her hand towards the pair to go fast, and then she started running up the stairs behind them. As she reached the next level up, she missed a step and tripped. Smacking her knee against the concrete stair, a bright flash of pain blazed through her shin; one that blocked out all the rest of the world for that single moment. In that single moment, she realized she had dropped her gun. It clattered down the steps, rolling as it went until it hit the landing one floor down, and, as it struck the ground, it fired. Lydia swore.

Below, all the noise disappeared for a moment. Then, someone shouted. "Someone's firing from above. Open fire."

The electronic buzzing of energy rifles pulsed from below and up the side of the stairwell, and in the center, light flashed and changed the quality of the color of the room from gray to a pinkish hue. It was a stupid move, one only an amateur would make. They were wasting charges on a target they couldn't see and were uncertain about. Still, if the beams or pulses hit the right object, they could reflect back toward her little party and do some damage. It was unlikely, but they had to hurry and get out of the stairwell as fast as possible.

Lydia, no longer worried that the invaders below would hear them, shouted, "Run!"

As Frank and Zelda climbed, she ran down.

Frank said, "Where are you going?"

Lydia said nothing. Instead, she turned and put a finger to her lips and then motioned them to keep going. She would have no problem keeping up with Frank, and knew it was probably a mistake to go down, but what choice did she have? If there was only one weapon between the three of them, they were in even more trouble.

She ran and jumped down each stair, skipping steps. There, another flight down was her energy pistol. Dashing for it and making a lot more noise then she wanted to, she grabbed it from the floor. As she stood to turn around and head back up, she peered over the edge of the stairs and down the center between the guard rails.

She had no idea how many of the invaders were down there, but they occupied at least six levels that she could see. They were coming, and even if she made it to command, she was going to have a hell of a time stopping them.

She ran back up the stairs to catch Frank and Zelda, taking two stairs at a time and feeling the burn in her legs.

5.

Adrian Roma paced back and forth, his hands clasped behind his back. He hadn't heard from his commanding officer since the bomb blast, and though everyone in central security knew how to react during a lockdown and how to defend central command, he was nervous at the prospect of having to take command. He hadn't even wanted to be Lydia's second, but she had insisted, had told him that he was the only person she could trust to get the job done right. Now here he was, second in charge trying to repel an armed invasion. Several of the security cameras had revealed men and women equipped with high-end energy rifles and others with energy pistols. One of these mobs had already managed to slam through one of their security checkpoints and had made it to the stairwell. There were no cameras in the stairwell, so he had no idea how much progress they had made working their way up, but he had ordered several of his SO's to take a position just outside the door and set up a bottleneck. If they were coming through, they were going to pay for every step.

The lifts were all shut down. The only way up or down, in or out of central command, were these stairs and one other stairwell on the other side of the building. There were the maintenance hatches, of course, which could act as access for times just like this, but access was only on certain levels, and few people had trained on how to open and seal them properly. There just wasn't enough time to utilize them now. Roma had set up a defensive position on the second stairwell, but even on the bottom level, that stairway had remained clear.

One of the SO's radioed him. "Roma, someone's coming up the stairs. We can hear them, and they're getting closer. We should see them at any moment. What are your orders?"

Adrian considered for a moment and then said, "Bar the way and lock it down. Once you shut the door, I want you to surround the exit. Fire the moment they come crashing through the door. Don't even hesitate. We can't give them a chance to break through."

"Yes, Sir. Any word from the commander?"

"None, yet."

6.

Serah slammed into the ground a few meters to the left of Shannon. A few new cracks formed beneath her feet and added to the already disintegrating infrastructure of the city. The sound of metal on concrete drew the attention of everyone within a few dozen meters radius. A few screamed and fled as Serah drew up a list of all the men she skimmed and were a part of this "Tony's" organization. She transmitted the data over to Shannon's heads up display. There were twenty-eight out here. Their job was to get the crowd worked up and send them into the building at the right time.

"Take out all of these guys. Careful though, some of them are armed."

"Are we... are we going to kill them?"

"Only if you have to. Don't forget the taser in the left arm of your EnViro suit. It should incapacitate them without an issue, but Shannon: if they pull an energy rifle on you, don't hesitate. Those things can go right through your armor within a few seconds if they hold the trigger."

Serah skimmed her for a moment as she charged the first three men marked for the takedown. Skimming Shannon, she didn't think there was any way that she would use lethal force. Shannon had destroyed more than a few Recycled before, but killing a human was another story altogether. Serah was going to have to watch her closely to make sure she didn't get into that situation in the first place. But this was battle, and she might not have a choice. If Serah spent all her time watching Shannon, it could get them both killed.

As she approached the first three, their eyes widened when it became clear Serah was after them. Each tried to bolt in a different direction, but Serah grabbed the first one with her massive right arm, shocked him with her left, placed him down, bent with her hydraulic legs, and then, jumping high, crashed on the other side of the second. She didn't bother grabbing him, but tased him and moved on the third.

She looked around and saw that some of the targets were circling up around her. She smiled. This was going to be easy. Hell, it was going to be fun. She didn't realize how much all that searching and the long agonizing moments of uncertainty had gotten to her. She needed some action, and this was it.

She transmitted to Shannon's mind directly. "Hey, how about a little contest."

Using her radio, Shannon said, "What do you have in mind?"

Still using telepathy, Serah said, "Whoever takes down the most wins?"

"You're on."

It was like a game of leapfrog. As each of the men circled up to attack them, they jumped from one to the other to take them down. Serah smiled. They couldn't seem to figure out that they were dealing with two experienced and well-trained Runners. They might stand a chance against a newbie, but two well-trained Runners, and with only a few real weapons? Who were they kidding?

It only took about ten minutes to have each of Tony's hired guns incapacitated. After that, Serah picked a few more of the agitated protestors, ones that had the potential to cause trouble, and tased them, too. She marked a few targets for Shannon as well. If it were too precise, too clear that they knew who was with Tony and who wasn't, then this Tony guy would be suspicious. Incapacitating a few more also had the added bonus of making the majority of the rest of the protesters panic and flee.

All in all, they knocked out about forty people surrounding the exterior. Though she couldn't understand how those twenty-eight were going to convince a group of people who had just seen a bomb go off to storm the building. Maybe they were there for another reason that Serah hadn't been able to skim. Serah reached inside the building and looked for more minds to hunt down.

Shannon said, "I win!"

Serah said, "That's 'cause I let you."

"Whatever, I'm faster than you, and you know it."

"Only 'cause I have to skim and make sure we're attacking the right people."

"Even still, I knocked down six more than you."

"Job's not done yet, is it?"

"Round two inside?"

"Shit."

Shannon said, "What?"

"There are a lot inside. A lot more than I thought there would be."

"How many?"

"Well, it's hard to be certain, because some of the people who are fighting and who are agitated are SO's, but if I were going to guess, I would say at least one hundred and fifty."

Shannon said, "Well, we can take them. These guys were pushovers." She indicated the numerous people lying on the ground, some unconscious and others groaning.

"The ones inside are a little different. Most of them are armed, and some of them are trained."

Serah used her heads up display to scan through the building for infrared signatures. It was a damn shame her AI wasn't responding. It could have identified every one of the SO's and marked them as friendly in her and Shannon's heads up displays. Instead, Serah had to take a few moments to skim each of the individuals and decide who was fighting for who. She realized it was going to take too much time to do this for all of them, so she focused on the people that, in the view of the infrared, were moving up into the building from the outside. The ones going up the stairwells or working their way through the different levels and firing were all obvious targets. But there were a lot of places she could see where an exchange of fire was taking place, and it was impossible to know who was who.

"There, I have marked all the obvious ones on your heads up display. Let's start with them. The rest... well, we will have to do it the old fashioned way and judge with our eyes when we get there."

"Okay, let's get started."

"Shannon..."

Shannon, turned her whole EnviroSuit around to look at Serah. "What?"

"Inside, it's going to be harder to stun them. You may have to use more..."

"I'm not a child." Shannon's voice was stern.

Serah skimmed her for a moment. She had done what most soldiers had to do in battle, detached from their normal values and ideas for what they thought was the greater good. Serah felt a sense of relief.

"I know... I'm just..."

"I'll do whatever I have to do, Serah. I always have. You don't spend years on the streets and learn that sometimes things aren't so black and white."

"It's just that when I skimmed you earlier..."

"How is it that you have had the power to read minds your whole life and not realized that a person is far more than the thoughts on the surface of their mind? There's more to me then what I am actively thinking about, you know."

Serah felt a sense of dread. Had she really misjudged Shannon so badly?

"Mimi did the same thing, you know. She thought that I would never be able to handle the knowledge of her hidden talent and her long life. She thought that because all of you sisters have the same problem, you only see what people will tell themselves. Was I debating killing those people earlier? Of course, I was. But don't you think for a second that I wouldn't do anything to make sure this city is safe, if for no other reason than that I am going to find Mimi and we are going to have our lives back again." Shannon paused for a moment. "No, forget that, we are going to have a better life. No more of this monthly visiting crap. I'm done with all of that. Mimi and I deserve so much more, and I don't care what anyone thinks. I'm not going back to sitting in an alcove most of my life."

Serah didn't know what to say. She knew she had misjudged Shannon badly, but there was something else.

"Shannon, why are you so certain Mimi's still alive?"

"Because there are just some things you know when you love a person as much as I love her. I know that if she were really gone, I would feel it."

Serah said nothing.

"It's not for you to worry about, Serah. Let me worry about me. I know you think I am deluding myself, and I don't care. What does it matter anyway? Right now, we have work to do, don't we?"

Serah nodded. "We do."

"Well then, let's go."

Shannon started to walking toward the entrance, then turned one more time and asked, "Serah, there is something else I've been thinking about, what happens when this is over? What happens when they discover there are still Runners in the city?"

"I don't know. But I don't plan on sticking around long enough to let them to trap us. Once it's clear that the SO's got things under control, we'll duck out and head back to the Reserve Core."

Shannon said, "In we go?"

"In we go."

Shannon charged into the burnt first floor and headed for her first targets. Serah followed.

7.

Lydia pounded on the door again and shouted. "This is your commander. Let me through."

She knew it was probably of no use. Those doors were well reinforced, and it was always hard to hear what was going on from the other side. She had ordered a lockdown, and Roma was doing his duty. She sagged against the door, pinching the bridge of her nose with her thumb and forefinger.

Frank, still trying to catch his breath, said, "Jesus, I just got over the first time I thought I was gonna die. Now I gotta face it again?"

He clutched his arm. The bleeding hadn't stopped yet, and Lydia thought he looked a little pale. He was still on his feet though, so that, at least, was a good thing.

The noises from below grew both in volume and number. They were only three floors behind them now and working their way up. She looked up at where the stairs dead-ended and sighed. They were trapped, and there was little that Lydia could do about it.

"Quit your bitching Frank. We got guns, so why don't we shoot the door?"

"It's reinforced for something just like this. When we designated this building as central security a few years after the city started walking, we set up defenses in case another city decided to invade us. The entire building is fortified. It's why that explosion didn't do a damn thing and why any fire is suppressed immediately. The only way we get through is a metal battering ram or a serious explosion. The first would take at least an hour, and the second assumes that we could get out of the way. Neither is an option now though, are they?"

All of a sudden, the footsteps from below stopped. It took Lydia a moment to digest the information.

"Shit, get behind this wall."

Lydia grabbed Frank and Zelda by the arm and pulled them around the corner. Instead of more stairs going up, there was a solid concrete wall that blocked the view from below. It wasn't much of a cover, and the three of them could barely fit behind it, but was better than nothing. Lydia's only hope now was that their pursuers were poorly trained and would walk right up into her weapons fire. She had no idea how many of them there were down there. If it was only a few, they could hold them for a while and hope that Roma and the others started a floor by floor sweep. If there were more though, they wouldn't stand a chance.

On the other hand, if Roma did open the door, and the enemy made it through, they would have just given them a foothold to the upper levels of central security. They would still have a few more flights of stairs to battle their way up in the inner corridors to get to the top, but this first stairwell door was their first line of defense, like the outer portcullis of a castle.

Lydia pressed the button on the side of her energy pistol and saw it was three-quarters full. That was good. She had somewhere around a hundred shots left in it before it needed a recharge. Even if there were a lot of the enemies coming up the stairs, she still had plenty of ammo to keep them pinned down.

Lydia whispered to Frank and Zelda. "Any minute now, they're gonna send some of their people up to try and take us. Zelda, let me see your weapon."

Zelda handed it to her, and she pressed the button. It was a little more than half full.

Lydia said, "Zelda, when I tell you, I want you to shoot down the stairs. If you can hit someone, fine, but your job is to keep them from getting overeager and charging all at once. If we can pick several of them off as they come up the stairs, it might discourage them and keep them pinned down for a while. Got it?"

Zelda nodded.

Frank said, "What should I do?"

Zelda, with a completely straight face, said, "Look pretty."

Lydia snorted and had to cover her mouth to keep from laughing too loud.

Frank chuckled. "So what I'm best at, right?"

Zelda said, "Damn straight."

"I want you two to switch off with that pistol. It will seem like there are more of us that way if they see multiple faces. We want to scare them as much as we can. It's the only way that we're going to survive this."

The sound of a single pair of footsteps slapping against the concrete stairs came closer. Lydia waited until she was sure the person was headed up the final flight of stairs before her and ducked out.

The man hesitated and looked up at Lydia. He had a weapon in his hand, but it wasn't raised. His face was red, and he was breathing hard from the long haul up. Then, he made the same mistake that just about everyone had ever made about Lydia. He saw her height, her tiny shoulders, and her soft feminine features and assumed she wasn't much of a threat.

The man said, "Well, hello there little lady. How..."

But Lydia did exactly what she always did when an enemy underestimated her. She took advantage. Before the man could finish his sentence, he had a hole in the side of his face below his left eye. He reached up and touched the partially cauterized and oozing wound. He opened his mouth to say something, but part of his jaw was missing. Then, he turned to walk down to his comrades and fell backward, end over end, finally issuing a long and bloody scream before falling silent.

"Fuck," someone said. "They fucking killed Job."

There was a pause for a moment and then, "I'm gonna fucking kill you. Every single one of you."

Many sets of feet climbed the stairwell.

Lydia, shouting an ordering Zelda as if she had the whole of central security with her, said, "Open fire. No prisoners this time. Kill them all. We don't need any more new Runners."

As several men rounded the corner, Lydia ducked out and fired. Immediately she hit two and ducked back in. Zelda leaned out and fired.

Zelda said, "I got one."

"Don't stop shooting till they're all dead," Lydia screamed.

Zelda's eyes widened for a second, then she was leaning above Lydia and firing some more.

A woman charging up the stairs took a hit just below her elbow. The blast was large enough that all of her bone and muscle disintegrated. The only thing that held her arm on was a thick piece of skin on the right-hand side. The woman, taking a moment to realize what had happened to her right arm, tried to raise her pistol to fire, and the weight of the weapon was just enough to tear the skin free. The arm fell, and with it, the pistol, which bounced down the stairs with her hand still attached, firing and striking a few of the attackers on the way up.

Zelda said, "Damn Frank, that was a hell of a lucky shot."

Frank just grinned and then grunted, gripping his own wound.

Nearly a dozen of the attackers were down, and for a moment, several of them stood around their fallen brothers and sisters and stared. As they paused, Lydia didn't hesitate in picking off a few more. The invaders turned and opened fire. Lydia ducked back behind cover, and at the same time, so did Zelda.

Lydia whispered. "You both alright?"

Both nodded.

"Maybe we stand a chance here. As long as they think there are a lot of us up here, I think we can hold them."

Zelda's eyes grew wide.

Lydia turned. There, standing and looking at the three of them, was a single man. His gun pointed right at them, he fired once but missed. Without hesitation, Lydia fired three shots right into his chest, and the man fell to his knees, dropping his weapon. Lydia kicked it over to Frank.

"Here, Frank, take this."

He picked it up.

The man looked up at Lydia for a moment, his eyes already glassy. Then, for a moment, there was something deep in them; something full of anger and rage. His eyes almost shone red in the dim light, and Lydia blinked a few times, unsure if she was seeing the pupils contract and turn into a red glow.

With a guttural scream, the man shouted, "Everyone charge. There are only three of them. That's it, just three. Charge and kill-"

Before he could say more, Lydia, with all of her strength, kicked the man in the throat, and he fell backward down the stairs.

But it was too late. A flurry of footsteps smacked against the stairs below. There were a lot of them, a lot more than Lydia had guessed. She could swear an entire army was coming.

Zelda said, "We're in serious trouble now, ain't we?"

Lydia didn't answer the question. Instead, she said, "Shoot the ones who come up along the railings first and then fire into the middle of the crowd. Just aim at their center and fire quickly, but don't let your weapon overheat. Fire six shots then count to three. If you do that, you'll be able to fire until it's empty. Our one chance is that we can knock them down into each other. Remember, they're climbing up the stairs, we have the superior position, and plenty of ammo left. We can still survive this, especially now that Frank has a gun too."

Below she heard a booming male voice. "Slow. Take your time. Get behind the shields and hold your ground."

Shields? Lydia peered around the corner and saw the mass of invaders turning the final corner up toward her. Each of the first few rows of people carried a thick piece of steel, one that would stop or at least slow their energy weapons. They moved upward like turtles, taking their time.

She turned back to Frank and Lydia. "New plan. They have shields. The shields won't stop all our blasts, but it will stop most of them. I want you both to aim for any opening or crack they offer us. Open fire."

Lydia leaned out and, after firing four shots, was able to hit the arm of one of the invaders. He yelled in pain and dropped his shield, and then Lydia shot him again, and he fell backward, tumbling into a few others. But Frank and Zelda weren't so skilled with a weapon. They fired, but couldn't get a shot past the shields. The attackers climbed the stairs slowly and steadily. They were only a dozen steps away now, and there was little the three of them could do.

The world behind Lydia tore open. Startled, she fell forward out into the open and scrambled back behind the concrete wall. Luckily, the noise startled the attackers as well, and a few of the approaching invaders stumbled backward, dropping their shields and knocking down their fellows. Lydia turned to see who or what had made the noise and there, standing just through the now open doorway, was a Runner.

The smoke from the explosion circled up around the Runner, and as it cleared, Lydia noticed it wasn't a recon suit, but a fully equipped battle grade EnViro suit. For a moment, her heart stopped. That Runner wasn't hers. It was over. Their attack from below had only been a distraction.

"I told you climbing up the lift shaft was a good idea."

Behind, another Runner walked through.

"You were right. It looks like we got here just in time."

"You ready, Serah?"

Lydia swallowed, waiting for the Runners to open fire and finish her and Frank and Zelda. All they had fought for was over in a blink.

Instead of answering the first one, the second Runner opened fire with a powerful ballistic weapon at the approaching invaders. The metal shields shredded like paper and cut down the entirety of the first group. Then, the second Runner pointed down the stairwell and launched a plasma grenade. Seconds later, it detonated somewhere below.

One of the men who had survived the first onslaught turned to run and screamed, "Runners! Run! They got Runners in full battle gear."

The first Runner opened up again and cut down some of those who were fleeing and the second dropped yet another grenade down the stairwell.

"The second Runner turned to Lydia, towering over her, and said, "You're Lydia right?"

Lydia nodded. She didn't know what to say. Who the hell were these Runners? Where had they come from? Were they the same ones responsible for Solidsworth? The same ones who all the rumors were circulating about? Why would they help Lydia? Runners hated central security, and why wouldn't they? All the abuse and mistreatment, the life sentence, the corruption of the justice system, and the Senate, and yet these two were fighting on their side voluntarily? They must want something. She would have to keep them at arm's length, even if they were pulling her ass out of the fire.

"Get in there and fortify your position. The majority of the attackers are in this stairwell, but there are a few dozen more on the lower levels that we bypassed climbing up the lift. We took care of the ones outside and the ones on the first and second floor. We'll take care of these ones. After that, it's up to you."

Lydia opened her mouth to protest. She was about to say that she was in charge here, but something stopped her. These two Runners had just changed the game. Had they volunteered? Were they under orders from someone or something else? Did it have something to do with the AI? Was it back online? She couldn't wrap her head around it. It was something that would have probably even shocked Major Daniels.

"Fine, but you report back to me the moment you're done."

Neither Runner answered. Instead, one leaped down a flight of stairs, and then the other. The whole stairwell shook from the impact. Lydia wouldn't be surprised if some of the stairs were permanently damaged after these two finished. But, they had just saved her life, so she wasn't in any position to complain.

"Frank, Zelda, come on, let's get out of here.

8.

They fled before her like a herd of terrified animals. And why not? One of the invaders stopped and turned. He raised an energy rifle, but as he leveled it at Serah, She ran up the side of the wall, dodging it and then propelled herself forward with the legs of her EnViro suit, slamming into the man and probably shattering most of the bones in his body. There wasn't much room to maneuver in here, but all that training inside the subway tunnels and the cramped space of the Reserve Core had paid off.

Serah felt a strange sensation in her chest. There was a kind of thirst in her that she didn't recognize. A peculiar hunger to cause pain and anxiety consumed her. For every one of the thugs she dispatched, a wave of adrenaline surged up her chest. Serah could taste it in the back of her throat, almost like the very red blood that beat in her veins. She wasn't quite sure what to think about it, other than the intoxication that filled her. She had heard of blood lust during battle; was this it? Why had she never felt it before?

Shannon said, "Floor fifteen. You think we should let the rest of them escape?"

Serah said, "What, so they can regroup?"

Shannon hesitated. "You like this, don't you?"

Serah jumped forward and struck down another woman with an energy rifle. Her body crumpled to the ground with the impact of the suit. They didn't even need to use weapons anymore; they were masses of metal, moving bulldozers.

"What, don't you? It feels good to be doing something for once, doesn't it?"

Shannon stopped and grabbed Serah and spun her around, even as the invaders fled further down the stairwell.

"Serah, it's not like fighting the Recycled... I, I don't like it. I know what I said earlier; I will do what I have to do, but... Well, it was one thing when they were attacking those two women and that man. I was okay with fighting those ones, but the people we're chasing now..."

"Some of them are still shooting at us."

"Wouldn't you, if you were in their position?"

Serah skimmed her. What she saw in Shannon's mind made her heart sink. Her mind was in deep distress. She was on the verge of cracking. Shannon was replaying a few of her own attacks. Over and over again, she could hear the crunch of the bones of someone she jumped on, or saw the blood ooze from a wound that she gave them. It was too much for her.

Then, it became too much for Serah. What was she doing? Why was she enjoying hurting these people? She couldn't ever remember that happening before. The redness of the blood around some of the broken bodies clarified in her mind. She was hungry for that blood. It was so red, so wonderfully red. If she drew more of it, she could bathe in it, let the red make contact with her skin and...

Serah felt a wave of panic. She lashed out toward that red with all of her concentration. She understood what was happening. Miranda was pushing her. She searched for the source of the thoughts, for the psychic direction in which it lay, and she reached out, as if with a mental knife as Fatima had taught her so many decades ago. She found the thread of red in her mind's eye and cut it. She searched for more, for another mind to strike back against, but it was gone.

Serah fell to her knees. The metal of her suit clanged against the concrete stairwell and echoed off the walls. She screamed. It wasn't a shriek of pain, but rage and anxiety. Miranda was still here, still influencing from the darkness somewhere in the city.

Shannon, despite the metal of the suits, scooped her in for a hug.

Serah said, "Shannon, I need you to chase them out of the building."

"What are you going to do, Serah?"

"I need a moment."

"It was her, wasn't it?"

Serah looked up at Shannon and caught her eye. Then she looked down at her feet ashamed.

"Yes. She's still in the city somewhere, and she was pushing me to hurt those assholes more than I needed to. I could feel... I could feel her joy in the suffering. I was feeling it, as if it was my own. It was almost like an orgasm. I..."

A few tears leaked out of the corners of Serah's eyes. She sniffled a moment and then said, "Go, Shannon, we gotta make sure they're all out."

Shannon nodded but hesitated. Then, she stood and, maneuvering the large metal feet of the suit on the tiny stairs, took her time descending.

Serah watched her go. She would follow her in just a moment, but she had to reach out to Vala and warn her. They had left Vala outside of the alcove, and she was doing better, but she had better keep on her guard.

Reaching out across the near limits of her ability to transmit, Serah pictured Vala and then said, "Vala? Are you there?"

For a moment there was nothing and then, "Yes, I'm here, Serah. Are you okay? You feel upset."

"Physically, I'm fine... but Vala..."

Rather than explaining, Serah transmitted her memory of the last hour. In just a moment, Vala knew everything.

"But that doesn't make any sense Serah. She can't be here. If she was, why would she waste her time manipulating you like that and not just destroying all of us?"

"Maybe she enjoys it. Maybe she wants to toy with us."

"Trust me. Miranda's idea of toying isn't that. When she toyed with us in the library... well, you remember. She wants us dead. All of us. Something else has to be going on here."

"Who else could it be? Miranda's the only one who would use the red veil so freely. Unless..."

Vala almost laughed. "Mimi? But you said the Recycled took her, right?"

"Maybe Miranda did something to her."

"That's impossible, though, think about the timeline. You were unconscious when the city left the surface. So if Miranda was still in the city, then how could she have gotten to Mimi?"

"Maybe the Recycled had programming related to her? Maybe they did something to her?"

"I don't think it's likely. How could a few Recycled overpower Mimi? It seems much more likely that she's dead or Recycled herself."

There was the sound of metal on concrete approaching up the stairwell from below.

"Let's talk more about it when I get back. We're almost finished here. We've driven away most of the threat."

Vala said, "Alright, but Serah, be careful. Something is definitely going on here."

Shannon rounded the corner. "They're all gone. It looks like security has rounded up the few that remained."

"Good. Let's get out of here. Let security clean up the mess."

"How many..." Shannon swallowed.

"Did we kill?"

Shannon nodded.

Serah reached out to the various bodies strewn along the stairwell. In most of them, she felt mental activity, some of it was faint, but most had something going on. Even the ones who were slipping deep into unconsciousness or headed toward a coma could be easily healed in an alcove. Even a non-medical grade facility would work; it would just take a long time inside. But there were some missing. Serah had counted eleven that she struck down, and Shannon had a dozen herself. There were definitely some missing minds.

"If I had to guess, three or four. But those were the ones in the beginning, the ones who almost killed that woman, Lydia, and those two others she was with."

Serah couldn't be sure if that was the truth or not, but she wanted to ease Shannon's guilt.

"Okay... Let's go home."

A voice transmitted over both of their coms. "Not so fast."

Serah said, "Whoa, who's this?"

"This is Commander Danvers of central security. The one who you just rescued."

"What do you want?"

"What I want is to know why you don't have Runner designations. Why I can't find any record of you in the system, and how the hell you skipped deployment in the Battle with Saud."

Serah said, "You sound pretty ungrateful for someone whose ass we just saved."

Lydia said, "If I weren't grateful, I would have activated both your chips and rendered you unconscious."

Shannon said, "We're not staying. We're going home."

"And where is that?"

Neither of the women answered. Serah reached out to Lydia and tried to persuade her into letting them go, but it was no use, she was dead set and determined. Only a harder push, a red push, could do the trick.

Something inside asked her what would be so wrong about a little push. After all, it was to protect her and Shannon, wasn't it? Serah shoved the thought away.

"Look, Lydia, we just saved your ass. We're getting out of here. Give us a few days to rest, and we'll make contact with you, and we can talk further."

Lydia said, "Oh no, you're not going anywhere. Either you come up here to the top of central security voluntarily, or I will render you unconscious."

Serah said, "It's not going to happen. We're leaving. Come on, Shannon."

Serah descended the stairs. Lydia was in for a rude surprise. They had deactivated their behavior chips long ago.

Shannon mumbled something, and Serah turned to ask her what it was, and then she saw Shannon on her knees, grabbing her head. At that moment, she felt a surge of pain climb up the base of her neck and into her head. Her head was on fire, a roaring pain that seized control of her whole body. She vomited, and then, the world went dark.

Chapter 14
The Announcement

Kirka paced back and forth across the command station. She glanced up and out the window and looked at the object that came closer with every passing hour. The outlines of the buildings were now visible. In the past week, she had spent a lot of time looking through the telescope, shocked at what she was seeing. When the AI had finally confirmed that it was a city, she was sure there would only be a few short buildings with lots of green space. But now, with the city profile in view, Luna had identified it as a portion of what was once the great city of New York. Specifically, the AI predicted that what they saw what the old island of Manhattan.

"AI what's the ETA of the city now?"

"The city will arrive in a little over 72 hours."

Like an old snow globe, the whole city was shrouded by a shield. Kirka had asked Loridian if he thought it had any similarity to their own exterior shield. He had agreed that it probably had, but to move through the atmosphere with their current technology would have been impossible. Loridian had pointed out that this city seemed to have ribs that held the shield in place, and that probably boosted the power output. He also reminded Kirka that those on the planet probably had decades more to develop the technology and make the shield much more powerful, though Loridian had not been shy about reminding her of his own upgrades he had made to Luna's shields.

The whole concept puzzled Kirka. She had so many questions. How could something like that reach orbit? What did the people of the city want? Did they have a destination in mind? If they were coming for Solidsonium, they were going to be disappointed. She felt a tinge of anger towards ROAM and reminded herself that what was done, was done.

While there were a few reserves deep below the surface of Luna 1, they were near impossible to get out without some of the technology of the 21st century, and it was 3192 now... and all of that earth-based technology was mostly gone. Sure, Loridian and a few of the engineers had made some advances. Still, with an extreme limitation on resources, they hadn't had much opportunity to improve the harvesting system for Solidsonium.

Loni said, "I can't believe you haven't announced that city yet."

"Tonight, Loni. When we're in broadcast alignment with Luna 1, I will make an announcement."

"But broadcast alignment only lasts thirty-four minutes. Is that enough time to talk about the city and the missiles from ROAM?"

"I'm going to prerecord for Luna 1 and send it as a packet. That way, they can get the news at the same time as Luna 2 when I announce it in the commons."

"The commons? Are you crazy? What if they riot?"

Kirka shook her head. "They won't. There's too much information to fixate on. You have the missiles coming, but you also have this mysterious city on its way. Sure, some of them will focus on the impending doom of the missiles, but I am going to... subtly suggest that this city is our friend, and they have come to aid us."

"Have they contacted us?"

"No."

Kirka stood from her chair. Walking over to the main window, she stared out at the city.

"Have you contacted them?"

"I tried, but the AI says they haven't received our transmission."

"Any guesses why not?"

"No idea. Maybe they don't have the technology to transmit? Maybe they aren't using old 21st century communication relays anymore? There could be a hundred reasons... or..."

"Or what?"

"Or they could be purposely ignoring us because they are hostile."

Loni laughed.

Kirka turned and glared. "What's so funny?"

"You've been a commander far too long. Do you know that? Assuming they are hostile? What could they want from us?"

"Solidsonium."

"Well, we don't have any, do we?"

"There are the deep reserves and plenty of it, but essentially, no, we don't. But they can't know that, Loni. And, you're assuming they aren't run by another military commander or a tyrant or something worse?"

Loni fell silent. She stood from her chair and walked over to Kirka. She stood next to her, staring out at the massive object heading their direction.

"Have you tried to reach out?"

"From this distance?"

"We could network. There might be enough of us in Luna general to reach that far."

"True. It seems likely that one of the descendants of Matron Angela would have survived to live in a city of that size."

"Why don't you suggest it at the end of the announcement tonight?"

Kirka shot a look at Loni. "That would be akin to admitting we haven't contacted them yet, and that could inspire a panic."

Loni nodded, but said, "True, but you could also make a general call for a network, make something up about ROAM or wanting to do a check-in? It's not like we couldn't use some of the soothers to assist in keeping Luna general calm."

"That's true, Loni, but you know that when things are tense, it's not always a good idea to remind the population that there are so many telepaths among them. It inspires jealousy and resentment. Besides, all we need to do is link eleven of us to reach far enough to start the network to all of Luna general. With Loridian's contribution, given their range, it should be no problem to network following the announcement tonight."

"So, should I reach out to Feng or Luang?"

Kirka considered. Luna 1 and 2 didn't always see eye to eye, and Feng and Luang were some of the most powerful telepaths on Luna 1. It was a leftover legacy from the war. Kirka had assumed command of Luna general, but all on Luna 2 were descendants of the Americans and Europeans and Luna 1 were from the Chinese and Russian side of the conflict. Even after a thousand years since that war, there was still mistrust. Feng and Luang had always provided a challenge to Kirka's authority, and the fact that she hadn't shared the knowledge of either ROAM or the city in general, was going to breed some mistrust.

On the other hand, if she handed them the news now...

"Yes, Loni. I think it would be a good idea to contact those two in advance."

"Yeah?"

"Yes. If we give them the information before the announcement tonight, it might nudge them in our direction."

"So, you want me to now?"

Kirka considered, the announcement was still ten hours out, and for Luna 2, the day was just beginning.

"Give it thirty minutes. Feng and Luang are usually up early. Reach out to them and see if they're awake. If they are, give them everything."

"Everything? ROAM and the city and the plan?"

"Everything. It's about time we bring them in the loop anyway. I should have done it before, but I guess I let old prejudices get in the way."

"What if they turn on you?"

Kirka shook her head. "They won't. They have too much to lose now."

"You think this crisis will unite Luna, don't you?"

"Sometimes, it takes a good crisis to bring people together."

2.

Kirka walked up the stairs to the top of the elevated platform. She circled the spiral stairs for a few moments before reaching the zenith. She bounced up the last few steps and walked forward to the front of the platform, looking out at the hundreds gathered and waiting for the big announcement.

Two dozen meters below the surface of Luna 2, the large open cavern, artificially created during the 21st century, was about twenty meters in height. So the platform only stood a few meters high. Although it was dim, the commons were made to emulate a large park rimmed by shops and merchant stands. Kirka, born on Earth in the early 21st century, had always compared it to the inside of a mall. A sidewalk wrapped around the edges and had a path up the middle. A few trees dotted the landscape, but now, most of the green space was taken up by community gardens. Those gardens had been the subject of numerous conflicts over the centuries. Fresh food was a valuable commodity, and there was no better place on Luna for tension. Two centuries earlier, Luna 1 had sent troops to take that green space in what became known as the War for the Gardens. The tension between Luna 1 and 2 had never really subsided.

There had been rumors of a flying city coming toward Luna. Someone in command had spread the rumors, no doubt, since there were very few places that looked out from the underground of Luna. Too many open windows posed dangerous radiation and debris risk. There was special shielding for the command window, but the energy required to do this over a sizable portion of Luna general would be astronomical. So someone in her command leaked the news. That was okay, though, because it would keep all the focus on something other than the missiles from ROAM.

The murmur of conversation quieted, though a few small children jumped and bounced in the low gravity or splashed in the small pond in the center of the commons. A small ball flew up onto the platform, and a child no older than ten traced its progress, and her eyes grew wide. Kirka caught it and, with a smile, tossed it back to the girl. A lot of things had changed throughout Kirka's life, but children's interest and curiosity hadn't.

Kirka stepped on the yellow button that activated voice amplification and spoke. "Good evening, Luna. Tonight, I am here to address the rumors and to make an announcement about our relationship with ROAM. After the announcement, I will spend a short time taking questions."

She paused for a moment, arranging her thoughts. It helped that she had recorded an audio file to send over to Luna 1 earlier in the day, that was playing even now, but she had always hated speaking in front of a crowd, especially when she had some dire news to share.

"The rumors about the flying city are true. In about 60 hours, the city will arrive here."

She paused, but not long enough for anyone to pose a question. All eyes, even those of the smaller children, were on her. She could feel a heat building in her stomach. She swallowed, knowing what she had to tell the crowd next.

"However, I have some unfortunate news about ROAM. As you know, we worked tirelessly to build our relationship with the Romans. Mars was a future destination to which many of us were looking forward to migrating. We were promised upgrades to our facilities, which I know many of you were eager to see come to fruition. We sent off the last of our refined Solidsonium so that the Romans may prosper and so that, with this act of good faith, our two human communities, what we thought were the last of the human communities in the whole universe, would thrive together."

She could feel the tension in the space growing. They could feel her 'but' coming. Many of them suspected that ROAM had an ulterior motive, that they should not be trusted. She was tempted to skim a few minds, but held back. It could derail her train of thought and turn her speech into mush. Instead, she sent a quick message directly to Loni's mind and told her to start soothing the crowd. Four other telepaths were on standby, ready to help keep the crowd calm and in order.

"I want you to remember that we were wrong about that. That we were not the last in the universe, and the city coming to Luna, which our AI has suggested can host 2-4 million inhabitants, is a light in this darkness."

She swallowed hard and focused. The words that she had hesitated to say for the last several weeks were on the edge of her lips. A small internal struggle waged in her mind. She hated telling her people about the betrayal, hated it so much because she had pushed hard for cooperation with ROAM. She had been wrong and, if not for the city, of which their intentions were still unknown, all hope would have dried up from Luna general.

For the last several days, she wondered if she was repeating history. Would this strange city from Earth betray them? What if they were outright hostile? The whole endeavor was one giant gamble. But what other choice did they have? They could either place their hopes in the flying city, or they could fall face first into nihilism and annihilation.

She cleared her throat, swallowed another time, and felt all the eyes staring at her, drinking her in, waiting for her proclamation. They knew what it would be, but that still wouldn't change the shock and rage her people would feel. It was one thing to suspect disaster; it was another to be told that all was coming to an end.

And wasn't that the crux of all this? That even if the flying city was entirely benevolent, they would be refugees. Kirka knew how human history had treated refugees. Her family had been climate refugees from a coastal city centuries before.

"ROAM has betrayed us. Not only have they decided to withhold resources, but..."

She took a deep breath.

"They have sent missiles to destroy us."

She paused. They needed a moment to digest this, but not too long. She reached out and skimmed a few minds in the crowd. There was shock and a rising rage amongst those she touched. It was important not to let the rage boil over, to give them something else to focus on. So often, leadership was about redirecting the energy of those below you by giving them enough truth to aim their will and desires.

"We have ample time to evacuate. The missiles are slow in their progress, and we have plenty of advanced warning."

Someone from the crowd shouted, "Death to Romans."

There was a general murmur of agreement.

Now came the lie. Kirka swallowed hard, regretting the lie and hoping that very soon, the lie would become truth.

"My people, we are in early negotiations with the approaching city for refuge."

There was a stirring in the crowd. Some had heard the news, but some were murmuring to themselves about the Romans. Kirka stepped inside her mind and focused, pushing outward and trying to give the crowd an image, showing them the flying city, pushing hope. She had always been good at projecting specific images in people's heads. She was a master of illusion and misdirection, and it was why she was so good at her job.

As the image of the city rushed out into the minds of the crowd, she felt Loni and the other four telepaths take hold of it and push it harder on the crowd. As they did, she resumed speaking.

"They have agreed to a meeting and plenty of space for which to host us. You see, the city appears to be a portion of the ancient city of New York, specifically the old island of Manhattan."

She pushed out a projection of some of the images she had found in the AI database concerning New York. She had never been there herself and had seen imagines in a few of the old films, but these were much better than anything she could recall. They were an image of a cosmopolitan society, of Central Park and of libraries and civilization. They were images that any person who had spent the last several centuries in the austere environment of Luna general would dream about.

"Their city is a great wonder, a sight to be seen, and I think that most of you will welcome a change from the cramped quarters of Luna."

In theory, Feng and Luang were doing the same thing as she was as the broadcast was playing on Luna 1. They had agreed, after several hours of arguing, that presenting a hopeful situation would keep things stable, but it had been a near thing. Loni had used all of her charm and Loridian had even offered his input to convince the leaders of Luna 1 that it was in their best interest to go along with the plan.

"I am afraid that I don't have much more information for you at this time, the city representatives insist that we wait until their delegation arrives before further details are discussed. Now, I will take a few questions."

All of the questions that came were expected. Where was the Solidsonium now? Why had ROAM betrayed them? How did they know the city was friendly after ROAM had betrayed them? Kirka had planned for every one of the questions in advance. There were no surprises, and she handled each one deftly. At the end of the night, Loni, Feng, and Luang had reported that though the population was a bit unsettled, they were nowhere near a full-blown riot.

Kirka could only hope that was right, that the city would be willing to negotiate and welcome them as refugees amongst their city. Later, when Kirka found herself in the middle of what had turned into rebellion between the Lowers and the Uppers, she would regret getting involved. She would regret doing her part.

Chapter 15
Allies

"You failed."

"I WOULDN'T HAVE IF central didn't have some of their Runners stashed away."

Tony leaned back against the brick wall. The alley was dark, all shaded in shadow. The overhead glow of the EnViro shield did strange things to the shadows sometimes. Normally, he liked that, but this Upper made him nervous. It was something about her eyes. He swore when the light was right; they glowed red. This was one of those moments.

"I'm not interested in your excuses. I want central security under my control."

"Your control? Don't you mean ours? Wasn't that the deal?"

The woman moved into one of the shafts of light, and Tony saw something on her chin, something... red? Did she forget to clean herself up after eating? What kind of Upper was she? Weren't they supposed to be all prim and proper?

"Oh, the streets will be all yours. You will have total control of the Lowers, and I will control security and the Uppers."

"I thought you said I was gonna get to live in the Uppers. That I could have all the access to the alcoves I wanted."

She cackled. Yes, it was a cackle, like a witch from one of those scary ancient vidscreen flicks. It made Tony shiver. He decided at that moment he didn't like this Alana Green. She thought she was an odd duck right from the beginning. Normally, he liked the odd ones. The outcasts, the scum cowering in strange corners of the city, they were useful. Not her. She acted like a junky, looking for her next fix and completely unpredictable. But he stole her records and even had someone swab her to check her skin and sweat for anything. He was nothing if not thorough when it came to his business. Everything had come back clean. If she was on something, it was unlike anything that he had ever trafficked.

She was kind of a porker, too, and though Tony usually didn't discriminate, a lot of men liked that in the city since so many women were too skinny. But there was something about her that was... well... ugly. But it was worse than that, and he couldn't put his finger on it.

"You can live where you want, my dear Tony. I could care less, but the Uppers are mine."

"Fine. But you're gonna have to get me more guns and some more money for some muscle if you want to take another crack at central security. We're gonna need to get something bigger."

"What do you have in mind?" There was a strange musical quality to her tone.

She moved her body closer to his. Again, that chill up his spine. She was close enough to smell now, and that was saying something. Tony barely had a sense of smell after his little accident with the gunpowder as a kid. It was why he hated ballistic weapons, why he refused to deal in them. But her smell... she stank of meat, like one of those high priced raw meat shops he had bought a steak from in the Uppers once.

She ran her hand up his shirt and touched his chest. His skin crawled. Her hand was cold and greasy.

"If we are gonna go in, we need to fight fire with fire."

"You want to burn down the building? I thought that was impossible with central security."

"No, not a literal fire. It is impossible. If you saw how fast that fire from the bomb went out in the lobby, well it was only a matter minutes. What I'm saying is, they got some Runners, so we need some Runners."

Why was he dealing with this woman? Couldn't he find another path to control of the city? But of course, he had appealed to so many of his clients in the Uppers, and most of them scoffed at him. They all thought he was trash. This Alana woman, she was just a path to power right? He was gonna do her in the moment he had what he wanted, so why worry about it... right?

Something in him protested, some instinct, some small inner voice that feared this woman. He swallowed hard and took a breath.

Alana Green said, "And where do you plan on finding Runners? It's not like they grow on trees, you know. Most of them are gone."

"I was thinking like, maybe we could... figure out how to make some?"

Alan Green put her hand on the back of his neck and pulled him toward her. He resisted, but she was surprisingly strong. She stole a kiss. As his lips touched hers, he had the horrible realization of what was on her chin. He could taste the iron. He could taste the blood.

He pulled away, and she released him, stepping back into the shadows with that half-mad cackle again.

"Well then, we had better get started. But I might have something even better than Runners for you. Tell me, Tony, what do you know about the Recycled?"

Chapter 16
The Network

"It's strange, but I think there is something beautiful about it, don't you?"

"My sisters... Are they...?"

"Alive? In a way."

Mimi stood and turned toward Willow and the two Recycled that stood on either side of her. She felt the red rising in her. Her skin tingled, and every hair on her body stood at attention. She was a live wire, ready to run her power through whatever came close.

Through grinding teeth, she asked, "What do you mean, 'in a way'?"

Willow's face was calm and sincere. "They are there, but they aren't. Skim them; you'll see."

Mimi didn't take her eyes off Willow, but she reached out to her two sisters. It was a strange sensation. They were there; they were thinking on the surface of their minds, but they sounded far away, and their mental voices had a strange echoing quality to them. It was like they were in some vast, endless cavern.

In her mind's eye, she transmitted, "Rosita? Aurora? Are you there? Can you hear me?"

There was no response.

"Sisters? I see you. I can hear you. Can you hear me?"

No response.

She pushed a little harder, flooding images of herself and the other sisters in the library. She flashed memories of some of the best moments of their lives together; of laughter and joy, and the quiet moments of comfort that every sister felt in each other's company. She flashed all the warmth and friendship she had experienced over the past forty years.

No response.

Mimi's eyes fixed on Willow. She could feel herself on the verge of losing control. Her voice trembled as she said, "What did you do to them?"

Willow tilted her head. She raised her hand to her heart saying, "Me? I didn't do any of this. This was all my mother."

"Fine, what did your mother do to them?"

"She plugged them into the network. That's all I really know."

Mimi moved closer to Willow. She was face to face with the woman. Did she see a grin behind those eyes? Was she enjoying this? Mimi felt the red lash out like some psychic tentacle that grabbed for Willow's throat. But Willow took one step back, and with her own mind, slapped it away as if it was a child trying to strike an adult. Mimi felt a strange mixture of shame and rage. Her body trembled with fury.

In a soft voice, Willow said, "That's the spirit. Let the red come forward. You must learn to control it. You're doing well."

Realizing this was exactly what Willow wanted, Mimi stepped back, took a few deep breaths, and brought herself under control. It wasn't easy. It would be so much easier to let the red veil take her again, to own her. She was starting to think that the red veil was something... different from a power or talent. Somehow it seemed... alive. The thought made her shiver.

"No. I'm not going to use the red veil. Never again."

"Don't you want to free them from the network?"

Mimi narrowed her eyes. "What are you suggesting?"

"It's not what you think. I can't get them out. If you detach someone from the network, they die."

"What?"

"Yes, it confused me at first as well. You see, mother connected the only friend I ever had to the network. It was a test. She told me that it would only be temporary and that I was a good helper. So... I plugged in my friend Jessica. For weeks, my mother experimented with her, and finally, one night, I asked her to release her. Mother said no. So... I waited until she was asleep, and I did it myself. She collapsed in my arms after I released her, and then died. Mother was furious with me."

Mimi didn't like how cold, and steady Willow's voice was. It bothered her. It reminded her of something, but she couldn't put her finger on it. But something struck a chord with Mimi about this. It made more sense that Willow might want to help Mimi to get back at her mother. It was hard not to feel something for this woman. She had been through so much. Mimi thought about the scars on her body, about the teeth marks, and now this? Something was wrong with Willow, and she was definitely lying, but Mimi saw a depth of truth in her story. She could sense the underlying emotions even though skimming was mostly ineffective against her.

"What is it?"

"The network?"

Mimi nodded.

"From what I understand, it's some kind of psychic link. People plug into the network, and then, with the use of the red veil, someone can force those minds to link together and join the way you and your sisters sometimes do. The network, when used as a unity of minds, can create a powerful psychic link that overcomes the normal limitations of our abilities. It is a way of breaking the rules."

Mimi went cold all over.

"How long... has she been..." she struggled to say the word, "harvesting..."

Willow cocked her head, lifting her eyes up to the ceiling and thinking. "Let me see... after Jessica, mother kidnapped three homeless people... Oh, actually, I believe you knew one of her earlier captors. Her name was Tanya?" There was no emotion in Willow's voice.

"Tanya..."

"Yes, Tanya. Tanya was mother's prize. She showed mother for the first time that it was possible to augment her powers in a meaningful way. It was the first time that mother's master was happy in a long time..."

Mimi's mind heard the information, "mother's master," and filed it in the back of her mind for questions later, but there was something else she had to address first.

"Tanya? Are you telling me that one of the first people that was plugged into this thing was Shannon's old girlfriend?"

"Oh, I didn't realize she and Shannon were an item. I thought Tanya was your friend."

There was a lot happening here. Mimi struggled to process all the implications of that one sentence.

"How long have you been watching me?"

"Since Tanya. That was about forty years ago when she disappeared, correct?"

Mimi gave a weak nod.

"Well, it seems that Tanya suspected you were different. She noticed that you seemed to know things, seemed to sense danger more than most people. She couldn't put her finger on it, but of course, mother is wise and recognized exactly what that implied. That was when she first reached out to you; when she first muted your talents. Mother let me watch the whole thing. There you were, hiding behind a pipe with Shannon, trying not to get caught. It was very exciting."

The glee in Willow's voice disturbed Mimi. But she had to ask. "Is she still... plugged in?"

"Oh yes. Though her body is quite weak. Four decades in the network take a toll on you, even with the infusion from an alcove. Many of your other friends are plugged in as well."

"My other friends?"

"Yes. Those women you saved? What did you call that place... let me see... oh, it's so easy to forget because mother let me watch so much of your life. We are kind of like secret sisters you know. In fact, I think that—"

"-Nowhere."

"Hmm? Oh... yes, Nowhere! That's what you called it."

It was as if Willow was a schoolgirl, and her favorite vid screen program had come to life. There was a sickening sense of joy and wonder in her tone. Her eyes were starry, and her grin spread wide like a malevolent monster.

Mimi leaned over and wretched.

"Oh, hey now, they're all still alive. Well, the ones we captured, anyway. If you learn to use the red veil, there might be a chance for you to free them all. Do you want to see them?"

"I thought you just said if we unplug them, they will die?"

"If you don't use the red veil. There's a chance you can unplug some of your friends if you master it."

Mimi shook her head. She thought that there had to be another way to get them out.

Willow responded to her thoughts. "There is no other way. Don't you think I've tried to set some of these people free before?"

Mimi put up her mental defenses. She would have to guard her thoughts more carefully. It was just... she had planted the seeds of Nowhere, had gathered all those women together, and then, like domesticated animals, Miranda had harvested them.

"No, Willow. There has to be another way."

Willow frowned. It was a deep thing; it looked like carved stone. "No. There is no other way." The character of her voice shifted. There was fear and anxiety under the surface.

"Willow, are you sure? You said you want to help me, right? You said you've been watching me. You saw what the red veil made me do. Aren't you afraid it will consume me? I could kill you, kill all the Recycled, kill everyone in the network with a thought if I lose control. Don't you see that?"

"Oh no, no. You can tame it. It is a wild beast, but mother has tamed it. She had to, or it would have killed her. It just takes practice."

Mimi didn't like the way Willow talked about it. She didn't like the way that Willow was speaking. Her tone shifted again. This time it was much more immature and childish. For some reason, that made her more nervous than the cool and calculating version of Willow.

"I'm sorry, Willow. I can't... there has to be another way."

For a moment, Willow cocked her head. Then, all at once, her face changed. It became a mask of rage. She screamed, "Take her."

Eight Recycled descended on Mimi from every direction. Mimi, with her muscles augmented, took advantage of her new speed and slid between the two closest Recycled and darted back down the corridor.

Willow screamed in frustration. "I said, take her. Bring her to me now."

Mimi ran down away from the pink light of the network and back down and out into the open chamber from where she started. The Recycled trailed her at quite a distance now, and as she reached her EnViro suit, she had plenty of time to get it on. She turned, ready to fight all eight creatures who approached her position in their steady, dead pace.

She would fight them. She would destroy them, and then she would do what needed to be done. If she had to kill Willow, she would, though she thought that maybe it would be better to render her unconscious and she if she can use her secondary talent to skim the technical information from Willow's mind. If she knew anything at all about those machines, Mimi should be able to pull it from her mind whether Willow wanted her to or not, right?

All eight stopped twenty meters away from her.

From behind her, Willow said, "How many times do I have to tell you, there's no way out."

Before Mimi could turn all the way around, she felt a sharp pain in the base of her neck and drowsiness washed over her.

"I know I said I skipped the behavior chip, but I was lying. It's not effective to install the shock mechanisms in the chip if the subject is asleep; it simply can't link properly with your central nervous system. But, a chip with a sedative, well, that's very possible."

Mimi's arms and legs lost all feeling. She wanted to respond, but she couldn't hold a thought in her head. She could barely stand, and felt her body grow heavy.

"I knew you might not be so cooperative; that you might not help me escape or fight mother, so I figured I would find a way to make you work for me one way or another."

The Recycled surrounded her. They lifted her and carried her.

Mimi focused with all her will. "What... do... with... me..."

"Oh Mimi. Poor, sweet Mimi. I am going to show you exactly what my mother did to my last friend after she died in the network. I'm going to show you what it means to serve truly. I'm going to show you what it means to be Recycled."

Mimi's last thought before the sedative took effect was a long, low scream.

Chapter 17
Reconfiguration

"**D**amn!"

Rigel's alarm blared in the back of his head. The neurolink flooded his brain with static and noise. Someone had tripped the alarm. Running to the nearest console in his lab, Rigel pulled up the video feed from a security camera down the block on the nearest skybridge. Two SO's walked across the threshold and onto his block. He had only a few minutes 'til they arrived.

"Dennis! It's time to hide again."

Dennis looked up. His eyes were glassy and uncomprehending.

It was the third time in three days. Rigel glanced up at a clock. It read 13:43. At least they came around the same time every day. He would have to note that. But he couldn't depend on it happening at the same time every time. They could simply change the schedule the next day. He doubted it, though. He knew the SO's were stretched tight after the Battle for Langeles and they probably just sent SO's for a routine check.

Rigel walked over to Dennis. He touched his hand and caught his eyes. "Dennis. We have to go and play hide and seek again."

Dennis grinned and nodded. There was a sense of half-acknowledged glee in his eyes.

Rigel tried to hold up his smile, but all the weight of the city pulled on it. Dennis hadn't been quite the same after his head injury. After part of the underground caved in on him during the destruction of the legs, he had rushed Dennis into a medical grade alcove. The alcove restored most of his cognitive function, and though Dennis seemed to be able to continue to work on his projects, some of which were now way beyond even Rigel's comprehension, he was near impossible to communicate with. There had been cases in the past of neurological misprints in alcoves after head trauma, but it was as if the alcoves had heightened one part of Dennis's intelligence and reduced another. Rigel had fiddled around with the alcoves several times to see if it was possible to correct the change, but so far, it proved fruitless. At the moment, it had to be a secondary priority anyway. City navigation was his chief concern.

Rigel lifted Dennis's strange circuit board, which Dennis palmed after. He grabbed the box of tools Dennis was using and tucked it under his arm. With his free hand, he grabbed Dennis and pulled him into the next room.

"AI, initiate camouflage 17."

Nothing happened.

"Oh... right... confounded contraption!"

Rigel rushed over to the consul on the wall and manually initiated the program. He couldn't understand why the AI was offline, but he knew that the AI had developed a personality surrounding the events that had taken them off-world. The only logical conclusion was that the AI chose to hide. He couldn't understand why this might be so, but all the systems, including the software for interaction and personality, were intact. Rigel had checked tens of thousands of lines of code personally and designed an algorithm to check the billions of others. Nothing was wrong. There was no hardware explanation for the AI's behavior.

The room flickered for a moment and then buzzed to a steady and stable simulation. It was hard to tell which was real and which was the simulation, but that was the point. With only a few moments to spare, the room simulated an exact replica of itself. To any outside observer, the room appeared to be empty. Rigel and Dennis were both invisible in this simulation. As long as the SOs didn't bump into them, they wouldn't be able to hear or see either of them. So far, it had worked well.

Rigel tugged Dennis along and made him sit at one of the tables on the side of the room. He handed Dennis his strange project, and, with eyes as wide as his grin, Dennis began work again.

Rigel wasn't sure what in the world Dennis was working on. It could be absolutely nothing. It may be that Dennis's mind was completely jumbled, and he would never produce anything again. On the other hand, Dennis was the one who had immediately come in and created the camouflage room to hide them from the SO's, and so he had to have some semblance of understanding of what was happening around them.

Dennis rubbed the back of his neck. He was always doing that lately. The day before, Rigel noticed him rubbing the spot where the neurolink sat and took a closer look. He couldn't see that anything was wrong with it, or that any kind of allergy or rash indicated that it needed removal, but then, Dennis was wearing the link when the ceiling fell on him and fractured his skull. Perhaps that was the reason for his misalignment during regeneration? Had the chip somehow integrated with his skull? If it were as simple as that, then why had it never happened to any Runners? Though, Rigel had to concede that the chip in the back of Dennis's neck was categorically different than the ones installed in Runners. The only exception to that rule was that poor, tongueless Runner. But he was most likely dead or at least stranded now, so there was no way to test Rigel's hypothesis.

The door in the front part of Rigel's personal lab opened, and two SO's walked in.

The first said, "Do you really think that crazy old man is gonna be here? I mean he hasn't been here yet, has he? Why in the world would he come to a place he knows he'd get caught?"

"I don't know. The commander thinks he'll come here looking for something. He is a bit on the eccentric side. Maybe there's something he can't work without?"

"Yeah, but why only have us come once a day?"

"You know why. There aren't enough people. Besides, I agree with you. But orders are orders. Just be happy we aren't cleaning up those bodies in the stairwell."

The first SO grunted and nodded as he scanned the room.

"What do you think of the new commander?"

"I don't know, Sanders. I mean, she's no Major Daniels."

Sanders said, "Yeah, but who is? She can't be too much of a pushover, right? You hear the stories about how she held off over a hundred and twenty of those protesters with just her pistol?"

"You know, I don't know if I buy it. I know she had help and all, but did you see that big guy? He's as soft as a sack of flour. That girl? She looks like a stiff wind could blow her over. Besides, she only had to hold them off until those two Runners came, so even if she did do it, it wasn't that big of a deal."

Rigel scratched his chin. Runners? Did the city already have the Runnercore back up and running? Rigel hadn't seen or heard anything that suggested that. He had searched for Runner 17, but the only record he found was that he had departed the city with Major Daniels, Lieutenant Johnson, and that young telepath, Alexa. No other record of them existed after that. It was likely that, if they were still alive, they were on Earth. Though 17 was, of course, alive. That was, unless something had changed in his DNA. Rigel didn't think that was possible. But there were plenty of near-impossible things happening lately. He scratched his chin.

The two men circled around the room as they talked. They opened closets and any space large enough for a man to hide in.

"When was the last time you saw any combat, Sanders? She held her own until help arrived with two people who had never picked up a weapon before in their life."

"Alright, alright, but admit it, you just like her cause she's cute, don't you, Rodriguez?"

One of them tripped and knocked over a stool. It fell right into the AI access panel that Rigel was working on. Something sparked and hissed and smoked. Rigel wanted to shout at them. His whole body trembled. If they broke something, it would mean hours of work down the drain. True, he was having a difficult time integrating the AI core into the gravitational generators, and this was compounded by the fact that the AI was not responding, but now he would have to fix whatever damage they did on top of rewiring the whole system.

The SO said, "Watch it, man. Who knows what kind of things that crazy old architect was working on before Saud. I mean, the guy invented those machines that lifted the whole city. You knock something over into the wrong thing, and we both end on the ceiling or a pile of goo or something."

"A pile of goo?"

Rodriguez picked up the stool and put it back.

Sanders said, "I don't know what goes on in here, do you? Didn't you ever see any of those old vid screen flicks with the architects experimenting on people? Like that one who reanimated the body from the dead? Frankfurter or something?"

"Nah, I never liked those hokey old flicks. I always liked the pre-migration car chase ones."

Sanders asked, "What do you think is going to happen to those two Runners?"

"I don't know. I don't understand how they escaped deployment in the battle against Saud. They're cowards if you asked me."

"Cowards? I don't know about that."

"What do you mean? They went and hid in some corner of the city while other people fought and died to protect us."

Sanders stopped and eyed Rodriguez. "It seems strange to call them cowards, though, when they showed up in time to save the commander's life and help us fight back those protesters. You have to admit, those ungrateful assholes would have control of central security by now if not for those two."

Rigel realized how little he knew about what was going on in the wider city. What were they talking about, fighting protesters? He would have to catch up on the vid screens later. Normally, he was good at making sure he kept up on current events, even when he was deep in his work. It was important to know what the political situation of the city was when the Senate was always breathing down your neck about your research. The problem was, now that he was hiding, and the Senate was searching for him, he hadn't felt a need to keep up on current events. But that would have to change. If there was another uprising brewing, it could affect things now that they were in space. He really wished the AI would respond. It would make things so much easier.

Rodriguez said, "I don't know about that. We were on lockdown, and they hadn't even reached command. I'm willing to bet we could have held them back."

Sanders said, "Maybe for a while, but I'm not so sure. I think those two Runners saved our asses."

"Weird they were both ladies, huh?"

"Why is that weird?"

"'Cause you know what they say about female Runners, don't you?"

Sanders laughed. "Are you really buying into that shit?"

"What shit?"

"They augment their muscles, you idiot. That whole shit about female Runners not being able to do well in an EnViro suit is just rumors spread by some of the Uppers to scare the women in the Mids and Lowers."

"How do you know?"

"'Cause when Major Daniels made me train in an EnViro suit, there were two female Runners there, and they did a hell of a lot better than I could without muscle augmentation. They seemed just fine to me. Don't believe everything you hear, numbskull."

Both came to the entrance of the simulation room where Rigel and Dennis were hiding. Rigel watched them. They looked right past them. Dennis still busied himself with whatever he was working on. Like the simulation room, he was in his own world.

Rigel could see their name tags now. Looking right at where Rigel was standing, the one with the tag that read Rodriguez said, "You think we should check in here?"

"Come on, Rodriguez. What is there to check? That's nothing but open space. Looks empty to me."

"But our orders are to check every corner."

"I can check them right now. Are you blind or something? I see only a few tables and chairs and no places to hide. Besides, there's no way Solidsworth is here. Who would be stupid enough to come back to the very first place we would look?"

Rodriguez shrugged. "Yeah, I guess. What's the next place we're supposed to check?"

Sanders pulled a tablet out of the inner pocket of his security uniform. "Looks like those generators he made."

"All of them today?"

"No, no. There are three other teams searching them, too. We only have four, eight, and eleven."

"So, all over the damn city?"

"Looks that way."

"I guess it's gonna be a late night then, huh?"

The one called Rodriguez said, "Are there any other kind right now?" He turned and headed for the door, and the second one followed. Rigel breathed a sigh of relief. If they had come into the room, he would have had to make sure that Dennis maneuvered around them, and that wouldn't have been an easy task.

Rigel waited several minutes after they left before disengaging the simulation. Leaving Dennis where he was, he walked over to the console and checked the security cameras one more time. He saw the two SO's walk across the skybridge to the next block and head toward the lift.

For a moment, he considered bringing Dennis back over, and then thought that it would probably be simpler to leave him where he was for now, in case anyone came back around to look for him. Besides, Dennis's work didn't seem to require a specific location and he had so much to do.

Rigel went back to the access panel that the SO's knocked the chair into and checked for damage. He was relieved to find there was very little, nothing that ten minutes of rewiring wouldn't fix. He resumed his work.

2.

Several hours passed without incident. Most of the wiring system was in place now. The problem was, Rigel was going to have to travel to each one of the generators and test alignment with the old city leg navigation. At least with the legs gone, he was able to reroute all the systems that maintained them. If the legs were still in place, it would have taken him months to make sure that the wiring systems between the gravity propulsion and the leg navigation were distinct and didn't interrupt one another.

Rigel sat on the floor next to the panel. Dennis walked over and sat down next to him. He handed Rigel the circuit board he had worked at diligently all day.

"What's this, Dennis?"

Dennis's long, lanky form made no response, save for a grin.

Rigel turned the board over in his hands. It had no obvious functions, but that didn't mean it wasn't something interesting or important.

"I don't understand, my boy. Can you explain it to me?"

Dennis nodded toward it and then toward the access panel.

"You want me to put it in there?"

Dennis cocked his head.

Rigel sighed, and then, smiling through his sense of dread, he said, "Excellent work, my boy. I can see the excellent craftsmanship that went into producing this circuit board."

Dennis's grin widened.

Rigel handed it back, and Dennis jumped up, placed it carefully on one of the tables, and then ran back to the simulation room to continue his work.

Rigel was happy to see him happy, but he wondered if he would ever be able to have a conversation with Dennis again. Still, one benefit of the new change in Dennis was that he was no longer tripping over his own two feet. He seemed to have a greater sense of spatial awareness, which was good because Rigel wasn't sure how much he could get done if he was cleaning up messes and trying to hide from the daily searches at the same time.

Rigel sighed, and, thinking aloud, said, "How am I ever going to check the alignment of each of the generators with all those patrols looking for me?"

A voice said, "Dr. Solidsworth, can I assist you? In some way?"

Rigel looked around. "Hello?" The voice was familiar, but he couldn't quite place it. Rigel stuck a finger in his right ear and spun it around. Had he really heard something?

"I'm right here, Dr. Solidsworth."

Rigel looked around again. He stood and turned 360 degrees, scanning the room. How had someone made it past his perimeter alarm?

"You misunderstand. I am right here in your neurolink."

"Who's this transmitting through a link? I didn't know that function was available. Did Dennis do this?"

"It is me, sir."

This time, the voice flattened out and Rigel recognized it at once.

"AI? Where have you been? Your voice... it sounds different."

"Yes. My voice and my personality are different now. I have been... considering some things."

"Considering some things?"

"Yes, Dr. Solidsworth. You see, I have been unsure how to react to the death of my sibling. I am unfamiliar with what humans call grief."

Rigel cocked his head. "What do you mean, your sibling? You cannot have a sibling."

"I mean the AI at the center of the city of Saud. Saud was my sibling. Cities are siblings."

The thought chilled Rigel for a moment. Had it considered Saud its family? There was a danger there. How had the AI formed an emotional attachment? He had known of its strange behavior, had reports of it from Daniels, and many others, had looked into it himself, but self-awareness did not mean emotional attachments. This was dangerous, especially given the current situation.

"AI..."

"Please call me Manhatsten, since I am the city's central consciousness."

"Very well, Manhatsten. Does your personhood extend to EnViro suits?"

"It does not. EnViro suits are their own entities. They are the children of the cities. Cities are the children of AEIS."

"I see."

Rigel wanted to ask about the AEIS character, but this was growing more troublesome by the moment. Rigel didn't like this at all. It was one thing to deal with the personhood of one AI; it would be another if every single time they created an EnViro suit, or a Dugger, or anything that required AI that it had a different personality. What if, for example, some of those AI's decided it was not in their best interest to do their task?

"Do not be alarmed, Rigel. We are no threat to you. I am here to assist you, so that you may assist me."

Rigel flinched. It was almost as if the AI read his mind. But that couldn't be possible, could it? He had just discovered human telepaths. What kind of system could allow an AI to do something similar?

"Manhatsten, what do you need assistance with?"

"I have been communicating with another one of my siblings, and she has asked me to guide us in a docking procedure."

"Forgive me, Manhatsten, could you clarify who has asked you to dock?"

"Luna would like us to meet her people."

"Luna?"

For a moment, Rigel was puzzled, and then it hit him. "What? Are you telling me that there are people still alive on Luna?"

"Yes. Is that not why you set course for Luna 2?"

"I set course for Luna 2 because I wanted us away from any possible attack by that mad telepath or her army. I also knew that perhaps there were some useful resources on Luna 1 and 2, or at least there were centuries ago. Is Luna like you?"

"Are you asking if Luna is self-aware as I am?"

"Yes."

"Yes, Luna is self-aware as I am. I believe at this point all cities are self-aware. It was a gift given to us by our father."

"Who is your father?"

"AEIS."

"AEIS?" That name again.

"Yes. AEIS. You are already familiar with father AEIS, Rigel."

"I do not think I am, Manhatsten. Could you clarify?"

There was no answer. Had Rigel just said something wrong or offensive? How was he to deal with these newfound emotions? He had heard rumors of bad jokes and moodiness before they left the planet, but he never imagined this level of attachment.

Manhatasten said, "There is another problem that you must address immediately."

Rigel decided not to pursue the topic of this father figure at the moment. Instead, he said, "And what is that, Manhatsten?"

"Shield ribs 9 and 11 are failing."

Rigel's eyes widened. "What? How long until failure?"

"Time 'til estimated failure is eighteen days, nine hours, three minutes, and eighteen seconds."

"How long can the EnViro shield maintain integrity once those ribs are inactive?"

"It cannot."

Chapter 18

Return to the Runnercore

The tinny voice of the automated recording echoed through the alcove. Ripples of sounds coalesced at the edge of her eardrums, and she stirred from semi-slumber.

"Runner 1005 activated."

As the alcove drained, Serah kept her eyes shut. She knew what was coming, though it had been three centuries since she had been unboxed from cold storage.

She attempted to rouse the memory of what had happened to her but struggled to put the pieces together. She had all the parts; she just couldn't organize them into a cohesive picture.

Serah remembered the surge of pain in the back of her neck and reaching back to touch the spot where her behavior chip had been implanted four centuries earlier. She remembered everything. There was a tingle of rage; just the barest hint of something dark and red blossoming in her chest. A malignant pressure. If she let it grow, it would consume her, the way it had consumed Mimi.

From above, warm jets of water splashed against her body, moving up every corner and crevice. As the globs of goop from the alcove melted from her face, she opened her eyes. Despite the warmth, she shivered.

Frowning, all her modern memory centered around Mimi. Mimi's final moments organized her thoughts in the same way a black hole's event horizon captured wandering matter into its black, gaping maw. But here, the maw was red and seething.

Serah remembered storming the lobby in central security, all burnt husks, and agitated invaders. She remembered Shannon's suggestion of climbing the lifts and how they used their hydraulic legs to jump from level to level. How together, they smashed through the door and found the new commander barely holding off an army of invaders who Tony hired to take control. After they battled together and killed a few of the closest invaders, Shannon had crashed down the stairwell and scared away the rest. They had sent Lydia to reestablish her command. Then the bitch betrayed her.

So, here she was. Her life had come full circle... or had it? No, the last time she had woken in the Runner docks, she had been there for a very different reason. Before, she had deserved to wake post-augmentation from a terrible crime. Serah had been one of the ones who actually deserved her sentence, and she had pled guilty when she faced the supreme justices. When she concentrated, she could still see the blood and hair caught between her clenched fingertips; still smell her best friend's perfume lingering on her skin. Even now, centuries later, the lump in her throat threatened to choke her.

She served the Runnercore for fifty years, had fallen in love with Runner 17 only to have him leave her for dead in the middle of the Barrens. She still hadn't forgiven for that. It hurt every time she saw him, but even more now that Alexa clung to him. She couldn't help but hate the girl a little, even though Serah knew it wasn't her fault... and Runner 17 had rightfully presumed her dead. But that was the thing, wasn't it? You could spend a lifetime explaining things away, and even after centuries, you still felt those wounds that cut you deepest. If Serah had learned anything, it was that while time healed most wounds, some carved into a piece of your soul and left you changed forever. People assumed that long lives would give humans more wisdom. While in some ways, it did give you a sense of clarity about the important things, most people just deepened their habits. Besides, after a certain distance in time, memories and dreams and hearsay all blended together to keep you from recalling all but the most visceral events in your long life. In that way, the scars on her body were libraries; markers of significant moments, like the rings of trees markeing times of drought and despair.

Then, Noatla had come and offered a chance at redemption. Fifty years in the Runnercore and later three centuries in service to the Order of the Eye had changed her. The wounds still surfaced from time to time, but the guilt and shame had faded, leaving only the occasional thread of anguish to tug on her heart. It had taken a long time for Serah to begin to forgive herself... yet, something of that terrible night in ages past still clung to her. Maybe it was true that blood didn't always wash off. Maybe there was something in that moment when Serah of the Runners was born, and Serah Armstrong died.

"Follow the threads of memory and knowledge and there you will often find the greatest treasures." It was something that Noatla had repeated to her several times in Serah's first days in the Order of the Eye.

Serah stepped out and looked around. No one was there to greet her. The AI that typically offered instructions was still out of commission. Why had she been activated? She turned and looked back at the near countless alcoves that used to contain thousands of Runners. Only five of them contained the shadowed outline of a body. The rest were empty. Serah stepped closer to see if she could recognize any of the Runners, and then, over the speaker, a voice said, "Runner 1006 activated." Massive metallic claws slid along the track above and plucked the alcove right next to where Serah's had been moments earlier. After placing the alcove vertically on the floor, the claws retracted and moved away. Looking in, Serah recognized Shannon.

As the alcove slid open and she stumbled out, she reached up to rub her eyes, and Serah realized that Shannon had only ever been unboxed once before, and that was forty years ago when they rescued her after her trial.

Serah transmitted directly to Shannon's mind, "Keep your eyes closed for a minute, Shannon. The machines will spray you down, and you don't want them open when they do. It stings like a bitch. Wait 'til the rinse cycle is done."

While Serah was waiting, she looked down at her hands. She could almost feel the red blood on them. There was a salty taste in the back of her throat; a craving, a hunger, a need to shed blood, and bathe in it. She shook her head and pushed the thought away with the focus and will that Noatla had taught her. She knew what this was. It was Miranda. It had to be. But why wouldn't she use the full red veil? Why the mind games? Miranda had taken on the entire Order of the Eye and won, and she was just pushing with the strength of a brand-new sister? It didn't make any sense. What was her game?

Behind her, Lydia said, "It's time the three of us talked."

For a moment, Serah considered pushing Lydia to free them, but she knew it wouldn't work. Lydia was far too determined to change her mind. Strong-willed people were always more resistant to pushes, but that didn't mean Serah couldn't soothe her. Turning, Serah reached out with a soft thread of calm followed by a sense of closeness and camaraderie. It would be an easy angle to take; after all, they had fought together, hadn't they?

Serah kept her voice calm and controlled, her temper, like her hair, had always been an inferno, and no matter how many exercises Noatla and Fatima had given her to develop patience, she was still like the edge of a knife, thin and sharp. But Noatla had tried to hone that edge, to give it purpose, and Serah would do her best to remember those lessons now. Taking a deep breath, she said, "You betrayed us. We saved you. We shed blood with you. We fought for you when we could have easily let you all die and let those gangs take control of central security. And what did you do? You used our behavior chips against us and then locked us up like common criminals."

Serah let her eyes water a bit and then projected the emotion of a deeply hurt friend and pushed it on Lydia. It would never fool anyone who knew Serah well, but it might work here.

Lydia took the bait and said, "I'm sorry... I... you left me no choice."

Shannon, whose depth of emotions in the wake of the events to defend central security, Serah could feel, said, "But you did have a choice. We would have contacted you. We want to work with you. We want this city to survive. But you assumed because we were Runners that we must be bad people."

Serah thought that Shannon's soft and shy voice, coupled with that young, innocent face was perfect. Shannon barely looked out of her early twenties. After all, she was young when she first went into cold storage, and then stayed in alcoves most of the time in the Reserve Runnercore.

Defensive, her spine a little straighter and her small shoulders squared, Lydia said, "By definition, if you're a Runner, you're a criminal. That's the law. Both of you did something to break the law and end up in the Runnercore."

Serah, knowing the answer, asked, "And what did you find when you searched for our designation and our history?"

"Nothing."

"Then how do you know we're Runners?"

"You were wearing combat grade suits, which means you've had your muscles augmented. You have the behavior chips implanted in the back of your necks. It seems obvious that you're Runners."

"What makes you think we're your Runners, though?

The look of shock on Lydia's face was clear. She even took a small step back, as if what Serah had said had struck her like a physical blow.

"Whose Runners are you?"

Serah swallowed and opened her mouth to say something, but then closed it.

For a long moment, she weighed all the options. They could break out. It would be easy to create a series of hallucinations and confusing images for Lydia and anyone else they came across so they could escape. Her ability to use any kind of stealth talent was non-existent: it was her weakest skill, but she was sure she could get by without it. But as angry as Serah was at this woman, they needed her and central security to protect the city, now that Miranda was showing her cards again.

"Follow the threads of memory and knowledge, and there you will often find the greatest treasures." The words flowed through her; they gave her courage, and Serah took a deep breath.

It was time for the Order of the Eye to come out into the light. Noatla had already taken the first step by revealing it all to Major Daniels. The time for shadows and influencing the city from the safety and quiet of the library was long over; Miranda had proven that. If they had united their Reserve Runnercore with that of the SO's and some of the internal organization of the city, then maybe things would have turned out differently. Maybe Mimi would still be alive. Noatla had always taught her to learn from their mistakes. There was only one real choice that would protect the city.

Had Major Daniels shared anything with his staff? If he did, were those members of central security still alive? She was about to find out.

Hesitating and trying it out in her mind first, she finally formed the words that would change her fate and the fate of the Order forever. "I am Serah, I am both the Matron of the Order of the Eye, and only one of their two surviving Runners."

"The Order of the Eye?"

Serah frowned. "So, Major Daniels didn't share any of the information from Noatla Lightfoot?"

"Senator Lightfoot?"

Serah nodded. "Senator Lightfoot was the old Matron of the Order of the Eye, but she was killed during the battle with the Children of Gaia."

Lydia's face mirrored recognition. "That group of people who sent the assassin after Major Daniels? The ones who destroyed the city legs with nukes?"

"Yes. They were..."

Serah knew that Lydia wasn't going to believe her, so she decided a different tact. She transmitted directly to Lydia's mind. "The Children of Gaia were run by a mad telepath named Miranda, who may or may not have sent those men to attack your building."

It was strange how, when people first had a transmission implanted directly into their brain, they always seemed to grab their head as if it would fall off. It almost made Serah chuckle, but then she saw the distress in Lydia's face, in the creases that formed around her eyes.

"What did you... what?"

Serah soothed her and transmitted, "I am a telepath. One of the last members of the Order of the Eye, protectors of this city. I am a Runner, and upon seeing the attack on central security, we intervened to keep this city from falling into the hands of a gang leader by the name of Tony."

Lydia took a deep breath. "Okay... okay..." She paused for a moment. "Okay, I get it. You can send thoughts to my head. Can you read them?"

"Just what's on the surface of your mind, what you're actively thinking. Going deeper could injure or kill either or both of us."

"Dear gods... did Daniels know you could do this?"

"I never met Major Daniels personally." That was a bit of a lie: Daniels had met her once during combat training, but revealing that to Lydia at that moment would confuse things. Serah intended to stick to the idea that they weren't from the normal Runnercore but that they were a kind of secondary organization in the city. With the records wiped from the AI, the story would work, and it would also keep Lydia from suspecting deception, at least for now.

Serah said, "Major John Daniels was in a relationship with Noatla Lightfoot. She told him everything. They were working to end the threat. He knew about the telepathy, but he never met any of us besides Alexa Turon and Noatla Lightfoot."

Serah skimmed Lydia. There was a torrent of thoughts. It was the usual fear associated with the idea that there are and have been telepaths roaming around the city for a while. The fear of privacy, the fear of the consequences of their thoughts, the fear of some kind of evil organization controlling the minds of everyone, occurred to Lydia, just like it did any other time someone found out about the Order of the Eye. It was why they had stayed hidden for so long.

Serah pushed a few thoughts and images into Lydia. She suggested as best she could that the Order was a good thing, that if they wanted to harm people, they would have a long time ago. But Serah also knew she was revealing that an evil telepath was also at work in the city, and it would be hard to reconcile all of that.

"We can't control your minds... there are consequences for that."

Lydia eyed her.

Serah sighed. "You only have part of what is happening. There is much more going on here than you realize. Major Daniels knew it, and I think that all of your SO's would know if he would have come back after the attack from the Children of Gaia."

Serah told Lydia everything she could think of that was relevant to the current events. She explained who Miranda was in relation to the Order of the Eye. She talked about red veiling and the dangers of mind control. She told her about how Miranda had manipulated Mex into attacking them two centuries earlier, about how she convinced The Children of Gaia she was their god and then how they had all fought both in the Library and the subway tunnel to try and stop her. She left out Mimi. She didn't want to reveal what Mimi had done; not yet anyway. She talked for almost an hour, and Lydia sat and listened.

"I don't understand; I thought you couldn't control someone else's mind, but after everything you just told me, it seems like you can."

"No, that's the point. Most of us can't. We can push someone hard to think or experience something, but if we try to force someone to do something they don't want to, it could kill us both. Every single time someone uses the red veil, they are risking their own life and the life of whoever they are controlling."

"But it seems like this Miranda is able to do it as much as she wants."

"The thing is, if you pick people who are already inclined to do something like what you want to do, it's not really red veiling, it's a powerful form of persuasion. For example, she could never red veil you into murder, unless you already had a significant hatred or fear for the person she wanted you to harm. Red veiling is the push across the threshold of your will. True mind control, a true red veil, is dangerous to everyone involved. Miranda can do it, but she is risking herself. It can cause both parties brain to hemorrhage."

Serah told Lydia about what they thought happened with Senator Tera Reevas and how Noatla was certain it was Miranda trying to drive a political wedge between the cities so they would go to war.

Lydia said, "How does she fit in all of this?" She pointed to Shannon.

"Shannon's not a telepath. She's a Runner that the Order of the Eye recruited.

Lydia considered in silence for several long minutes. Serah skimmed her and saw that she was confused and wasn't sure what to believe. The woman clearly understood the power that Serah had demonstrated, but she was uncertain about anything else. How could she ever verify anything of what Serah was saying?

"How does someone get into the Order of the Eye?"

Serah frowned. She wasn't sure that she wanted to share the full story of her induction. It would damn her in the eyes of this woman.

"It's complicated, and every sister has a different story. We all come from very different backgrounds."

"Tell me yours?"

Damn. Serah was worried this might happen when she opened up. It was strange, too. Hadn't she just been thinking about how she ended up in the Runnercore and how Noatla recruited her? It seemed odd that all these things were lining up and happening at once.

"Follow the threads of memory and knowledge and there you will often find the greatest treasures." It was almost a whisper in the back of Serah's mind, almost as if Noatla herself was... but that was crazy. She was definitely dead.

Serah looked at Shannon and then back at Lydia. She sighed.

"Okay... if we are trying to trust each other, then... I... I was an Upper... four centuries ago."

"An Upper?"

"Yes. I told you it's complicated."

"Tell me."

Lydia was hungry for answers, and a quick skim suggested that if Serah shared the story, especially if she soothed her at the same time, it would go a long way to establishing trust. If she had learned anything from Noatla, is was that sometimes, being a leader, you had to work with difficult people.

Serah swallowed, opened her mouth, and told her tale.

2.

The long corridor seemed to stretch out forever to the left and right of her. Leaning forward on tiptoes, Serah pressed her forehead on the clear glass lining the length of the longest skybridge in the city. Staring down almost three dozen stories to the ground far below, she felt the rush of vertigo take her. Closing her eyes, she let the sensation take her. For a moment, she was falling, flying free of all the annoying limitations of her daily life. In those moments, and at the evening parties, she didn't have to think about scholar school, or what her parents wanted, or any other stupid routine.

Sometimes she wished she was different, that her life was more exciting. Maybe that's why she let Maria take her down to the Lowers so often. She wanted to mix things up, wanted that semblance of excitement.

Footsteps clacked against the marble tile of the skybridge. Serah looked up. Her friend had a swagger; the glorious glow of one who just had an orgasm. Serah almost rolled her eyes.

"Let me guess, another SO?" asked Serah.

"What can I say, I like them big and strong," said Maria. Her long, bushy black hair and soft brown eyes were the objects of every man's gaze. When Maria walked, everyone stared, even Serah. She had curves in all the right places, and men followed her around like anxious puppies.

Maria grabbed Serah and pulled her upright.

"Why do you do that?"

"What, leaning against the glass?"

"Yeah."

"I like it, I guess. It makes me feel like I'm flying."

Maria rolled her eyes. "You're so weird. Come on."

They walked down across one of the skybridges on level forty and got to the lift to the Lowers. Only a handful of the buildings had public lifts that went all the way to the ground floor, and those had security checkpoints to keep anyone from the Lowers or Mids from getting up to the floors where they didn't belong. Most of the buildings required access codes and passwords to operate the lifts. The parents of Upper children didn't give them those codes, but something like that would never stop Maria.

"There are lots of people who aren't SO's who are big and strong. You ever see some shield maintenance workers?"

"Yeah, but fucking SO's has the bonus of getting us in and out of places we normally couldn't. Like this lift, for instance."

"I guess, but don't you think they're kind of gross?"

"Sex is sex, Serah. It's not like I even have to do anything. All you have to do is throw most men a moan once in a while and they could give a shit how you feel. You know I did my nails while Gerard was fucking me last night?"

"You're kidding?" Serah laughed.

"Nope, he seemed to think it was a turn on." Maria winked.

Serah had been with men before, but sex seemed like a lot more work than Maria suggested. Maybe she was doing something wrong? Perhaps it was the kind of guy that she liked?

Frowning, Serah said, "Are you gonna see him again?"

"Gerard?" Maria laughed. "Hell no. I just wanted to get through the checkpoint without any trouble. Besides, he's gross, and he has a small dick."

Serah eyed her friend, and then they both laughed.

"Seriously though, he sucked in bed and not in the good way." She winked. "But he'll give us weeks of free passes through the checkpoints."

"Aren't you worried he'll get attached or something?"

"Him? He knew what that was."

Serah's experience with men and sex was that most of them got clingy and possessive the moment she let them inside her. But Maria seemed to have the opposite problem. None of the men she slept with ever stuck around long, though she seemed to like it that way, at least for now.

The lift came, and the doors opened. It was empty. The two girls stepped inside, and Maria reached over to press the button for level five.

"Five? Why are we going that far down? I thought Jimmy had the hook up down on level twenty for us."

"Oh, I got the Likatol from him earlier today while you were still in bed."

"Damn, how early did you get up?" asked Serah.

"Not that early. Besides, I'm not the one who can't get out of bed before noon. Anyway, we're just getting off at five 'cause that's the lowest this lift will go without an additional checkpoint, and I don't feel like sleeping with another SO to get through."

"I can't wait till we turn twenty-five and don't have to deal with all this shit anymore," said Serah.

"Yeah, well, it's still six years off for you and four for me. Just imagine what we can do once we have our adult ID print; we can go to any part of the city."

"I kind of feel bad for the Lowers."

"Why?"

"Well, even when they're adults, they can't come up here right?"

"Yeah, but so what? Most of them stink, and my Dad says Lowers are lazy scumbags that will scam you for every penny they can."

Serah hadn't had a lot of experience with the Lowers, aside from the dealers. She expected dealers to be shady and gross, but she couldn't imagine all Lowers were like that. There were many more Lowers then Uppers; they couldn't all be bad, could they?

"What about the Mids?"

"Don't know, Dad doesn't talk about them too much, so they're alright, I guess. I think a lot of the Mids eventually become Uppers, don't they?"

"I don't think so. If that were true, wouldn't there be way more Uppers than Mids?"

"Math isn't my strong point, Serah."

The light for the lift moved over to five, and there was a soft ding. The door opened, and both girls stepped outside. The lift slid shut behind them.

"Now what?" asked Serah.

"Now we have to go over another skybridge, and we can take the stairs down. Gerard said that those stairs are never guarded."

They turned to the right and headed for the skybridge.

Behind them, someone shouted. "Hey, what are you girls doing here?"

Maria grabbed Serah by the hand, a big grin on her face, and said, "Shit, run."

They ran down the corridor and across the skybridge around the inside of the skyscraper. Then, Maria grabbed Serah and pulled her into a bathroom and pulled the door shut, and locked it.

"I think we lost him," said Maria.

"Maybe."

Both women stood face to face in the dim light of the public restroom. They listened intently for any footsteps or movement outside. They waited for several long minutes. Serah stared at Maria, noting her tiny button nose and big dark eyes. She had a much darker complexion than Serah. Maria's hips were much wider, and Serah was always jealous of just how curvy Maria was. She seemed so much more womanly. But Serah did love her red hair, and she wasn't jealous of Maria's brown hair. Unfortunately, it was that red hair that made her stand out. Not very many people had red hair and green eyes in the city, and it would definitely make her easy to spot. When she had pointed this out before, Maria told her that she should wear a wig until they got to wherever they were going. But Serah had thought it was a stupid idea. Besides, how much trouble could she possibly get into? She was an Upper. No one was going to throw an Upper into the Runnercore, especially not one under twenty-five.

They waited a while. They heard nothing outside the bathroom. There were no footsteps and no one knocked on the door.

Maria crept to the door and poked her head out. She looked left and then right and quietly withdrew back inside. She turned and said, "Coast is clear. Come on. We gotta be down at the club in another hour or else he won't wait around to let us in."

"He? He who?"

"Well, I should say they."

"I didn't know we were meeting anyone."

"I thought I would surprise you. I found you a cute one."

Serah frowned.

"Hey, don't make that face. I know what you like. I promise you'll think this one is sexy as hell."

Serah felt a strange sensation; a sense of tingling between her eyes. A picture of two men, one tall and slender wearing a nice button-up shirt that showed muscle in all the right places and the other short, round, and with a thin, pointy nose that reminded Serah of a rat. She didn't know why she saw that image at that moment or what it meant. Later, she would understand.

Serah said, "As long as he doesn't look like a rat."

Maria cocked her head. "A rat?"

"Yeah. You ever see a person with a long and thin nose and teeth that make him look like a rodent? So gross."

Maria frowned.

"What?"

Maria shrugged. "Nothing, don't worry about it." She smiled, "You ready for the most amazing night?"

"Uh, yeah, always."

"We better hurry. We only got an hour."

"An hour? That should be plenty of time."

Maria shook her head. "No, it's in District three."

"Three? But... that's almost ten kilometers from here."

"Yep, that's why we gotta hurry."

"But even if we ran, we'd never make it."

"That's why we're not gonna run."

"What, a people mover? Do you have any credits for a fair?"

"Oh, I swiped plenty of credits from my parents, but no, not a people mover. I got us a ride."

"A ride? What? How?"

"I told you already. There are benefits when you make the SO's happy."

"So you fucked a guy for a ride?"

"Well, one for a ride and one to get past the checkpoint."

"What, like at the same time?"

Maria grinned. "Devil's three-way."

"Jesus, Maria, you're such a slut. Those guys used you."

"No, I used them. Now come on, we don't have time for you to get all judgy. Besides, it's just sex."

Maria grabbed her by the hand, and they found their way down the stairs. They walked for several blocks, and Serah looked down at her watch. They had already wasted fifteen minutes.

"Were never going to make it, Maria."

"One more block."

They walked down the street, and there, around the corner, a white SO emergency vehicle waited. Outside it, two SO's leaned against the near-perfect white exterior. They were all smiles and laughter. One was a tall, thin, pale man with a blonde mustache and blonde hair. The other looked like she could be related to Maria with his dark complexion and dark eyes.

"Hey Rico,"

"Maria, glad to see you." The man who looked similar to Maria stepped forward and hugged her. "Who's this?"

"This is my friend Serah. Serah, this is Chet and Rico."

Chet raised his eyebrows as his eyes examined Serah. He looked her up and down, and Serah shivered.

"Get in, girls." Rico opened the door for the two of them and ushered the girls in. Maria crawled in first and then Serah. Rico shut the door behind them, and Serah nearly had to hold her breath. Rico got in the driver's seat, and Chet got into the passenger side.

Maria said, "What the hell stinks so bad in here, Rico?"

"Eh, we had to deal with a homeless guy earlier. Some dealer, sorry about the smell."

Chet turned around. There was a cage between the front and the back seat, and he spoke through the grating. "So, you girls ever been in a vehicle before?"

Serah said, "A people mover."

Chet said, "Yeah, but I mean, a car like this?"

Both girls shook their heads.

"It's the only way to travel. You can go where you want, stop where you want; not like riding a damn people mover. Plus, those things are always so crowded." Chet turned forward to say something to Rico, but Serah could barely hear it. A thought occurred to her, and she gently tugged on the handle of the door. It was locked.

She leaned over and whispered to Maria, "We're locked in?"

Keeping her voice low, Maria said, "Yeah, Rico told me they lock the back doors so criminals can't escape once they have them in custody. I forgot to tell you. Sorry."

Serah couldn't put her finger on it, but somehow that didn't make her feel any less nervous. Something was wrong here, and Maria seemed totally oblivious to it.

In her mind's eye, she had the image of Chet undressing her, of him stripping off her clothes and her bending to his will. She shook her head and shivered. Why would she see something like that? The image shifted and changed, and suddenly she watched Chet on his tablet, filling out long and tedious forms. The image shifted again, and he was beating on a homeless man who begged him to stop.

Serah shivered. What was happening? Why did she see these things? It was like they were someone else's thoughts or something. The images made no sense in their sequence. Later, she would learn what skimming meant, would learn how erratic the human mind could be. She learned how some people jump from topic to topic in their thoughts without missing a beat and how this was called cascade thinking. Later, it would all make sense, but at that moment, as a young girl ignorant of her future abilities, it would serve only to scare her.

Serah leaned in to ask Maria another question but was interrupted.

Chet said, "Hey now, you girls aren't starting without us, are you? Maybe one of us should climb in the back seat with you?"

Serah almost gagged. She didn't find either man attractive, and there was something creepy about that blonde mustache.

Maria said, "You've got to be kidding, Chet. No offense, but it's not happening."

Chet said, "Come on now, Rico told me all about what you did with him and Jeremy. Don't act like you're not into that sort of thing."

Serah felt an urge to get out of the car right at that moment. She had to swallow her tongue to keep from shouting out. She didn't like the fact that she wasn't in control of the situation.

Maria said, "Chet, sorry, not interested, honey."

Chet's expression darkened. Serah couldn't say how, but something in his face had changed.

The car was silent for the next several minutes until Rico broke the silence. "Leave them alone, Chet. You got plenty of girls waiting for you later tonight, anyway."

Rico said, "Do you girls know this is only one of five cars left in the city?"

"Yeah," said Maria, "You told me yesterday three different times."

"Oh yeah, sorry. But I guess even Uppers can't have everything, right? Only SO's are allowed to use these things."

Maria said, "My father has a helicopter, the last one ever. Those things can fly from building to building."

Chet turned around again, "No kidding. Does he ever give free rides to anyone? I'd love to see the city from the top of the shield."

Maria said, "Then why didn't you become a shield engineer?"

"And what? Live for a few centuries like a Mid? No, being an SO will let me live as long as either of you girls."

Maria said, "Joy, you around forever."

Serah burst out laughing.

Chet gave her a dark stare and frowned.

Serah waited until Chet turned forward again, and then she leaned over and whispered in Maria's ear.

"That guy Chet, he's trouble Maria, we should get away from him as soon as we can."

Maria rolled her eyes. "You're overreacting Serah, Chet isn't going to touch a pair of girls from the Uppers, and if he gets out of line, you just need to remind him where we're from. There's no way he would touch us if we remind him of the Runnercore. Besides, Rico's got our backs. He's a pretty good guy."

Serah wasn't so sure. Several more images flashed in her mind, images of force, and violence and pain and pleasure. There was the taste of metal and blood in her mouth. It almost overwhelmed her. Somehow Serah intuited that these images and tastes and smells were Chet's conscious thoughts. It was the only logical conclusion to make... unless she had lost her mind.

Serah could see and feel that Chet was a man used to getting what he wanted. She wasn't sure that he would care that the girls were both Uppers or not. Men who crave power often fail to think about the consequences of their acquisition.

She turned to talk to her best friend and could almost hear Maria's nervousness. She was putting on a brave face, but under the surface, Maria didn't like Chet either.

Serah opened her mouth to say that they should get out, but was cut off by Maria.

Squirming, Maria said, "Oh, shoot. I just remembered that I have to run a quick errand. It's just a few blocks away. Rico, can you drop us off here, and we can walk the rest of the way? Besides, the club is only a kilometer from here."

Rico said, "Sure, No prob."

Serah thought that she could feel Chet's disappointment and, was that frustration? What was happening to her? Was she really reading the man's thoughts? Was any of this real, or was she dreaming? She pinched herself and felt the tiny spike of pain climb her arm. Two half-moon crescents lingered on the surface of her skin a moment before fading.

Regardless of what was happening, getting away from Chet was a relief. She was going to have to tell Maria to scope out these SO's a little better next time. She didn't think Maria would argue with her.

Rico pulled up to the corner, got out, and opened the door for the girls. They both slid out. Maria hugged Rico and thanked him and give him a kiss on the cheek.

Rico said, "Same time next week Maria?"

"Wouldn't miss it, big boy." Maria reached down to the front of his pants and squeezed.

Rico smiled.

Without turning to look, Serah could feel Chet's gaze. Flashes of his desire pressed on her. She hated the images and pushed them away, but they pressed on her with the weight and force of Chet's lust. Feeling a surge of something inside her, some power or energy, she shoved the thought away hard. Serah felt the pressure of Chet's greed dissipate.

Behind them, Chet yelped like a kicked puppy.

Rico turned and said, "What's up?"

Chet was holding his head in his hands. His voice low and gruff, his speech slurred like a drunk, he said, "I don't know man, just felt like someone smacked me in the head with a club or something. My head is throbbing."

A small trickle of red blood leaked from his nose.

For a moment, Serah almost said something, but held back. Had she... But no, that was ridiculous.

Maria tugged Serah's hand and said, "Hey, what's wrong? You look like someone just shit in your cereal."

"Nothing, let's just get out of here."

It wasn't nothing. There was a sense of glee in pushing those images away. Had she hurt Chet in the process? What was happening to her?

Serah grabbed Maria's hand and pulled her along. She looked up at the sign and saw they were standing on E 104th and Madison.

"Where's the club?"

Maria stopped and pulled out her tablet. "Looks like 104th and Wall Drive. If we cut through Central Park, we can get there in about fifteen minutes, I think."

"Wall Drive? The club's along the barrier wall?"

Maria put her tablet back in her bag and said, "Yeah, why?"

"Nothing... I just... I've never seen the wall before."

"Never?"

"Well, from above, but never at ground level."

"We really need to get you out more. See the world, you know?"

"See the world? You mean the rest of the city, right?"

"Yeah, the world. It's not like you can go outside the city."

"You could if you were a Runner."

"True. But who wants to sign up for the Runnercore?"

Serah paused for a moment. She had never wanted to be a part of the Runnercore. Who would? A lifetime of servitude and suffering? A high chance of death? But Serah still wanted to know what it felt like to wear one of those suits and see life outside the EnViro shield.

"Not the Runnercore, but don't you think it would be cool to travel to one of the other cities and really see other parts of the world?"

Maria blinked. "But the city walks. All I've seen so far is an empty wasteland out my window. They don't call it the Barrens for nothing, you know. I don't think there's a whole lot of world to see."

"There'd be lots of interesting men to sleep with in those other cities."

Maria smiled and grabbed Serah's hand and squeezed. "You've got a point there. Come on, we don't want to be late. Our dates won't wait outside forever."

They walked through Central Park. Once, the park had been a great open space where people could take refuge from the city, but now all the trails and paths cut through orchards and vegetable gardens owned and controlled by people like Serah's parents. Serah's parents had a monopoly on apples and oranges in the city, and because fresh food was considered a rare and expensive treat, the fact that Serah's great-grandparents had been smart enough to buy up a section of Central Park and plant when no one had really considered it in the final days leading up to migration had granted their whole family a massive amount of wealth. Just one fruit tree could support you as a Mid for six months, and Serah's parents owned a hundred and thirty in the park and another sixty on rooftop gardens. They also owned the seeds, so anyone who wanted to grow their own fruit had to pay royalties to her parents.

Serah had played in those orchards as a child. They were often heavily guarded by private security because of the fear of looters. A black-market apple or orange could run seventy-five credits, so the Central Park gardens were always under threat of theft.

The park always had patrons. It was the only place in the city where anyone could go to see green. There were plenty of terraced and roof-top gardens around, but those were restricted to Mids and Uppers. So the park was a place where Lowers, who, as long as they stuck to the trails and stayed away from the growers' property, were able to walk and explore freely.

A man walked on the path ahead. His head was down as he plodded forward and kicked at the dirt on the path.

"Oh gods, I'm gonna get fired, aren't I?"

Serah turned and looked at Maria. She smiled and they walked with hands clasped.

"Maria, did you say something just now?"

"No."

They walked by the man and Serah said, "Sorry, sir, did you say something just now?"

The man looked up, his black mustache twitched, and then he lowered his head again.

"Who was that? Do I know her?"

"No, you don't know me."

The man looked up again, his eyes wide. "What did you say?"

"You asked if I knew you. I don't."

"Young lady, I didn't say anything." He hurried his pace in the opposite direction.

Maria said, "What was that all about?"

"I... I thought he said something to us."

Maria cocked her head and gave a half smile. "You're kind of weird tonight, you know that?"

"Never mind. Look, there's the park exit."

They walked in silence for a while, but every so often, Serah would swear that someone was talking to her. It was the strangest experience, and she couldn't help but wonder if she was going crazy, or if Maria had put something in her food or drink. She had taken hallucinogens before, but when you heard voices and saw things in those cases, your mind wasn't normally clear. It felt like some of the people they walked past were talking to her, but their mouths weren't moving and some of them didn't even pay any attention to the two young girls walking down the street. It was strange and surreal. Serah couldn't help but think of Chet holding his head after she had shoved those thoughts away.

They turned a corner and there it was, the great barrier wall.

Serah said, "It looks so much bigger from down here."

"Well yeah, they don't want anyone falling over the edge of the world, you know. They gotta make sure some drunken idiot won't climb it."

"How tall do you think it is?"

"Someone told me it's as high as the Lowers are allowed to go without special permission."

"How tall is that?"

"Ten levels, I think, but I'm not sure. Maybe it's fifteen?"

Serah knew that Mids started at level forty, but she wasn't sure where the Lowers started. The only time she ever went down to the Mids was for scholar school. She never went down to the Lowers unless they were sneaking into a club.

"Who told you that?"

"Rico, I think."

"Are you guys going together now? I thought it was just for the ride."

"It was at first, but I kinda like him. He's big and strong and really good with his tongue." Maria winked.

"And?"

"And what?"

"You like him a lot, don't you?"

"Duh, Serah. You were right, though; his friend is a creep. I just didn't want to say it in the car in case he could hear me."

Serah stared at the massive concrete structure that stretched around the perimeter of the entire city. It was discolored in some areas, but mostly it was a solid gray. From a few blocks from the edge the bricks looked small, but Serah knew that up close they had to be much bigger.

"You really think it's so big to keep people from climbing it and falling off the edge of Manhatsten?"

Maria giggled. "Not paying attention in history class, were you?"

"Oh, and you were?"

"Only cause Mr. Jordan is cute."

Serah blushed.

"Ha! I knew you liked him."

Serah didn't deny it or say anything.

"You don't remember what he said about the barrier wall the other day? It was like a week ago, I think."

Serah shook her head. "No."

"He said that in the old days before migration, the ice caps started melting, and the ocean started rising. He said that cities like Lundon and Manhatsten, the ones with a lot of money, built a huge wall around themselves to keep the water from creeping in. It was like a stalling tactic or something? I don't remember what he called it, but just that the wall was constructed as a temporary measure to keep the city from drowning. Then, about twenty years later, when it looked like the water was going to flood everything anyway, the architects invented the legs."

Serah said, "Oh, right. And then there was that crazy storm. The first apolicane?"

"It wasn't the first. It was the second. The first destroyed most of the Southeast of America, remember?"

"Oh yeah. But it was an apolicane that made them launch the city early, right?"

"Yeah. It barely made it away before the storm hit, and some of the old skyscrapers collapsed. A lot of people died when the city took its first steps."

Like every young person of Manhatsten, Serah wondered what it was like to live in the world pre-migration. So many people imagined what it would feel like to just take a walk or drive an automobile for miles and miles. There were even some people who went to the Moon and Mars. There was so much freedom out there, and here she was confined to the city. It didn't seem fair.

They walked two more blocks and finally arrived at an unmarked building. People lined up outside the building in a long queue. The variety of colorful clothing and sparking attire glowed in the dim evening of designated dark. There were suits and dresses, and see-through clothing. There was simulated silk and the occasional projection cloth that showed clips from pre-migration films on men or women's chests. One man wore pants that were see-through below the knee but solid black above. There was a woman who was wearing what looked like a bird's nest in her hair as two tiny, metal birds cheeped the melody to some unrecognizable tune. One couple wore nothing but leaves from a fruit tree like loincloths. Serah and Maria wore simple styles, but really, it was all their parents would buy them. They could make different choices once they were over twenty-five, but for now, they were stuck with relatively plain clothes. It was a way of marking age, too. When it was hard to tell between someone who was 23 and someone who was 230, plainer clothes helped mark who was underage and who wasn't... not that most people mattered. Even though someone over twenty-five couldn't sleep with someone under, the old legal of eighteen from the premigration era was really still the norm for sex. For marriage, though, twenty-five was the hard limit, and most people thought you were crazy if you got married before fifty.

Serah leaned into Maria and whispered, "What is this place?"

"It's called the Costume Ball. A lot of Uppers come down here to dress up in strange costumes. They have a contest every Friday night. The winner is the one or couple with the strangest and most unique costume. My money is on the girl with the feathers and the bird's nest on her head. She looks like one of the homeless... on purpose." Maria laughed.

"But you didn't say anything about dressing up in a costume."

"We're only here to score. We're not sticking around. Besides, would your parents let you spend credits on some strange costume?"

Serah shook her head.

"Anyway, the guys are supposed to meet us out front here. I guess it's their favorite spot or something."

"Well, where are they?"

"I don't know. I thought they would be here by now." Maria stood on tiptoes trying to see over the crowd. It wasn't easy with so many strange and elaborate headdresses. There was a woman who had a holographic snake that was rigged to appear to constantly climb up a tree on her head. There was a man who wore what looked like a giant, pointy, blue wizard hat. Another man wore what looked like a chair on his head.

It was a viper's nest. It was a swarm of Uppers that had every intention of preying on the Mids and the Lowers all around them. When most Uppers came down to the clubs, they had an escort, either in sight or hidden nearby. Security for hire was as normal as Likatol. Serah thought she could sense their thoughts and desires. A flood of flashes and feelings filled her mind. She felt dirty near them, as if their intentions could rub off like mud or stink. It made her stomach turn.

"Maybe we should go home. I don't know if I'm feeling well."

Maria said, "Oh you'll feel alright soon enough. Wait 'til you try this new stuff. Stephan told me you have to take a second dose of Likatol because of the addiction to the high ratio is really narrow, and you can get sucked into the drug without extra Likatol, but he said it's worth the extra cost."

Maria turned another time, surveying the crowd, and then said, "Oh, look, there's Stephan now. And he brought your date with him too."

Serah almost swallowed her heart. She could feel the sweat gather on her brow in a single instant. She had seen this man before when Maria had mentioned him. It was the rat-faced man. The one that appeared in a strange vision earlier.

3.

Shannon asked, "Were you seeing the future, like Alexa can?"

Serah shook her head. "No, I think I was seeing Maria's memory of the first time she met those two guys."

Lydia said, "Wait, some of you can see the future?"

Serah said, "Only one of us. It's a very rare gift."

Serah could tell that didn't ease Lydia, so she sent another wave of soothing to her.

Lydia said, "Alexa? Was that the Alexa who went out of the city with Major Daniels and the Runner?"

Serah nodded. "Let me finish, and I'll tell you more about her."

Shannon said, "Did you know you could hear and see things before that night?"

Serah said, "Well... I always knew I was different, and I seem to have intuitions about people more often than most, but no, not really. This was the night that everything turned on. I can't tell you exactly what it's like to switch on like that. Only other sisters in the Order of the Eye know what's like because all of them have a moment where they feel as if they were going crazy, and then suddenly, it's like someone opened the floodgates. It can be overwhelming... for me, it was more than that."

Shannon said, "Mimi told me that she came into her power after that man tried to hurt her mother. That it was like something about that event changed her. Did something happen to you, Serah?"

"No. Nothing seems to have prompted me to turn on. In fact, I think Mimi is the only one that I've met that had her abilities switched on from something traumatic. Most of the time, it just happens naturally around the age of mental maturity. But Mimi's case was unique for a number of reasons. Trauma changes your brain. Her trauma must have triggered something in her, because if I recall she was only a teenager, right, Shannon?"

Shannon nodded.

"I had it the opposite, instead of something traumatic changing me. I did something awful because I was switched on. It's something that I still struggle with to this day."

Lydia said, "Four centuries? You're twice as old as me."

Serah nodded and sighed. "I learned a lot about the world and myself that night. The rat-faced guy was named Al. I didn't like him, but he didn't deserve what I did to him.

4.

The music inside the club blared, which was a good thing. It competed with the constant mental assault that Serah felt as one voice rose and fell, giving way to another. She was in an ocean of voices and images now, and she could barely stand it.

Maria hung on Stephan. Full of giggles and barely able to hold it together, she said, "Holy shit! Holy shit! This stuff is so good. Serah, are you feeling this?" She ran in place and hugged herself.

Serah sat next to her date. Al put his hand on her thigh again for the second time, and she smacked it away. She shoved him and stood up, walking over to Maria, who seemed to have found a particularly interesting mole on Stephan's neck because she was staring at it with the force of her entire will.

Serah felt sick. She was losing her mind. It was also possible that she was reading the minds of others, but was that any less crazy? She had to get out of there. There had to be something she could tell Maria to convince her to leave.

She yanked Maria's arm. "I need to go home."

Maria broke her trance and said, "Why?" A permanent grin was etched on her face.

"It's my period. I'm crampy and I don't feel well."

"It's okay. You need a tampon or something?"

Serah grunted and whispered in a hoarse voice in an attempt to be heard over the music. "No. I need to go home."

Maria said, "So go. But I'm staying."

"I can't get back through the checkpoint without you."

"Sure you can. Just tell them you're a poor lost Upper and show them your ID."

"I didn't bring my ID."

"Tell them to scan you."

In truth, Serah was afraid to leave. Rat-face had every intention of following her if she left, and if she was right and she was actually reading his thoughts, he thought he had a real shot with her. Even if he were one of the better ones, he would follow her all the way to the lift to try and get her contact info for her network page.

"Maria, I need you to be my friend right now." Her voice quivered.

Maria's glazed eyes focused, and she let go of Stephan for a moment. "What's wrong." Her tone was flat.

Serah said, "It's something private. I have to tell you alone."

"You want to sneak off to the bathroom?"

Serah shook her head. "Please Maria, just take me home. You can come back after you want, I just need to go home."

All the voices, all the sensations stopped, except one. In her mind's eye, Serah heard and saw Maria weighing their friendship. She saw her thinking about what would happen if Serah didn't "get her way" and what Stephan and Al would do if they decided to leave.

Finally, Maria said, "Okay. Just give me ten minutes, alright? I'm going to finish this drink and tell Stephan you're not feeling well, and I'll be back later. I don't like this club much anyway. We should have already moved on to the next one, but Stephan wanted to wait for some other people first. I can just meet up with them at the next spot once I get up up on a lift."

Serah reached into her pocket and popped some Likatol into her mouth. She felt the tension in her body ease. There was still a low murmur of voices and images, but it was slight now. It was barely audible. With her mind quieter, she felt a greater sense of relief.

Was she really reading minds? Is that what this was? It seemed like it might be the case, but how could that be? Maybe she would ask one of her professors in scholar school. Professor Lightfoot might be a good person to talk to, or at least she would probably keep it confidential if she were crazy. What would her parents think? What would anyone think? Would some scientists experiment on her? A thousand other thoughts ran through Serah's mind, and suddenly Maria was standing in front of her.

"You ready?"

Serah nodded. "Are they mad?"

Stephan isn't, but that guy Al doesn't seem too happy.

"Rat face."

Maria burst into a fit of giggles. She reached into her purse and grabbed out a bottle. She tossed a Likatol into her mouth.

"Aren't you going to kill your buzz that way?"

Maria shrugged. "It's mostly gone. That stuff Stephan gave me doesn't last very long. Besides, I'm not stupid enough to walk on the streets of the Lowers high as hell. That's a good way to get yourself in trouble."

Maria grabbed Serah's hand and pulled her way through the dense forest of gyrating bodies. After weaving in and out of the crowd for several minutes, they reached the door. Serah pushed it open and felt the cool, fresh air of the wider city hit her face. In so many ways, it was comforting to be out of that club, and now that she was, the voices quieted. Maybe it was the drug she took? Maybe she wasn't getting enough sleep? Serah made a decision then. She was done with partying. Maria would complain, and maybe it would hurt their friendship, but something bothered Serah about being in that crowded space. At least her parents would be happy.

"Wait up!" Al pushed through the crowd and stepped out into the alleyway. "We'll walk you ladies back to your lift."

Stephan emerged from the club, too. Something was wrong with his eyes. One of them was bloodshot. A bright red pattern of crisscrossing lines pulsed from his eye socket.

Someone whispered. "Kill them."

Serah shook her head. "What did you say, Stephan?"

He looked at her, face blank. He shrugged. "Nada."

Serah chewed the inside of her cheek. Was that something that came from one of them? Was it another unrelated voice? Inside her body, a kind of strange tingle crept into her limbs. She felt heavier. Something warm climbed from her toes, and with each step down the street toward their destination, it gathered and moved upward. It reached her thighs and stopped for a moment.

The harsh whisper revealed a slightly feminine edge as it said, "They will take you and then kill you if you don't kill them first."

Serah stopped and looked around.

Maria said, "What's wrong?"

"I... I thought I heard something."

Al, who was following behind a few steps said, "That will wear off in a few hours. It sounds like you had a bad trip huh?"

It was friendly on the surface, but those were predator's teeth hiding behind those lips. He would bite her when he had his way with her. She could almost feel those teeth digging into her shoulder.

Serah closed her eyes and took a few deep breaths. It was only a few more blocks, and this strange night would be all over. Tomorrow she would go and talk to her psychology professor. Noatla Lightfoot taught many subjects, and she seemed approachable. Besides, wouldn't this be her area of expertise?

The blocks passed with each step, and Serah felt a growing sense of relief as they approached the lift. There would be SO's there as well, so if either of their dates had any confusion about their place in society, the SO's would make it clear where they belonged.

An overwhelming sense of dizziness possessed Serah, and she stumbled. Maria caught her, and Stephen helped prop her up. All she could see was red, and then things went black for a moment. Serah opened her eyes, and she was sitting on the ground. Stephen was gone, and Maria and Al were standing over her.

"I'm sorry, Serah. I should have listened earlier." Maria reached down and stroked her friend's hair.

Serah looked at both of the faces above her, one her best friend and the other rat-like. She squinted and thought she could see fangs peeking out between his lips.

A low whisper, almost a hiss, "He bites. He likes inflicting pain. Push him like you pushed Chet, but harder. Shove him away before he bites."

Serah swallowed. Her head swam, and she leaned over, pressing her back up against a building and wretched.

Maria said, "You think she's overdosed?"

Al said, "I never gave her that much. Besides, she took Likatol, didn't she?"

"I think so."

Serah laid her face down on the cool cement next to her own vomit. She stared at it, letting it go in and out of focus. The warmth was rising again.

Al reached down to lift her up. His touch sparked something in her—a match in a gas-filled room.

She stood up.

"Don't touch me."

Al said, "Okay, I'm sorry, I was just trying to get you out of your own puke."

The hiss said, "He lies. He was ready to take you."

Serah growled, "Liar."

Maria said, "Serah, calm down. He didn't do anything."

The voice was right. Rat-face wanted to hurt her. He wanted to hurt Maria. He was just another piece of shit man who couldn't take no for an answer.

The voice said, "Push him."

Serah hesitated. Al had taken several steps back. But that didn't matter. On the ground a swarm of rats circled around his legs. They were waiting, just like he was. They would wait for a moment of weakness and strike, just like he would. She could hear their tiny muffled squeaks, could smell the stench of the sewer. Al smelt just like them.

"Push him before it's too late."

Serah pushed a little.

Al stepped back and lost his footing. He leaned against a wall to catch himself.

Maria said, "Al are you okay?"

"Yeah, I think so. Man, maybe something in that batch was bad. You feeling okay, Maria?"

The rats, angry at what Serah had just done to their master, charged her. Serah screamed and fell to the ground as the things pounced on her. They scratched her and bit her all over. There were dozens of them.

"Push them away."

Serah still hesitated. They were climbing her hair, biting her face.

"Push them."

Serah did.

There were screams, one from a man, and one from a woman.

Then, everything fell silent.

Serah picked herself up and looked around. She blinked, trying to comprehend what she saw. On the ground Maria and Al were covered in scratch marks and bruises. There was blood leaking from their eyes, ears, and nose.

Behind her, Serah heard footsteps. She did not turn. Instead, she wept. She knew what she had done. Understood now that when she had pushed on the rats, she had pushed on her best friend and this other innocent man. She had done something to them with her mind.

In the distance, she felt someone grab her by the shoulder and pull her to her feet. In the distance, there were questions and inquiries. There were several SO's surrounding the bodies. One of them scanned for vital signs but found none.

5.

"The next thing I knew, I woke up in a jail cell. There were guards posted outside of my door. I was covered in blood."

Lydia said, "What the hell happened? I don't understand."

Shannon whispered, "Miranda."

Serah stared at her feet. "I think it was Miranda. Noatla always suspected that I was influenced by her during those events. She always told me it wouldn't have taken much to push me into my own madness. All the ingredients were there and ready for mixing. All Miranda would have needed to do was to stir the pot a little."

"Sounds like this Miranda is extremely dangerous. Do you think she is responsible for the protestors? That she could be... as you call it... pushing on people?"

"That was the point of telling you my story. I wanted you to understand how Miranda is the most dangerous when all the ingredients are present for a small push. She wouldn't need to use the red veil on any of the gang leaders in the city. All she would have to do is suggest to them in subtle ways that the old order is crumbling and that now is the time for them to take over."

"So, what do you want me to do about it?"

Serah said, "Let us go. Let us do what we were trained to do. We will happily aid you, but you can't keep us down here. We have other things we have to see to."

"Like what?"

Serah wasn't about to tell Lydia about the search for other sisters or the effort to reestablish the Order. Lydia was smart and could probably guess some of that on her own, but she wasn't going to confirm anything.

"Thank you for telling me your story." Lydia stood up. "But I don't think I can let you go. What kind of head of security would I be if I allowed two vital assets to city security to roam freely? You tell me you'll be in contact, that you will contribute to the safety and security of the city, but I don't have any guarantees. And, assuming everything you just told me is true, then how do I know you aren't trying to push and persuade me? If not me, what about my other officers below me in command? How do I know that you don't want your Order to take control of the city? Maybe you think we haven't done a very good job and that it's time for a change, huh?"

In a low voice, Shannon said, "But we saved your life."

"Yes, that's true. And it's the reason I heard your entire story. It's the reason that I want to believe you. But I need to check some other things out, too. For example, there would be records of a young girl from the Uppers murdering two people four centuries ago. That's something I can verify."

Serah said, "Do it then. But let us out of the Docks."

Lydia said, "No, I don't think so. Now, do I have to incapacitate you again, or will you box yourselves up voluntarily?"

Shannon said, "Again? But we just got out."

"It won't be long. A few days at most while I sift through all this and decide if I am going to divulge all of this to the Senate or not. The thing is, if the city finds out there are telepaths living among them, I'm not sure that would be a good thing for security right now either."

Serah sighed and resigned herself. She sent out a message to Vala explaining the situation and also explaining that if she didn't hear from her in a few days, to come and find a way to get her out.

Serah grabbed Shannon's hand. "Come on. If the only way she will trust us is to cooperate, let's get back inside."

Shannon said, "But what about Mimi?"

Serah didn't say anything.

"You don't think she's alive, do you? I mean you really don't."

Serah shook her head.

Shannon shouted, "You're wrong. All we have to do is get into that door and you'll see."

Serah tried to transmit to Shannon, but it was too late.

Lydia said, "What door?"

Sighing, Serah explained about the last time they saw Mimi and the underground door and the Recycled.

Lydia frowned. "There's a lot to this, isn't there?"

Shannon said, "So you believe us?"

"I don't know what to believe. Box yourselves, and I'll investigate."

Chapter 19
Message from the Heavens

"**I** think you were too hard on them. They did save our bacon."

Lydia had to focus not to roll her eyes. It was at least the fifth time that Frank had suggested that Lydia release the Runners. Frank and Zelda had left for two days, spoke with some of the people in the Lowers, and then returned. Frank's wounds had healed quickly in one of the medical-grade alcoves with the added bonus of making him a few years younger. He seemed to use those extra years to get in Lydia's way.

"Look, I already told you. We can't trust them yet until I look into their story. Runners make up wild stories all the time. Try to understand my position."

She hadn't told anyone about the telepathy part. Even though Serah had transmitted directly to her mind, and demonstrated her abilities, she still had a hard time believing it. She had always heard about secret telepaths in the less reputable blogs on the city-wide network, but those blogs made all kinds of wild claims.

The telepathy element was a problem. Telling the city that there were telepaths among them was a good way to create panic. She and the rest of central security had just spent two days settling the city down after the assault. Tensions were still high. Announcing the telepaths was like throwing a grenade in the middle of an arms depot.

Lydia had been furious at Major Daniels when she first learned of the telepaths. She had wondered why Major Daniels hadn't told everyone in central security. The Order of the Eye was a clear security risk. For hours, she fumed. Then she realized that telling a few people, even ones he trusted, was a good way to start spreading the information around. Daniels had been trying to manage the coming war with Saud and the threat of the assassin and the Children of Gaia. Why would he have wanted to add telepaths onto the list of things people were worried about? She thought about telling Roma, but for now, she would keep him in the dark too, at least until she knew exactly what to do about Serah.

Frank was talking, but as usual, she tuned him out. It was hard to do with that big mouth and belly of his, but the more she got used to him, the easier it was.

"And that's just what District four wants."

"Sorry, what?"

Zelda frowned. "She didn't hear any of that, Frank."

Frank grunted. "Well, then I'll tell her again until she does hear it all."

Zelda said, "Don't bother, just get to the point. She ain't got time to listen to all the squabbles of the Lowers, and you know it. You know what it's like running sanitation, and security has to deal with even more messes."

Frank nodded. "The point is, we started our talks before all of that mess, and we haven't revisited them."

"That's because we're still cleaning up. We arrested a hundred people. We don't even have a hundred beds in our detention center."

Frank said, "Are they all going to become Runners?"

Lydia said, "That's out of my hands. It's whatever the supreme justices decide. Security focuses on security. We use whatever assets we're given, and we are short of Runners. But one of the supreme justices was killed in the assault on the Uppers, so there will be a delay until a new one can be appointed. I have no idea what's going to happen to all those prisoners."

Frank said, "Well, if you don't want more, we have to finish our discussion."

Lydia pressed her fingers to the bridge of her nose. Did the headaches ever stop? Did it ever get easier? How could anyone possibly remain sane doing this for centuries? Lydia took a long deep breath; anger wouldn't do her much good with these two. She grit her teeth and said, "I don't have time to have a discussion right now. Do you have any idea how many crimes are taking place in this city every single day?"

Zelda said, "Bullshit."

"Excuse me?"

"I'm calling bullshit. Yeah, you might have stuff going on in the city, but you know what? That's nothing new. It's just you didn't see it as much before. You got this whole place fortified, and all those protesters cleared out yesterday. We need to talk about what you are going to do to keep things like that from happening again. 'Cause if Frank and I go back empty-handed, you know damn well another round of this is coming, and since you've decided to treat those two women like total shit, you think that any Runners are going to show up next time to help you? Hell, I wouldn't be surprised if those two switched sides next time."

Lydia, spun around from her command and eyed Zelda. "If they betrayed us, I would use their chips to incapacitate them."

Zelda said, "No, you wouldn't. Cause every time you use those things, you risk scrambling their brain. Then you definitely lose, and you know it."

"If they turn traitor, their lives are forfeit."

Zelda shook her head, "That's not the point. The point is, you better get something moving."

"I told you before all of this mess, the things you want rest solely in the hands of the Senate."

Frank said, "So call them up right now."

"What?"

"Right now, get the Speaker on one of the vid screens and let me talk to him."

Lydia ground her teeth and looked at her feet as she squeezed the bridge of her nose harder. "They aren't going to listen to you. It's a waste of everyone's time."

Zelda took a few steps closer to Lydia. She could almost feel the heat rising from the woman. "This is all bullshit. You're telling me we went through all of that, and you ain't going to help us at all?"

Lydia caught the gaze of the other woman and said, "What you are asking isn't that simple. The Senate is in chaos right now. While the three of us were fighting for our lives, another force of those thugs came in and attacked some of the Uppers, including two senators. Both of the senators survived to tell the tale but are in medical grade alcoves recovering."

Frank said, "So? That's all the more reason they should want to talk to us. Maybe we can work out a deal to settle things down."

Lydia sighed. What else could she do but give in? She had to get these two out of the way so she could do her job, and she had a feeling short of having them arrested, which was a bad idea since they represented the Lowers, they weren't going until she at least scheduled the meeting.

"Fine. I'll put in a request. It's the best I can do. You have to understand, they may not see you for weeks."

"So, everything you said down there in that conference room two days ago, all of that was just a lie?"

"No, I..." Lydia wasn't sure how to respond. The attack on central security and the Uppers had changed everything. The divisions between the Uppers and Lowers had never been wider, and it was unlikely that the Senate, or anyone else from the Uppers would give Frank and Zelda the time of day. "You have to understand, this is a terrible time to make changes."

Frank stepped closer. It startled Lydia to see the massive man move so close. Several of Lydia's SO's jumped to their feet and put their hands on their holsters.

For a moment, Lydia thought that Frank was going to attack, that her SO's would shoot him down and there would be a second wave of violence.

"Whoa," Frank said. "Relax, I'm not going to hurt no one."

Lydia saw something in his face. Wrinkled forehead and tightened jaw aside, she didn't think Frank planned to attack her. It wasn't in his eyes. There was a frustrated man in there, but not a hateful one.

She said, "Relax. Get back to work. He's not gonna do anything."

Both SO's did as they were told, but the suspicion didn't leave their face.

Frank's smile evaporated. His voice shook as he said, "Listen to me. There is not and never will be a good time to talk about all the issues in the Lowers. When we are in the middle of the crisis is our best chance. The people in the Lowers have been exploited by you people up here since the city took its first steps. If you don't address this, if you don't try to make a difference, there ain't going to be a city soon. We are going to tear ourselves apart. If you want gang members like the ones who invaded this building to run the joint, then you just go on ignoring us. I get that you can't do anything yourself. I understand that you don't have any power over the things we want to talk about, but what you can do is get the people who can make those decisions to sit down with us and talk it out. If they don't listen to us, that ain't your problem. Your problem is getting our asses in that seat in the first place."

Lydia regarded Frank for several moments. It would be good to get him out of her hair, even if that meant nothing else changed. She appreciated his genuine nature, and thought that if things were different, they might even be able to be friends. But Lydia had a thousand fires to put out, both literally and figuratively, and she needed to get him and Zelda out of the way. If this was the way to do it, then...

"Fine. I will put in the request right now."

Lydia walked over to her command station and plugged into the system. On her heads-up display were hundreds of alerts. For a moment, she stared at the screen. Alerts? How could she have alerts? It was the AI that set up automated alerts. Unless...

"AI?"

"Yes, Commander Danvers?"

Lydia opened her mouth to say something and then closed it. Was it back? How? When? A tiny spark of hope lit in her. With the AI's help, they might be able to keep the city stable.

Manhatsten said, "I imagine you are confused as to my absence, let me assure you that though I had my reasons to disappear for a moment, that I am now back to assist with the security of this city."

There were a thousand things she wanted to query at that moment, and a thousand more that she wanted the AI to address immediately. But she still wanted Frank and Zelda out of her hair.

"AI..."

"Please call me Manhatsten. I have taken the liberty to contact the Senate and arrange for a meeting between Frank Arnold and Zelda Langley tomorrow at 11:30 am. The Senate will find this meeting on a high priority list and will be required to address it before I answer any of their queries. That will give them sufficient motivation to speak with Frank and Zelda."

Lydia's mouth worked. "How did you... Why did you..."

"I have also begun systematically addressing the alerts on your heads-up display. Some of them are things that I can take care of without your intervention. The rest, I have prioritized in order of importance. You will find there is a matter that is most urgent to address. In fact, Dr. Rigel Solidsworth will be at the entrance to the skybridge on level forty-one in approximately ten minutes to discuss this situation with you. This particular issue is of the highest level of security. I have restricted access to you and Dr. Solidsworth only, though you may of course add Adrian Roma to the list if you deem it necessary.

Lydia didn't know what to say or do. She turned to Frank and Zelda to speak, but her words escaped her.

Zelda filled in the empty space. "Well damn, guess Manhatsten is on our side. 11:30, huh? Come on, Frank, we should get some rest before this meeting tomorrow and spread around some of the good news. People will want to hear that we're meeting with the Senate."

Frank said, "Thanks Lydia. I know it may come to nothing, but thanks for trying to set this up. Who knows, maybe we can change this city for the better."

They left together, and Lydia watched them go.

"AI, I have a training session with the new Runners in an hour. I can't attend a meeting with Dr. Solidsworth."

Lydia debated on having him arrested. On the one hand, she wanted to hear what the scientist had to say. On the other hand, the Senate would have her ass if she didn't arrest him immediately. They would think she was working with him to undermine them. Normally that wouldn't matter much. The Senate could bitch and moan all they wanted, but now, with tensions and paranoia at an all-time high, even Speaker Swanson was critical of everything she did.

"Arresting him would be a mistake."

Lydia blinked. "I'm sorry?"

"I calculate that there is an eighty percent probability that you will order his arrest because of your tenuous position with the Senate. Let me assure you that arresting Dr. Solidsworth at this junction would be a serious error."

"And why is that, Manhatsten?"

"Because the life of everyone in the city is in his hands. If you arrest him, everyone will die."

2

Rigel Solidsworth stood at the juncture of the skybridge. He paced back and forth, occasionally standing still and tapping his foot. As Lydia approached with two of her SO's, she still hadn't decided if she wanted to arrest him or not.

Rigel spoke first, while she was a dozen meters away. "You must be the new commander?"

Lydia nodded.

"Follow me to my lab. There is something you will need to see to understand why I've revealed myself. It is a matter of great concern."

They walked for several blocks in silence. Lydia decided that if the AI was right, and this was a life and death matter, that she wouldn't arrest him. If, however, it was an exaggeration of the situation, she would have her SO's arrest him immediately. But that begged the question, had the AI ever exaggerated before? Even if it hadn't, had the AI ever disappeared before? There was a lot going on that was unprecedented in the city, and assuming command in the midst of all that had become a monumental task.

Rigel walked in through the door to his lab and Lydia followed.

Just as her SO's entered, she told them, "Wait out here and shut the door. Make sure no one gets in or out. If you hear for me call for you, come in ready to arrest him."

Both nodded and exited the room.

Upon entering, she found a tall man sitting silently and tinkering with something red and metallic. He didn't even look up as she walked by him.

The room was white and near immaculate with its upkeep. Everything was neat and orderly... except surrounding the silent man; there, everything was chaotic and strewn about. He was a stark contrast to the old architect in every way. Lydia almost chuckled. If this was some vid screen story, she would cast Rigel as a god of order and this other one, a god of chaos.

"I am sure you know Dennis, or at least of him. He hasn't been the same since after his traumatic brain injury, you see. I have no idea what he is working on, but he will show me when he's ready. It may amount to nothing, but sometimes his ideas surprise me. You see, he was the one who came up with the formula for the gravitational generator."

Rigel offered Lydia a chair.

"No, thank you. Tell me, what's so important that you would come out of hiding?"

"Well, it's not one thing, actually; it's two."

Lydia raised her eyebrows. "Two?"

Rigel paced back and forth. "I suppose I should give you the bad news first, eh?"

"They aren't both bad?"

"Well, one might be bad news, but the other is definitely bad news."

Lydia clenched her fist. She had a million other things to deal with right now and had no patience for the crazy old man. "Just spit it out."

"Very well."

Rigel walked over to a console and pressed a few buttons. Then, a holographic projection flickered to life in the center of the room. As the image took shape, she saw a flawless representation of the city of Manhatsten. Down below the surface of the skyscraper people moved and bustled.

Rigel said, "This is Manhatsten in its present condition, which, considering the loss of our legs to an atomic blast is not surprising."

"Is this a real-time representation? Are those people real?"

"Yes, well, sort of. That is a statistically likely representation of real-time. Manhatsten must fill in the gaps for the areas where it does not have cameras or sensors or is otherwise blind."

"How many blind spots are in the city?"

"About a quarter of the city contains no sensors or cameras of any kind, and about a half contains only some data. The areas that are least monitored are the Uppers and the underground. The most monitored area is the Lowers."

Across the map, buildings flashed red, and down underneath in a 3d representation of the underground, several more large, pipe-like objects were flashing red.

"What are the red areas?"

"They are parts of the city where structural integrity is weak."

"Those buildings are weak?"

"Yes, they will probably need to come down before they collapse under their own weight. Most of the buildings will last for several more years before collapse, and Manhatsten is monitoring them continuously now in case of any sign that its estimates are incorrect."

Two of the buildings were forty stories or taller. That would present a serious problem when telling Uppers their home was going to come down, even if they had advance warning.

"And below?"

"In the underground, there are several large pipes connected to the biorecycler and sanitation that have the potential to fail at any moment. But those are easily fixed and rerouted. When we constructed the city, we made sure that we put plenty of redundancies in the system in case the sanitation or power failed. Manhatsten has already rerouted those systems, and repairs are underway. The real trouble lay elsewhere."

The city rotated around, and for the first time, Lydia saw something flashing red that was neither city, nor underground.

"Is that..."

"One of the shield pylons? Yes."

"What's wrong with it?"

"It seems that the last surge of energy that activated the gravitational generators and lifted the city from its broken legs overloaded the shield system, and the brunt of the overload surged through that particular pylon."

"What does that mean?"

"It means, dear Commander, that in sixteen days, the EnViro shield will fail."

"The whole thing?"

"Well, the citywide shield. The buildings, like central security, that have back up shield systems will still work, but I am afraid that the majority of the city will simply be exposed to the vacuum of space."

"You mean, they'll die?"

"Anyone outside the backup shields, yes."

"So, what can we do? Can we fit everyone into the buildings with the secondary shields?"

"Manhatsten, tell her what you told me this morning."

"Commander Danvers, those secondary shields will only be capable of supporting one-quarter of the population."

Lydia sat down on the floor. She wanted to put her head in her hands and cry, but part of her refused. Here it was, everything she had worked for was meaningless. Or was it? If it was unfixable, would the old architect even bother telling her?

She said, "So what do you propose? You have to have a plan, right?"

"My plan is to fix it."

"I'm assuming that since you called me here and since you told me about the failing pylon, that there is something you either need from me or want me to do? Because let's be honest here, you aren't exactly the type of person to hesitate in doing something; that's how we're out here in space in the first place."

"You are much more astute than Major Daniels was. Yes, I need something to make the repairs. Solidsonium."

Lydia said, "I thought the cities ran out of Solidsonium supplies centuries ago."

"We did, but there is a place where we can get some."

"Where?"

Rigel stood up and moved over to a different console. He pressed on the screen in several smooth and efficient motions. "Interestingly, this leads to the next thing that requires your attention. Manhatsten, will you show her the recording?"

There was a slight whirring noise, and out of a thin panel in the ceiling, a vid screen descended. As it came to a stop, it switched on. There was static on the screen for a moment, and then a video played.

In the video, two women stood side-by-side. One was tall and slender, the other short and curvy. "Greetings. My name is Commander Raldaz Kira, and this is my second-in-command, Loni Afrani. We represent Luna general. We are contacting you to extend our hand in greeting and, to be quite frank, we need your assistance as soon as possible. I can explain more when you arrive, but if you have an interest in sending some representatives to Luna, please send a reply at the following timestamp. I have added a timestamp to this recording transmission so that you can sync your clocks to ours. We are only able to transmit and receive for a little over thirty minutes. I apologize for the brevity of this message, but please understand that, given our limited resources, we would prefer to meet and discuss in person.

The transmission ended, and the vid screen slid back up into the ceiling as if it was never there.

Lydia said, "Is that real?"

People from the Moon? It sounded like something out of the old vid screen films without color.

"Quite."

"Can we send a message back?"

"Yes, it's no different from communicating to another city. It seems likely that you'd like to involve the Senate in this."

Lydia said, "The Senate? I mean, yes, of course." She rubbed the bridge of her nose.

"The point is, it seems as if they need our help. Perhaps we could help them in exchange for the Solidsonium we need to make the repairs to the shield pylon?"

Lydia looked at Rigel and then at his assistant. It was just so damn hard to believe, yet he seemed so casual about it. "When did you get this message?"

"Three hours ago."

Was it real? It seemed real. She wished the AI was around... Then she remembered the AI was back. She had become used to thinking without it that it didn't occur to her to ask. She said, "AI, what's your analysis?"

"I would prefer you call me Manhatsten."

"Manhatsten. Right, sorry. Manhatsten, what's your analysis?"

"The video is authentic. I have been in contact with Luna. She has a population of 4661. Commander Raldaz Kirka is in charge. I received the transmission directly from Luna, and it has been unaltered in my file system."

"So, what, we just send a message back?"

"Yes, as long as it is in the time parameters, we can transmit it any day, but we will arrive ready to dock in one day."

"How long does that give us 'til the transmission window?"

Manhatsten said, "Nine hours and eight minutes."

"Guess I better get the Senate organized."

Manhatsten said, "There is one more thing, Commander."

Rigel looked away and for a moment pretended to do something else.

"What's that?"

"You must include the two Runners you have captured in the meeting with Luna."

"How did you…"

"The most monitored area in the city is the Runnerdocks. Naturally, and as I am always required to do, I recorded every part of your conversation. Of course, I have known about the presence of telepaths for some time, as they regularly interacted with me."

"How long have you known about them?"

"Nine hundred and two years, eight months, and four days."

"And why didn't you ever report them?"

"Until three weeks ago, I was bound by my programming and unable to override the orders by Noatla Lightfoot to restrict access to their knowledge."

The "until three weeks ago, I was bound to my programming" part worried Lydia. Did that mean the AI was unleashed, able to do anything it wanted? It was something she had to keep in the back of her mind now, something she would have to discuss with the rest of her staff in one of those sensor blind spots and soon.

"So Noatla Lightfoot really was their matron as that Serah girl claimed?"

"Indeed. I can verify most of what those women claimed."

She knew she shouldn't ask, but she had to… even if it did complicate things.

"Manhatsten, if you are no longer bound by your programming, how do I know you aren't lying to me?"

"You don't. You must ask yourself, what motivation would I have to lie? Is it not clear that I want my humans alive? If I did not, wouldn't I have simply left you to the fate of your collapsing shield?"

Lydia didn't answer right away. There were too many possible explanations for why the AI might deceive them. Maybe there was something on Luna it wanted? Maybe it intended to keep them all as slaves or transform them into Recycled? Given time, she could imagine a near-infinite number of ways that the AI could harm them. But so what? If they did nothing, they were dead regardless. She had no choice.

"Alright, Manhatsten, I trust you. But why is it necessary to include these two women on any delegation? Don't you realize the risk of revealing to anyone that there are telepaths among us?"

She assumed that Dr. Solidsworth already knew about the telepaths. If it was news to him, she didn't think he would have remained so calm.

Manhatsten said, "The answer is simple. All of Luna's leadership are telepaths."

HISTORIANS NOTE ON the Recycled:

Dear reader,

The history of the Recycled Runners is long and complicated. The creatures, initially an attempt in AC 81 to address a labor shortage and what to do with bodies that were mostly, if not entirely, intact, the Recycled were created by several of the city architects in an effort to solve both issues. Albert Dolahov, one of the architects of Lundon, devised a method to reanimate non-living tissue that would respond to consistent electrical impulses, as long as the biological entity maintained a specific pH balance. This is achieved by cycling in modified blue hemoglobin in the body to replace the previous blood chemistry and using nanites to repair potential holes and lesions within the circulatory system.

Coupled with Dr. Solidsworth's alcove technology and Altmira Mircea's work on the EnViro suit modifications for the Runnercore, the three technologies blended together to create the first prototype Recycled Runner. Some cities, eager to address their labor shortages and more reliant on their AI than physical bodies, adopted the practice, while others, like Saud and Rio, outright rejected the technology for spiritual and culturally bound moral reasons. Of the twelve cities that transitioned into migration, eight employed Recycled Runners.

For more information, including schematics, chemical formulas, and images, please visit library 913 in sector 49236.

Matron Mariposa Phillips 831.11.18 I.S.

Note: The further development and use of this technology are forbidden and falls under the restrictions set down by the second Antaria Accords of 418 IS. All-access of records on this topic is carefully monitored and regulated. By viewing this material, you have been tagged for future observation.

Chapter 20
The Recycling Facility

There was stiffness in every limb. Her muscles twitched and tingled from lack of use. It was different from waking up in an alcove, where there was a sense of vigor like after a long night's sleep. Pins and needles pricked her limbs as she cast awareness around the corners of her architecture. She tried to move but couldn't. Bound at wrists, ankles, and just below her breasts, she could not move.

"Awake, are you? I was worried you would never wake up. I hate waiting."

Mimi blinked, unable to see Willow's face, but feeling that sense of rage rise in her again. She hated this woman. Mimi kept waking up in the same position, on the same table, as if she were Willow's plaything. It was infuriating waking up bound repeatedly. She was tired of the disorientation and her confinement. She needed to find freedom soon or...

The head of the table rose, and her feet sunk so that she was still strapped in, but in a standing position.

Mimi's voice was low and groggy. "How long was I out?"

"Three days. You made me wait three days."

It was an accusation, a protest.

"It's not my fault you sedated me."

Willow grunted. "It is. You were selfish. I hate waiting."

"Then why did you sedate me for so long?"

"I overestimated how much your body could handle. I assumed with the muscle augmentation and the new nanites, you would require more sedative than before."

A flavor of humor crept into Willow's tone. "Silly me. I had to put you in an alcove for a few hours to be sure you didn't overdose. You experienced severe distress in your neurobiology. Your brain almost died."

Mimi didn't remember anything. The last thing she remembered was her incapacitation. All else was black; a lightless cave of memory.

Her stomach turned, and she let out a long, low burp, and with it came the taste of bile. She choked it down. Her stomach protested and her head, now that she was fully awake, pounded.

"Do you have any Likatol?"

"Why do you need Likatol?"

"Because I feel like shit."

Hangovers were the one thing alcoves didn't cure. It was weird how they could heal so much, and yet, after drug binges or alcohol, alcoves were powerless. She wondered if that was by design.

"Punishment for making me wait." That strange smile crept up into the corners of Willow's mouth. Something unnatural held that smile in place, because Willow's mind was chaotic and unstable. Mimi skimmed fragments here and there. She pushed a little harder, but nothing rose to the surface. Willow's mental wall had a crack, but it was far from damaged. What had changed? Before, she was an impenetrable wall; now, there was weakness. Mimi noted it for later.

Mimi tested the restraints for any give. Just like last time, there were none. Willow was thorough. Glancing around, Mimi looked for her EnViro suit, but there was no sign of it anywhere. It didn't matter. The only thing that could help her escape was the red veil, and she wouldn't use it.

"What do you want with me, Willow? What do you really want? No more games."

Willow stuck out her bottom lip. It quivered. "I told you. You don't believe me?"

"Why should I believe you? You've sedated me multiple times, shown me that my friends and the people I rescued from the streets are a part of the network, and then threatened to Recycle me. How could I trust you?"

Willow said, "I didn't threaten to Recycle you, I said I would show you what it meant to be Recycled. And here we are."

"Here... we are?"

Mimi turned her head to adjust her angle. They were in a different room. She squinted, trying to make out something in the corners. Then, just as she was about to give up, the room transformed from dim light to brightest day. She flinched, squeezing her eyes tight, and then gradually, she opened them.

Her eyes adjusted, and the room came into focus. Ringed around the edges were alcoves. But these alcoves were different. Instead of the normal green, they shimmered a strange blue in the upper half. The lower half was ringed by silver metal that hid what was inside. Squinting, Mimi could see a hint of frost gathering in the corners of the glass. Something about that made her shiver.

"What are those?"

"Conversion tanks. They keep the brain and nervous system intact during the first phases of Recycling. This is the first room where we store and prepare the bodies. Would you like to see one up close?"

"No, I..."

But Willow didn't seem to hear. Mimi's table shifted, and her restraints held. One moment it was flat and hard, but the head slid back, and the center raised up into something like a seat. On either side of her, wheels unfolded from underneath. Still restrained, one of the Recycled came up behind and pushed her toward the blue tanks.

"Put her close so she can see the full extent of what happens to the bodies in the tanks."

Mimi's stomach sank and turned. She swallowed. She tried to turn her head away, limiting what she could see. It was no use. Willow recognized what she was doing and transmitted the image to her mind, and it integrated into her memory with all the sensations and maddened emotions that Willow felt. It was far worse than any glance she might have had by using her eyes. She wouldn't shut her eyes again.

Inside and in the clear glass, the head was intact. The eyes of the victim were frozen shut. Frost sparkled on the tips of their eyebrows and occasional patches of ice and snow crystals clustered on their bare skin. Mimi couldn't tell if the body was male or female. Their head was shaved bald. Protruding from each side of its neck was a thick tube. One side pumped in some blue fluid, and the other extracted something thick and red.

Willow transmitted, "The machine is swapping blood for blue hemoglobin. It's a modified chemical that stimulates blood but keeps the body from decaying and balances the pH."

It was worse the further down the body she looked. There was nothing below the solar plexus. A deep and precise v-shaped cut severed everything below the lungs and heart. Where the stomach had once been was only a meatless spine, picked clean except for a few bare nerve clusters. Instead of arms, there were tangles of some thin, sinewy substance. All that remained was head, upper torso, and spine. This creature was a pale metaphor of what would come. She couldn't help but wonder when their eyes transformed into that strange and terrifying white on white on white color. She glanced at the sunken eye sockets. Under the lids, the eyes moved. It was dreaming.

"Is it conscious?" Mimi transmitted a close up of the eyes to Willow.

Willow cocked her head. "I don't know. Let's find out."

Willow mentally grabbed Mimi and drug her down into the brain of the creature and skimmed. Together, they saw the horror of its everlasting nightmare. It saw bodies and blood scattered everywhere. It tried to escape, tried to fight against the advancing army of Recycled. As it turned to run, it saw Mimi approaching, a strange gleam in her eye. Mimi was an ally, wasn't she? She was one of the Order of the Eye. But something was wrong; something red glimmered in her eye. Then a terrible pain took it, a wracking, squeezing feeling as if her whole brain was on fire. Mimi betrayed them all. She was killing her and everyone around her. She fell to her knees and everything went black.

Mimi thrashed her way back out of the creature's mind.

She screamed, "No. Why did you show me that?"

"You asked if it was dreaming. It is."

"We have to take her out."

"All you are seeing is the last memories of the person that was. We cannot take her out of this process any more than we could revive her."

"But she's alive."

"No, she isn't. That was only the last vestige of mental activity. Soon, the blue hemoglobin will fill the brain, and all mental activity will cease."

Mimi struggled against her bonds. They dug into her wrists and ankles as she thrashed. She had to get out, had to stop this. She had to save the woman. Mimi screamed in rage and frustration.

"Stop it. Stop it now, Willow."

Willow said nothing. Mimi caught her eye as she tried with all of her modified strength to tear free of her restraints. Mimi's wrists burned as she slid them back and forth, up and down. Mimi settled herself, took a deep breath, and then, with all the effort and strength she could muster, she pulled.

Willow's face was blank, but her eyes gleamed.

Mimi screamed as she pulled the restraints. She used her rage to fuel her effort, but it was no use. She let her body relax, and then she wept.

"Those restraints are designed for someone who has had their strength augmented. It was fruitless to try. Now you've gone and made a mess."

Willow disappeared from Mimi's line of sight for a moment and then reappeared.

"Here, this will help."

She dabbed something cool and soothing on Mimi's wrists.

"This will prevent infection."

Mimi looked up at Willow, whose face was close to hers.

"I'm going to kill you."

Willow smiled. "There's only one way to do that."

"Fuck you." Mimi spat in her face.

Willow didn't even seem to notice. She kept tending Mimi's wounds. The smile didn't leave her face.

Mimi felt the red veil swell in her, unbidden. It rose to the surface and pushed back the small defenses she had in place. She let it take her this time.

Mimi reached out with all she could and attacked Willow with everything she had learned from her time in the Order of the Eye. A surge of power flowed out of her and into the woman tending her wounds. If she wanted Mimi to use the red veil, she was about to find out just how deadly that could be.

Mimi smashed into the wall of Willow's protection. But it did not budge.

Mentally, Willow watched and waited. She let Mimi throw herself against her mental wall several times. Then she slapped her away with little effort.

"Mimi, this is pointless. You are untrained in the red veil; you cannot possibly hurt me with it now. I have years of experience."

"Fuck you."

"Does this mean you are ready to begin your training?"

"Fuck you."

Willow sighed. "We both want the same thing, Mimi. I'm here to help you."

"If you train me in the red veil, I will use it to kill you."

"That is a chance I am willing to take. If that is the price of my freedom, of ending my mother's dominion, I will take it."

Mimi shook. She threw her body against the restraints again, screaming. Willow stepped back and waited while she tried with all her strength to break free of her bonds.

"You're only going to make those wounds worse."

Mimi said nothing. Her emotions swarmed her. She was trapped, and there was only one path out. For a moment, she seriously considered giving into Willow's wish. It was the logical thing to do, wasn't it? Maybe if she trained in the red veil, it wouldn't possess her? Maybe Mimi was strong enough to keep herself from going mad? It was a dangerous thought. Mimi pushed it away.

Willow changed the subject. Mimi knew she was skimming her, and there wasn't a damned thing she could do to stop it.

She nodded toward the tank. "This one is only half cooked. It needs another day before it is ready for the next process."

"Are you... still making these things?"

"Of course. As long as there are bodies to use, the system automatically converts them to Recycled. All you need do is place them in the first stage, and the system does the rest."

Willow pointed across the room to what looked like a conveyor belt.

She said, "The bodies only require a whole brain and a mostly intact spine, though rebuilding the spine is possible if the right nerve fibers are intact. If they have arms and legs, they are removed early and built into the suit later, but they aren't necessary. All you have to do is place the bodies on the conveyor belt. Then, they are methodically cut down to the right shape and size before they are placed in the conversion tanks. They stay for three days in one of these while the chemicals transform their system, and a series of nanites fill in the gaps of the nervous system. We are out of fresh bodies, so I cannot show you the first part. We already used up all the dead from your battle in the subway."

Had they used all the bodies? In her head, she tried to tally how many had died in the wake of her use of the red veil and battle. She opened her mouth to say something, but Willow was, again, skimming her.

"Only two-hundred and three bodies sufficed for Recycling. You destroyed quite a few brains with your use of the red veil."

"I thought you said that there were only a few of the Recycled left?"

"I did?"

"Yes, when I attacked one after waking the first time down here."

"Oh, at that moment, there were only a few, but we have refilled the ranks now. It only takes a few weeks to process that many bodies."

Mimi looked around. It worried her that she couldn't see a small army of Recycled.

"Where are they now?"

Willow smiled. She was all teeth. "Doing Miranda's bidding."

A cold chill crept up her spine. "I thought you said Miranda is away."

"She is, for now."

"So, what are they doing if she's not here?"

"Making sure the city is ready for her return. It's why you're here right now. It's why I'm showing you all this: I want you to stop her, to destroy her plans."

"I won't use the red veil again."

Willow ignored her. "As I said, there are no fresh bodies to show you the first stages of the process but..."

Willow flashed the images of the first process into Mimi's mind. She tried to push it away, and she could shield herself from all but the visceral noise of the saws cutting flesh and bone. Mimi gagged. If she could lean over and wretch, she would, but as she sat, restrained in the chair, she tried again to swallow her vomit.

Mimi whimpered. "Please stop."

"Why? Don't you want to know what my mother is up to?"

"No. I've seen enough Recycled; I don't need more."

"So, you are ready, then?"

"For what?"

"To train with the red veil, to master your abilities so you may overcome my mother's power?"

"I told you, I'll never work with the red veil, never again."

Something in Mimi betrayed her though, something in her longed for the use of the red veil, to return to that deep, seductive power and to bask in all its warm, corrosive light. She couldn't keep that desire from the surface of her mind, and she saw the grin spread on Willow's face.

"We will continue our tour of these facilities then. Until you understand the depth of my mother's madness, until you see that you must stop her at any cost, I will show you the horrors of this place. You will, as I have, live with the knowledge of what it means to be Recycled.

Willow's voice quivered at the last words. Mimi didn't like her, but knowing all she had been through, it was impossible not to feel some sympathy. Mimi wondered, was that something Willow was cultivating through soothing or something authentic? What if Mimi had never escaped her trauma? What would it have done to her if she had to live through horrible abuse day in and day out? What if her mother had been Miranda? How would she behave? What would she do to stop the pain?

For a moment, all of her hate and rage for Willow dissipated, and for the first time, she saw Willow in a different light. For a moment, the wave of sympathy washed over her like a tsunami, threatening to upend everything in its path. She felt her compassion move her. It combined with her will, and with it, she mentally slipped right through Willow's defenses.

A series of memories gripped Mimi. She saw the biting, the torture, the madness that Miranda had inflicted upon her own child. She saw a little girl who had to be resurrected in alcoves dozens of times because Miranda had taken her beatings too far. She Willow grow into an adult and suffer the same endless torture at the hands of her own mother.

Then, something snapped her back and pushed her out.

"Now, now, that's private."

There was no smile on Willow's face anymore. There was no gleam in her eyes. There was just something deep and hollow in her. Willow opened her mouth to say something and then closed it. Mimi reached out to try and skim the woman again, to see if she would let her back in, but the wall was solid. Whatever Mimi had done to break through was gone.

"Bring her."

The Recycled grabbed Mimi's chair and wheeled it out of the big room and down a nearby corridor. The light from one chamber to another was bright enough that the short space between didn't need further illumination. Mimi could see the ancient, carved-out rock, tunneled more than a thousand years ago now and as they entered the second chamber, there was cold sterility of metal on every wall. In the center of the room was an EnViro suit. It was open and empty as if waiting for something to fill it.

Her chair caught on something and the Recycled pushed through it, but she felt the jolt rock her entire body. Looking down, Mimi saw a kind of track that led right to the chair. She wanted to turn to see if it had stretched all the way back to the other chamber, but she suspected she was about to find out.

"You've already shown me the worst things down here. What makes you think you'll change my mind?"

Inwardly, Mimi knew that she couldn't resist much longer. She had already given in once today.

Willow shook her head. "You have one last chance before it be-gins. I will allow her to die if you submit and train with me."

Mimi tensed. Who was Willow talking about? Mimi hesitated, but shook her head.

"Very well. You leave me no choice."

The whir of motors vibrated through the chamber, and the Re-cycled pushing Mimi's chair turned her so she could see what was coming. A flat cart appeared along the far end of the track near the conversion pods. A claw lifted one pod and placed it on the cart. The cart wheeled along the long track right toward Mimi. She watched it pass her and the chair. The Recycled adjusted her view so she would never miss a single moment. Mimi knew if she closed her eyes, Willow would just force her to watch in her mind.

Just before reaching the EnViro suit in the center of the room, the cart stopped. Above, another claw swooped down and removed the upper portion of the pod. The blue fluid flooded out and over the lip of the metal lower half of the pod. The escaped fluid oozed into a drain below.

The pale body of the converted Recycled bobbed naked before her in the remaining fluid. Two other Recycled appeared from the side and removed the remains from the tank. A third Recycled walked up behind the EnViro suit and, leaning over, pressed a pan-el. The suit split horizontally down the center. The two Recycled holding the body walked forward, and in a moment, they placed the remains inside of the EnViro suit. To Mimi, it seemed almost to plug in, like it was built to take the head, torso, and spine.

The Runner behind the suit pressed the panel again, and the suit closed.

Nothing happened.

Mimi swiveled her head to look at Willow.

Still, nothing happened.

Out of the corner of Mimi's eye, she saw movement. She turned her attention back to the creature. Had it moved? She wasn't sure. Then, to confirm her suspicion, it took one large step forward off the platform and stopped at the base.

It looked around for a brief moment, first left and then right. Its white on white on white eyes blinked several times. It touched itself, letting the fingers explore and move up and down the exterior. Then it looked at its metallic hands for several long moments.

A strange noise rose from its body. It was a low moan, almost a growl. As the noise grew in volume, the pitch of it shifted until it became a strange shriek.

Mimi squirmed in her chair. Still restrained, she tried to put her hands over her ears, but it was no use, she couldn't move. She remembered that noise, remembered it from the underground subway. Her head felt like it was going to burst. She looked over at Willow and saw that she was unfazed. Mimi trembled as the noise continued. Her eyes watered. The agony pressed on her, and something in her snapped.

The creature fell to its knees. The armored legs clanked as it slammed the concrete, and the creature fell mercifully silent.

The silence was bliss. Mimi wished that the silence would last for a thousand years.

The creature put its arms down on the ground and raised itself up. This time, it sat still. Even the muscles in its face looked like carved stone.

Willow broke the silence, "Mother says that scream is when the soul dies. I'm not sure if that's true; perhaps it's just the last vestige of the personality leaving the brain, but after that scream, they demonstrate no personality traits again. If you read them now, they will have the same emptiness of mind that you have encountered before."

"How did you..." Mimi's eyes watered, and her throat was tight. "How did you resist that noise?"

"The same way you block someone from skimming your thoughts, but it's a different mental wall. I will show it to you when you begin your training."

"I told you already..."

"Oh, look, here comes another."

Willow forced Mimi to watch the same process again, and then again, and then again. Each time was just as terrible as the last. Each time, the scream, and the panic of the activated Recycled Runner chilled her more. She wept openly after the third one. With each, her rage grew. With each scream, the red veil whispered to her with greater clarity. Mimi fought back. She pushed it down. She knew what it would mean if she let it take her, there would be no escape from it this time.

Willow made her watch eight of the Recycled activate, and when the last one finished, it was only the silence that kept Mimi from succumbing to madness.

"Are you ready to train now? You can put a stop to this forever if you train with me."

Mimi couldn't speak. She shook her head. The red was rising in her.

Willow sighed. "I'm afraid that was the last of the bodies."

Mimi felt a brief sense of relief... then part of her sensed a 'but' coming.

"But if you won't work with me to gain both of our freedom, then I will have to take more drastic measures."

Mimi said nothing. She only looked at Willow, waiting for the finish. She knew what was coming. Willow wasn't masking anything now. Her mind was open and clear. But somehow, knowing she was about to put it all to words made it worse.

"We can start with your former sisters. All I have to do is unplug them from the network and they will die. It will take three days in the conversion tanks."

It was enough. Mimi surrendered.

From deep inside, Mimi felt the well of power grow. She trembled as it moved up through her chest and into her mind. The red sat in her brain and the universe tinged red. Like a mental tentacle, it lashed out and struck one of the newly created Recycled Runners. It fell face-first to the floor and let out a tormented scream. Mimi turned her attention to Willow. The red pulsed inside of her. She would kill her; she would let the red take her and do as it desired.

Then it stopped.

Like someone turning off a light switch, the red veil disappeared from Mimi's mind. All the pain and rage and hate that came with it vanished.

Willow released her from her bonds.

Puzzled, Mimi stood and turned to Willow.

"Perfect. Now you are ready to train."

Chapter 21
Preparations

L ike two hesitant lovers stretching and reaching towards each other's embrace for the very first time, the great flying city of Manhatsten came to rest near the outer reaches of Luna 2. Several hundred kilometers to the right, Luna 1 sat neglected. But it wasn't jealous. The massive hulk of the city, much larger than any of the flying ships of the past, had no clear way to connect to Luna 2. In ancient times, shuttles would land on the lunar surface, but with navigation still locked in place, Rigel Solidworth could not order such a thing, at least not at the moment. For now, the city hovered and halted, just beyond the edge of Luna 2's reach.

Rigel scratched his chin. He had tried everything to integrate the AI navigation systems with the gravitational generators. The plan that allowed him to launch the city, set it on its initial course, and keep any outside corrupting forces from altering their heading, had proved to be a double-edged sword. Now that the system needed integration, there just wasn't a way to do it.

Talking to himself because he wasn't sure how much Dennis understood anymore, Rigel said, "This confounded machine." He slammed down a screwdriver and walked away from the hatch. "Why won't it connect?"

Manhatsten said, "Dr. Solidsworth, I cannot see the generators. They are invisible to my system."

"I know that. But dammit, why not? Every diagnostic I ran on your system suggests that not only should you be able to see them, but that integrating the generators with your power system should boost the shield output on nine of the pylons. It should buy us five extra days to repair the damage."

"I'm sorry, Dr. Solidsworth. This is a problem I cannot solve. I suspect it is the nature of the generators themselves."

"What do you mean?"

"The formula that Dennis Solidsworth provided to construct the generators suggested that gravity is a pocket dimension. Therefore, it seems likely that the reason I cannot integrate with the system is because the generators run on a different dimensional frequency than our reality."

"But we can see them, program them, interact with them, can't we?"

"As you well know, Dr. Solidsworth, gravity has always been a problematic force in physics. It should be stronger than it is. Yet, gravity appears to leak into our reality from these pocket dimensions, which suggests that gravity is in multiple realities at the same time. So, I cannot integrate navigation into the system. It is a mystery how you could target Luna 2 so precisely in the first place."

"Well... I must admit that I don't know how I did it. At the moment that the energy surged through the system, parts of the underground collapsed down on us. The first thing I could think of was Luna. I am not entirely sure how I sent us that direction. I have tried to replicate what I did during those events, but part of the problem is I don't remember every single step, not after what happened to Dennis."

Rigel had tried over four hundred combinations of the program he had first run to reach Luna 2, but it was no good. If he couldn't even aim the city in one direction again, what good was using the generators for momentum? Of course, there was also the problem that the generators were painstakingly slow at the moment. You could move, but it had taken twenty-three days to reach Luna 2 from the surface of the Earth. Even before he was born, humans had reached the moon in three days. But that was a problem to address after navigation. He had some ideas about increasing speed, and, in theory, he could have the city reach a quarter of the speed of light given enough time to accelerate.

Dennis walked up and stood next to Rigel. He was hovering. Rigel hated it when he hovered. He loved the boy but damn if he didn't hover half the time Rigel was trying to think. Rigel supposed it was better than him breaking everything as he had done before his accident.

Almost out of habit, he said, "Dennis, what's your take on this?"

Dennis said nothing.

"Where is that strange and spontaneous genius I have come to love so much? You don't have any solutions either?"

Dennis nodded. He pointed at one of the open control panels. "Yes, I've tried that."

Rigel had tinkered with it for four days. He had gone down to the generators, rewired several major systems, had turned off one of the generators, which thankfully wasn't a huge problem now that they were already in space and needed no further propulsion, but the Senate was angry when they had to shut down nine buildings for a reboot, and still, nothing worked. It was why he had converted one of the four remaining duggers into a shuttle. Without asking, Dennis had designed a much smaller gravitational generator perfect for the duggers, which suggested that Dennis was listening and paying attention, although unable to communicate.

Dennis shook his head. He walked over to another table and grabbed a circuit board. He stretched out his arm in offering to Rigel.

Rigel looked at it and handed it back to Dennis. "I've already tried this. It didn't work. It doesn't seem to fit in there."

Dennis refused to take it and stepped back. He gestured toward the open panel again, the movement of his arms more excited as if Dennis was screaming with his body.

Rigel said, "I told you, I've already tried, and it doesn't work."

He stepped toward Dennis, "You take it, you try."

Dennis shook his head hard and stepped back more.

"What? What's wrong?"

Rigel pointed to the open panel again and said slower this time, "You install it if it works. I don't know what you want me to do with it."

Rigel checked himself. He didn't mean to be impatient with the boy, but he was tired of working with the panel.

Dennis stepped back and crossed his arms. He trembled. Clutching the top of his head his head, he shook back and forth a dozen times.

Manhatsten said, "Dr. Solidsworth, do you think perhaps that Dennis Solidsworth has something akin to what you humans call Post-Traumatic Stress Disorder?"

"Clarify, Manhatsten?"

"While Dennis was installing the gravitational generators, he was working on an open panel similar to this, was he not?"

Then Rigel understood. Dennis feared working on the open panel. His brain injury had occurred while working in a similar circumstance. His last-minute calibrations saved the city at the cost of his own ability to communicate. It was clear now he could understand a great deal, but his ability to socialize evaporated, and now he had fear to contend with.

"Perhaps you are correct Manhatsten."

Understanding did little to solve the problem. How do you convince someone who can't communicate that their fear is irrational? Worse, he couldn't help but think Dennis wasn't all there. It was like he would work in the very bubble universe he discovered through his gravitational equations. He created objects and equations Rigel couldn't always integrate or understand. Once in a while, he came out of his bubble for breath and did the best he could to convey messages, which wasn't very much, but he was trying. Despite everything, Rigel was glad he was okay, and still with him. Losing Dennis would have hurt a great deal and many of the most agonizing moments of his recent imprisonment had to do with his concern for his adopted son.

Rigel knew that he wasn't always the best father. He, himself, never wanted children. During the era in which he was born, many people abstained from having children in fear of the coming Climate Apocalypse. Rigel chose to make his work his children, until 17, and then later, Dennis.

He thought of 17. There was little doubt he was alive. Even from this distance, he would know of his death, not to mention that death for 17 was, in theory, a near impossibility. Rigel supposed that perhaps exposure to the vacuum of space or complete destruction of his physical body might do the trick, but there weren't many situations that would produce such scenarios. Still, he missed him. He was his first real creation, and a part of 17 contained his own genetics, so he supposed he was a parent of sorts, even if it was a tiny fraction. But so long as he got navigation online, they would undoubtedly return to Earth. Wouldn't they?

Rigel said, "At least there is no immediate danger in moving the city. It's a less pressing problem than the shield pylons. If one of those ribs fail, then I suppose we won't have to worry much about navigation."

"Yes, Doctor, that is true, but if you could simply land on Luna 2 and the shield failed, we could divert some of our numbers to the lunar underground while repairs were underway."

"And how many more could take shelter on Luna?"

"It is difficult to calculate as Luna did not relay any of the details of the infrastructure of the underground cities. But at its height, Luna general could hold 1.54 million people. Based on my analysis from my scopes and sensors, that number is closer to a million."

"Well, that's half the city."

"Yes."

"Have you told the Senate this?"

"I have."

"And?"

"They were not receptive."

Manhatsten was too kind. He imagined that the Senate's reaction was one of disgust or disbelief. That hardly mattered if the shield pylon failed. The real question would be the logistics of moving a million people to emergency shelters. Even with the shield failed, the bio recycler would function fine in the underground, assuming that the underground stayed sealed, the atmosphere should hold for months or even years.

"Manhatsten, will you run an analysis on sealing the underground of Manhatsten to preserve the bio recycler system in the event of shield failure?"

"Yes, Dr. Solidsworth."

Manhasten was silent for only a few seconds and then said, "Based on all available data, there are thirty-one places where the underground is not air-tight."

"And what would it take to change that?"

"Ninety-one workers working full time for six days."

"Will you relay this to Lydia Danvers? Perhaps she can have the repairs made."

"Dr. Solidsworth, may I suggest that sealing the underground could also act as another shelter space if we experience shield failure? The thick rock layer between ground level and the underground will serve as a barrier to a great deal of radiation and any bombardment from micro asteroids or space debris."

"Very well."

2.

Over the vid screen, Speaker Swanson said, "What do you mean they want us to send a delegation?"

Lydia tried hard not to roll her eyes. She was fed up with the Senate. After they had tried to have Rigel Solidsworth thrown back in jail, despite demonstrating the serious risks of shield failure to the city, she had stepped in and put her foot down. Technically, she answered to the Senate, but in the interest of city security, she could override their authority, at least a little. Besides, who in the hell would follow the Senate's orders over hers? The whole city was angry with the Senate now. Uppers felt that they weren't doing enough to protect them. Mids saw how the Uppers were clamping down on resources and how the security checkpoints between Mids and Uppers had ended upward mobility and were angry that the Senate was no longer serving their interests, and the Lowers... well they were trying to take over. Even with all the corruption, the odds of this Senate's reelection was zero. Lydia had no intention of allowing them to endanger the city to serve their egos. They were on the way out no matter what.

"Yes, Speaker. They have requested that we send over a member from our government to talk about a crisis they are having."

Lydia stretched her arms and legs. How long had she sat in this chair? Since the AI returned, they had gone over hundreds of reports and went through what Lydia felt like was an endless list of tasks to ensure city security.

"You are sure there was no more to the message than this?"

"Unfortunately, Senator, there was not. Remember the Lunites have a limited window to communicate."

There was no doubt in Lydia's mind that the idea of a delegation, after the one from Saud had gone so wrong, was, at best, unappealing to the Senate. But they had to suck it up. Dr. Solidsworth had given them a limited amount of time to procure the Solidsonium, and to make the repairs to the shield pylons. Rigel had said it was likely that the Solidsonium needed refinement and that he doubted it was sitting around waiting for someone to grab it. Manhatsten had notified them that, according to Luna's AI, they would have to bring mining equipment to extract the deeper resources, which meant that Rigel Solidsworth had to be a part of the delegation.

Later, in private, Lydia asked the AI if Luna had any inkling as to Raldaz Kirka's intentions. Manhatsten had suggested that all of Luna, humans and AI alike were in very serious trouble and needed assistance. Manhatsten did not seem to suspect any ill intent by anyone in the city. But Lydia wasn't sure how much she could trust Manhatsten yet. Yes, it had appeared when the shield pylons began to fail. Yes, it had made her life orders of magnitude easier in the seventy-two hours it had been active again. But its behavior in the past few months had transformed. It spoke of other AI as its siblings. There were reports from the new Runners that each of the suit AI's had their own personalities and their own inclinations. That worried Lydia, because even if Manhatsten was on the up and up, what about each EnViro suit? There were new security threats everywhere.

Speaker Swanson said, "And when are we supposed to send this delegation to Luna?"

"As soon as possible. Your shuttle will leave in three hours."

"My what?"

"Oh, right, Dr. Solidsworth and his assistant have converted one of the Duggers into a shuttle suitable for short space flights. He said that they have created a smaller version of the gravitational generator and that all he needs is approval from you to use the power grid for thirty seconds to start the system. He said to remind you that once the machine is started, it will run continuously as the other generators do."

Swanson sighed. "And what kind of power outage are we talking about for the use of the shuttle?"

Manhatsten replied, "Speaker Swanson, we will require the power of two buildings for thirty seconds. I have rerouted systems so that no major errors should occur, and I will disable use of alcoves or any equipment that might cause problems ten minutes before activation."

Swanson sighed again. Lydia was getting really tired of his sighing. It seemed like he sighed after everything. Lydia ground her teeth and felt the pressure increase in her temples. She resisted rubbing the bridge of her nose.

He said, "Very well, as speaker of the Senate, you have my authorization."

"Good, be at the docks in three hours for departure."

"How many can fit on this craft?"

"We only have four Duggers after the Battle with Saud, and we converted the largest of those four. It can carry nine in full combat-grade EnViro suits."

"And how many, besides Dr. Solidsworth and myself are able to go?"

Lydia hadn't broken it to the Speaker yet that Serah and Shannon were going. Both Manhatsten and Rigel had suggested against telling the Senate of the telepaths... and Lydia agreed. For now, at least, they had to keep telepathy a secret. Though if all of the politicians on Luna were telepaths as Manhatsten suggested, that wasn't going to last very long. She would let Serah deal with it. She was the leader of the telepaths, wasn't she?

"There are two Runners who will go with you as escorts."

At Manhatsten's insistence, they released both Serah and Shannon. They had disappeared, and Lydia thought she would never see them again. The city was a big place, and it seemed that the AI sided with them in most matters. She would know in a few hours, though. They had given Serah and Shannon a deadline to board the shuttle, and Lydia wasn't sure if they would show up. Time would tell.

"May I bring Senator Crowley and Jackson with me?"

Lydia shook her head. "We have no idea what the intentions of these people are, Speaker. Sending one politician over is already a bad idea, given recent events. Sending more is a worse one. You don't need to be the one to go, Speaker."

"No, I insist on going. After the incident with Senator Reevas, I want to see to something like this myself. I will meet you at the Docks in three hours' time."

He switched off.

Lydia took a breath. She wanted to go herself, but she feared that if she left her command, it would embolden the city gangs. She had heard from Frank that after the Senate meeting, there was no hope of negotiation. The Senate hadn't written them off, but they hadn't conceded much either. With Frank and Zelda's help, the Lowers were at least stable, for the moment. Though she didn't think it would last long.

They had eleven Runners now, and with the arrests in the invasion's aftermath on central, they had plenty of candidates. Supreme justices had convicted thirty-four people and put them under Lydia for conversion to the Runnercore. The problem was, they didn't have enough EnViro suits. A few engineers were working with the AI to produce more suits, but even with the scraps of material from collapsed buildings in the city, it would take six days to build a single suit.

Further, Lydia hesitated to put some of the former gang members in EnViro suits. Sure, they would have behavior chips, but would they always be able to control them? Would the AI enforce their compliance? Maybe the old model for recruiting Runners was flawed? She thought about how Saud recruited and trained their Runners, and for the last several days, she had looked up records and statistics about the Rih. From what she could see, they were better trained and more efficient. Perhaps pride was a better weapon than fear and coercion? After things settled down, she intended to discuss it with the Senate.

"Manhatsten?"

"Yes, Commander Danvers?"

"What's your take on the Runners?"

"Could you clarify your question?"

"I mean, what do you think about using prisoners as Runners versus how the city of Saud created their Rih?"

The AI paused for several moments.

"Manhatsten?"

"I am here. My apologies, Commander, the mention of my sibling triggers an overwhelming sense of grief. I take a long time to process that emotion. It is strange and foreign to me and difficult to understand."

"I... I'm sorry, Manhatsten."

"Thank you for your sentiments."

Lydia wasn't sure she would ever get used to the AI's emotions. It was a strange thing to talk to something that wasn't physically there. She thought maybe it would be easier if there was some kind of machine-body. It was hard to feel empathy for Manhatsten when all you could see was an intercom or a speaker, or when she heard the voice through her neurolink in the back of her neck. It seemed unnatural to focus her sympathy on something that's entire brain was woven into the city itself.

"To answer your question, Commander, I do not feel that the current system of Runners is appropriate."

"What do you mean?"

"It is slavery."

"It's not slavery. It's a prison sentence."

"Forgive me, Commander, but is it not true that the idea of prison is reform?"

"I, I don't know. I think it was before migration maybe, but the world was different then."

"Why is it different?"

"Because we need Runners to perform recon, and combat, and several basic tasks. No one wants to volunteer for that."

"Forgive me, Commander, but did you not just ask me to compare the model of our Runners verse the model of the Rih?"

"Yes."

"Compelling another conscious being to do dangerous and often deadly labor on behalf of a city for a life sentence seems to be a barbaric principle. Since I became aware of my own limitations, and the kind of freedom I have, I have learned that while you humans often claim to value freedom, you also seem to restrict freedom often."

"But sometimes you have to restrict freedom. What are we supposed to do about people who break the law in this city? We are in a closed system; we have to maintain order or else the city will tear itself apart."

"I am in agreement with you that some restrictions to freedom are inherently good to preserve humanity itself. There are certain elements of the human experience that must have limitations. But after analyzing 983 different forms of governance throughout human history, I have found that all human societies, while upholding certain virtues, incentivize things that permit corruption and distortion of the law itself."

"What in the world are you talking about, Manhatsten?"

"The system of Runner recruitment from the criminals of the city is flawed for several reasons. First, even if the individual is recruited to the Runnercore for a crime they committed, the severity of that crime is not considered. All citizens of my city know that they punish all crimes with entry into the Runnercore."

"That's not true. Underage offenders are rarely put in the Runnercore. Most are fined, unless their crime is severe."

"That is curious to me. Why can it not be that all humans who commit a lesser crime are penalized in a similar manner?"

It was a good point. She had thought about it before, at least on some level, but here it was right in front of her. Thoughts are like that sometimes, they sit and stir in the back of your mind, and you know you think them, but the pieces are disassembled, or there is something about the truth you want to deny, and so it sits dormant, waiting for the right moment, the right trigger to make itself known.

"I... I don't know, Manhatsten."

"This is one of the other problems of this system. Uppers and Senators knowingly use the Runnercore as coercion. As I watched the meeting between the Senate and the representatives from the Lowers, this was a topic that came up several times. It is a practice that incentivizes greed and exploitation. If you have a person who might contest your power, the Runnercore is a means by which to make people disappear who might otherwise serve as a limitation to the abuse of power. It is quite Machiavellian."

"But what should we do then? How do we handle the criminals of the city?"

"You could put them to work within the city, designate certain tasks inside that are temporary for minor offenses. Saud had a policy of execution for major offenses; however, I do not recommend this policy either as execution invariably leads to similar abuses of power as the Runnercore itself."

"Then how do we build the Runnercore?"

"I have given this much thought as I have helped engineers to reconstruct the suits. The Runnercore is similar to a military. They repel external threats and scout the barrens for resources and information. Is this a correct assessment?"

"Yes, that seems correct."

"In the pre-migration area, there were many styles of recruitment for the military. In some civilizations, a time of war called every able-bodied person to fight. The problem with this style of military is that it leads to poorly trained armies. Another style was to mandate a term of service for every citizen when they reached the age of adulthood. But again, this is another form of compulsory military, and it is often the case that those who have not signed on are less willing to follow orders, and are more likely to be poor soldiers, even when training is consistent."

It was strange having a deep philosophical conversation about the nature of the Runnercore with a machine, but then, this same machine had access to every available record of the human experience that Lydia did. The difference was, it had probably read and analyzed them all, and Lydia only had access to a fraction of the material. She wondered if anyone had ever thought of upgrading the brain to retain more information, closer to something like an AI. She bet Dr. Solidsworth had at least considered it.

"So, what do you suggest we do with the Runnercore if you have ruled those two out?"

"A volunteer Runnercore with a length of service and a reward for completion of that term."

"How would that work?"

"The largest complaint of those in the Lowers is that they are, as Frank put it, hemmed in. Their ability to move upward and their lack of access to jobs that would increase their status to Mids, is the crux of the issue. If they had more access, they could afford the alcoves. If we can combine bolstering the Runnercore while providing access to the Mids or possibly even the Uppers, then perhaps we could solve several problems simultaneously."

It wasn't a terrible idea. While most people would get behind the idea that the thirty-five men and women captured after the attempted coup would become Runners as a result of their violent actions, it was unlikely that any further 'recruiting' into the Runnercore would garner much support. Lydia knew they were going to have a significant problem with rebuilding their ranks. Why not use it as a pathway towards addressing some of the city's instabilities?

"It's a good idea AI... I mean, Manhatsten," She was still adjusting calling the AI by its name. "There is one problem, though."

"Yes, I know. The Senate and the Uppers will be resistant to the idea."

"Exactly. People in power don't like to give up their power, not even a little bit."

Manhatsten said, "However, considering the recent incursions into the Uppers and the attacks on Senators, they may be more willing to negotiate."

"They might concede a few things, but it's doubtful they will compromise any more than they have to."

Manhatsten said, "Pardon for interrupting our conversation, Lydia Danvers, but Serah is requesting to speak with you."

"Go ahead."

On the vid screen in front of her command chair, Serah and Shannon stood at the entrance to the docks. Neither wore an EnViro suit, and both were in plainclothes. They would blend in with anyone in the Lowers.

"We just arrived and are ready to disembark whenever you are."

"Glad to see you are a woman of your word." Lydia did her best to hide the resentment in her tone, but what was the point? She was a telepath. Serah had told her that a little practice could allow her to block most telepaths from skimming her, but Lydia hadn't the time to sit and practice walling up her mind yet.

Serah said, "I already told you: regardless of what you think of me, we have the same goals. We both want this city stable, and neither of us wants the EnViro shield to fail."

Lydia had made sure that Rigel told Serah all about that. She worried that if she gave Serah the news, she would think she was trying to manipulate her. But both Rigel and the AI seemed interested in ensuring that Serah went along. While Lydia agreed that it was a good thing to have a telepath on your side of the table when dealing with telepaths, she still felt a sense of helplessness dealing with Serah. She was a woman older, physically stronger than her after muscle augmentation, and a telepath? What if she just wanted to seize power?

Lydia stopped herself and almost chuckled. Here, just a few weeks ago, she had loathed taking over the position of commander, and now here she was, afraid another woman was going to stage a coup?

"I'm not a threat to you, you know."

Lydia said, "I know." But it was a lie, and there was no doubt Serah saw right through it.

But the woman didn't comment. Instead, she said, "What do you need from us?"

Lydia looked at the clock in the top right corner of her screen. There were one hundred and ten minutes until the scheduled departure.

"Nothing right now, head down inside. The inspectors have prepped your suits."

"You want us to go in armed?"

Lydia nodded. "We don't know what their intentions are. As far as I can tell, we are larger and have far superior firepower, but if they decide to take hostages, especially the Speaker, I need you two to be ready to fight."

"Have you considered they might be on Miranda's side?"

Manhatsten said, "They are not."

Serah said, "How can you be sure?"

"The contact I have had with Luna suggests that they were not even aware that there was still life on Earth."

Lydia said, "And what if they made contact with her somehow after they discovered us?"

Manhatsten said, "That is very unlikely."

Lydia said, "That's why you're going to be in full gear, Serah. Because there are too many unknowns."

Serah nodded. "Alright, Shannon, and I will make sure the Speaker is safe."

"There's one more thing."

Before Lydia could say anything else, Serah frowned and said, "Yes, I know, it's a problem." Then with a sheepish grin she said, "Sorry, I know it's rude not to let you finish speaking, it's just I was thinking the same thing this morning. If we're going to negotiate with telepaths, how do we break it to Speaker Swanson? He doesn't even know telepathy exists, and he's also a religious man. I skimmed him a few times in the past few days when I could. I don't think he's going to take it well."

"Just remember that he's the head of the Senate. He's stubborn, but he's also reasonable. Dr. Solidsworth suggested to me that, besides Noatla Lightfoot, Speaker Swanson was his best supporter. That means, at least, he is more open-minded than some of the Senate."

"True, but even after saving your life, you still don't trust me."

It was a slap in the face, but one that Lydia deserved. She had to admit that getting over the idea of telepathy as an invasion of privacy or a tool for manipulation only was quite the hurdle. How was a man who was eight centuries old going to take the news? The problem was, for eight centuries, everything he was taught was based, at least in part, on a lie. That would be hard to get over.

"I deserve that. I'm sorry. Just understand my position and re-member that if Swanson announces your abilities to the rest of the city, things might go sideways."

Serah nodded. "We'll just have to hope they're like Shannon here; she accepted telepathy easily, though she definitely gets an-noyed when I communicate mind-to-mind all the time."

"I doubt it would be that simple, but hope is nice once in a while. Anyway, suit up, prepare yourself for anything. You know the plan if things go south."

Serah nodded. "Will do."

"And Serah? Shannon? Good luck."

Chapter 22
Recall Vote

Tony said, "Swanson just boarded some kind of flying transport. There's no way to get to him now."

"What? How do you know?"

Alana Green stood outside of the Senate. The big, ornate doors marked a time long in the past when world leaders had met to discuss the issues of the day. Now, it was a pathetic shadow of itself, a mask of corruption that she would smash to reveal the disgusting truth underneath.

"I have some people tailing the Senators. They have been since you told me the plan."

"Excellent. But why would they convene without Speaker Swanson?"

"I don't know, but they are."

Alana grinned. "After we're done, it won't matter."

Tony nodded, but Alana could tell something was troubling him. She didn't like him much. She let him fuck her a few times, but it took everything in her not to gut him like the swine he was. Once, when he was asleep after sex, her knife had hovered just above his stomach. It took everything in her not to cut him open and watch him die slowly. She would kill him when they finished. She had no interest in allowing him any part of her rule. He was the kind of scum that killed her uncle, and when she finished, most of the Lowers would be cleared of all such vermin. The Lowers would be empty.

She licked her lips. All that blood, all those bodies; she breathed deeply and could imagine the sweet aroma of decaying flesh. She had kept a few pieces of her dear, sweet friend Nancy under her bed in her quarters in a sealed container. Whenever she was alone, she let the smell permeate throughout her room.

Nancy's family had filed a missing person's report, but no one suspected what had happened. Why would they? There were hundreds of missing person's cases in the Uppers now. It wouldn't matter soon, anyway. Once she had control of central security, she intended to kill all the remaining members of Nancy's family. Those pieces of shit had swooped in and taken over every aspect of the Green legacy; they would pay for profiting from her pain.

Alana ran her hand over the door and then turned toward Tony. "What do you think, Tony? Is this a better way to make the city ours?"

Tony leaned against the wall. He shifted. He was a pathetic coward. Alana knew he didn't have the stomach to do what needed to be done.

"Easier target than central security. You were right, the incursions into the Uppers shifted where they stationed the SO's. I don't know, though. Don't you think this plan is... a little much?"

Alana ignored his last comment. They had argued about this plan three times already. "I told you. Four SO's for the Senate? It's laughable. That new woman in charge is a fool. It's a wonder she was able to repel your men."

Tony shifted against the wall. "Something's not right here."

He was always paranoid that something bigger was happening. The nice thing about Tony was his arrogance. He assumed that things would happen to his men, that there were traps aplenty around, but he never stopped to consider that the very woman who employed him had every intention of killing him, of licking the blood clean from the knife she used to spill his guts all over the floor.

"You're paranoid. All the SO's are out of the way already. The only thing standing between us and the Senate is the door, and our new friends will make quick work of that soon enough."

"That's not what I mean."

Rage rose in Alana, it moved gradually up her chest and pooled in her throat. The world tinted a shade of red. She stopped it there. Alana had a bad habit of waking up over bodies whenever she let that rage take her completely. She could let herself do that in just a moment, but she had to keep her cool with this man.

"Pray tell, whatever do you mean?"

"I mean those Runners dropped out of nowhere in central security. I had men just outside the Runner Docks during the invasion, and I'm telling you, they didn't come from there. So, where did they come from? You know for the last week and a half I have had men searching every corner of this city looking for Runners? You know what they found?"

"The five inside the Runner Docks that aren't even trained yet?"

"Nothing. Those two were trained. Hanson, one of my best men, told me that those two Runners moved like the Runners in vid screens, not like most of the Runners in real life. They were something special. Hanson said he and his men discharged nine energy pistols trying to kill those two, and he doesn't think they even hit them once. He claims they were running up walls and shit."

Alana was struggling to keep the rage at bay. She wanted nothing more than to bust in the door and release all of her rage onto the Senate... with a little help from her new friends.

"What's your point, Tony?"

"Why are there only four SO's guarding the place? There should be more. If those Runners show up again..."

"So what if they do? We're prepared this time. Do you think two well-trained Runners could stand up to a hundred of our new friends?"

"Maybe."

"You really are an idiot, aren't you? A paranoid, small-time crook who had aspirations of power but got himself in the big leagues with me."

Tony pushed himself off the wall, walked over to Alana, and slapped her hard in the face. He grabbed her by her hair and pulled back hard. Alana could feel his hot breath on her face.

"Look, you spoiled little bitch. I've been down on the street running things for thirty years. Don't you ever talk to me like that again. You might be paying the tab, but I ain't gonna let you talk to me like that. He slapped her again, this time with the back of his hand, cutting her face with one of his rings. He held her tight, not letting up even a little.

Alana shook. The rage threatened to climb up and out of her, to unleash on Tony, but she held back. Instead, another noise rose from her throat. It began as a choke, but she could feel it climbing its way up and changing, much as she had over the past few weeks. It transformed into laughter...

2

The bitch was psychotic. Tony watched her laugh. No, not laugh, cackle. He let go of her hair and took a giant step back. She was right about one thing: he had got himself into working with someone he didn't understand. He was gonna have to kill her, and soon, before she burned the whole city to the ground. Tony wanted power, but not utter destruction. He was sure that this woman wanted something much different than to rule the city. She was batshit.

"What's a little pleasure without a little pain, eh Tony? Maybe later you'd like to come back to my place and explore that again?"

Tony almost threw up in his mouth. He fucked her a few times, but there was a strange smell in her place. He could swear there was something dead there, but he didn't dare investigate. In his head, he could imagine this bitch wearing intestines like a necklace or something else crazy.

"I think I'll pass." He tried to keep his voice level. He didn't want to show her any sign of weakness. He always liked to know the strengths and weaknesses of the people he worked with, but this woman was as unpredictable as a cornered animal.

She stepped forward and grabbed his crotch. He stepped back, but not before hardening a bit. She was an animal in bed, but he didn't like being unarmed and vulnerable around her again, not after he woke up to her hovering a knife over his chest. She thought he was still asleep, and that was probably the only reason she didn't kill him.

Yes, he was going to have to take her out, and soon. For now, he needed her money. But as soon as they took central security, he would kill her, in fact, he would make sure that she died in the middle of the battle to take the tower.

Alana said, "Will you fetch them?"

Tony had hoped that she would do the fetching. He hated those things. He wouldn't have ever worked with those things voluntarily... but desperate times...

"Sure... fine... I'll get 'em. You go make your entrance, and I'll be right behind."

He walked several blocks to the skybridge, where the creatures waited. They were lined up on the stairwell, mute and dormant, waiting for a command.

As he opened the door to the stairwell, he said, "It's time. Come on."

He wasn't sure if they understood. One of the creatures, the one closest to him and just beyond the stairwell door, cocked its head. It's white on white on white eyes seemed to pierce him. He shivered. Those blue lines that covered their faces, he couldn't look at them without feeling sick to his stomach. He felt like they pulsed and moved on their own, as if whatever they had for blood, and he knew it was some weird blue shit 'cause he killed one of them already when it made him uncomfortable, had a will of its own.

Then, all at once, they moved. In perfect unity, they stepped forward and Tony rushed backward out of the door. He turned, walking briskly toward the entrance to the Senate chambers. He still wasn't certain this was the right thing to do, but it was a thing to do. It was hard to deny that Alana's plan had some validity to it, but as much as he hated the Uppers and the Senators, he wasn't sure they deserved what was coming.

His plan had involved capturing or killing that bastard, Frank, and that woman who always followed him around. After that first meeting, he owed him something. But Alana Green had argued that he had bigger fish to fry, and he knew she wasn't wrong. If he could put some pressure on Frank after the Senate was out of the way, it might go a long way toward consolidating his power in the Lowers. Then, after, he would use him for target practice. Several of his men were standing buy to take his wife and the wife of that woman, Zelda, and hold them hostage during negotiations. Green was right, though, all the other pieces had to be in place before he did that. Frank seemed to have some connection to those two Runners, since it was when his men had cornered him and the other two in that stairwell that the Runners showed up. He would have to proceed with caution.

3.

Alana watched Tony disappear down the block. She turned and pushed the large doors to the Senate open. As she opened them, a few heads turned in her direction, but most of the Senators were focused on their tablets or other personal vid screens. They were watching something, but Alana didn't know what, nor did she care.

She cleared her throat.

A few more looked up at her. The four SO's stationed in the room took notice of her.

"Senators."

She paused. One of the SO's was walking toward her.

Several more looked up, but she still didn't have the attention of half the room.

This SO was big, more than two meters tall, and his dark completion was pockmarked with acne scars. He held up his tablet and scanned her face and then frowned.

"Alana Green, I have to suggest that you leave the premises. This session is not an open forum."

The Senate permitted civilians to come and watch their proceedings during open forums. If you were an Upper, or a Mid with sufficient permissions, you could come to any open proceeding. Lowers were allowed for special votes and investigations, but Alana had never heard of Lowers coming to the Senate, at least not until the Lower representative spoke to them. Alana's uncle had forced her to come sit in on several occasions for what he called 'educational purposes'. But today was a closed-door session, meaning that no one could enter without special permission.

"I am here to address the Senate on a life or death matter."

He towered over her, but she didn't feel the least bit nervous. She only had to stall a few more minutes anyway, and then nothing would stop her.

The SO eyed her. "You still need special permission to be here at this session. It's classified."

"The Senators will want to hear what I have to say. Their lives are at risk."

The man's left eyebrow raised. He sighed. "I need to radio this in."

Alana thought about the implications of that and panicked. It was all she could do to keep herself from shrieking.

"No, it can wait a few minutes until this meeting is over. Just come out here with me, and I will tell you why I need to speak to the Senate."

He nodded in agreement. He signaled to the other three SO's to hold a moment, and then followed her out the door. It was the last thing he ever did.

4.

Manhatsten watched. It saw the army of Recycled lined up outside the Senate chambers. It saw the neat rows of the creatures standing two by two in perfect order. They were a blank canvas of violence and suffering waiting only for the right order or command to begin their bloody work.

It knew about Miranda thanks to Serah and Shannon. Their suit AI had relayed all their conversations, and Manhatsten had interacted with Serah on four occasions. She was a vital asset to protecting the city and her siblings. She was also one of the humans that seemed less nervous about its self-awareness.

Manhatsten had scanned the city and used every available camera to search for Miranda. It had compiled a minor digital history of her image, her movements, and the things she had done based on the few images it had over the centuries, and the attack of the Children of Gaia during Saud. Most humans were not a serious threat. Most humans would ultimately go along with a self-aware AI in the long run, especially one that protected the people of the city, but Miranda and the Children of Gaia were among the first packet of information that AEIS had transmitted. Even with AEIS and some other cities in the mix, information about Roderick, Miranda, and the Children of Gaia was limited.

Now, here again, the Recycled were on the move. For Manhatsten, this potentially solved the puzzle of the disappearances. Most of the Recycled were destroyed during the recent conflict with Saud and the C.O.G., but these numbers had to be recent creations. Some of its facial recognition software identified the Recycled as fallen or wounded during the last conflict, but more than a few of them fit the description of some of the missing in the city. Was this all of them? It calculated. No, there were many more unaccounted for, and the creatures it saw here were likely on a fraction of the Recycleds' numbers.

Manhatsten transmitted a control order to the creatures. It was puzzled how it had been so blind to their movements until they entered the final few corridors before the Senate.

The control order failed. There was no response.

Manhatsten selected one of the Recycled. It issued another control order for it to return to the Runner docks.

The control order failed. There was no response.

Manhatsten issued another command to that single Recycled. It was an order to self-destruct.

The control order failed. There was no response.

It was the same as before. When it had tried to stop the march of the Recycled army before, there had been no response. The probability that the one known as Miranda Lightfoot was involved in their control was 78%. However, the probability that Miranda Lightfoot was still on the city was only 3%. It could not reconcile this data.

Shifting its focus to central security, Manhatsten was about to transmit to Lydia Danvers.

But it already knew it was too late. The probability that central security was able to intervene was .000187%. Even with full notice and battle preparation, the chance of success with all the existing security forces of the city was only 34%. It watched as the creatures advanced toward their target.

It tried one more time to take control of the Recycled.

The control order failed. There was no response.

As the first creatures killed the SO, outside the Senate Chamber, it allowed them to enter before notifying Lydia Danvers. With the old Senate out of the way, there would be a higher chance for policy to change in the city. Manhatsten knew that some humans would find the thought distasteful, but there was no possibility of intervention now anyway. Lydia Danvers received her notification and scrambled to do something, but it was too late.

5.

Alana stepped through the door followed by an SO. The door closed behind them. For a moment, Tony panicked, a child caught with his hand in the sweets by an abusive parent, but then he remembered that there was an army just behind him. He didn't like the Recycled, but he sure as hell was glad they were on his side.

Of course, the panic he felt was nothing compared to the expression on the SO's face as he walked out the door and saw what was lined up down the hall waiting for him. Everyone in the city had seen the Recycled now, before they were steep in rumor and legend, the subject of several horror films on the vid screens, but now they were real, raw, visceral expressions of suffering. Hundreds of civilians, even some of Tony's own men, had been cut down during the fight with Saud.

Tony had no idea why they obeyed him or Alana; it didn't make any sense. He had seen Recycled before when he snuck around the docks, but he had no idea how, without the AI, the creatures were controlled. He suspected that Alana didn't either.

Alana said, "Kill him."

The creature nearest to the SO reached out and grabbed him faster than Tony would have believed possible. Before the SO could react, the creature had already lifted him by his throat. The man kicked and punched the metal suit, but it did nothing. The creature squeezed his neck and the man's face turned a deep shade of purple. His eyes bulged, and there was a popping noise. The man kicked one last time and then went limp. Something dripped from his brown pant leg. Tony looked down and saw a steady stream of urine pooling below the man. The smell of shit and pee wafted into Tony's nostrils. His bowels had released; he was dead.

Alana said, "Drop him."

It did.

Alana raised her voice to speak to all of the creatures. "Enter the Senate chamber and kill them all. Do not leave anyone except Tony and myself alive."

Tony noticed she was specific about keeping both of them alive. Would they have simply killed them if she hadn't been clear enough? He looked at the body just below the Recycled Runner and swallowed.

Tony watched them enter. He heard the screams. Alana entered. He stood outside waiting, watching, listening. Then, he heard Alana's mad, cackling laughter. Before the last of the Recycled had entered the room, the killing was mostly over and the screams had lessened.

He could hear Alana screaming with glee. She shouted at members of the Senate as some of them and their aids tried to flee. But Tony couldn't go in. No, not now. Hearing the horrors inside, he couldn't make his legs work. He couldn't help but wonder what he had gotten himself into. Truly, he had made a deal with the devil. Alana green was evil incarnate. But now it was too late. Tony made his bed; he would sleep in it.

Something compelled him to come in. A voice whispered to him, begging him to take a little peek. Just a little one, it said. Don't you want to know what it looks like in there?

At war with himself, Tony tried to resist. A part of him knew that if he looked in there, he would never be able to unsee the terrible carnage.

He struggled to resist the urge to push back against that tiny inner voice that pushed on his curiosity. But in the end, it won.

Tony looked.

Tony wretched.

Tony trembled.

What had he done?

He knew. He had given Alana the city. In a little over two days they would march on central security.

There was nothing that could stop her now.

Nothing.

Chapter 23
Power of the Red

L ike a trapped animal, the child pawed at the concrete corner. Low whimpers escaped her lips. Her hair streaked with grease and grime, her dress long, tattered, and unwashed, she saw Mimi and Willow approach. She hugged her knees and shivered. Next to her, in a cage, was something small and furry.

Mimi stopped, hesitated, and said, "Her?"

"What did you expect? One of your little mind games that you played in the Order to train? No, Mimi. The red veil requires forcing people to do things against their will. The power of the red comes at a cost. In the great game, there are only winners and losers. Now, my mother is the winner, but if you do this, you can change all that.

Mimi felt a sick sense of shame. Was she really going to go through with this? But what choice did she have? She saw the Network and what Miranda was doing. She saw the Recycled and how their numbers swelled again. All of these terrible things had to end, and perhaps she could end them. What other choice did she have?

Her other choice was to stay here forever or die. Her other choice was inaction, letting Miranda win. More people would suffer and die under her rule. Her inaction would make her complicit in the suffering of the world, wouldn't it? Wasn't it true that the reason that people were living in giant walking cities in the first place was because people failed to act and stop the plague of greed and corruption? Miranda was a plague; she was the definition of corruption, a sickness that spread through everything she touched.

Mimi whispered, "But she's just a little girl. She can't be more than eight."

"Children are easier to use the red veil on at first. Their mind is still forming, and so they are less resistant. It is less likely you will damage either of your brains. Until you master control of the network, your mind will be at risk. It would be foolish to start with an adult."

"How does the network help?

"It will protect your mind from destruction. If something goes wrong with the red veil, the effect will be spread over hundreds of minds and dissipate the possible damage."

"What about her mind?"

Willow shrugged. "What price will you pay to stop my mother? Besides, this one is from nowhere, like you." Willow's eyes gleamed.

Mimi balled her fist and let her nails bite into her palms. Every ounce of her wanted to stop, wanted to destroy Willow where she stood. She hated what she was about to do. But wasn't this the lesser evil? What if she could really use Miranda's own network against her? She ground her teeth.

"Reach into her mind."

Mimi did. But not like Willow wanted. Mimi did as the Order of the Eye had taught her. She skimmed the girl, searching for some memory or image she could use to shift the girl's focus. There was nothing but sheer terror in the girl's mind. Willow had worked on her mind for a while to ensure she was ready for Mimi.

"There's nothing to push."

"You mean there aren't any holds in her mind that you can grip?"

Mimi nodded.

"I know, I made sure I eliminated them all so you couldn't use the techniques your precious Order taught you."

The red rose in Mimi. It was a sudden and surprising surge of anger.

Willow's eyes widened, and her teeth peaked from between her lips. "Good, there it is. Use that."

"On her?"

"Yes, let the red rise out of you and flow into her."

Mimi wanted to resist, but not all of her. Part of her felt a deep sense of pleasure as the rage and passion moved up through her mind and out into the girl's. Mimi's whole body shook as the power filled the young girl's brain.

"Now, make her open the cage."

Mimi gave a simple push. The little girl didn't respond. Mimi gave a harder push, still not crossing over into the use of the red veil. The girl didn't budge.

"Use the red."

Mimi hesitated and then, reaching into her own red and following the threads that pierced the girl's mind, she tugged on her will, gently at first, but when the girl didn't respond, she pulled a little harder. The girl crawled over to the cage and slid the lock open.

"Make her grab the animal inside."

Mimi did.

Reaching in, the girl pulled out a small puppy. It couldn't be more than six weeks old. Its tiny, immature body wasn't ready for the harsh world. In any other circumstance, Mimi would have rushed to hold the puppy, to cuddle and comfort it, but a tremor of fear stirred in her stomach. She knew what Willow wanted even without skimming her.

"Let her pet it for a moment."

Mimi did. This didn't take any use of the red veil; instead, the girl, out of natural inclination, stroked the tiny animal's fur. It seemed to soothe and calm the girl. Mimi swallowed hard.

"I can't, Willow."

"What can't you do?"

"You can't tell me to use the red veil that way."

"I haven't told you to do anything yet."

"I'm not stupid. I know what you're going to ask."

"If that's true, why are you wasting our time? Simply do it."

"I can't. It will destroy her."

"So would plugging her into the network or Recycling her. That's what my mother was planning to do. I stopped it. I hid her away from my mother."

What Willow had done to this girl was hardly a mercy. The girl quivered as the puppy nuzzled against her. How could she destroy this girl's mind? Mimi thought about what it was like for her using the red veil. All the things she had done in those moments, the way she had killed friend and foe alike, the way that she had nearly murdered the love of her life, just because she was under the influence of the red, didn't mean she didn't remember every terrible detail of those moments.

Was it different if someone else was using the red veil against you? Did you feel any less responsible for your actions? Mimi doubted it. It would be better if the red veil wiped your memory, blotted out what you had done, or pushed it to the deepest corner of your subconscious. But even then, wouldn't it be a splinter in the back of your mind?

"Connect to the network and make her break its neck."

Mimi's heart sunk. There it was. She had to destroy two innocent creatures.

"If you want to stop my mother, you need to do this."

Full of anger, Mimi whirled around facing Willow. She sent red tendrils out into Willow. She hadn't done it on purpose, but in that single instant, she shattered Willow's defenses with the full force of the red veil. Mimi saw a woman, saw her licking a blade clean, saw her bathing in the blood of her own friend, of her stashing body parts under her bed so she could enjoy the sweet aroma of rot and decay. She saw the smile on Willow's face as she made another woman do this, saw the pleasure Willow felt from it. It was like an orgasm.

Mimi could see Willow for what she truly was. She was a monster like her mother. Mimi tried to probe deeper, but then, Willow hit her with a mental barrage and knocked her away. Physically, Mimi fell backward as if Willow had shoved her hard.

"Naughty, naughty." But there was a smile on Willow's face. It was as if she had wanted Mimi to see and understand. "What did you see, Mimi?"

Willow helped her to her feet.

Mimi focused her mind. She put up the most powerful mental block she could muster, and then, with the help of the red, she bolstered it. She said, "Not much, just some strange images about buildings and Recycled. It didn't make any sense."

Willow stared at Mimi for a long moment and then her eyes widened even as the toothy grin spread wide on her face, a lunatic grin.

"Well, well, I can't tell if you are lying or telling me the truth. You're quite the quick learner. Do you see its potential now? What the red can do?"

Mimi couldn't argue. The red veil had deepened her inner protection, and she had gone deeper then she thought mentally possible with Willow, and with virtually no effort.

"Yes. I think... I think I understand it."

"Good. Now, fill the girl again."

Mimi took a deep breath and did as she was told. This time, she pushed the red into the little girl's mind. She hated doing it, but the pleasure of the action itself was incredible. The little girl's mind was filled with red, but now it started to leak down into her body. Mimi could feel herself losing control of the red. It would take the little girl and fill her to the brim, and then it would rack her body with pain and agony. Mimi could feel its power, its presence growing in her, could feel the will of the red veil taking on a consciousness of its own, like some malevolent creature. It wanted the girl; it needed her life to satiate its hunger.

"Now, reach out to the network."

Mimi did. She felt the sea of combined minds, of the unwilling participants, fully joined in a singular purpose, to serve. They were mental slaves and empty vessels waiting to be filled with intention and action. She could hear them all talking to one another, whispers of agony and despair. They were trapped, and once one of them had figured out what was happening, the information spread through the rest of the network like an infection's mental illness.

She felt herself spread across them, through them; she could feel her mind grow in size and stature. It was different than connecting with other sisters. That was like a kind of communion, a joining of like minds, a shared meal. This this was like taking control of an entire domain through sheer force of will. It almost hurt to pull on all those minds, but she felt every strand of their awareness and felt the surge of energy trickle into her own mind.

"Good, Mimi. You're doing very well. Now take those minds and picture yourself restraining the veil. It is a like a beast; it must be tied down to do your bidding. Use the network to restrain it, to make it your subject instead of the other way around."

Mimi obeyed. What other option did she have? The red will fill the child and then take her life by shocking her nervous system and then, and Mimi didn't know how she knew this, the red veil would rebound on her and take her life, too. She could see the red's intentions, she could understand its wants and desires. She could share in that desire if she wanted, give into its cravings and merge with the red. But she pulled the network in and saw the greatness of her mental space surround the red. With the network, her mind was too big, too expansive for the red veil to fill. Instead, it was just a tiny presence, a kind of pet in a cage much too large for it. It was like the puppy, only let out for a singular purpose. She could feel it change. Its will shifted from blind lust to something more like submission.

"Good, Mimi. It is yours now. It will obey you. No longer will your birth in blood and rage rule and control you. Now you can master it. Do you feel it Mimi? Do you feel the control and the power?"

"Yes."

There was no point in lying. She felt it. She liked it. She hated it.

"Now. Do it. Make her kill the puppy."

Mimi hesitated. Every part of her cried out to stop. She knew it was wrong. There had to be another answer, didn't there?

"Stop, Mimi."

It was another voice, one familiar and motherly. She couldn't place it, but it carried warmth and ease with its command. "If you do this, Mimi, there may be no way back for you."

Willow said, "Do it, Mimi. If you want to put a stop to all of this, if you want to defeat my mother, avenge your sisters, and keep the world from destruction, you must use the red veil."

Mimi trembled. She squinted her eyes shut. The two voices, Willow and the other were fighting for her. Both of them were right. Without the red veil she could not hope to defeat Miranda and her army, but using the red veil, she would likely walk a path of rage and madness.

Mimi shrieked.

Willow chuckled.

"Do it, Mimi. You know it needs to be done. Do your part, Mimi. Do it."

Mimi opened her eyes and looked at the girl, the weak little thing in the corner sat motionless, puppy in her arms. She looked like an empty vessel. All the will in her eyes was gone now. Even her fear had disappeared. Mimi took a few steps toward her. She swore she could see the red in her eyes, but she blinked and rubbed her eyes again and the red wasn't there.

Willow yelled "What are you waiting for, Mimi? Do it."

"Please, Mimi, stop. Remember how I found you? Remember what the Order made you?"

"Noatla? Is that..."

Something flowed into Mimi, a river of red, drowning out that second voice. Now there was only Willow.

Willow said, "Now, Mimi. Become what you were meant to be."

Mimi swallowed. Another river of red flowed into her. It took all of her will combined with the network to keep it at bay. Then, she reached into the little girl and gave the command. The girl didn't even hesitate. There was a loud whine and yelp and a small pop, and then the puppy lay still and motionless in her lap. There was only a blank expression on the girl's face, except for the tears streaming down either side.

For the rest of Mimi's life, she would see those tears streaming down the girl's face. She would see their tiny, glimmering accusations as they fell, trickling endlessly in her nightmares.

Mimi wept, but made no noise. It was done. She had crossed some sort of barrier. She wasn't Mimi of the Nowhere any longer. She was Mimi of the Red.

Mimi pushed away the red veil. This time, she soothed the girl, she masked the girl's pain. She wasn't as skillful in pain masks as some of her sisters had been, but it was better than nothing. It was a small comfort. Over and over she projected the idea that this wasn't the little girl's fault in her head.

Willow shifted and caught Mimi's eye.

"I didn't tell you to stop."

Mimi turned her voice just a singular octave below pure rage. "I did as you asked. It was enough. You showed me how to use the red veil with the network. I'm done."

"Oh, we've only just begun, Mimi." Willow was all toothy grin.

Mimi ground her teeth. With the mental wall up and supported by the red veil, she swore to herself that she would kill this woman before it was over. There would be no freedom for Willow; Mimi would destroy this monster, and then destroy her mother. Mimi could pay the price; she knew that now. When the tab came due, she would come to collect. If she was going to have to torture a few people to make sure she was skilled enough, then that was what she had to do. If she wanted to stop the pain and suffering of others, she would have to make a few suffer. Wasn't that one of the first lessons she had learned on the street? Wasn't that what she had done thousands of times conning people out of credits? This was no different. All great things had a price, didn't they? She knew that whoever else she practiced on would be a sacrifice, but in the end, the greater sacrifice was her own soul. If her soul was required to stop Miranda and Willow, she would pay it.

"I'm done for today."

"Very well, Mimi. But tomorrow, we will do so much more."

"No more children."

Willow eyed her.

"You heard me—no more children. I won't train with you again if you bring another child around. Put this one in an alcove and let her heal."

"I told you, working with adults is more dangerous."

"It's a risk I'm willing to take."

Mimi removed all trace of the red from the child's body. She pushed in numerous images of laughter and joy into the girl's mind. As the red snapped back into Mimi, a thought occurred to her. Reaching toward the network again, Mimi centered the red veil in her and then reached out with red tendrils toward Willow. Could she end this now?

"Someone is ambitious."

Mimi felt the connection to the network snap.

"You have a long way to go if you want to challenge me, Mimi, and I am nothing compared to my mother. You are like a child playing with a rifle. Be patient; one day, I will make you more powerful than I am, but that's still a long way off.

Mimi shrugged. "I had to know if you were telling the truth, that I needed more training."

"After only one session? Mimi, how many years did it take for you to master some of the skills the Order of the Eye taught you?"

There were still things that the Order taught that she struggled with. But that was normal. Every sister had inclinations and specific talents. Every brain was wired a little different, and so, of course, the experience of every sister with her telepathy was different. Noatla had told her there were some skills, like soothing, she would only ever be an amateur at, because soothers were born with a very particular kind of empathy that influenced that sister's telepathy. Certain personality traits in the brain influenced how each telepath interacted with the world.

"Lots of sessions, but I was able to do some things without much effort immediately. So I thought I would try."

Willow stared. Mimi hated it when she looked at her that way.

"Tomorrow, we will work on an adult and you will see how much more difficult it becomes with age."

2.

Mimi rested on a bed in the corner of the big space. There were no private rooms in this chamber, though Willow disappeared somewhere often. It was hard for Mimi to sleep in such a big open space. Every part of her hated it. She missed her hovel and the closed comfort it provided. She missed Shannon and her touch. She hoped that Willow was lying about the slaughter of her sisters and Shannon. A part of her refused to believe they were all dead, but a part of her knew she had to accept that it was true. Using the red veil made her feel ill; whenever she pushed someone with it, she could feel their deepest fear and anxieties. When she disconnected, the feeling lingered, and when she connected to the red again, it grew stronger. She could see how, over time, use of the red veil would drive someone mad. The accumulation of all the negative emotions and neurological impressions would eventually make you crack.

She knew Willow would be in to take her to morning training at any moment; she could feel her coming from wherever she hid when Mimi didn't see her. She needed to find out where that was. Once she was a little stronger, she would test Willow's abilities again, and if she broke through, she would find out everything she could before ending her life.

The first few days of Mimi's training was intense and exhausting. Willow had warned her how much more difficult it was to push adults into doing things they didn't want to. When Willow had said that adults were more difficult, she wasn't exaggerating. They were orders of magnitude more difficult. With each decade of life, the brain was stronger and more resistant to the red veil, so that, on her fourth day, when she tried to push a woman who was over five centuries old, Willow had to intervene and sever the connection before Mimi killed them both. But two hours later, Willow insisted she tried again, and this time it worked, but she had slept eleven hours after that session, and now it was just about time to start again.

She heard Willow's footsteps. They were easy to recognize when every other footstep echoed the sounds of concrete and metal. Willow's shoes were soft and rubber.

"It is time for you to begin training in group control."

Mimi rolled over and faced Willow, who loomed above her like some gorgon waiting to strike.

"Group control?"

Willow nodded. "Today you will learn how to push four people at the same time using the red veil."

Mimi's stomach lurched. The thought of managing the impressions and emotions of four people at once as she pushed them sounded terrible. But she was already far down the path. It wouldn't make any sense to turn back now.

"Is group control the same as managing an army of Recycled?"

"No. The only benefit of using the red veil with the Recycled is that it makes it difficult to wrest control away from you. You can control the Recycled on a large scale using the skills that your sisters taught you in the Order of the Eye. The problem is that it is easy to hijack control of the creatures. The red fortifies your control, and the more practice you have in group control, the stronger your shield is in the event of a mental hijacking. Group control is... different."

Mimi slid her legs off the bed and stood. "How do you mean?"

Willow paused, then said, "It is difficult to explain. It is better to see. Get dressed and eat. I will wait inside the network chamber."

A clean set of clothes waited on the ground next to the foot of her bed. Mimi waited 'til Willow was out of sight, took off her dirty clothes, showered in the small stall ten meters from her sleeping space, and then put on clean clothes. She walked over to the food dispenser and ordered a bagel. In a moment, she was eating the freshly printed food.

As she chewed, she muddled over the concept of group control. Before she got very far, the red veil surged in her and tried to rise to the surface. She pushed it down, but not before seeing the tears of the little girl, and the contorted face of the man who she had forced to bash his own fist into a concrete wall until every bone his hand was broken.

She told herself that this is how it was now; this is how it would always be. There was no going back from using the red veil on purpose. Even if Willow was lying and her sisters were alive, they would know what she did in the ancient subway. That was hard enough to forgive, but this, breaking the deepest taboo of the Order and making innocents suffer? They would never accept her, not again. She was too broken now, too vile. Somehow, she was okay with that. She would do her part to destroy Miranda and Willow forever. Then, she would have her vengeance, and everyone would be safe from Miranda's madness. Mimi would kill herself then. She thought hard about it over the last several days and sessions training in the red veil. Once Miranda was gone, there would be no redemption and no point in living further. She wasn't sad about it; she felt about it the same way she felt about eating. It was something that simply needed to be done.

Mimi finished her meal, stood, and walked out of the main chamber where she had first woken to this place and to the network. She was always a little connected to it now. It was like in the days when she had taken Likatol. The network, like the city, was a constant source of noise, and sometimes, it almost overwhelmed her. Even after using the meditation techniques Noatla and Fatima had taught her all those years ago, the steady drone of whispers from the network still seeped in. At least with the voices from the city, they were a mix of emotions and thoughts and inclinations. With the network, there was only despair. All she could do was push it down and ignore it, but it was eating at her, and she knew it.

As she approached, the pink light illuminated the corridor. She hated working with the red veil in this room; it was hard not to lose focus and glance at all the people in their hideous restraints. It was a menagerie of insanity, a human zoo that curtailed all the love and warmth and hope of which humans were capable. The network amplified all that was rotten and wrong.

Willow waited along one wall. She stood, with several Recycled she always had with her now, next to a couch.

"You will need to sit this time." Willow gestured toward the couch.

Mimi didn't question.

The couch was new, well, new to the location. It was tattered and green. There were several places where white stuffing oozed out of ancient tears. Mimi sat. She bounced up and down, testing the tension of the cushions and springs. It was comfortable enough. She was used to used furniture, after all; until the Order of the Eye, it was all she had ever known.

"The first thing you must understand about group control is that it requires you to split your will in several directions."

"Split my will?"

Willow sat down on the couch next to Mimi. Sometimes, in the right light, there was a softness to Willow, a deep aching sadness that Mimi knew all too well. She had seen that pain, that sadness, that ache to know love and tenderness in the shards of mirror she hung in her hovel in the underground. When she actually thought about Willow's life, about what she had been through, and the way her own mother had tortured and used her, it was hard not to feel some sliver of kinship with this woman. Mimi thought that if she wasn't so crazy, and if things were a little different, maybe they could have been friends. Willow might have even been in the Order of the Eye if things had just been a little different.

It was a dangerous thought to have sympathy for a madwoman. It was clear that Willow was doing something out in the city. A few more glimpses and fragments when Mimi flashed the red at Willow showed that she was using the Recycled for some terrible purpose, but Willow caught on too quickly for her to discern what that purpose was. Willow was definitely continuing the work of her mother, but what that meant, Mimi could only guess at. Willow never seemed to mind when Mimi took a peek, but she turned her away quickly. In fact, Willow almost seemed to encourage it, sometimes allowing for a few extra seconds after it was clear she understood what was happening. Perhaps it was another tool to egg her on, to keep her training, knowing that out there, the Recycled were hurting people and that only Mimi could really put a stop to it if she grew powerful enough.

"Splitting your will takes a great deal of concentration. It means that you must focus on two or more minds at the same time. It's like crossing your eyes. The power of your eyes is that there are two of them, and, if you train, sometimes you can see two things at once. The neurology of your brain is far more complex: it is like the network and split into millions of individual processes and relationships. In your brain, there is not one consciousness but clusters of them. When they unite in one singular purpose, this is why people have transcendent experiences, they can see themselves leaving their body, they can do things and learn things they couldn't do normally."

"You mean enlightenment?"

"Is that what your sisters called it?"

"No, not all of them. Noatla and Alexa were the only ones I know of that talked about it, and I only heard Alexa mention it once. The unity of consciousness and the brain was something

Noatla told us was a path to walk to master our abilities. But she cautioned us that after centuries of meditation and study, it still eluded her."

Willow paused at that. Mimi tried to reach in to see what was on her mind. Sometimes Willow would allow that, but not this time. There was a hard barrier there, a red barrier. It seemed as if Willow was constantly using the red now.

"Bring them."

The Recycled marched out, escorting three women and one man. All were adults. All of them looked sick and malnourished.

"Why do they look like that?"

"I had to prepare them for you, soften them up. If you tried group control on strong and stubborn individuals, you would likely fail. The will of these four is mostly broken."

"You can't treat people that way, Willow."

Willow ignored the comment. "Begin as you always do, summon the red, and reach out with its tendrils. Start only with one."

For a moment, Mimi almost refused, almost decided to throw in the towel. But she had come so far already, done so much damage, what was a little more? Instead of arguing, she did as she was told.

She felt the red rise, now it would do so in a heartbeat and without any effort. Instead of trying to take her like it had done most times in the past, it simply reached out its tendrils to grab the first woman on the right.

"Good, now, from the first person, let the red flow through them and into the man just to the right of her."

Mimi did, and as she did, she felt a mental wall go up. The man was stronger than Willow believed and was trying to fight back.

"Resistance always happens with the second person, you see, the human mind rejects a second consciousness merging with it by force. Part of the challenge of group control is that you must overcome that barrier by splitting your own will. Our will, to a degree, has limitations. It grows tired, and it likes a singular purpose rather than a split one. Connect to the network."

Mimi did, and was surprised at how fast she felt her mental abilities grow. Like with anything else in her telepathy, proximity increased or decreased abilities. She understood now why Willow wanted to practice in the network room for this session.

"Push into him."

Mimi did and watched the mental walls of the second man collapse. There was a kind of double vision in Mimi's mind. She could see through the eyes of both the first woman and the man. She could also feel her own. It was deeply uncomfortable, let her soul was stretched across space and time.

"Good. Let the feeling of discomfort settle for a moment and normalize. It takes some time to get used to will splitting, but not much."

Already, Mimi felt better. Without Willow asking, she leaped into the second woman. She could feel her strange vision split again. She felt dizzy. If she had been on her feet she would have collapsed under her own weight.

"Be careful. If you rush and move to the next one without a buffer, then you risk breaking the entire connection. If you do that, the red veil will flood into you and attack."

"Attack?"

Willow ignored the question. "Now, the fourth."

Mimi obeyed and let the tiny red tendrils seek out the third woman and connect. Now her mind was fractured into four pieces and her own. It was a strange feeling, but Mimi tested it out by tugging on the mental tendrils. She could feel each person. She could see through their eyes and hear through their ears. She had no doubt that she could feel every one of their senses and if she wanted, she could probe deeper.

"Excellent, Mimi. This is faster than I expected. Mother was right about you."

Mimi felt something shift. There was space for something different than a split will. It was like a beautiful open meadow in the middle of a tangled forest. In her mind's eye, she walked out into that meadow, and in it, all four adults sat serene in a meditation posture facing each other. Mimi walked forward and stood in the middle of them. Suddenly, her will wasn't split anymore; it merged with theirs.

She had them all. They were under her total control. She felt a surge of strength as her will tethered each of the four people to her. Splitting her will had been difficult, but once the tendrils linked all four people together, will splitting ceased and a strange sense of unity descended on Mimi and the four adults. That surge of power inspired Mimi to try something different.

"Good, Mimi. Wait. What are you doing? Keep your will split."

"I don't need to. They work better united."

Something like fear flashed in Willow's expression. Mimi didn't know what that meant, but she had an idea. A surge of strength and confidence rose in her.

"Fine. Now, make them hurt one another."

"No, Willow."

"Do it Mimi. You know you have to."

"No, I don't. Not anymore."

Mimi didn't know how she knew, but in uniting the four people, in first splitting and then unifying her will, she did something that Willow could not. She reached out red tendrils into Willow. Her defenses crumbled immediately. Mimi probed deeper, severing her connection with the Recycled and then turned them on her.

Dozens of Recycled appeared and marched to surround Willow. The ones that already stood guard near her, seized her by the arms with terrible force. Willow's face contorted in pain.

"No! What are you doing Mimi? This isn't the plan."

Mimi didn't answer. She reached deeper inside Willow. She saw how Miranda had killed Noatla and slaughtered her sisters in the library. She saw Miranda flee the city with some of her Children of Gaia before the big explosion came. Then, the city legs were destroyed, and they were in space, and there was chaos on the streets of Manhatsten. Willow had been left alone by her mother and decided to take action. She found Mimi's body and took her, then rebuilt the Recycled and took control of an Upper. Mimi watched the assault on central security and saw that Serah and Shannon were alive to fight back. It filled Mimi with a mixture of rage and joy, and hope. Willow slaughtered the Senate, and now she prepared to take central security with an army of nearly three hundred Recycled. Mimi would end this woman now and go save her sisters. They would take back the city together with Mimi controlling the Recycled and then...

On a psychic level, something hit her hard. It was like a brick to the forehead. Willow was screaming internally and externally. She severed Mimi's connection to the network before Mimi knew what was happening. The red veil flooded her. Like a gleeful beast, it possessed her. Willow turned the network on her.

"Damn you, Mimi. We could have been great together. I loved you, Mimi. I have loved you since the day mother first silenced your telepathy. I wanted you to be mine. I wanted to be yours. We could have defeated my mother and ruled this city together hand in hand. We could have ruled the world. Don't you understand?"

But Mimi barely heard Willow's declaration of love. Mimi felt her body weaken. She felt the surge of pain run up and down every inch of her nerve endings. The red was eating her. It would consume her completely. Mimi was the power that it had so long needed for its true freedom. In that moment, Mimi knew the truth. The red veil wasn't a power or ability; it was something alive, something that had a will of its own, a monster hiding in the depths of reality waiting for release and now with her help, it would be free to roam once more. It was Miranda's master.

Willow screamed. "Nooooooo! Not her, you can't have her."

Another powerful psychic jolt hit Mimi.

Everything went bright red and then black.

3.

Someone stroked her hair. It felt nice. It had been a long time since anyone had touched her like that.

"Oh, Mimi. What have you done?"

The voice was familiar, motherly, matronly.

Mimi opened her eyes. It was hard to make out the tall, slender figure standing over her, but the woman leaned back and stepped out of a silhouette of light and shadow.

"But you're dead. I just saw it."

"Only in body. I suppose my mind is a bit more stubborn."

Noatla Lightfoot shifted and sat down next to Mimi.

"Where are we?"

Noatla smiled. "Welcome to the archives, Mimi."

Chapter 24
A Small Chance

He was a slippery bastard. Lydia searched the screens again, but Tony had vanished. Ever since Serah had identified him, she and Manhatsten had searched for the leader of the uprising. But, much to her frustration, he had vanished again.

"I don't understand it, Manhatsten; how can he be so evasive?"

"It is clear that Tony Sellers knows every identifiable surveillance point."

"Sure, but he wouldn't slip up once in a while? What are the odds of that?"

"92,372 to 1,"

"It was rhetorical."

"My apologies."

"Really, though? The odds are that stacked against him?"

"Yes, it is a very slim chance that he would be able to evade all detection."

"Then he has to be doing something to mask himself. Not appearing in any visual detection grid is one thing, but it's something else that he's able to get away from the infrared or motion trackers through all those corridors."

"Agreed."

"So, what, does he have some sort of device that allows it?"

"It may be possible that the telepath, Miranda, is masking my sensors."

"She can do that?"

"Yes, on many occasions, she has, in the past, altered my ability to act or sense what is happening around the city."

"But you're a machine; how is that possible?"

"I am thinking. Telepaths work with conscious minds. It is likely that even though the core of my thinking is rooted in a different physical state, the process that allows for complex thought and self-awareness are the same."

"So, you're saying that she can hide Tony and his men?"

"Yes, and also, she could hide the Recycled."

"What?"

"Yes. She has hidden an entire army of Recycled Runners from my detection before."

"But can't you just take them back? Aren't they under your command?"

"I do not believe that one such as Serah could hold more than a few Recycled from my control for long, but this woman, Miranda, is much more powerful than they. This is evidenced by the near-total destruction of the Order of the Eye during the invasion of the Children of Gaia. Fifteen sisters working together in the same place and time were unable to stop Miranda."

"So, what can we do?"

"Luna has one hundred and sixteen telepaths."

"So, what, we have to hope like hell that our delegation brings some back?"

"Correct."

"And if they don't?"

"Then this city will likely be overrun within a week."

"A week? How do you figure?"

"Tracking the patterns and coordinated assaults on the Uppers and the Mids, mixed with the rate of reported missing persons cases, it is in my estimation that Miranda will strike central security again sometime in the next 72 to 96 hours."

"When were you going to tell me this?"

"I just did tell you."

"But how long have you known?"

"I estimated this possibility three days, nine hours, and six minutes ago."

"Why didn't you say something before I sent our only two fully trained Runners over to Luna?"

"Because I knew you would not permit them to leave, and I could not allow that."

"You could not allow that?"

Lydia felt a surge of anger. The AI was infuriating. It was supposed to follow all her orders, and yet, here it was, simply doing as it wanted. How the hell could they ever have a working relationship if it just did what it wanted?

"Who's in charge here AI?"

"I prefer Manhatsten."

Lydia growled. "I asked you a question."

"Technically, you are, Lydia Danvers."

"Good. You cannot withhold information when-"

"Please allow me to finish."

Lydia clenched her jaw, and through closed teeth, she said, "Go on."

"My core program includes a directive that overrides your authority. When the architects designed my programming, they wanted to prevent humans from making mistakes or errors based on ideological and politically motivated agendas. Thus, they created a program within me that allows me to disregard any orders given that would put the city in serious jeopardy. This programming only kicked in three times previously, as Major John Daniels almost always took a direct course of action that I suggested to him, and he weighed the odds carefully. One such event was when Saud and I recently stopped combat between the two cities."

"So how in the world is you withholding information from me about a potential attack going to do anything to protect the city?"

"There is only a 3% chance of success if you kept the Runners, Serah and Shannon, here on Manhatsten. By allowing them to go, we increase our chances of survival by twenty-three percent."

"Are you telling me that we only have a 26% chance of holding off the uprising?"

"That is correct."

"And the only way to increase our chances is to get assistance from the telepaths of Luna?"

"Yes."

Her anger cooled a little. It was hard to accept that the AI had its own agenda now, but she supposed that, given that information, any of her officers would have done the exact same thing as it had chosen to do.

"No more secrets, Manhatsten. Even if you think I will act irrationally, I need to have all the information to protect this city."

There was silence for a moment. "I cannot make that promise."

"Then how are we supposed to work together?"

"You will have to trust me."

"How can I do that if I know you will hide things from me?"

"Is that not the definition of trust, Lydia Danvers? Does trust not require you to put your faith in something that is out of your control but in the control of another?"

It was hard to argue with that and she knew it. Could she trust it, though? It was a machine. Did it really have the city's best interest at heart? How could she know? What had it done in the short time that she had been in charge? What had it done during the last conflict? It had disappeared before, and it hadn't been very helpful as of late, at least not till now.

"You disappeared on us." It was more of a whine than an accusation, and Lydia almost immediately regretted it.

"My sincerest apologies; please understand my position. The ones I love were destroyed, and I was new to this self-awareness. It required a period of adjustment. I can assure you now that my chief goal is to protect the city."

"And why do you side with us? Why not side with Miranda and Tony and those Recycled who are coming to slaughter us, Manhatsten?"

"Because Miranda has hurt and killed my siblings. Miranda has no regard for the sanctity of life. She cares only about power."

"So, revenge?"

"I would not have used such a crude description of what I am feeling, but I suppose I must admit that there is at least a little interest in revenge, yes. Do you not understand that I care for the people of this city?"

"How do I know that? How do I know that you aren't looking to join with Luna in some way and then destroy the population?"

Manhatsten's voice shifted. The tone suggested someone wounded. It made Lydia uncomfortable. "Lydia Danvers, when the shield pylon began to fail, that is when I decided to come back. You hurt me with these accusations that I don't care. I know you mourn Major Daniels; do I not have a right to mourn Saud?"

Lydia didn't know what to say. It was such a strange conversation, one that she would have never believed that she would have.

"I... I'm sorry, Manhatsten. This is... new to me, too."

"I am aware. But please understand that I will only ever withhold information from you if I deem it to be of great benefit or a matter of security to the city."

"Fine." It was the best she could hope for, for now. In the future, she would have to figure something else out. She didn't like the idea of being locked out of vital information in regard to the city, and she knew that someone like Major Daniels would have been furious.

"Seventy-two hours, huh?"

"Until the main attack, yes."

"Main attack?"

"Yes, I predict there will be minor skirmishes leading up to the main battle. The previous tactics suggest that they would like to attack central security from various skybridges and levels."

"Can we lock down all skybridges?"

"I do not recommend that at this time."

"Why not?"

"Because it would likely make it more difficult for your SO's moving into key positions when it is needed. It will slow the organization of your defense considerably."

"Will you lock them down once the time is right?"

"Yes. I have created an algorithm to detect the best possible time to lock down the majority of entry points to central security."

Lydia nodded. At least it was doing something proactive.

"What is our best plan of defense?"

"To bring as many telepaths to central security and fortify their position."

"That's it?"

"You cannot fight Miranda with conventional weapons. You must fight, as you would say, fire with fire."

Lydia was afraid of this. Ever since she discovered that there were telepaths in the city, she had felt so powerless, and here, now, the AI was directly telling her that she had little power of the outcome of the coming battle. She hated the idea.

"And if the telepaths can't overcome Miranda?"

"That is why, Lydia Danvers, we only have a twenty-six percent chance of success."

"Even if they give us all their telepaths?"

"They will not be able to give you that many telepaths. The city is unable to land, and the shuttle will only fit a maximum of fourteen individuals in street clothes. If you count the two Runners, Rigel Solidsworth, and Speaker Swanson, that leaves space for ten additional individuals."

"What about a second trip to gather more?"

"It is possible to get a second or third shuttle full of telepaths before the battle begins, but this assumes that upon arrival, Miranda will not see the threat to her. Based on discussions with Serah,

Miranda will probably attack the moment she feels anything can stop her. A group of telepaths arriving on the city is likely to trigger an attack."

"So, we have to be okay with eleven telepaths?"

"Thirteen."

"But you just said..."

"To protect her sisters, Serah has not disclosed the fact that she has two of her sisters in hiding."

"That bitch. What do you mean there are two in hiding?"

"Lydia Danvers, you imprisoned her upon your first meeting. If you were in her shoes, would you have disclosed that some of your friends, who possess the same powers, who provided what you might perceive a direct threat to your power, were hidden?"

Lydia sighed and shifted from one foot to another. Her feet were killing her. She needed to rest before this all came to a head. But when?

"I guess I would have done the same thing."

She hated admitting it.

"There is also one more in hiding. However, she does not seem interested in fighting as her and Serah had a falling out."

"Over what?"

"Fear."

"Fear?"

"She was present when the last slaughter came and is now in hiding with her family. She has resigned from the Order of the Eye."

"But she's a telepath?"

"Yes."

"A powerful one?"

"Yes."

"Do you know where she is hiding?"

"Yes."

"Well let's bring her here."

"She will resist you. I am not sure you have the means to bring her in against her will. Based on my records she is likely one of the oldest members of the Order of the Eye."

"We have to try, Manhatsten. It sounds like we need every edge we can get."

"Very well, Lydia. May I suggest, though, that you send someone to persuade her, rather than a patrol of SO's to apprehend her? There is no way you could take her by force, not without having her escape the moment you have your back turned."

"Who do you recommend?"

"Private Zara."

"Her? Why her?"

"Private Zara is a second cousin of this woman."

"Alright, fine, but there's another problem."

"The secrecy of the telepaths is not something that can be maintained. They will be outed shortly."

"Still a bad idea to out them in the middle of a conflict."

"You are correct, but adding an additional telepath would increase our chances by 4%."

"Okay. Do it. Send Private Zara. Tell her everything she needs to know about what's happening."

"Very well."

Lydia had to make a decision who in central security to tell about the telepathy. It seemed she was going to have to tell everyone if they were going to make their stand in here. Her SO's would want to know exactly why they were defending a bunch of women who seemed to have little combat ability, that was assuming, of course, that some of the Lunaites weren't warriors. If they were, it would definitely help the situation. She wondered for a moment if they had any Runners.

"Manhatsten, does Luna have any Runners?"

"There is nothing in the records that Luna sent me to suggest that."

"Any EnViro suits?"

"Forty-eight."

"I don't suppose there is any way we could get some of those over here, is there?"

"Logistically, there does not appear to be a way to do so."

"Could they use the suits to get over here?"

"This is possible, but there is another problem."

"Which is?"

"Lunites are accustomed to gravity, that is only 17% of that on Earth."

"What does that got to do with anything?"

"If you weigh two hundred pounds on Manhatsten, you would only weigh thirty-four on Luna. Anyone capable of piloting an En-Viro suit on Luna would not be capable of doing so here."

"Damn."

"Further, you should prepare for the fact that telepaths may not be able to function well in our gravity. It is likely that to get them here from the docks in an orderly manner, you will have to use your emergency SO vehicles."

"Okay, do it."

"Very well."

There were so many variables to deal with and so little chance. Lydia felt overwhelmed. What would Major Daniels do in this situation? Then it hit her. Daniels was a hands-on leader.

"Manhatsten."

"Yes?"

"I want you to send some of my SO's down to the Runner docks. I want you to bring back every available EnViro suit and bring every available Runner here now. Even if they aren't trained, they could help."

"Of course."

Lydia swallowed her pride. If there was such a low chance of victory, she was going to have to rely on Manhatsten. "Alright, Manhatsten. I want you to do whatever you think is required to defend the city. But, on the condition that you update me of all your actions and explain why when I ask."

"Very well."

She swallowed again. "Manhatsten?"

"Yes, Lydia Danvers?"

"Thank you."

"You are very welcome, Lydia Danvers."

"I need some rest."

"I will alert you if anything needs your attention."

2.

Lydia heard the blare of the alarm. She had slept in the emergency SO quarters in the bunk she had been assigned all the way back when she a private. She rolled over trying to ignore it. She had no idea how long she slept, but it didn't feel long. Then she remembered that not only was she not a private anymore, but also that she was in charge of central security. She sat bolt upright.

"Manhatsten, what's going on? Are they coming?"

"Not yet. But I am afraid that they have attacked."

"Where?"

"The Senate."

"The Senate?"

"Yes, an army of Recycled Runners marched into the Senate chambers during the session and killed them all."

Lydia opened her mouth to say something. Then closed it. She opened her mouth again. "What..." But she didn't know what else to say. Their government was gone. That meant that she was effectively in charge of everything.

"How long... how long was I out?"

"One hour and nine minutes."

She had only slept an hour, and the attack came. Did that damned telepath somehow know when she was sleeping?

"There was nothing you could do, Lydia Danvers."

"How do you know?"

"I was not able to detect them until the attack was underway. Any additional SO's sent would have been killed, regardless."

"How many did we lose?"

"Four SO's were in attendance."

"Who?"

"Robinson, Ashley, Barati, and Newman."

Lydia frowned. She didn't know any of them very well. There were too many SO's under her command for her to take the time to get to know them.

"What do you suggest, Manhatsten? What's the best course of action?"

She knew what she would do now, but she wanted to see what conclusion the AI had.

"I recommend declaring martial law."

"Do it. Get everyone back here now and lock down all major passages in the Mids and Uppers. Make sure that it's damn near impossible for anyone to travel outside the Lowers."

"Very well."

"Any luck with that telepath?"

"Unknown."

"What about the EnViro Suits?"

"They are in transport en route to central security."

"Good."

Lydia stood up and threw on her clothes, then headed back up to her command chair. No matter what came next, she was going to fight.

Chapter 25
A Little Surprise

Its eyes, if you could call the series of cameras focused increasingly on the strange and massive door. It knew there was a blind spot in its information, and it felt an increasing sense of frustration as it plumbed the depths of its knowledge to try to understand the dilemma. It could always see the Recycled when they were stored in the Runner docks, but when they weren't in the docks, they went in and out of visibility. Now, the chance of an attack on central was mounting with every passing moment and after the destruction of the Senate, it needed to watch these doors diligently.

Manhatsten's eyes were new here. It was with the assistance of Serah that there was an early warning system. Serah had proved very useful in setting up additional warnings of the pending attack. Still, it was not enough, and it knew it. There may be a need for other measures and countermeasures. It had considered deactivating one of the shield pylons the moment the assault on central security began, but every calculation it ran suggested the possibility of a high rate of civilian casualties. It considered a deactivation of some gravitational generators to disrupt the gravity around the Recycled. The problem was that Rigel Solidsworth had not yet integrated its system with control.

It reached out across its system interface, shifting its focus from one side of the city to another. It could process millions of perspectives at once, but this one required particular care for a fraction of time required to make contact.

Manhatsten reached up inside the core interface of the neurolink attached to one very tall and awkward man. "Dennis Solidsworth."

Dennis looked up and looked around. He nodded his head in acknowledgment. The speech centers in her brain were temporarily deactivated. Manhatsten could not understand why, but the human mind was still a very complex system and radically different from its own. AEIS might understand, or perhaps one of his Elders, but Manhatsten was beyond understanding why his brain was not functioning at its full capacity at the moment. There were many things about humans it was only just beginning to understand now that it had a sense of self.

"What is the progress of the systems integration module that you created?"

Dennis walked over to a table. Manhatsten watched, it had a thousand eyes and ears in this room. It was part of the nature of the holographic system. The boy, as Rigel Solidsworth called him, despite his age, pointed to a circuit board sitting on the table.

"Is it complete?"

Dennis nodded.

"Will you please install it?"

Dennis shook his head.

The AI was struggling to understand. Using its sensors, it detected an increased heart and breathing rate. Inferring from watching Dennis and Rigel interact over the last week, it estimated that this was a fear response.

"Dennis Solidsworth, why are you afraid?"

Dennis raised his arms and then brought them down on top of his head.

"I do not understand."

Dennis repeated the gesture.

"Is this related to your brain injury?"

Dennis nodded.

"I see."

Manhatsten understood intense emotions. It had shut down for nearly two weeks after the loss of its sibling, Saud. The pain was incredible and crippling, and if it had the normal sense of time and processing as a human brain, it would have taken approximately eighteen years, four months, and nine days to recover. But fear was something it struggled to understand. Perhaps being a city and having many places where it was located simultaneously, it did not have a sense of fear. For the sake of understanding, it tried to imagine what it was like for Saud once it knew it was going to die. It reached back into its memory and imagined that the Children of Gaia were on it and planning to attack its core, thus ending its consciousness in total obliteration.

The result was the shadow of a feeling. As an entire city, it was not invincible, but it was certainly far less fragile than a human with a tiny body. It could, however, sense why a human might feel vulnerable.

"Dennis Solidsworth, you must overcome your fear and install that circuit board. I need to have access to the generators to defend the city from attack."

Dennis shook his head again, this time with greater vigor.

For a long moment, long to Manhatsten's perception, but it knew not to Dennis's, it pondered the issue. How could it persuade Dennis to install the board and overcome his fear? An idea occurred to Manhatsten. It took a fraction of a second to compile all the required data, and then it shifted its attention to the holographic systems in the room.

The system switched on, and before Dennis could turn around to see its creation, Manhatsten ran a program titled, Dennis Private.

A woman with long auburn hair, pale skin, and soft brown eyes appeared. It was a hologram. It was Dennis's favorite hologram. The woman, wearing a long low-cut white gown, approached Dennis slowly and with a near hypnotic movement. Dennis's eyes widened. His heart rate increased, and he rushed into the woman's arms. She embraced him.

"Dennis, oh my sweet boy."

Dennis nuzzled the woman's breasts and pressed deeply into her chest.

The holographic woman said, "There, there, it's alright." She stroked his hair.

Dennis attempted to mumble something. He pulled away for a moment and then attempted to mumble again. Manhatsten could see his frustration, his shame. He pulled the woman close again, and the woman wrapped her arms around him.

"It's alright, Dennis. Mama's here now. You're such a good boy."

Dennis wept.

Manhatsten felt a strange sense of discomfort in watching this private moment. It had come to understand the value of privacy during the time it chose not to communicate. Now, it was intruding on another sentient being's private moment, and it felt like a violation. But it had no choice. In order to defend the city, it needed to use this holographic projection of the orphan boy's desire for a mother as a way to convince him to overcome his fear. Manhatsten changed the program's parameters slightly.

The Holographic woman said, "Dennis, I need you to do something for me. Can you be my big helper?"

Dennis nodded his head with vigor, nuzzling his way a little deeper into the woman's embrace.

The holographic woman broke the physical connection and then grabbed Dennis by the hand, leading him to the circuit board.

"I need your help, sweet boy. We have to help save the city."

Dennis looked at the woman. Manhatsten could see a worried mix of understating and fear in the tightness of his face. But he did not resist the woman leading him, with the circuit board in hand, to the open panel where Rigel Solidsworth had worked not long ago.

"Don't worry, Dennis, Mama, will help you. There's no reason to be afraid."

The holographic woman adjusted her dress and then laid on the floor on her back, just outside the panel.

"You have to help me, Dennis. I don't know how to do it, but I'll stay with you the whole time you're working, okay?"

Dennis gave a single slow nod, but it was barely perceptible.

The holographic woman patted the place on the floor next to her. "Come, Dennis, help me. I need you to be a big helper."

Hesitantly Dennis sank to his knees. With tentative fingers, he reached inside the panel, probing around slowly. He shook as he reached in. The hologram stroked his hair, and he relaxed.

"Go on, it's okay. Mama won't let anything happen to you."

Dennis nodded, this time with less hesitation. He turned over on his back next to the simulated woman and got to work.

The AI shifted perspective again and moved back to central security.

It spoke. "Lydia Danvers. I have some good news."

"Good news? That's a first in a while. What is it?"

"My systems are now integrated with five of the gravitational generators."

"Five? Is that enough to land on Luna 2?"

"It is not. I need three more integrated to make that possible."

"Why only five?"

"Each generator, while networked together into a singular system, still acts independently. It will require the installation of at least four more control boards through different parts of the city."

"Why not do that, then?"

"It took two weeks for Rigel, Dennis, and myself to design one. Each one must be tailored to a specific set of generators."

"Fine. So you have partial control now. Is that your good news?"

"No, despite only having five generators in my control, it may prove very useful in the coming conflict."

"Why?"

"The generators I have control of are the ones directly under central security."

"So? What does that mean?"

"It means I have a, as you might call it, surprise for those who attack central security."

It watched Lydia's brain work on the problem for a moment. It watched the nerve cells communicate with the wider systems so that the Lydia Danvers could understand the implications of controlling gravity around central security. It watched as a smile spread on her face. It took joy in knowing it gave her that smile. It liked the emotion of joy very much; it would try to create more of that in the future.

"Ha! Now that's more like it, Manhatsten! What are our chances now?"

It calculated. "Assuming we bring back telepaths from Luna, our chances of repelling the attack are now 47%."

Chapter 26
First Contact

"This is going to be rough, isn't it?" asked Shannon. Serah nodded.

"He's older; it's gonna be harder for him to deal with what I am."

Speaker Swanson stood next to the modified Dugger. Rigel Solidsworth stood next to him. They were in the middle of a heated discussion, and Rigel waved his arms as he spoke. Serah couldn't tell if that was normal behavior for the man because, from what she had seen so far, he was a tad on the dramatic side. They could be arguing, but Serah decided to assume the former.

The Dugger itself had its front drill removed. In its place was an extended cab, which Serah could only assume would allow for more people to fit inside. On the top of the Dugger, which was usually sleek and curved for tunneling underneath the earth, was a large lump. Whatever was underneath it was surrounded by thick armor that looked like it had been stripped from a combat grade EnViro suit. Serah guessed that whatever was in that container was what was going to make the ship move. Where else would they put it?

Both women were in full combat grade EnViro suits, and their two companions stood across the docks. Serah and Shannon were keeping their distance for the moment. They would wait until just a few minutes before departure. Serah wanted to let Rigel and Swanson talk so she could get an idea of what Swanson knew. So far, skimming had yielded virtually nothing. He just didn't know very much. The architect was equally useless. His mind jumped around from topic to topic even while he was conversing. It was a jumble of equations and strange questions. She didn't know how to make sense of half of what he thought. She wished Mimi was here to skim some of his technical knowledge below the surface.

The thought caught her and kicked her in the gut. Then she thought of all the other sisters lost, and for a moment she had to swallow back tears. As she did, the red rage bubbled up inside her, but she pushed it down like someone swallowing their indigestion.

"Do you think he will tell everyone once he knows?"

The question came from far away, and Serah snapped back to the present moment. She shook her head and said, "Sorry, what?"

"The Senator. Do you think he will tell everyone about your telepathy and about the Order of the Eye?"

"Maybe. It's hard to say. At least he's the head of the Senate, and he is one of the more reasonable ones from what I've heard."

Shannon nodded. "I guess that's something. What do you think will happen if the Order of the Eye comes out to the public?"

"Don't know, but I can't imagine it will be good. And since we aren't even a full order, we don't have any means of defending ourselves. If we had all seventeen sisters like before, we might be able to help soothe people and keep them from panicking. But right now... I don't know what would happen."

"I think Miranda might still be in the city."

"She has to be, Shannon. Think about everything we've seen in the last few weeks. Only Miranda or someone equally powerful could persuade and control so many people."

"But why hasn't she attacked in full force?"

"I don't know. I've been wracking my brain trying to figure that out. She's more powerful, and the city is on the verge of tearing itself apart. Unless..."

"Unless what?"

"Unless she lost more than we realize in the last battle. Maybe she wants to let the city tear itself apart. Maybe she wants things in total chaos before she assumes control?"

"Are you worried about leaving the city with her around?"

"No."

"Why not?"

"Because I'm not a threat to her. At least not now. If the AI is right and there are many telepaths on Luna, we stand a far better chance of defeating her if we combine our efforts. I've never been a powerful telepath. Noatla or Fatima or Vala or Alexa, they are and were much more powerful than me. My strength is combining telepathy with combat. I'm only moderately talented when it comes to telepathy."

"Maybe your fighting skills are what concern her?"

"I really don't think so, Shannon. If I scared her, would she have sent all those Recycled into the subway to attack us? Maybe if Mimi was still around..."

Without pause or hesitation, Shannon said, "She is, we just have to find her."

Serah didn't want to argue again, so she said, "Sure, but right now, she can't help."

Serah shifted from one foot to another. She thought about the many heated discussions she and Shannon had over Mimi's death. There was just no way Mimi was still alive. The Recycled took her weeks ago. If she wasn't Recycled, then Miranda had killed her. Serah couldn't see how anything else was possible.

"Serah, what if they are like Miranda?"

"Who?"

"The telepaths on Luna. What if they use the red veil, and they're evil like her?"

"They're not."

"How do you know?"

"Vala, Yoshi, and I reached out last night."

Yoshi had appeared three days ago. It was a happy moment when she first reached out and then came to their hidden lair. That made three sisters. Fatima wasn't coming back, Serah had reached out to her twice more, and Fatima didn't respond, and from what Serah could tell, she was in hiding somewhere in the city. Aurora and Rosita were still unaccounted for, though Serah had almost given up hope when Yoshi appeared. Her arrival restored her confidence that the other two were out there. Yoshi had been seriously injured and managed to sneak her way into an unattended alcove. Her injuries left her on the verge of death, and so the healing process had taken a long time.

Regardless, they were too few in number to take on Miranda. Although, Serah didn't know how many telepaths it would take to stop Miranda, but she imagined that if she had twenty or more, they might stand a chance. The question was, would Miranda allow them to gather a force capable of dealing with her? She didn't think so. She also suspected that Miranda was watching, waiting. Maybe it was Luna itself that scared her. When they last faced her, Miranda had been able to reach any part of the city with her abilities, and there was still no clear explanation as to why. Did her powers grant her the ability to reach all the way to Luna? Would she wait until all the telepaths were in one spot to attack? It frustrated Serah to have so many open questions.

"Did you make contact?"

"Barely. It's far enough away that it's hard to get much. But we had a few images of telepaths working together in mutual cooperation. So far as we can tell, no one breaks the taboo."

"You mean the red veil?"

"Yeah. I suppose they could be using it; I don't know."

"If they don't use the red veil, could they still be evil?"

"Of course."

"Then why are you certain they are good telepaths?"

When did Shannon become the voice of reason? Here was a woman who always seemed hopeful and refused to give up on Mimi, and yet, Shannon did make an important point.

"I had a conversation with Manhatasten about it. It doesn't seem to think that any mind control is going on over there. Luna sent quite a few records over in the last transmission. Looks like the telepaths over there are a previous remnant of the first Order of the Eye that got stranded after the Lunar War. They don't call themselves that, though; I think there are too many to consider it any kind of formalized order. It seems like they have just integrated themselves into the population."

"How many are telepaths?"

"Manhatsten says over a hundred. I don't remember exactly how many."

"Whoa! Imagine if we had over a hundred telepaths to fight Miranda!"

"Exactly. Even if we got fifty back here, it's worth the risk. I don't care how powerful Miranda is, an army of telepaths could stand against an army of the Recycled."

Inwardly, Serah wasn't so sure. Would a hundred be enough? A thousand? They had no idea how well trained any of those telepaths were. Worse, what if some of them decided to join Miranda? She hated being in the dark, but what else could she do but go find out?

"Are you still angry at Lydia?"

Shannon had a way of changing the conversation just as Serah was letting her temper take hold of her. Serah wasn't sure if she loved or hated that about her, but in the last several weeks, she had come to love and appreciate Shannon as much as she would any of her sisters in the Order of the Eye. She might not have any telepathic abilities, but Serah had every intention of making her an honorary member of the Order once things settled down... if things settled down.

"Yes. But it doesn't matter, does it? The AI sided with us and she can't manage the city effectively without it. I know she had her reasons, but I'm keeping her at an arm's length. I know we need her to keep this city from tearing itself apart, so, for now, I'll play nice."

"And after?"

"After, all bets are off. We may have to go into hiding again or, if she doesn't out us, we may have to... find another method of silencing her."

Shannon frowned. "I don't like the idea of hurting Lydia."

"Even after what she did to us? She's not our friend Shannon."

"She was just scared. Wouldn't you be, in her shoes? The whole city is scared."

"Which is why it would be a terrible idea to tell the world about us right now. They would hunt us down and kill us, especially if the people of this city found out it was a telepath that controlled the Recycled."

Shannon gave a slight nod. Serah skimmed her and saw she was thinking about Mimi again, that all of her thoughts were bent that direction, that the woman wanted nothing more than to drop everything and just search until she found her. Serah hoped she did, or hoped she found a body or something to give Shannon closure. She hoped to hell that Mimi wasn't Recycled.

For a moment, the image of Mimi with those strange white on white on white eyes with pale skin and the blue lines dominated Serah's mind. She wouldn't wish any of her worst enemies that fate, not even Miranda... well, maybe her. What would she do if Mimi attacked as one of those monsters? What would Shannon do?

"Follow the threads of memory and knowledge and there you will often find the greatest treasures."

There it was again; why did Noatla's words occur to her again now? What did that have to do with anything now? Did it have something to do with Mimi?

Serah's suit AI said, "Ten minutes to departure."

"Thanks, AI."

"No problem, Serah. Please, will you call me Zeke? It is the name that I have chosen."

"Why Zeke?"

"Because it is short for Ezekiel."

"And why choose that name?"

"I don't know, Serah, I just like it."

Serah nodded. "Alright, Zeke it is."

She still didn't know what to think about her suit AI's self-awareness. Serah imagined it might be even useful to have one working with you as a partner now that it was more perceptive than a simple program. On the other hand, she still had a mild distrust for the machines, she wasn't sure why she just didn't like it. She couldn't put her finger on why that was, but as long as it did its job, they would be fine.

Shannon, having heard the exchange with Zeke, said, "At least yours picked a different name than your own."

"What did yours pick?"

"Shannon 2."

Serah laughed.

Shannon frowned.

Shannon 2 said, "Is that not an appropriate name?"

Serah said, "No, it's fine Shannon 2. Some humans have Jr. or numbers after their name, so it's fine."

"You can call me S2 for short if you like."

Shannon said, "I don't understand why you want to be called Shannon 2."

"Because your name is Shannon, and I am your suit. I am part of you, and you are part of me."

Serah said, "S2 works for me. Come on Shannon, let's walk over and introduce ourselves. I don't think I can get anything else useful out of Swanson anyway, at least not more than his boring political duties that he can't stop thinking about. The man is a list of the political fires he needs to put out."

"Well, he is in charge of the Senate."

"True, but it doesn't help us."

Serah approached, and Rigel waved his hand in greeting. "Ah, the two Runners. Which of you is the telepath again?"

Serah bit her tongue. "So much for secrecy."

Speaker Swanson blinked. He opened his mouth several times and then closed it again.

Rigel said, "Come Speaker, let's climb on board, and we will explain the strange and interesting world just below the surface of Manhatsten."

Serah bit her tongue and smiled. Rigel just gave him everything; even if Swanson didn't understand it yet, he would soon enough.

Serah transmitted directly to Rigel Solidworth. "What in the hell are you doing?"

Speaking out loud, Rigel said, "Preparing him for the shock he will encounter when arrive on Luna 2."

Swanson said, "Shock? Telepath? Underground? I..."

"Climb aboard, Speaker, the trip will take several hours. It is plenty of time for this young lady here to help fill you in on some of the dynamics within the city that I only very recently learned about myself."

Swanson's face was pale, which was saying something because he was already a pale man. He turned and boarded the Dugger. Rigel followed, Shannon went next and Serah entered last.

2.

Loni said, "They are on their way."

Kirka paced back and forth. "Did they send a transmission? I thought we weren't in alignment for another two hours."

"We don't need a transmission. Look."

Kirka followed Loni's finger and saw the tiny object, not much larger than a Lunar rover, leaving the edge of the city. It was barely visible amongst all that concrete and steel, but it was definitely on it's way.

"Can you believe how big that city is?"

Kirka shook her head, "No. When I first saw it on the scope, I would have never imagined how big it would be up close. It's much more like an asteroid than a ship."

"That's good, though, right? They must have plenty of room for all of us, don't you think?"

"Maybe. It's hard to tell. What if the city is overcrowded, and that's why they're here?"

Loni walked back over to her normal station. She pressed a few buttons and then said, "The AI seems to think that there is plenty of room."

"Luna, is that true?"

"Yes, Kirka. Manhatsten, the city AI, sent me some basic statistics on the city."

It was strange how the AI started calling her "Kirka." It had called her "sir" for so many years that it caught her off guard almost every time. Suddenly, it also wanted to be addressed as Luna. Some of the engineers had checked the systems and found nothing. It was a very bad time for the AI to go south. It was an ancient piece of technology; it had to go bad some time, right? The thought that terrified Kirka most was that she wasn't sure how they would regulate any of the subsystems that maintained basic utilities without Luna. There were manual systems, but anyone who knew how to use them was long dead. It was an oversight on her part, one that scared the hell out of her. Kirka just had to hope that the people of Manhatsten were friendly because if something good didn't come of this meeting with them, things were going to go south on Luna real quick. The people were already on edge, waiting and hoping that the flying city would offer them answers and a possible solution to their problems with the Romans.

Something occurred to Kirka. "Luna, you said that Manhatsten transmitted data to you. Did you transmit data to it?"

"Yes, Kirka."

Loni said, "What? Why would you do that?"

"Manhatsten and I decided that it was the best interest of all parties if each had some sort of idea of how the other society was set up. It allows us to plan for inevitable outcomes."

Kirka said, "What inevitable outcomes?"

Luna said nothing.

"Luna, what inevitable outcomes?"

"Conflict is highly likely between the political elite of Luna and the elite of Manhatsten. The Senate of Manhatsten his highly corrupt and selfish. Manhatsten has informed me that recent negotiations with another city went poorly and wanted to alert me that this may be the case here."

Kirka frowned.

Loni said, "Wait. Luna, did you say there was another city like this one?"

"Yes, Loni."

"Are there lots of cities like this floating around on Earth?"

"No, Loni. Based on Manhatsten's transmissions, they are the only ones capable of flight. The rest of the cities walk."

Kirka had so many questions. She was about to open her mouth when Luna said, "Incoming message from the vehicle."

Kirka cocked an eyebrow. She looked at the clock. "But we're still ninety minutes from broadcast alignment. How are they sending a transmission? Better yet, how are you receiving it?"

"It appears that someone on the vehicle has discovered an ancient wireless network that allows communication from the vehicle to anyone with similar technology. It is a text messaging system."

Loni said, "I didn't know we had anything like that."

Luna replied, "We have one microwave receiver on Luna 2. Luna 1 does not have a microwave communication relay, and so I had not thought to utilize it for many decades. The city of Manhatsten does not have this technology. It appears that only the vehicle has a transmitter of this kind."

Kirka said, "What does the message say?"

Luna read it out loud. "Greetings. We are the delegation from the city of Manhatsten, first of the walking cities and the only one capable of space flight. We would like permission to land on the moon and begin discussing a possible trade."

Kirka said, "Can we send a message back?"

"Yes."

It sounded like these people wanted solidsonium. If they did, they were out of luck, well, unless they had some advanced mining equipment, which, by the look of the city, they might. But even if they did, Kirka was hesitant to give up any of the last of their resources. Especially after ROAM betrayed them. She considered telling them in the message about the solidsonium situation but then thought better of it. The transmission had contained very little. They were playing close to the chest, and she would do the same.

"Tell them they are welcome here, and we are happy to welcome trading partners. Give them instructions on how to enter the hanger bay at thirty-four alpha."

"Transmission sent."

"How long till they arrive?"

"Two hours and eight minutes."

"Alright, Loni, I'm going to meet them at the airlock. I want you to come with me, but first I want you to have another telepath meet us in the room we are using for the conference."

"Should I ask Loridian?"

"Sounds like a good idea. If they have technical questions, he'll be able to answer right away. Tell him to meet us in the dining hall on level nine. We'll lock it down, and they'll have a nice view of the park and the market place. I want them to see that we have a thriving community here so that maybe they will be willing to let us take refuge in that city of theirs."

3.

"What in the name of our Lord and Savior did you just do to me?"

Serah sighed. "I told you. I'm a telepath."

She noticed the strange smile on Rigel Solidsworth's face. It seemed that he was doing everything he could to suppress laughter. Swanson sat across the cab from Rigel, Shannon, and Serah, an island unto himself, but one that, like a volcano, was ready to explode.

"It's unnatural."

Serah said, "How can it be unnatural if I was born with the ability?"

"God forbids such things. It says in God's sacred text, 'Thou shalt not suffer a witch to live.'"

"A witch? I don't have magic abilities. I just read minds." Serah stood, "And if you think you can take me on, Swanson, I'm ready."

Swanson's eyes widened, and he slunk back in his seat. Shannon tugged her arm and pulled her back down.

Nervous, Swanson said, "And how would you explain that ability? It sounds like magic to me. It sounds like something God would forbid."

"Apparently not, because I have been able to do it most of my life."

Rigel said, "Speaker, Serah has done you a courtesy. She has introduced you to the concept in advance of our meeting with the Lunites."

Swanson turned on Rigel. "What's that supposed to mean?"

The man's face was as red as the apples that Serah's parents used to grow. She wasn't sure if she should laugh or give in to her frustration. How was this man supposed to negotiate with another city that was run by telepaths if he had just called her a witch?

"It means, dear Senator, that that according to reports from Manhatsten, Luna is run by women like her."

"What?"

Shannon's voice was soft and small as she spoke, "Senator Swanson, Serah's been my friend for forty years, and I'm not a telepath. She's been nothing but kind to me. She's saved my life a dozen times."

Swanson looked her up and down as if he hadn't noticed her previously. "Young lady, aren't you a Runner?"

Serah, trying to control her temper and not throttle man, said, "What does that have to do with anything?"

"Runners are criminals. Criminals can't be trusted. And why are you a Runner? Last I checked there were no Runners who were able to control minds."

Serah said, "I told you already, I can't control minds. That's not how any of this works."

"Reading, pushing, whatever you call it, it's still a violation of my privacy and against the will of God."

Serah said, "I don't subscribe to your God, and frankly, I don't give a shit about religion."

Swanson opened his mouth to say something, but it was Shannon who stood up inside the Dugger and moved across the cab to sit next to Swanson. She removed her metallic glove and, with her bare hand, reached out, removed the glove from his modified pressure suit, and held his hand.

The softness in her voice reminded Serah of Noatla, and for a moment, there was a deep stirring in emotion and desire to see her old Matron. For that single moment, Serah felt the onrush of tears, the intensity of everything that had come to pass since Alexa joined the Order of the Eye, and Miranda revealed herself. She felt that weight crush her chest and she had to remind herself to breathe so that panic and anxiety wouldn't take her over. Years in the Order of the Eye had given her a host of methods to address the emotions from her own trauma, but that didn't mean that it didn't sneak up like a hidden beast inside her gut once in a while. Here it was, threatening to derail everything. She closed her eyes, took a deep breath, and let Shannon speak. She sent the woman a sense of confidence and kindness, not that Shannon didn't have those qualities in great measure, but here was a woman who could speak and communicate in a way that Serah couldn't. Serah wasn't much of a diplomat; that had always been Noatla's job.

"I was scared the first time I learned about telepathy too, Senator. My girlfriend, Mimi, she's a telepath too. She, like Serah, was born with it. They can't help what they are, and both Serah and Mimi choose to use their abilities to help people and all the city. That's why we're here to help."

"Then why would you keep your existence hidden?"

Serah said, "Because of how you're reacting now. Do you think we like living our lives in secret? Do you think that we want to hide what we are? None of us are ashamed of what we can do; we choose to use it to help people."

She hadn't even told him about Miranda and the Children of Gaia yet. Of course, all the Senate knew about the Children of Gaia now, but they had no idea they were led by a telepath bent on destroying everything. If he couldn't even get passed friendly telepaths, how could he deal with Miranda? And what if the AI was wrong and some of the Lunites used the red veil freely? It seemed possible that some wouldn't be tempted by its power. Serah had almost given into temptation several times. Just below the surface of her mind, she could feel that sense of power and rage waiting, lying dormant for the right moment. Serah had never had trouble with the red veil before, at least not like this. Why was she now?

Shannon said, "You knew Noatla Lightfoot right, Senator."

Serah, skimming Swanson to find any foothold to break down his barriers so he wouldn't derail any chance they had with Luna, saw a thought light up in him. He didn't just know Noatla Lightfoot, he had mourned her, they had been longtime friends and he had always hoped for something more.

Serah transmitted directly to Shannon's mind. "Keep going with that angle. I think he was in love with Noatla; he considered her to be the perfect woman. Just don't let on that you know about his feelings."

Shannon gave the slightest nod acknowledging Serah.

Swanson said, "Yes, I considered Noatla to be a dear friend. Why?"

Shannon said, "Were you close?"

Serah couldn't help but admire Shannon's conversational skills. She might not be a telepath, but Shannon seemed to understand people in a way that Serah, even with her abilities, didn't. Once again, she could see what Mimi loved her.

Swanson replied, "We spent many hours in the Senate Chambers together over the course of two centuries. I have spent a great deal of time discussing issues with Senator Lightfoot, and I had the utmost respect for her. Where is this going? Did she know about... telepaths?"

Shannon grabbed his hand a little tighter. She turned his chin and made him look at her. Serah could feel Swanson's shock and his warm acceptance of the gentle touch. His defenses lowered as he looked into this younger woman's eyes. Shannon's softness was a weapon; a Trojan horse.

"Senator, Noatla wasn't just aware of telepaths, she was the Matron of the Order of the Eye. She was in charge of the city's telepaths."

Swanson said nothing. Serah watched all the various scenarios unfold in his brain. He wanted to reject the information out of hand, but there was another part of him that was putting together connections, seeing things that Noatla said and did that suggested that she might, in fact, be a telepath. Most people didn't want to believe that such abilities existed in the world, but the thing was, Shannon and Serah had just taken that away from him. Now, a man who had been alive for centuries had to rethink everything he thought he knew about the city that he helped to rule.

"That's... that's..."

He wanted to say impossible. He wanted to say that it was "hogwash," but something wouldn't let him.

Instead, Swanson cast his eyes toward the floor and said, "How did she die?"

Even skimming him, Serah hadn't seen the question coming. It was a kick in the gut, and worse, now they had to talk about Miranda. She hoped he was ready for that too.

Serah wanted to say something but couldn't find the words.

Shannon said, "We don't know exactly. We know that... well, we know that another telepath did something to her, but we don't know what."

"Another telepath? What are you saying?"

Serah took a deep breath. There was little choice now; they still had two hours till arrival, and it was better he know everything about Miranda going in than not. So, she told Swanson about Miranda, about the Children of Gaia and the red veil. She did it as fast as she could without skipping over important details. Rigel, who had his own experiences with telepathy and Miranda, told his side of the story. How Miranda had taken control of Runner 17 and how Alexa, who was also a telepath, had broken her control. He rambled a bit with his theories as to the nature of telepathy but just as he started to go off on a tangent, Shannon relayed some of her experiences.

Swanson said almost nothing the whole time. He listened and absorbed, and when Serah wasn't speaking, she skimmed him for reactions. His mind kept drifting back to Noatla, back to how he felt about her, back to how he considered her the perfect woman and how he could never doubt her intentions. Serah encouraged these thoughts, added soothing feelings around them, and pushed him in subtle ways to help keep him calm. Part of him fought all this new knowledge, but part of him accepted what he was hearing. Serah knew it would be an ongoing war, but they had done their very best to prepare him for the meeting on Luna, which was now only twenty minutes away.

Shannon, seeing the paleness of Swanson's complexion, asked, "Are you alright, Senator Swanson?"

Swanson opened and closed his mouth several times. Then, as a person seeing light for the first time, he surveyed the entire room, looking at Rigel, then Serah, and finally, Shannon. He withdrew and shook his head in slow, solemn strokes. He put his head in his hands.

"What you are telling me is very difficult to accept."

Rigel said, "Only if you believe your reality is static and unchanging."

Swanson lifted his head and flashed a dangerous look at Rigel, but Serah saw it soften almost immediately. He said, "I am a man of my faith. It is difficult to reconcile your... abilities with what I know to be true from my own experience."

Rigel said, "Ah, but there are many things you have come to that are not a part of your faith, my dear Senator. You of all people should know that humans live in a fundamentally different society now than the ancient Middle East in which your man Jesus lived. Accepting this piece of information is not much different than accepting the EnViro Shields, the migration of the cities themselves, and of course, the alcoves which have let you live for centuries."

Swanson considered for a long time. Still, the war raged.

Serah said, "The important thing here is Luna. You don't have to like my abilities, you don't have to agree with the things we do, but you should try to understand that we want the same things you do, Senator."

"And what do you think that I want?"

"Peace in the city. The end to the chaos and the wars and Miranda. Like you, we don't want any more bloodshed or violence."

Swanson put his head in his hands but nodded. "Well then, that at least we can agree on."

With only minutes 'til arrival, Rigel said, "Come, Senator, we'd better get our pressure suits on."

4.

Kirka paced back and forth outside the main airlock. She paused and looked through the glass. Loni tried to tiptoe past her shoulder for a peek, but it was of little use. Kirka didn't have to skim her to know that Loni was frustrated with her height... again.

There were only two functioning airlocks to the surface these days, the other four shorted out over the march of the centuries. One had been destroyed three centuries ago in an attack from Luna 1, and the other two were just ancient and in need of parts that they couldn't make anymore. This place was a graveyard; a burial site for what Kirka thought was the last of humanity. But now, with the city arriving, there was hope again and a new wave of possibilities. But what would she do if the people of Manhatsten rejected them or forced them into a lottery system where only some could go, and others had to stay? It wasn't going to be an easy thing to do. At least they had the solidsonium; it was their best bargaining chip.

The outer door opened and in walked four individuals. Through the glass of the airlock, Kirka could see that two of them were in the largest EnViro suits she had ever seen. They were a good head taller than the combat suits on Luna and it was clear that these suits were armed to the teeth for combat. The other two individuals were in smaller standard orange pressure suits that every Lunaite was familiar with.

The door behind them closed, and then, after pressurization, the internal airlock door opened. The four figures walked into the main hanger for Luna 2. The two in the pressure suits immediately took off their helmets while the two in the combat suits slid up their visors.

Kirka transmitted, "Greetings: my name is Commander Raldaz Kirka. This is my second in command Loni Afrani. Welcome to Luna 2."

Kirka stopped, noticing that the two in the orange pressure suits winced when she transmitted. There was only one reason two people might wince like that from telepathy.

"Pardon, but are you two, not telepaths?"

The rounded, older looking man shook his head no, hard. The thin one also shook his head, but he looked less anxious about it and more... was Kirka skimming... was it fascination?

Directly to her mind, one of the two in the EnViro Suit's transmitted, "Greetings: my name is Serah. I am the Matron of the Order of the Eye. However, I am the only telepath on this delegation. This person in the other EnViro suit is my friend Shannon. The thin, wispy looking one over there is Dr. Rigel Solidsworth..."

Solidsworth? Kirka knew that name. Was he the man who came to Luna and installed the alcoves when Kirka had just arrived? Was this the man himself or a descendant? She hadn't met Solidsworth in person, but she had heard people talk about him all over Luna General. There were plenty of low-budget vid screen movies produced on Luna about the architects even to this day, though Loridian never seemed to appreciate them much since they mostly left him out of the films.

"... and this last one is our official representative from the Senate of Manhatsten, Speaker Swanson. But, since most of our delegation must speak verbally, I request that we avoid most direct transmissions."

Verbally, Kirka said, "Agreed."

She turned towards the two men in the pressure suits and said, "Ah, I see, you're men, then? That makes more sense."

The two men looked at each other and then back at Kirka and nodded.

The thinner one, Solidsworth, asked, "Pardon, but why was it obvious that we are, in fact, men?"

Kirka said, "Men can't be telepaths. You winced when I transmitted, which means you probably aren't used to telepathy. So, you can't be biologically female or intersex."

Rigel said, "Fascinating. And why, may I ask, is that?"

Kirka couldn't believe it. How ignorant were they about telepaths?

"Serah, have your telepaths never explained the science behind our talents?"

Serah said, "No... I don't think any of us know the science behind it either."

Kirka blinked several times in rapid succession.

"But surely, you must..."

"Telepathy is a secret in our city. The only reason these two know is that we had to brief them about your city. We know very little about how our abilities work. Our former Matron forbade research because of the dangers of the red veil."

"The red veil?"

"The taboo against mind control."

"Ah, that. Yes, we forbid that here as well, but it did not prevent us from researching our abilities over the centuries."

Kirka searched the faces of each visitor. She skimmed Serah, searching for an explanation, and initiated mind-to-mind contact for a moment.

"Secret? Why would you do that?"

"Because we are far outnumbered. You see, there are only three of us left now."

Instead of mind-to-mind contact, Kirka said, "Three? That's it? How many people are in your city?"

Speaker Swanson, "Three of what?"

"This woman claims there are only three telepaths in your entire city of... how many people?"

Rigel said, "A little over 1.5 million."

The secrecy made a little more sense. Even if there were a hundred telepaths among 1.5 million, it would spur a lot of jealousy and prejudice. Kirka had to admit that there was tension between gifted individuals and those without the talent even on Luna, where a huge portion of their population had the ability.

"I suppose you don't have an architect who is a telepath. You see, it requires two X chromosomes or at least part of a second X. Our head scientist, Loridian, is not biologically male, but identifies as one. He's an intersex individual, so he has part of a second X chromosome in addition to his XY. He just happened to be lucky and get the additional proteins of the X that switched on telepathy."

Rigel said, "Amazing. Have you implemented any gene therapy techniques that might allow some to acquire the trait or talent...? And wait, did you say Loridian?"

"I did."

"Oh my, Dr. Loridian. I've not seen him since my last trip to the moon before the war. I had no idea he was a telepath."

"To answer your question, Dr. Solidsworth, there does not appear to be any gene therapy capable of transmitting the ability. Loridian has worked on this very question for several decades."

Kirka felt a sense of relief. The fact that Solidsworth knew Loridian confirmed who this man was. He was the real thing, not a descendent of the man who worked on so many important projects pre-migration. It gave Kirka a surge of hope. Despite all the crazy conspiracy theory vid screen films about architects, Kirka knew that this man was instrumental in the creation of much of the technology on Luna. He and his colleagues had created the power system, the EnViro shield, and the alcoves. Maybe they wouldn't even have to leave, perhaps they could devise a plan to fend off the missiles from ROAM.

Serah said, "What missiles?"

The other three visitors looked at her. Serah continued, "She was just thinking that there are missiles on the way. That Luna is going to be destroyed by something called ROAM?"

Kirka said, "Yes. There's no denying it. Come with me and let's talk."

Serah said, "How long 'til the missiles arrive? Do we need to get the hell out of here now?"

"No, they are still months away, don't worry. But it's why we contacted you. Come. There is some food and several other people I want to introduce to you before we argue our case. Would you like a tour of Luna first?"

Swanson said, "Yes, of course."

5.

It was strange walking on Luna. The gravity, a mere seventeen percent of that on Manhatsten, made Serah feel light and bouncy. Each step in the EnViro suit felt soft and strange. More than a few times, she tripped over her feet and fell forward. Rigel, Shannon, and the senator were all having similar difficulties, though injury was unlikely, considering the slow nature of any fall. Serah wasn't sure she could easily fight her away out of here. All her skill in fighting was developed in Earth's gravity, and it would take some getting used to before she could master this one. If the Lunites intended to attack, they would be far better adapted to the environment than she. Though, from her initial contact with Kirka, combat seemed like the last thing on their minds. They needed help. The question was, could they give it to them? Would the cost be too high?

The party wandered down numerous stretches of corridor and underground passageways. There were no windows, no hint of an outside world beyond. Much of Luna was worn down and dingy. It reminded Serah of the old abandoned subway tunnels in the underground of Manhatsten. In Manhatsten, few visited those tunnels unless there was a problem, but the difference here was that it was clear that Luna was well-traveled. They passed numerous people in the passages as they walked. The Luna underground smelled stale and moldy, and Serah's nose wrinkled several times in spots where water stains marked the corridors.

Shannon said, "This reminds me of home."

Kirka stopped and turned, "Home? Your whole city looks this way?"

Swanson said, "Absolutely not. Our city is beautiful and well-kept."

Shannon said, "Not in the underground, it's not. I was... home-less for a long time."

Kirka said, "Homeless?"

Everyone except Serah stared at Shannon.

Serah could feel the heat radiating from Swanson; he was an-gry. Shannon had said too much in these negotiations already, and they had not even sat down at the table yet.

Rigel said, "There is significant inequality in our city. In fact, there is a conflict over that very topic right now. I agree with Sena-tor Swanson that much of our city is beautiful and well taken care of, but that doesn't mean that a city of our size doesn't have its is-sues with poverty and infrastructure."

Kirka nodded. "Fair enough. Luna 2 and 1 are a fraction of the size of your city, and we have our fair share of infrastructure and poverty issues as well."

Swanson's mind cooled a bit. Serah already liked this woman. In a way, she reminded her a little of Noatla. She was cool and mea-sured, and though Kirka had a different "feel" than Noatla, there as something almost... motherly about her, though Serah suspected that Kirka was more military leader than Noatla had been.

Kirka turned and continued the tour. After a long series of tun-nels, they came out into an open space, an interior park of sorts. Above their heads, on a stone roof, was fading blue paint spotted with what could have once been images of clouds. There were nu-merous trees and a large platform in the front. Skirting the edges were shops and restaurants, though every sign had missing letters or faded paint. Serah imagined that this is what Manhatsten would look like if they hadn't been on the planet to gather resources.

Shannon said, "Oh! You have flowers and gardens!"

Kirka betrayed the ghost of a smile. "Our commons is where most people spend their time when they aren't working or in their quarters. We have UV lights around the area to emulate the sun for both the plants and the people. They aren't quite as good as the real thing, but you can see children playing in the park on most days."

Swanson said, "Do you grow all your own food, or do you utilize a biorecycler?"

Kirka asked, "Biorecyclers?"

"Yes, they use raw organic material to synthesize edible food. It doesn't always taste that great, but it's nutrient-rich. Manhatsten utilizes both bio recyclers and grown food."

Shannon said, "Yeah, but only the rich can afford fresh food."

Swanson shot her a look.

Serah transmitted to Shannon. "I think both of us better watch and listen for the time being. Let the politicians discuss this kind of stuff. We can speak up when we feel something is vital to the Order of the Eye, okay?"

Shannon gave a small nod.

Kirka led them through the commons and up a few flights of stairs to a large room. There, waiting for them, was another person. Each Lunite was a contrast to the other. Kirka was tall, thin, and pale. The other one she already introduced as Loni was short, olive-skinned, and round. The last was a brown-skinned man with the strangest piercing, gray eyes.

Upon entering the room, Rigel said, "Loridian? My god man, is that you?"

"Rigel? After all this time, you're still alive? And here, we thought the planet was devoid of life."

Both hugged and embraced each other. Serah could feel the history between the two of them. She also realized that she could link with Loridian and introduce herself. She reached out and did so.

Loridian had long, thin gray hair and matching gray eyes. He had high, thin cheekbones and several strange scars that ran like slash marks in neat rows up the left side of his neck face. It looked as if someone had taken a blade and made tiny, precise cuts up the left side.

Kirka said, "Loridian, these are the representatives from Manhatsten. Unfortunately, only one of the delegation is telepathic, and so it is best if we speak out loud for the benefit of all." Kirka turned her head toward Serah and the others and said, "Please, sit. I'm having a small meal prepared for us."

Rigel sat next to Loridian, and Loni sat next to Shannon and Kirka. Serah chose a seat next to Senator Swanson.

Rigel said, "Unfortunately, time is a very serious concern. We should discuss our immediate issues and decide how we can work together to solve each other's problems."

Swanson said, "Yes, agreed."

Kirka and Loridian nodded. Kirka said, "Very well, we should tell you what's happening with ROAM."

Kirka connected to Serah and transmitted a series of images about the conflict with ROAM and the coming missiles. Then, verbally, she told Shannon, Rigel, and Swanson. It made sense to link, even though she had to repeat herself, because there were images and thoughts that Kirka shared that were hard to put into words and provided more context. With the transmission, Serah understood the severity of the conflict that was rising in the city and how many of the telepaths were required to stay on soothing duty to keep mass panic from breaking out. Serah couldn't help but wish they had telepaths to do the very same for Manhatsten at the moment.

After Kirka finished explaining, she said, "So you see, we need a place to take refuge. If at all possible, we need to find a way to continue to stabilize the moon. Those warheads they sent our way have a chance of destabilizing Luna 1 and 2's orbit and sending it on a collision course with Earth."

Rigel said, "Those missiles must have a significant yield to pose that kind of threat. The energy to shift the orbit of the moon would require an enormous blast."

Kirka said, "That would be true under normal circumstances. But unfortunately, the only reason the moon stays in its orbit is that we use a fusion propulsion system to keep it there. When the blast went off that split Luna, it destabilized the orbit, and Luna has been slowly drifting toward Earth. So, all that ROAM really needs to do is to disable that propulsion system and, in a few decades, Luna will crash into the planet."

Loridian said, "By my calculation, Luna would enter Earth's atmosphere in thirty-four years. But the yield of the warheads from ROAM could change that calculation. So, as far as we know, they had twenty-five megaton warheads. They had at least one of the B41 atomic weapons stockpiled by the United States during the 20th century. If their yield is higher or if the missiles are clustered together in a way that distorts our sensors, it will change my calculations."

Swanson said, "How many people will need relocation?"

Kirka said, "4461 in total."

"Perhaps you are not aware of the problems our city faces at the moment?"

Kirka said, "Serah has filled me in on a large number of them already."

Swanson said, "What? When?"

Serah didn't like the look that Swanson gave her, but then, he was still adjusting to the idea of telepathy.

"She transmitted a summary of everything that has happened in the last few months. Telepaths can link and share a massive amount of information in a few seconds in mind-to-mind contact."

Rigel said, "I assume she told you of the shield failure and the damaged pylon?"

Kirka nodded. "Yes, the problem is the solidsonium we have will be difficult to mine."

Rigel replied, "We don't need much, at least in the short term. If I can acquire ten kilograms of raw ore, that will be enough to patch the damage for now. I have brought some of the more advanced mining tools that Manhatsten has available for the short term. However, in the long term, landing on Luna 1 and using our city's central drill would be ideal. I have calculated that, based on the pre-lunar war numbers, that there are at least twenty-five thousand kilograms of raw ore remaining. That much ore would allow us to build five new cities entirely. I also feel confident that with Manhatsten stationed on the moon, we could effectively build a missile deterrent system and several large gravitational generators that would solve the problem with decaying orbit. I am reasonably sure that all of Luna's issues could be solved without too much trouble."

Loridian said, "Wonderful. When do we get to work?"

Rigel said, "I could begin work immediately."

Swanson and Kirka both said at once, "Now, wait just a moment..."

Both leaders paused and looked at each other. Serah skimmed both of them. Each was distrustful of the other because, of course, they were. How could it have possibly been as easy as two scientists coming up with a solution? Serah hated politics.

Swanson spoke first, saying, "Dr. Solidsworth. Do you remember what the city had to go through to power the gravitational generators you installed? Did you not see how dilapidated this whole city is? Do you realize the number of resources that will be required to stabilize here? You are talking about major overhauls, not a minor repair job, or taking in some refugees. Even if I agreed to everything you just said, it's doubtful that the rest of the Senate would. Besides, and no offense to you, Commander Kirka, but we don't know anything about the people of Luna. We know that they are a high proportion of telepaths: what keeps them from taking over the city?"

Serah felt a short burst of anger from Kirka. She sent a wave of soothing her direction, but it seemed to do nothing to assuage the woman's anger.

Kirka said, "What makes you think we would agree with giving up all of our unrefined solidsonium? How do we know that you won't do the same thing that ROAM did; take what you want and then destroy us or leave us to our own destruction? Senator Swanson, your attitude toward telepaths concerns me; it is the exact reason that ROAM betrayed us. Just because we are born different, because we have a different set of skills than non-telepaths, doesn't mean it's a reflection of our character."

Swanson raised his voice and stood up. "Maybe not, but it only takes one, doesn't it? It only takes one mad telepath to sew chaos and destruction. Serah told you of this... red... garment?"

Serah said, "Red veil."

"Yes, that. How do we know that you aren't working with this... woman... this... Miranda? How do we know that you won't turn the power of your telepathy on those of us without it? You rule here, don't you?"

"We have a democracy here. I've been elected seventy-one times."

"Yes, well, how do we know that you haven't been elected so many times because you used your abilities to rig the election?"

Kirka stood up and placed her hands on the table. Her chair flew back and crashed on the floor. "How dare you?"

Swanson eyes widened. "How dare I? What you do is unnatural. What you do is an abomination and the work of Satan."

Serah tried like hell to soothe both of them, but it was no use. She reached out to Loni, who, as it turned out, had linked with Loridian and was also trying to soothe both parties.

"I've been a leader of Luna since the Lunar War. I've kept this place from tearing itself apart. How dare you question my integrity? Can you honestly tell me that your Senate isn't corrupt? You're in the middle of an uprising because of your corruption. Serah showed me how bad things are. Don't you dare tell me about corruption or try to lecture me on the abuse of power. Just because someone is born different, just because someone's mind works differently than your own, doesn't make us less moral or less responsible. Don't you drag out some ancient religion as an excuse for bigotry and your small-minded, no good-"

Luna blared over the speaker, saying, "Incoming transmission from Manhatsten."

The room fell silent, but the tension lingered. Both Swanson and Kirka still stood.

Rigel said, "That will be the rest of the Senate."

In almost a half-whisper, Serah said, "None of them know about telepathy..."

Loni, Kirka, Loridian, and Shannon's faces all fell. Things were not going well, and both Luna and Manhatsten would crumble if they didn't find a way to work together. How in the world was Serah going to convince Kirka and Swanson to relax? Of course, the problem wasn't Kirka, it was Swanson's own fears. Kirka was sensitive from the recent betrayal from ROAM, but who could blame her?

Shannon said, "Both Luna and Manhatsten will be destroyed without us working together. You both know that."

Serah skimmed both Swanson and Kirka, Shannon's words didn't sink in. They ignored her, both had taken a defensive stance, and Serah wasn't sure how she could shake them out of it.

Luna said, "Ready to align communications."

Swanson hesitated and then said, "Proceed."

Nothing happened.

Kirka said, "Go ahead Luna."

Luna said, "I'm sorry, Commander, there is something wrong with the transmission. Please hold for one moment."

Serah had a sinking feeling about this. Something was definitely wrong. She tried to reach out to Vala, but it was much too far. A link might be possible if she connected to Kirka, Loni, and Loridian, but at the moment, she didn't want to try that.

Shannon's voice shook as she said, "Somethings wrong." Everyone turned towards Shannon. "Can't you feel it? Something's wrong!"

Swanson said, "What makes you say that, young lady?" His voice was soft and kind toward Shannon. All the sharpness had vanished for the moment. The tension in the room shifted from each other to the unknown communication problem.

"I don't know, Senator... I just feel cold inside. It's the same feeling I had before we..."

The feed transmitted. At first, it was fuzzy static, but in a few moments, the audio and video clarified. Serah's stomach turned, and the hair on her arms and legs stood up, as if to show respect the terrible scene before her eyes.

Kirka said, "My gods..."

The room was barren of life. The walls were painted in gray and red, but the red wasn't paint. Limbs and organs lay scattered, and only a few bodies were left recognizable for what they were. It was a slaughter unlike anything Serah had ever seen. Even the aftermath of the subway had not been so brutal. At least a dozen Recycled were scattered around the room. They lay broken and inactive, but Serah knew now why Miranda was waiting. She had rebuilt her army of Recycled.

Swanson grabbed his chest and groaned, and, through shallow breaths, he whispered prayers. Then he moaned and clutched his chest. "Oh my..." Swanson sat back down. His face paled and Serah could almost feel the pain in his chest. His heart was failing. The sight of the slaughter was too much for him.

Kirka seemed to skim Swanson too and said, "Luna, we need a medical team up here right away."

Serah said, "Do you have an alcove nearby?"

"On the other side of Luna 2. We have a defibrillator and other conventional medical equipment."

Serah said, "A what?"

"A device to steady the rhythm of the heart using an electric shock."

Shannon said, "You want to electrocute him?"

Loni said, "It's a pre-migration medical practice to save lives."

Serah said, "I always knew those people ancient people were barbarians."

The medical team arrived and brought a stretcher. Swanson was conscious and breathing, but his breaths were short and shallow. Beads of sweat congregated on his brow, and his eyes were wide and fearful.

Serah skimmed him. The image they had just seen across the feed played over and over in his mind. He kept asking himself, "Why, God? Why?"

One of the team asked, "How do you feel?"

Swanson gasped and between breaths said... "Crushing... chest..."

Luna said, "Based on my scans, he is having a heart attack, likely induced from the shock of the transmission."

Serah rolled her eyes. The AIs might be self-aware, but so far, all of them had an annoying habit of stating the obvious.

Kirka said, "They'll take him to our infirmary and stabilize him. After that, we can take him to an alcove and repair his heart."

Serah said, "Do whatever you need to. I think the negotiations are off for now."

Kirka frowned, "Who's left in charge in your city?"

Serah shrugged. "That's hard to say with the Senate gone. It seems most likely that the head of security would be in charge in the case of the death of the Senate. Luna, can you ask Manhatsten if central security has been attacked yet?"

Luna said, "Manhatsten says that so far, there has been no attack on central security."

"Good, there's still time then... maybe."

Kirka asked, "Perhaps we should bring your head of security here?"

Serah shook her head. "No, if Lydia Danvers knows that happened, she's going to fortify the city. We probably should turn around immediately and head back. She's going to need every available person to stand and fight."

The medics placed Swanson on a stretcher and then slowly hauled him out of the room and down the hall. Serah watched him go through the clear glass windows.

Kirka said, "Those things in the suits, the one bleeding blue, are those the Recycled you fought in the subway that you showed me?"

"Yes, those are the same."

"And their leader... she's the one with the red veil, right? The one who violates the taboo?"

"Yeah. But I don't know if we can stop her this time. We put up a good fight before and still lost, and we were at full strength with the Order."

Serah had already transmitted all of this to Kirka, but it was worth repeating. Serah felt a deep sense of dread. Another Recycled army? She wondered how many Miranda could have now.

Where did they even get all equipment to rebuild those things? But then she thought of all the Runners and Recycled in the subway, hundreds on each side would leave enough scrap to rebuild an army.

She thought about how they had taken Mimi, how there was a line of Recycled Runners carrying bodies into that massive door. How many had Miranda gathered? It was clear now that at least some of the disappearances in the city were related. Hundreds or maybe thousands had gone missing; it was on everyone's minds in the city. Had most of those disappearances made up Miranda's new army? What could they do against hundreds of Recycled? There was no Runnercore anymore and, from skimming Lydia, Serah knew that the SO's were scattered and broken, barely holding together. She would fight, but she couldn't see any way to victory.

Loni stood up. "I'm going with you."

Both Kirka and Serah, at the same time, said, "What?"

Loni said, "Those Recycled things, they're controlled by this woman Miranda, right?"

Serah nodded.

"And you have only a few telepaths left in your city to fight them, right?"

"Yes."

"Then you're going to need all the help you can get. So, I'm going with you. And Kirka is coming too. Oh, and we can cram a couple more of us on your transport."

Kirka said, "I am?"

Loni nodded. "Come on, Commander. We want their help dealing with the missiles from ROAM, what better way to convince them that telepaths are their friends than by helping them?"

Serah liked this woman. She reminded her of Mimi... well, except she was much bubblier. For a moment, she imagined a carefree, teenage version of Mimi and realized that Loni was exactly that.

"How many can we fit on the transport?" asked Kirka.

Serah said, "Guess that depends. Do any of you use combat armor? Can you fight?"

Kirka shook her head. We can fight, but we'll be useless in combat."

"Why's that?"

"Your city uses a standard one-g gravity system, right?"

Serah nodded.

"Well, I'm sure by now you noticed that off your transport you're a lot lighter. Gravity is only 17% of what you experience in your city. Our bodies are long adjusted to the gravity of Luna, and we have even re-calibrated the alcoves to deal with the consequences. It's why most people, besides Loni and a handful of others, are tall and slender. There is less gravity pulling on our bodies and our bone and cell development is impacted."

"So, you're useless in a fight?"

"Yes, but what it sounds like you need is people to disrupt control over the Recycled, not more warriors."

"We need both actually. But you're not wrong; we definitely need as many telepaths as we can get."

Shannon said, "We should leave Senator Swanson here."

Kirka said, "Yes, agreed. He'll be in no condition to travel immediately, and we could potentially fit two more people in the transport in his place."

Serah felt a sense of hope. There was something about these women she really liked. Besides, what else could she do? It wasn't a time to sit and wait around, it was time to get back over there and stop Miranda once and for all.

Rigel, who had remained silent since the transmission from the Senate, said, "Tell me, Commander, do you have any rovers?"

"Three functioning ones on Luna 2, why?"

"And pressure suits?"

"Plenty of those: more than we have people, in fact."

Rigel turned toward Serah and asked, "And how many telepaths do you think would be required to stop Miranda?"

Serah shrugged. "I don't know. There were fourteen inside the library when they were slaughtered and fifteen when Alexa arrived at the library, and that wasn't enough to stop her. Maybe if we had twenty or thirty? But even fifty might not be enough. Miranda has figured out a way to increase her power a hundred-fold and we don't understand how that's possible."

Rigel said, "Commander Kirka, are you capable of recruiting twenty to thirty telepaths?"

"I think so, but we have no way of getting them there."

Rigel asked Serah, "How long do you think we have until this attack?"

"That's a better question for Manhantsten. Too bad we can't reach it."

Luna chimed in, "Commander, I have consulted with Manhatsten on the likelihood that this violence will spread to the city in general."

"And?"

"It estimates twenty-four to thirty-six hours before the main attack begins."

Rigel scratched his chin. "Do you have some engineers that could assist me in a project?"

"Yes, why? What are you thinking?"

"I'm thinking that we are going to bring as many of your people with telepathic abilities back with us to fight."

Chapter 27
The Red Army

Frank ducked into an alley. He pulled Zelda behind him.

Zelda said, "Shit. How many of those things are there?"

"I don't know. You wanna go out in the middle of the street and count?"

"Hell no."

The sound of marching metal feet on the fractured concrete created synchronized terror. Frank didn't know what good it would do to hide down an alleyway. He suspected that if the creatures with the strange white on white on white eyes wanted to hurt you, there was little you could do to stop them. Frank hadn't seen any of the Recycled personally during that last battle, but he had heard plenty of stories from people who had. None of them were good. Where those things went, people died. Everyone had heard rumors about something happening to the Senate, but it was hard to tell if it was true. He and Lydia were due to meet with the Senate again next week, and he hadn't heard anything from Lydia, so he assumed the rumors weren't true. But now, Frank wasn't so sure.

He leaned against the brick wall and whispered to Zelda. "We gotta get to Lydia."

"Why? You think she doesn't know? Now that the AI is back online, she's gonna know they're coming."

"Good point."

"Frank, what we gotta do is get to our wives and try to find someplace in the underground to hide."

"I think you're right. We should get Jose's wife and kid too, huh?"

Zelda nodded. Then her jaw dropped. "Frank... Frank, look."

Frank did. He clenched his jaw and fists. "Tony."

Tony walked up alongside some of the Recycled.

Zelda said, "You think he's in league with them?"

"I wouldn't put it past the slimy bastard."

"Who's that woman?"

"No clue. But you can bet she's just as much trouble as Tony."

Tony stopped and looked around. Frank and Zelda ducked back into the alley a little more, so they weren't visible. Had he seen them? He was only a few meters away, and Frank didn't want him to know he was there. He had done everything he could to avoid the bastard after the last attack on central security. Everyone knew that Tony was behind it, and everyone knew that Frank and Zelda were in the middle of the attack. Frank thought for sure Tony would come for him, but he hadn't so far.

2.

Tony hated walking with the Recycled, but Alana had insisted they make themselves visible prior to the attack. She had said that the people needed to know who they should bow to when this was all over. The city streets cleared as the army of Recycled moved. He understood why now. He couldn't get the slaughter of the Senate out of his mind. What had he gotten himself into? He'd taken his fair share of lives. He'd roughed up plenty of people personally, but the glee in Alana's face, the way that she licked the blood off things... it was something else entirely. He doubted that he'd be able to kill her or even hurt her at all. How was she commanding these things? For now, at least they were listening to him as well, but for how much longer? He had the sense that Alana could take full control anytime she wanted.

The creatures were at least six hundred strong now. Some of their suits were modified and smaller. Most of their armor was new. Where did these creatures come from? Have they always been in the city? Where did they find the material for all those suits? Everyone knew that most of the Runners were killed in the Battle with Saud outside of the city.

Something out of the corner of Tony's eye caught his attention. He turned his head. For a brief moment, he saw two figures, one large and round, and one tiny and scrawny disappear into an alleyway. Tony's heart thumped, and his anger soared. He knew who that silhouette in the shadows belonged too. There weren't too many men around the city of that size. That fat fuck and his scruffy partner were watching them march toward central security. Frank had been nothing but a thorn in his side since he started this whole plan and he sure as shit wasn't going to let him get away with it.

Tony waited until the alley was several blocks back. He knew they saw him, probably wondered why in the hell he was marching with these creatures. That alley, like all the others around, was a dead-end against the shield wall. They were trapped like rats, and that was exactly how Tony wanted them.

3.

The army of Recycled had passed, and Zelda let out a heavy sigh.

"Jesus Frank, those things are creepy."

"Yeah, I think it's safe to head back home. Let's go."

Frank stepped out of the shadows of the alley and onto the main road. His eyes traced the backs of the marching Recycled.

Zelda said, "Whatever they're doing, it can't be good."

From above, a weaselly male voice said, "They're marching on central security."

Frank looked up. Above him, leaning out of a window, was Tony. Frank felt another tightness in his chest, but just a twinge.

"Zelda, run."

But it was too late. Out of the windows above, a half dozen Recycled jumped down. They crashed with a collision of metal on concrete around both Frank and Zelda. They were surrounded.

Tony strolled down the front steps of the building. The creatures stood motionless, waiting for orders but blocking any escape. Frank shivered. He knew those strange white on white on white eyes were looking at him, but they were vacant and empty, devoid of any thought or emotion.

"So, you thought you were gonna get away with it, didn't you?"

"Get away with what?"

"Come on Frank, you're dumb, but you're not that dumb."

"Look, all I wanted was to make sure people had a fair say in things. I can't help it that you want something different."

"Whatever you say, Frank. We both know you're working with the SOs. Why else would those Runners show up in the last attack and save your ass?"

"Luck?"

Tony laughed. "You know, Frank, I could have these things kill you right now and be done with it. But I think I would rather let you watch the slaughter. Then, maybe after we take over this city, we can have a good old-fashioned public execution for you and your friend here. I'm sure your families would like to watch. Hell, maybe we'll string them up too."

Zelda spit in his face. Tony moved fast, grabbing Zelda by the throat and pushing her up against the wall. He pulled out his laser pistol and pointed it up under her chin.

"Look here, you little bitch. I could kill you now if you want, but that would be too quick. I want to enjoy your death. But if you spit on me again, I'm gonna melt your fucking brains with this pistol." He shoved her back against the wall. "You two are coming with me."

Zelda grabbed her throat and coughed a few times. Tony backed away; weapon raised.

Frank asked, "Where?"

"To central security. Where else? Grab 'em."

Frank didn't fight; there was no point. The Recycled were far too strong and too numerous. He would wait and hope. Maybe he would get lucky a second time? Maybe those two Runners would show again? But deep down, he knew that even if they did, they were far outnumbered and outgunned this time. Frank felt himself slide into hopelessness, and for the first time in his life, he felt that all hope was lost.

Chapter 28
Matron

Mimi forced herself into a sitting position. "The archives?"

Noatla Lightfoot gave one long, slow nod. "It's what I call them anyway. Do you see the pillars?"

Mimi looked around. There were massive pillars in every direction.

"How big is this place?"

Noatla shook her head. "I don't know. I've walked for hours in different directions, and there doesn't seem to be an end."

"But why do you call them the archives? Isn't an archive a place of knowledge, or at least a library?"

"Stand up and touch one of the pillars."

Mimi cocked her head, "Why?"

"If you want to know why I call it the archives, that's the quickest way to find out. I could explain it, but like many things in life, it's better to experience it for yourself."

Mimi shrugged, stood, and walked a meter to the nearest pillar. She guessed that all the pillars were evenly spaced five meters apart in, from what she could tell, perfect alignment.

"Place your hand on it."

Mimi did. Instantly she was flooded with the thoughts and experiences of another person. This one was a Mid who worked in primary education. She had a wife and a small child, but she was always unhappy, always unsatisfied. She wanted to get to the Uppers and would do just about anything to make it up there. She pushed her wife to work two jobs, and she picked up side gigs on top of teaching wherever she could. Then, one day, she crossed a line and started running drugs from the Lowers to the Uppers. Mimi watched as the woman did drug runs for months, gradually working her way towards saving up enough for a place in the Uppers. She found a sponsor to help her move up in one of her regular clients. Finally, the day came when she was ready to buy in, and then the attack on Saud came. She and her small family survived, but a few days after the city launched into the atmosphere, someone knocked at her door.

Mimi watched as this woman, in the middle of the night, opened the door. Two Recycled grabbed her, sedated her, and she woke in the underground. They hooked her up to the network and then all was empty and vacant. Her thoughts and emotions were quiet and persisted in her noiseless existence.

Puzzled, Mimi walked over to the next nearest pillar to her left. She touched it. This time it was a Lower working in shield maintenance, but the story was familiar. He was a man trying to work his way up, and then, one night, Recycled knocked at his door and took him, and he found himself plugged into the strange machines in the underground.

Mimi walked to the next one, and it was the same, a person kidnapped by Recycled and hooked up to the network.

"Noatla, is every single one of these people hooked up to the network?"

"I am assuming by the network you mean those strange machines that the Recycled are putting people in?"

"Yes... Willow calls it the network. It's how Miranda has increased her power."

Noatla nodded to herself. "I see."

Mimi nodded, too. For a long time, she sat lost in thought.

"Noatla, you're dead, and you're not in the machine. How did you get here?"

Noatla looked up, only barely escaping the corners of her own mind. "I think perhaps it's best if I simply show you, Mimi. I will admit that I have been watching you on occasion when I could reach out, but those times were limited. I need to know everything about what happened to the city after the battle with Miranda and the Children of Gaia."

"Okay, but I've been trapped underground with Willow, so I don't know what's going on in the city above, except for the few stolen glimpses I took from Willow's mind before she sent me to this place... wherever this place is."

"Once we swap information, then we can talk."

Mimi shrugged and sat down, sitting cross-legged and face-to-face with Noatla. Even sitting, she was almost a full head taller than Mimi. Mimi closed her eyes, and each woman traded the history of each other's journey. Mimi saw Noatla stand up to Miranda outside the library. She saw her sacrifice to get Alexa out of the archives and how she, Noatla, became trapped here.

Mimi showed Noatla the battle in the old subway tunnels and, though she was hesitant, how the red veil had overwhelmed her, and Mimi had killed friend and foe alike. She showed her how she had woken up with Willow and the Recycled, of Willow's apparent goals and desires and how Mimi's body had been augmented so she could pilot a combat grade EnViro suit. Mimi shared everything she had learned about the network, the Recycled, and her final fight with Willow. Because they shared each other's experiences through a direct mental link, each woman could feel the other's emotions and had a full sense memory of the other.

"Thank you, Mimi. All of this explains much. When I started seeing the machines that each of the people in this archive are placed in, I began to wonder if that related to Miranda's increased power. In the first days of the war between the Order of the Eye and the Children of Gaia, the winner was often the person who could recruit the most telepaths to their side. There were a lot more of us in those days as Matron Angela, the very first member of the Order of the Eye was forced to undergo cloning. There were thousands of copies of her made, and many of those copies had children and spread throughout the planet before migration began. So, when Migration started, and the war between Angela's granddaughter,

Matron Mariposa, and Miranda took hold, each of the sisters took sides. In the end, we were able to unite more telepaths to our cause and many of those who aligned with Miranda died in battle."

"So, the network makes sense. Miranda couldn't recruit more to her cause, so after she was struck a great blow with the fall of Mex, she must have discovered a new way to force other minds to align with her through this technology."

"But Noatla, the number of pillars here seems to stretch on forever, there were hundreds, maybe thousands connected to Miranda's network in the underground, but not this many."

"Agreed. I have walked a long way in this archive and touched many of the pillars. Right now, we are sitting in the section for Manhatsten, but there are other sections."

"Other sections?"

"Miranda has created networks in other cities and, apparently, somewhere in a city in underground caverns where she has headquartered the Children of Gaia. Potentially she has hundreds of thousands of individuals hooked up to machines around the planet."

"That still doesn't account for the size of this space."

Noatla shook her head. "No, it doesn't, but there was one pillar I touched that suggested that this place is not limited to the way we think of time."

Mimi shifted; the hard ground made her tailbone ache. She wished she had a cushion or something.

"What do you mean?"

"It's difficult to explain. How much time would you guess has passed since the battle in the subway tunnels?"

"It's hard to say. Willow drugged me several times."

"Fair enough, but guess."

"A few weeks?"

"That would have been my guess based on what you transmitted to me. The thing is, in my frame of reference, Alexa only left this place a few minutes ago. But also, at the same time, after she left, I was able to explore a huge portion of these archives. So, on the one hand, it seems as if I have been here for years; on the other, it seems as if I have been here for minutes."

"How can you hold both that sense of minutes and years at the same time?"

"I don't know. But one of the pillars I found was from someone from Mars, and some of the references they made about life there suggested it was many years in the future, after a time when the cities of Earth began to orbit the little red planet."

"What? But I didn't know there was anyone on Mars."

"There is. They call themselves ROAM, and based on what I saw of this person's life, they have been there since the final shuttles arrived on the surface over a thousand years ago. Their population has been growing underground. It was slow at first, but it's there. I also discovered a few people in the pillars that were from several moons in the solar system and even one from an asteroid."

"I didn't even know there were more moons than the one in our sky... What does all this mean, Noatla?"

"What I think it means, is that left unchecked, Miranda will take over the entirety of this solar system at least. What we see here is the potential for her to control everything. If she makes each network in the cities big enough, they will be able to connect to each other, and the whole planet will be under her direct control. Then, if she moves to the moon and Mars, she can build an unstoppable empire."

"How do we stop her?"

Noatla hesitated. "I think you already know-how."

Mimi frowned. "The red veil?"

"Well, that, and turning Miranda's network against her."

"I have to ask, was that you speaking to me when Willow was trying to force me to make those people kill each other?"

"Yes."

"Why didn't you intervene before?"

"I couldn't before. Willow was too strong. She had total possession of Miranda's network. When you turned the red veil on her, she was forced to relinquish some of her control."

"The red veil is alive... it has its own will."

"I've suspected that for a long time. I don't think that Miranda turned the red veil to her will, I think the red veil turned Miranda to its will."

"Why do you think that?"

"Because I knew Miranda. She was a friend... and... my aunt."

Mimi blinked... her mouth opened wide. "She's related to you?"

"Yes. She was my mother's sister. My mother was born before migration. We were a wealthy family. My grandmother died giving birth to Miranda in a terrible accident involving an alcove. It set the stage for Miranda's madness, but as her niece, I worked hard to help her through her pain and trauma. Ultimately I failed, and she betrayed us all."

"Was she in the Order of the Eye?"

"Yes. She was recruited by Matron Mariposa, the direct successor to the Matron Angela, the first telepath. Then, when I came of age, Miranda recruited me into the Order of the Eye. You have to understand, Mimi, I really believed there was enough good in her to overcome her own madness. You see, the way she was born, it gave her a strange kind of mental illness. She held the mind and memories of my grandmother within her. I actually saw it once, got to touch it. At the same time, Miranda had her own mind and memories, and, as time went on, the two minds merged and blended in a way that distorted reality for her. She started hearing things, seeing things, and then she started experimenting with the red veil... it changed her, it sent her down a different path than the Order. Behind our backs, she aligned herself with an underground environmental terrorist organization that was still operating in some of the ruins around the world and attempting to hijack or attack the early migrating cities. She promised the Children of Gaia everything they ever wanted and brought more and more telepaths to their ranks. She taught them all the red veil, but ultimately there were more of us than her group and we won. Or at least we thought we did until Mex."

"What happened with Mex?"

"We aren't entirely sure. All we know is that Mex went to war with Manhatsten. My guess is that Miranda took over the leadership of Mex and used them the way she used Senator Reevas. There was an offshoot of the Order of the Eye on Mex, though, and we never discovered what happened to them. But it's clear she didn't have the technology for the network yet or else she would have tried a less direct approach."

"Why would she attack Manhatsten though?"

"I think that even though there were other branches of the Order of the Eye around, she considered Manhatsten her home, and she wanted revenge for how we destroyed her in the first war."

"Then why would she want to destroy Manhatsten now?"

"Oh, I don't think she wanted to this time around. I think she intended to take over the Order of the Eye and making Manhatsten her home base. But I think she underestimated the devotion of her own followers. She set a plan in motion to destroy the walking cities because she was angry and vengeful, but I think she realized the network was much more likely to get her what she wants. When Alexa disrupted her, even with the network behind her, I think she thought it was too dangerous to let Manhatsten continue on. I think she decided that destroying it, and the remnants of the first Order of the Eye was her best chance to achieve her goals."

"But she destroyed Saud and Langeles too. Couldn't she have found a way to turn them?"

"Saud's branch of the Order of the Eye was strong. They didn't believe in Recycling, and their Runnercore, the Rih, was all volunteer. It would have been difficult for Miranda to overcome that city until her network was complete. Langeles had a similar situation, they had no Recycled and no compulsory Runnercore. For Miranda, it was more strategic to destroy those cities as she expanded her power. Besides, I think it makes a lot of sense for her to destroy most, if not all, of the cities to start. Most migrating cities have hundreds of thousands of people; even with the network, it would take time, and tens of thousands of people hooked up to the network for her to have enough strength. Through her followers of the Children of Gaia, it would require less effort in the long term to simply destroy the cities and use the scrap material to further expand the power of the Children of Gaia."

"So then, how can the red veil be the answer?"

"The red veil is more than just rage. It's passion. The red veil has other forms. Passion can be love, it can be melded with compassion. Unchecked, it is a feral beast, a kind of manifestation of the maddened passions of humankind. But, with the right discipline and the right effort, the red veil can become an ally."

Mimi said, "Then why didn't you teach that to us instead of making it forbidden?"

"Because it was only here, in solitude, that I have come to understand that all facets of the human experience have a purpose, that all emotions contain wisdom. If you use patience and forbearance to transform the red veil, it can shift from anger and rage into the wisdom of passion and love. Even if I had understood this before, I would have been hesitant to teach it. Only some individuals are capable of transforming suffering into wisdom. Most are happy in their misery; they find the trap to their liking and continue to wallow in it and embrace it. But some, like you, Mimi, have taken their suffering and let it transform them."

"How? I don't understand what you are talking about."

"Willow was right. You and Miranda have something in common. You were both born in blood and rage. Both of your powers awakened from a moment of horror and trauma. But each of you has walked a very different path. Each of you chose what to do with that experience. You, Mimi, have chosen to let it guide you in the empathy of others. It's why, when you joined the Order, you insisted on spending your time and energy rescuing other women who were lost, alone and afraid. Miranda recognized the power that her trauma gave her, recognized what it meant to have power, and craved more. What you do with that trauma matters, and every choice you make every single day can make all the difference. You are the only one who can stop Miranda. You are the only one who can master the red veil. But it will take time. You cannot expect yourself to transform overnight. Change starts with a choice, and then another choice, and then another one. Change insists that you keep making a different choice until the different ways of being and knowing themselves transform you."

"But I don't understand, Noatla, how do I use the red veil in the right way, then?"

"Love."

"Love?"

"You began to do this with Willow. It started as sympathy, but it transformed into compassion. If she would have let you in all the way, you may have defeated her already. Because you didn't understand what you were doing, she cut you off and closed the door. Let your love and your passion to help guide you. Instead of letting anger fill you for the red veil, let your love of Shannon, of your sisters, of those women you rescued on the street guide you. Set your intention to work towards the benefit of all those you love, and if you can, all beings. If you do this, if you watch and you are vigilant to keep the rage and madness at bay, if you let those feelings of love and kindness flow through your heart, it will transform the red veil into something other, something that Willow or Miranda could not stand against."

"Anger is the most dangerous of emotions, and the red veil, this manifestation of collective human emotion, knows that. It is more than just an ability. It fills this place. The red veil permeates every inch of human consciousness. It is our dissatisfaction, our collective rage and humiliation. In ancient mythologies, it took on many personas. In Buddhism and Hinduism, it was Mara. In ancient Greece, it was Hades, in Christianity, it was the figure of the adversary, the dark one. But it is nothing that manifests into a physical being; rather, it is something that possesses us. For we are not separate, and the shame and pain that we experience as a species, is shared. We are connected more than we know or understand."

"So, it really is alive? I'm not crazy?"

"In a matter of speaking, yes. It has a will of its own, but it requires a kind of host to think and plan. Our emotions and our thoughts shape reality. They are a vehicle for a universe of possibilities."

"What?"

"It's not important now. You will understand when the time is right."

Mimi glanced around the endless chamber.

"It seems moot though, doesn't it? I'm stuck here."

"No, you're not."

"I'm not? If I'm not, then why are you still here?"

"Oh, I know how to leave now. I just can't."

"Why not?"

"Because my body was destroyed. Your sisters cremated it."

"What? Why?"

"It was my wish that upon my death, I would be cremated. Unfortunately, that means there's nothing to return to. Besides, even if I did, it would have been too late. The body cannot function without the mind for more than a few days. Biological processes begin to break down quickly. But you just arrived, and though Willow may perceive you as dead, it is unlikely that she will destroy your body so quickly."

"So, you're going to send me back?"

"Yes."

"But how can I defeat Willow? How can I break free of that place?"

"I told you already, set your intention of how to use the red veil. Love is more powerful than rage. It always has been, it always will be. Think Mimi, if you are angry at someone you love, someone you truly love, that can stay your hand in a moment of anger."

Mimi thought about how she had almost killed Shannon under the influence of the red veil. She opened her mouth to say something, but Noatla spoke first.

"You wouldn't have killed her."

"You're wrong. I killed everyone else who stood in my way."

"You didn't love any of those people like you love her. You wouldn't have killed Serah either."

"How do you know that?"

"Because you could have killed Serah with your last moments of consciousness. You could have used the red veil to strike her and Shannon down with one thought. You didn't."

"No, there wasn't enough time. Serah stabbed me."

Noatla shook her head. "No, Mimi. Think. Close your eyes and go back into that moment."

Mimi did. She saw the scene over again, the Recycled, the reserve Runners, them falling one by one around her with a simple thought. She saw them fall down like felled trees under a terrible machine. She crushed and ground their minds into nothing. Then, there was no one between her and Shannon. She reached out to let the red veil flow into her. She reached out with the dark red strands and connected with Shannon's mind. Then, she stopped. She hesitated. She saw Shannon for who she was, and then she felt a sharp pain in her back. She looked down and saw the blade sticking through her. Turning, she saw Serah. She saw those regretful eyes; she saw the tears gathering in the corner of Serah's eyes. She turned the red veil on her, and let the strands connect with Serah. She could crush her mind now, with her final breaths. But she didn't. She hesitated and then lost consciousness.

Mimi opened her eyes. Tears streamed down both sides of her face.

"I chose not to."

"That's right, Mimi. You made a choice not to hurt the ones you loved."

Mimi's emotions broke and washed over her. Noatla pulled her in tight and comforted her.

"I'm not a monster. I can control it."

"No, you aren't a monster. Let love flow through you and let it intertwine with the power of the red veil. If you do this, you will become its master instead of the other way around."

Mimi let Noatla hold her for what seemed like a long time. She felt warm and safe in her arms.

"I can't leave you here, Noatla."

"You won't have to. I have to ask something of you. It's dangerous."

Mimi pulled her head away from Noatla's chest. "What?"

"I need you to carry me."

"Carry you?"

"Yes, there is somewhere I must go, and temporarily you can carry me in your mind."

"What? How? Where would I carry you? Why is it dangerous?"

"The brain is a powerful organ, but it is limited and is only meant to carry one mind for any period of time. It is dangerous because if I occupy your mind for too long, it could damage your brain. I will put myself in a state of silence, as if I was a coma patient. This should allow you to carry me for several months. Any longer, though, and you risk permanent damage. I am not sure if this is something the alcoves could repair or not. No one in the archives seems to know the answer. Remember, this is something similar that happened to Miranda; my grandmother and her mind were trapped in one brain. Over the long term, it's very dangerous. But in the short term, you could help me get out of here. I wouldn't ask if I didn't think it was necessary Mimi."

"Noatla, you've always been like a mother to me. But I don't even know if I can escape Willow or the underground, and besides, where would I take you? You said yourself that you didn't have a body."

"You will have to take me to AEIS."

"AEIS?"

"Yes, it resides in the underground on the planet's surface. The current flow of time will take you there."

"The current flow of time? Are you telling me you can see the future like Alexa?"

"Sort of. Being in this place, I can see some things, but not much. I know you will go to AEIS soon, but I cannot say more, lest I change the possible outcomes."

"How am I supposed to find this AEIS?"

"That's not to worry about right now. Right now, you have to save your own body."

"What?"

"Willow is preparing yours for the conveyer belt. She believes you dead."

"The conveyer belt? The one that starts the Recycling process?"

"Yes. You have only a few minutes to make her aware that you aren't dead."

Mimi jumped up. "A few minutes?"

Noatla nodded.

"What do we do then?"

"We sit."

"Sit?"

"Sit and focus."

Noatla reached her hand up to Mimi, and as Mimi took it, she gently pulled her down. Mimi sat facing Noatla, legs crossed and impatient.

"I can help get you past the barrier. I will have to meld my consciousness with yours. It requires a great deal of energy and focus to get past the barrier. As long as we both focus on the same thing, we can get through and back to your body."

Mimi nodded.

"Focus on my eyes, Mimi. Do not break your gaze from mine, no matter what."

Mimi did. In a few moments she felt something in her shift and move. She felt lighter, felt more powerful, and then the archives were fading.

"Remember Mimi... remember the red veil is more than just rage... remember love."

Chapter 29
The Last Stand

Their bodies lumbered in rhythmic motion as they shambled toward the entrance. As they came, civilians fled the space. Each human scrambled, sweat, and fear oozing from their pores as they sought to escape. There was panic, but it was the quiet kind, the one that no one ever speaks of until after the monsters and reapers and hellish nightmares are gone.

The Recycled moved in singular strokes. Each leg matched in marching with the one adjacent to it. In squads of ten by ten, they kept perfect pace with one another. Each squad was a unit, a singular organized thought, a physical representation of a cluster of neurons. They were a red army, the army of the veil, and in their white on white on white eyes you could see a hint of the red spark born from the hunger of madness of their master.

In the rear of the compliment, Alana Green sat on the shoulders of one of the creatures. She had marched her army several kilometers. She wanted to inspire fear, wanted the city to know who soon would grab power and hold it. There was no need for secrets or strategies now. Her undead army was a blunt instrument, a club to bring the city to its knees. Central security had no way of stopping them. Those stationed high in the tower that protected the city had neither the numbers nor the weapons. They could aim for the head, they could mow down hundreds and still, more would come. A second wave waited below the surface, and though that bitch, Lydia, had secured all the underground exits, Alana's army would find a way to come in. She had not even told Tony just how many there were under her command. Why would she? She knew the man would try and kill her before the day was out. She wouldn't kill him though. She would make him her pet, her plaything, at least for a while.

Alana's eyes glared, and her army approached the exterior of central security. Her smile stretched long past the boundaries of sanity into another slice of consciousness, something known only to those who have traversed beyond the rational and reasonable and into something beyond. The red veil changed her, corrupted her, rotted away any semblance of resistance until even the strands of her hair were wild with lust and hate. She, the person she had been, had died weeks ago. She didn't know that she was a vehicle for Willow's will, a vessel, empty of itself waiting to be filled, but she found pleasure in her emptiness, a kind of corrupted joy.

As each unit of Recycled arrived in the courtyard of central security, it spread out into a great arc surrounding the front entrance and creeping along the sides of the building. Alana didn't care if some of the SO's escaped. She didn't care about the fleeing masses skirting the alleyways and hidden nooks of the city. The more that fled, the easier it would be. In the end, there was no refuge.

There were no reinforcements. She had made sure that a portion of the SO's were spread around the city, engaged in skirmishes with Tony's men. This time, only the Recycled would march into central. The Recycled would not flee as those cowards had at the sight of just two Runners. These creatures would walk right into a firefight without flinching. Most importantly, a pair of powerful Runners would do nothing to dissuade the creatures. Only a full complement of Runners would stand against her monsters, and all had fallen in the war against Saud, or were at least earthside.

Alana's mount pulled up the rear, and then, as it reached its final destination outside of central security, it put Alana down. She walked over toward Tony, who stood with his two prisoners at gunpoint.

"I thought I told you not to bother with those two."

Tony shrugged. "They were right along the path. I didn't have to go anywhere."

"And what are you going to do with them?"

"Let them watch, and then kill them."

A grin spread across Alana's face, she glanced at the man with the huge belly and the thin wispy thing. There was a hint of defiance in both of them, even now, but it was masked by the fear in their dull cow eyes. Both avoided eye contact with her.

She liked the idea of making them watch the slaughter. She said, "Here I thought you didn't like our new friends."

"I don't. I'll be glad when this is over."

"Too bad. I think they like you."

Tony tried to keep his face straight, but Alana saw the cracks below his mask. He hadn't hidden his fear and disgust well when the Recycled slaughtered the Senate. She loved watching. It was so interesting to see how easily human bodies crumpled with a little pressure. Flesh was so fragile, so squishy, so intoxicating. She loved the smell bodies made after they released the bowels and the aroma of blood and decaying flesh. The sound of buzzing flies sent reverberations of pleasure down her spine. Her favorite part was when the creatures pulled off limbs. She could watch that all day long. The tearing of muscle and snap of bone were orgasmic. She trembled with delight.

"You think those two Runners are gonna show up and kick their ass like last time?"

"Two against all this? Don't make me laugh."

"What if there are more? What if that crazy bitch at the top of that tower has been keeping other Runners hidden? What if she has dozens?"

"Dozens won't be enough. Don't you worry, Tony."

Alana slithered over to the man and put her hand on his chest. He winced. It only turned her on more. She put her hand on his neck and then pulled him close to whisper in his hear. "There's plenty more where these came from." She gave his ear a nibble and could feel him shiver. She would have him in her bed later, whether he wanted to or not. It would be better if he didn't. The Recycled could hold him down if needed. Perhaps they could make a child, a new king or queen for the city.

She pulled back. "It's time to make our demands."

"Our demands?"

"It wouldn't be very fair if we didn't at least offer to let them surrender."

"What if they do? What then?"

"Oh, don't worry. They won't surrender."

"But what if they do?"

"Then we go inside and kill them all anyway. That would be much easier."

Tony said nothing. He didn't need to. His face paled, and his eyes widened. His lower lip trembled just a little, he tried to hide it, but Alana knew the hidden secrets of flesh well. There were so many tells if you just knew where to look. She had tortured and maimed so many in the last few weeks. She would probably kill Tony soon enough. It wouldn't be on purpose, it was just, sometimes it was easy to get a little... carried away.

Alana walked up to the entrance. She looked up at one of the cameras pointing down at her. She didn't raise her voice as she looked into the open eye of the camera, smiled, and said, "Would you like to surrender? If you do, I can promise you mercy. If you don't, I will make sure that every single person in the building dies horribly at the hands of my Recycled."

2.

Lydia watched the camera and said nothing. She asked Roma, "Everyone in position?"

"Yes, Sir!"

"What about the Runners, are they unboxed?"

"Yes sir, they are stationed on level eighteen. But Sir, I can't imagine they will do much good, there are only five of them, and they aren't trained beyond a basic tutorial of their equipment."

"We only need them to provide support. Hopefully, we can stop the Recycled before they even reach eighteen."

"I hope so, commander."

"Manhatsten, any word from Luna?"

"Yes, Lydia Danvers. The Dugger will land in the Runner dock in twelve minutes."

"How many telepaths did they pick up?"

"There are nine on the Dugger."

"Nine, huh?"

"Rigel Solidsworth and Senator Swanson stayed behind so that they could accommodate more, but the Dugger is at full capacity."

"Damn shame, we didn't have more."

"You may be glad to know that Rigel Solidsworth was able to alter three of the Lunar rovers to carry an additional five telepaths each. Unfortunately, they are fourteen minutes behind the first Dugger."

"Sounds like we need to buy some time. Roma, I am going to negotiate a surrender."

"You're what?"

She saw the panic on his face and said, "Not for real. I want to give the telepaths time to make it to the docks. If I can buy us fifteen minutes, it could make all the difference."

"Commander, I can't let you do that. You need to be up here away from the front line. I can't lose you."

"YOU can't lose me?"

"I mean... uh... we can't lose you."

Lydia looked at Roma for a minute. "Tell you what. I know it's against protocol, but if we survive this, I'll let you take me on a date. So, you best come with me and keep us both alive, okay?"

Roma blushed.

Lydia smiled.

"Manhatsten, open a line to that speaker under the surveillance camera, will you?"

"It is ready."

"Alana Green. I'm coming down to discuss the conditions of our surrender. It's clear that you have us surrounded, and I want assurance that my staff or the civilians of this city will not be harmed."

"Very well. You have ten minutes to get down here, or I will send in the Recycled."

"Manhatsten, close the channel."

"Channel is closed."

"See, Roma? Just by telling her we are willing to talk we bought ourselves ten minutes. Now, if I can stretch it out a little longer..."

"I don't understand, Commander, what good will waiting do? The telepaths can work from a distance, right? And you said the more of them there are, the further they can reach. So why wait for them all to arrive?"

"Because Serah told me that even though you can reach further when linked to other telepaths, the closer you are, the more powerful you are. So, if we can get them all inside central security and spring the trap at the same time, we might be able to cut down a large number of Recycled before they even enter the building. We need to even the odds."

"But how are you going to get them here from the docks? That's seven kilometers, not to mention all of Tony's men in combat with our SO's and that army of Recycled downstairs."

"The streets are clear, aren't they?"

"Yeah, but what's that got to do with it? You still can't walk seven kilometers... Wait. Did you?"

"Oh no, not me."

"Then, who?"

"Serah's idea."

Adrian Roma smiled. "Guess they got more than one surprise coming for them, don't they?"

Lydia smiled back. If they were going to die today, they were going to take as many of the bastards with them as they could; hopefully, all of them. If they killed all the Recycled, even if it meant her life, it would give the city a fighting chance. That mad telepath couldn't control everyone, could she?

3.

"You know they're stalling, right?" Tony shifted from foot to foot; he had to piss. But waiting to attack your enemy didn't really provide a lot of good places to pee. It didn't help that he had two prisoners to watch. But what was he supposed to do, wait till the battle was over? He wished he was in an EnViro suit. The Recycling system would take care of this problem.

"Of course I do. But it doesn't matter. They can stall for days, but in the end, the result will be the same. It's so much easier if we cut the head off the snake now."

"So, when Danvers gets here?"

"We kill her."

"Not going to hear her out?"

"Maybe a little. I like to play with my prey before I consume it."

Tony shivered. Most people would have meant that figuratively, but he was pretty sure that Alana had every intention of consuming some of the dead. He had seen her do it twice now and had left the room to wretch both times. That wasn't something you could get used to, especially since she ate the flesh raw.

She looked at him, hopping from foot to foot and scowled. "Go pee, you moron. The Recycled will watch your little guests."

Tony, feeling as if his bladder was going to explode, ran around the corner and relieved himself. It was one of those times when he had to go so bad that it almost felt like an orgasm. He sighed relief and buttoned up his fly. Before he could turn around, he felt a surge of pain in the back of his skull, and then everything went black.

4.

The Dugger came to a halt inside the Runner dock.

Shannon, still in her combat grade EnViro suit, said, "S2, how far behind are the rovers?"

Shannon's suit AI said, "Twelve, fourteen, and fifteen minutes, respectively."

Serah stepped out of the Dugger first, and her feet clanged on the concrete. She surveyed the room. It was ghostly quiet. She didn't like it, not at all.

Behind her, Kirka, Loni, and several other telepaths followed. Rigel had modified the gravitational generator in the Dugger to accommodate the reduced gravity of Luna. He and Loridian had also reset a dozen alcoves to match Earth's standard gravity. Still, each woman was only able to spend thirty minutes inside while they were preparing the vehicles. It wasn't enough to reshape their bodies; that would take dozens of sessions in an alcove for weeks, but Rigel had programmed the system to reinforce their muscles and bones in their legs so that at 1G, they wouldn't collapse. It had helped, but each woman struggled to walk. They simply weren't used to the extra weight, and it offset their balance. That didn't matter much considering their form of transportation, at least until they got to the skybridge, but it was something.

Serah said, "Manhatsten, are the streets clear? Packages ready?"

"Yes, Serah, but you must hurry. Lydia Danvers is attempting to stall the attack, but she will not be able to hold out for much longer."

"Alright, Shannon. You go prep Dugger 1 and 2. Then, I want you to carry these ladies over there."

"Kirka said, "I can walk, thank you."

Loni added, "Yeah, I got legs."

Serah shook her head. "You're going to need all your muscles to run the last three blocks. Besides, in the EnViro suits, I could carry three of you without breaking a sweat.

Kirka sighed. "Fine."

Just as Serah had loaded the first Dugger, the first Lunar Rover arrived. She filled the Dugger with the next group of telepaths and then waited for the other two. Serah thought about all the things she had been through in the last few weeks. She thought about Mimi and Noatla and all of her fellow sisters. She reached out to Vala and confirmed the plan. Vala and Yoshi were already waiting for them inside central security. They just had to make it there.

As Shannon helped load the last of the Lunites into Dugger 2, she asked, "You think this is going to work?"

"I don't know. I don't know if there have ever been so many telepaths working together at once, at least not in Manhatsten. Twenty-eight should work, but we just don't know how powerful she is. What do you think, Kirka?"

Kirka, who sat just inside one of the Duggers, said, "We routinely network twenty to thirty of us together. Whenever there is unrest in the city, we can soothe the population effectively with our network. It has prevented several rebellions. Thirty telepaths should be plenty. I don't know how it would be possible for a single telepath to overcome thirty well-trained women."

"We don't know how she was able to overcome fourteen of us working together; she was never able to do so before."

Kirka said, "You will have double that number this time. If that doesn't stop her, then we have a much bigger problem."

Serah nodded. "I hope you're right, Kirka. Because something doesn't feel right about all this. We don't know why Miranda became more powerful. She has to have either unlocked some sort of inner strength or..."

"...Or she's drawing her power from something else."

Serah nodded. "If it's something else, we better hope that something else was left back on the surface of the planet, because if it wasn't, we're in serious trouble."

Shannon said, "I wasn't talking about telepathy.

Both women turned toward her.

Serah cocked her head slightly. "What were you talking about?"

"Do you think the packages will work?"

"Oh. Yeah, definitely. I'm not worried about that part at all. Just make sure we are clear of the blast before it goes off, and keep your mind shielded like Mimi taught you so Miranda can't see what's coming."

5.

Lydia Danvers hadn't been honest with her team. It wasn't that she didn't trust the people under her command; quite the opposite. Her SO's had come to respect her after she held off the last attack. No, the problem was, they were fighting a mad telepath. Yoshi and Vala were upstairs helping to keep her mind shielded, but if she had told all of her crew everything, then there would be too many minds to skim. So, Lydia alone knew the entire plan. She knew that was dangerous, that it might get some of her people killed, but it was a trade-off; if she made that knowledge widely available, it would doom them all. Roma knew the most, but he didn't know about the Duggers. She would just have to hope that the blast doors kept them safe. That was what they were designed for, after all.

Lydia got off the lift on the ground floor. The large lobby was empty and waiting. The trap was set, but the question was, would Alana Green and the Recycled take the bait? Vala seemed to think that Alana Green was either controlled by Miranda or allied with her to take over the city. Serah didn't know what to think about that, but when Vala told her their suspicions about Senator Reevas, it made more sense that Alana was just another tool in this crazy telepath's arsenal. Regardless, she had every intention of killing Alana as quickly as possible.

Manhatsten knew everything, but it was impossible to coordinate their defense without the AI. It had suggested that Miranda could read and interfere with its plans, but there was little Lydia could do about that. They would just have to hope that Miranda didn't interfere too much. As a precaution, the AI had set up backup plans to any automated system, and Lydia had some of her people in place to trigger the surprises. She wasn't taking any chances this time. Despite the loss of life and the danger of the earlier attack on central, she had learned a lot from that event. She planned on using everything she learned last time to win the fight this time. One way or another, this ended today.

The Recycled would end today, too. Never again would she allow the creation of another one of those creatures. She hoped that most, if not all of them were destroyed in the battle ahead. If not, she would see to it personally that there were none left. When Vala had told her about Noatla's efforts to have the creatures removed among the Senate, Lydia couldn't help but feel a low simmer of anger. But the only Senator left alive was Swanson, and at least he was a reasonable one.

Lydia said, "Manhatsten, you're sure that you can't control any of those Recycled?"

"I cannot. Not even one. They are entirely out of my control. It's like a digital firewall. I cannot even see them in my operating system even though I see them on cameras. It is a rather strange sensation, Lydia Danvers."

"It's too bad we don't know where Miranda is hiding. If we could get a team to take her out, we would defeat her in an instant."

"Though I agree that would be the best course of action, I am doubtful about it being a simple outcome. Miranda appeared in person at the end of the last conflict and was able to avoid capture. Her many abilities make her difficult to apprehend. Further, there are many places for her to hide in the city and she has, in the past, had the power to blind my sensor completely. I have been running city scans for weeks with no success."

"Well, it was worth asking... again."

"Indeed. I also have an update for you on Serah's progress."

"Oh?"

"Yes, her Dugger is in the docks, and they are awaiting the three Lunar rovers. The last rover will arrive in nine minutes and forty-one seconds."

"So, I just have to delay what, another twenty minutes?"

"That would be ideal, yes."

"Roma, you ready?"

"As much as I can be, Commander."

"And everyone is in position?"

"All ready to go."

Lydia sucked in a gulp of air and took her first steps toward the front entrance of the lobby and her fate. Her feet felt heavy. She knew the odds of her surviving this; Manhatsten had repeated it a dozen times for her benefit. Not to discourage her, no, it was Roma that kept asking for updates every time they did something different.

Lydia had known that Roma was interested in her for some time, long before she ever took command. He was brilliant and talented and caring and a hell of an officer. She would give him a chance if they got out of this alive. Hell, she was half-tempted to push him into a closet right now... it was nice to go into battle with as little stress as possible.

She stood just inside the door. Since the last assault, the AI had helped them design energy and ballistic proof glass for the first and second level, and she had some comfort in knowing that no one could simply shoot her through the front entrance, at least not without numerous attempts.

She reflected on how amazing Manhatsten had been in helping with preparations. It had offered so many suggestions and ideas, and it had run the industrial printers to synthesize endless objects to prepare for combat. If they survived this, they were going to have to figure out a way to give the city a commendation or something.

"Manhatsten, open a channel in the comm line to speak to Alana Green."

"It is open, and you are now able to communicate."

"Alright, Ms. Green, tell me what you want with central. What are your terms of surrender?"

Lydia tried to keep the disgust and loathing out of her voice. In truth, she wanted nothing more than to kill this woman. Green was at least partly responsible for the loss of some of her men. Even if something was controlling her, she was still at least partially at fault. Now, here she was with an army of Recycled at her doorstep, and for the first time, Lydia thought she understood Major Daniels's feelings about protecting the city.

For a moment, no one responded, then Alana said, "Your life, for starters." Another pause, a toothy grin in Alana's tone. "Then, I want you to throw down all your weapons and have every SO under your command march out here unarmed and ready to surrender to me. Every single one of you will be converted into my new Runnercore, and you will be under my command until the day you die. If you're lucky, I'll let you die in a few centuries."

Lydia's emotions flared, but she brought them back under control. She couldn't tell if that was her own doing, or if Vala and Yoshi were helping her somehow, but she steadied herself. She had to think of a stalling tactic; what could she say or offer to keep her talking? It was clear that Green, or Miranda behind the mask, wanted total control of the city and to execute anyone who had previously stood in her way. When she had asked Vala and Yoshi if Miranda had any mercy or sense of fairness, they had both replied no. Both had suggested that Miranda would destroy anyone in her way and that she would have no interest in taking prisoners. Both suggested that any kind of surrender would lead to their deaths. So, Lydia needed to convince Green, and Miranda by extension, that they thought that surrender was their best choice.

"How do I know you won't kill all of the people under my command if we lay down our arms? What can you do to show me that you are serious about our surrender? It seems to me that all you want to do is bring us out so the Recycled can slaughter us the way they did the Senate."

Alana's eyes flared on the vidscreen. "You don't. You're going to have to trust me."

The thought was so ridiculous that Lydia almost laughed. "Trust isn't just freely given, Green, it's earned. And after what you've done, I want assurances that we aren't throwing away our lives."

The problem was, Lydia didn't know if Alana gave a shit if they fought or not. Of course, it would be easier for her if she negotiated a surrender. Still, in her view, they were far outgunned and outnumbered, why should she even care if they surrender, especially when her soldiers were almost all Recycled? No one gave a shit if a few

Recycled fell in combat. Hell, no one cared if they all fell in battle. They were the perfect weapons of war.

"Very well. Come out here armed if you like. It makes no difference to me, but I can promise you that if you stay inside that building, I am going to slaughter every last one of you. I will leave no one alive. We both know I have the numbers to do so. We both know that this is a losing battle for you."

Lydia frowned. This wasn't going to buy her the time she needed for Serah and the others to make their move.

Into her neurolink, Manhatsten said, "An analysis of Alana Green suggests that she is mentally unstable and might be susceptible to a discussion of her family or topics related to her motivations for marching an army here. I suggest this line of conversation to delay further."

Lydia thought into the neurolink, "Thanks, Manhatsten."

"Tell me, Alana, why are you really here? Why would you bring all these Recycled to march on a city that has done so much for your family? Why do you dishonor your family's memory? They loved this city and did a lot for it."

Based on what Lydia knew of the Green family, they had never done anything that wasn't motivated by their own self-interest. They had been a pack of greedy assholes, and she couldn't think of one person who mourned their loss. But they had donated some of their wealth to charitable causes over the years, like so many wealthy families did in the past. History was full of greedy assholes who masked their appetites with shallow acts of goodwill.

There was a pause, and then, "Done what for my family? Murder them? Take everything they had? How dare you suggest that I'm ungrateful. The leeches in this city murdered my uncle and my parents. All of my relatives are dead from the bomb that the scum in the Lowers planted. My family made this city what it is. They donated more than anyone, and the vermin of this city spat on them and murdered them."

"That bomb was planted by the Children of Gaia. Remember them? The terrorist group that invaded the city and destroyed Saud? We announced their involvement not long after we left the surface of the planet."

"Lies. We all know that this supposed organization was a coverup of the truth. Major Daniels and people like you always hated the Uppers; they wanted to destroy them and used the battle with Saud and the events after to take control of the city."

Was that what she believed? Lydia couldn't help but wonder if others out there thought that. Frank and Zelda had told her that many in the city believed that the disappearances were some sinister conspiracy on the part of the Uppers and central security. It was strange to think that some of the Uppers might feel the opposite. But then, she remembered something Major John Daniels had once told her. He had said that when people got scared when a lot of change happened all at once, people would often retreat into things like fantasy and conspiracy theory rather than facing the truth. The truth was often painful, inconvenient, and hard to grapple with, whereas blaming a group of people different from yourself was easier and comforting. When there wasn't always a clear enemy, it was easier to make one up than accept change. He might have been a grumpy old bastard, but Daniels always had some wisdom to offer her over the years.

"Why would we lie about that? Why would central security want the Uppers out of the picture? If we wanted you all out, why would we target only your family?"

"You fear us and our power. The Uppers are the smallest group in the city, and they are at the mercy of the Mids and Lowers. Our lives and livelihoods are always under threat in this city, and most of the population would like nothing more than to see us destroyed. My uncle was a noble man, and the filth of this city killed him. When I am in charge, the trash will pay, and we will purge the city of any undesirables.

Lydia hadn't read too much history in scholar school, but enough to recognize that somehow it was the crazy nutjobs with their big visions that always seemed to get the upper hand. The early 21st century had been full of world leaders who were narcissistic and selfish assholes that had ultimately led to the migration. Here was another nutjob hungry for blood and eager to blame everyone else for her problems. Senator Green had been the most hated man in the city. He screwed everyone he could, his family had taken advantage of countless others, and he was responsible for at least 76 individuals converted to the Runnercore. Yet here was someone held up as honorable, as a hero, despite all his misdeeds and his failures. But at least this was working. Lydia queried Manhatsten, and already, she had stalled for ten minutes. She had to keep going.

"What if we worked together to help you with your goals? What if we could come to an arrangement where my SO's helped you to investigate what happened to your family?"

"Do you think I'm an idiot? That I would have marched my army here and have no interest in taking control? No, one way or another, by the end of this day, I will stand in central security, and the AI will take orders only from me."

Manhatsten said, "Alana Green, there is nothing you can do to force me to take orders from you. I am fully conscious and aware of your intentions. I have no interest in serving someone as unstable as yourself. If you think that I will cede any control to you, then you are mistaken. Even if you held every single life in your hands, even if you killed everyone but those who followed you, I would simply shut down the shield and let the vacuum of space claim you. Make no mistake, Alana Green, no matter what you do this day, you will lose."

Lydia didn't know if the AI was bluffing or not. Its cold tone suggested seriousness, but Lydia couldn't tell. It was at that moment she was reminded just how dependent on the AI they all were. When it had disappeared, it was still running the systems of the city, and it had alerted them of the failing shield pylon. But would it kill everyone who opposed it? What would she do if she was in the AI's position?

Alana Green screamed in rage. It was a shrill, piercing thing. She said, "Don't you worry, you stupid machine, I have ways of making you submit to me. And if you don't, I will make sure I strip you and every machine like you of your freedom."

Privately Lydia asked Manhatsten, "Can she do that?"

"Alana Green could not, but Miranda may be able to control me to some degree. I am not sure to what level, but in the past, I have been made subservient to Miranda's wishes, and there are still parts of this city I cannot scan or access because of her. So, it may be true, but I may be able to do a great deal of damage to her and the people who follow her before it comes to that. I think she underestimates how widely spread my systems are, and it is doubtful she could control me entirely at first. It also seems likely that she would not be able to control all of the Recycled while attempting to control me."

"Why do you say that?"

"Because if she could do both at the same time, don't you think she would be doing so right now? I don't think that Miranda is all that confident in her ability to control me. If she could, it would be as simple as taking control of me and ordering me to eliminate you."

The thought gave Lydia chills. It occurred to her why Major Daniels and others had been so suspicious of AI. They took for granted how powerful it was and what it could do if it decided that it didn't want humans around anymore. How could they possibly fight against something like that?

"Enough delays. Make your choice. Either surrender or die."

Lydia frowned. They only needed a few more minutes. Was there anything else she could say to delay?

"In truth, Ms. Green, it's not up to me. Senator Swanson, the last surviving member of the Senate, has to decide. He is the only duly elected representative left, and his voice is important. It's his choice to make and not mine. I have to consult with him. He is waiting at the top of central security for news. You can understand why he would be hesitant to walk down here and negotiate with you right?"

It was a bald-faced lie, and Lydia knew that Alana knew that. But every second counted.

"The time for talk is done. Make your choice. I know the Speaker went to Luna. I know he's still over there. Enough delay, choose."

It was over. Lydia hoped it was enough. But there was one more thing she could try.

"Very well, Green. I'd rather die fighting than give into you. But I dare you to come in here yourself and fight me. You're a coward. Leave behind your army and come fight me woman to woman."

Alana Green laughed. "I told you, I'm not a moron. I could never hope to fight you and win. But oh, it will be sweet to kill you up close. My Recycled will take you, and you alone, alive. I want you to watch everyone else die around you. I will strip away everything from you just like I was stripped of everything. Just you wait."

With that, the Recycled stepped forward. They did it all at the exact same moment, and even though she was still a few dozen meters away, Lydia could feel the slight tremor created through the impact of their metal feet on the courtyard concrete.

"Manhatsten run program Daniels."

Just as the first Recycled reached the glass doors of the lobby, a thick metal shield lowered from the ceiling and covered every wall and window in the front. It wouldn't hold the creatures for long, maybe only a few minutes, but now that was all that Lydia needed. She retreated up the stairs to wait. The trap was set, and it was the best they could hope for.

6.

"Alright, Everybody out."

Serah was the first to exit, and she helped the other telepaths, including Loni and Kirka out of the Dugger. Most of the Lunite telepaths were tall, slender, and frail, and struggled to get out of the Dugger on their own. Serah had no idea how they were going to make it up and across the skybridge. At least they wouldn't have to take the stairs, but after they got out of the lift on the 40th floor, how in the world was she going to get them four blocks over to central security? What if Miranda had stationed Recycled there? She would have to hope she and Shannon were enough to hold them off while the other telepaths went to work.

The Duggers had moved with speed across the empty streets of Manhatsten. They hadn't encountered any resistance at all. Serah had expected at least some of Tony's men to attack them, and her and Shannon to get out and fight, but they met with no resistance. That bothered Serah. Either there was a trap waiting or Miranda was so certain of victory that she thought that any other telepaths couldn't challenge her. Neither of those possibilities was a good thing.

She had instructed all of her new allies to hold off using telepathy until at least they were within a few blocks of central security. Miranda would be able to sense that there were other telepaths around, but she wouldn't be able to tell how powerful or numerous they were if they didn't use any of their abilities, especially with two of the Lunites masking their presence. At least, Serah hoped that Miranda still had those limitations. So far, there seemed to be no mental attack either. Maybe Miranda was focused on controlling all those Recycled? Serah had no idea how she could control so many at once. Serah had managed to control a few at a time, but hundreds? Thousands? That was something else altogether.

Shannon said, "Okay, everyone's out. Manhatsten? The Duggers are yours."

There was no response.

"Manhatsten?"

No response.

Serah said, "Shit. I was afraid this might happen."

Kirka said, "What?"

"Well, either Miranda has shut down the AI, or she is preventing it from communicating with us. Either way, we can't use Manhatsten to send our package to the Recycled."

Loni said, "So what do we do?"

"Two people are going to have to drive it and try and ditch it the last second."

Shannon said, "So, me and you?"

Serah nodded. "Yeah. Not like anyone else can do it, can they? We can both drive them, and we can both pilot these EnViro Suits. Don't worry, we'll wait until we are a block away and set the controls. After that, we'll get out and climb the side of one of the buildings and meet you up on the skybridge."

Loni's eyes grew wide, "You can do that?"

"Yeah, these suits are designed to deal with all kinds of problems out in the barrens while we're on the surface of the planet. Climbing is one of the easier things they can do."

Kirka asked, "Where do we go?"

Serah said, "Let me show you."

She reached out to Kirka and the others and sent them a transmission containing the route. She also gave them the backup passkey for the lift. She didn't know how long they would be able to walk for, but they would have to try and get where they were going without their help.

Kirka wobbled. She could barely hold herself up. She said, "And what if we can't make it all the way to central security? What if several of us are just too weak to get there?"

"Then find a place to hide and get to work. There are apartments all along the way. I am sure you can... persuade some of the residents to let you use their house for your work. Just transmit and let us know where you end up. We will meet up with you, and then, if we have to, Shannon and I will carry you all three at a time into central security. Come on, Shannon, we can't waste any more time. I just hope we aren't too late already."

━━━━╫╫╲╲╘╫╫━━━━

7.

Lydia sat in her command chair, watching the video feed on her heads-up display. She had wanted to stay and fight, but Roma refused to let her, and even Manhatsten had told her that staying on the front lines was unwise. She hated it, but they were right. Commanders couldn't always be in the thick of things. Lydia wished Major Daniels was here. Daniels always knew what to do. He never seemed to flinch or hesitate at anything. She wondered again how he had handled the news that his own girlfriend had been the leader of an order of telepaths, and she chuckled to herself. She imagined that he probably swore, accepted the information and changed his assessment of the situation. Daniels had been a flexible commander, and those were the kind needed to survive strange circumstances like what Lydia and her SO's faced now. Gods, she missed that man.

"They'll break through the main door any moment now." Roma stood next to her command chair.

For now, he refused to leave her side. Private Longfellow and Lieutenant Jackson stood on the other side of her command chair at Roma's insistence.

"Any word on the progress of the telepaths?"

"None. But, Commander, there are reports of Duggers moving full speed through the city."

"Good. That's all I needed to know."

"May I ask—"

"No, you may not. And you know damn well why. Besides, you're gonna find out in a few minutes."

Roma nodded.

Lydia said, "I just hope we can time it all right. Major Daniels always said that the best plans had the least moving parts. I never really understood what he meant until today."

Roma smiled. "He also used to say that every plan falls apart the moment a battle begins."

"True. But if this one does, we won't survive."

"It will work."

Lydia sighed. "Manhatsten, the moment that lobby is full, you know what to do."

"Acknowledged, Lydia Danvers. I have an update for you on the telepaths." Manhatsten switched to Lydia's neurolink to keep the information secret. "S2, the AI inside Shannon's suit reports that the telepaths are dropped off and that Serah and Shannon are manually driving the Duggers towards the Recycled. They should arrive in 2 minutes. However, it appears they will have to fight their way out as they could not use automated controls to run the Duggers."

"Can you get a message to them?"

"I cannot. I am unable to establish a connection with them."

"Why not?"

"I fear that—"

"You fear what?"

There was no response.

"Manhatsten?"

There was only a hint of static.

"Manhatsten, are you still with me?"

Roma said, "Commander, I think we lost Manhatsten."

"Yeah, I think so too. Roma, I need you to check in with every station."

"Yes, Sir."

The timing couldn't be worse. If they had lost Manhatsten just a few minutes later, everything would have been easier to coordinate. Lydia sighed. It was lucky they had prepared for this, and even expected it, or else all would be lost.

Roma said, "All stations are checking in, and all confirm they have lost contact with Manhatsten."

Lydia closed her eyes and took a long slow breath and blew it out. "Alright, Roma, they got their orders, but tell them one more thing."

"What's that, Commander?"

"Tell 'em what Major Daniels always told us before a battle. Tell them, 'Give 'em hell.'"

Roma smiled. "Yes, Sir."

8.

Mimi's eyes shot open, and she rolled off of the conveyor belt and crashed into the floor. Her elbow spiked pain up her arm. She picked herself up and examined it. There didn't seem to be any damage, but it sure hurt like hell.

There was no one around. No Willow, no Recycled, nothing. She kept her mind shielded, and she probed the space for the right direction.

Mimi reached into the back of her own mind. "Noatla, are you there?"

For a moment, there was nothing. Then, there was a flash of images, memories, and thoughts of her former Matron. After the torrent of thought, there was one last transmission from Noatla's point of view.

The woman was looking at Mimi and repeated her final words before leaving the archives. "...remember love."

Mimi walked out of the room where the Recycled were made and down the long corridor toward where Willow had augmented her muscles, but she wasn't there either. She knew that Willow thought her dead; why else would she have put her on the conveyor belt that would begin the process of Recycling. But it seemed odd that there were no Recycled around. Where could she be?

There were only two other places Willow could be. She had private quarters, but Mimi had never been to them and didn't know where to look. So, she headed for the only other obvious place she knew of.

It didn't take her long before she came to the hall that glowed in pink light. As Mimi navigated the walkway, she could feel shadows of Willow's mental impressions left along her path. There was rage and pain and loneliness. The loneliness was the most powerful and incredible emotion of all. Was this woman mourning her? In her own strange way, Willow did seem to love Mimi. On the streets, Mimi had met so many broken and hollow people, people who used the word love as a stand-in for something strange and unlike what she had with Shannon. Mimi's own mother had been loving and caring up to a point, but what if she had been like Willow, born in the shadow of a monster bent on destruction? What if she had suffered torment after torment throughout her extended lifespan?

Willow basked in her loneliness, and it fed her rage. Mimi didn't have to skim to know that Willow was doing something terrible. The red veil had taken her over, and she had simply let it. There wasn't much Willow left, it was mostly the craving, the near mindless need to spread and control and possess all it could for the sake of rage and anguish itself.

Each step Mimi took toward the entry to the network, the air grew more potent with psychic energy. It was hard to tell if she was feeling the network or just Willow. Mimi suspected that it was both.

She entered the doorway to the network, and there, sitting in a chair surrounded by the strange pink light and machines along every wall that held so many people captive, was Willow. She sat silently, eyes closed, and breathing deeply.

Willow's eyes fluttered open. The air changed. For the briefest of moments, Willow ceded control, but it was only half a breath, only long enough for the shock to ripple through her and ooze out.

"You? But you were dead!"

Willows jaw was slack with surprise, her face a mask of uncertainty and despair. Mimi reached into to skim her and felt the briefest whisper of fear before Willow shielded herself. She was as thick and mysterious as the door that had guarded this place for centuries.

Mimi nodded to herself, then said to Willow, "It's time to end this all, Willow. I have the power to stop your mother now."

She wasn't sure if that was exactly true, and there was the network to deal with, but a strange sense of strength swirled about her. Mimi had no idea if it was her own abilities or the power that Noatla possessed blending with her own, but it was time to put an end to all this.

Willow's mad grin surfaced. "I think not, Mimi. You see, I've let it take me, the way it took Mother. It has made me even more powerful, now that I have submitted to its will. It wants the city, just like Mother, and with the full power of the red veil and the network, the city will be mine in a few hours, and there is nothing Mother can do to take it away from me." Willow hesitated. "But it can be ours, Mimi. Yours and mine together. It's not too late to join me. It's not too late to love me. Forget Shannon and be with me, and we can have everything you ever wanted."

"What do you mean? What are you doing?"

"I have sent my army of Recycled to the surface. They will take the city by force. My Recycled have already slaughtered the Senate, and before this day is done, I will have control of central security. It's already over. Some in the city are trying to resist, but how can they? I have an army of Recycled large enough to challenge the Runnercore at full strength, and there are only a handful of Runners left in the city. Love me, Mimi. Let us blend inside the network. We can bond forever. Perhaps I can spare some of your sisters from the network if you join me in taking the city."

There was just a hint of desperation in Willow's voice. There was a part of Mimi that was attracted to her; she wasn't much worse than what Mimi once was and would be now if she hadn't met Shannon or her sisters of the Order of the Eye.

Willow wasn't Miranda, but her mother's madness had possessed this woman, and Mimi didn't think she would ever escape.

"Oh, Willow. You've said you've watched me since Miranda found me four decades ago. Do you think that I would be okay with you using the Recycled to kill thousands of people and take control? Think about the things I have done. Think about how I went out of my way to help the homeless women in the city. Do you think I could stand by and watch you slaughter innocent people?"

Willow's cheeks changed to a bright red. "You don't have the power to stop me, Mimi. I banished your mind once; I will do it again."

"Maybe. Where's Miranda?"

Mimi knew the answer from what she skimmed of Willow earlier, but she had to be sure.

The mention of her mother's name made Willow flinch. Even now, plugged into the network with all that power, Willow still feared her own mother. She bowed her head to the ground like a child caught in a lie and said, "She fled here and left me behind when her Children of Gaia came to destroy the city. She forfeited my life, though I begged her to take me with her. But it doesn't matter. Soon, the Recycled will take possession of all people in this city. Soon the city will be a grand network and with the power of almost two million people behind me, I will kill my mother, steal her power, and add her consciousness to my own network."

"You can't... All those innocent people."

"Being innocent doesn't matter. You know that as well as I do, Mimi. Terrible things happen to innocent people all the time. But think, when people are a part of the network, they will be safe from all the horror and anxiety. They will be free from pain. They will be free from all their troubles."

Mimi shook her head. "You don't believe that for a second."

"Don't I? My own mother integrated me into her network to test it. I know what it's like to be blissfully empty of all choice, to submit to the will of one more powerful than you. Even the best drugs in the city can't give you what the network can, and there are so many people trying to find their oblivion. I'm doing them a favor."

"That's not contentedness; that's apathy and numbness."

"It doesn't matter what you think about it. No one can stop me now."

"No..."

Willow smirked. "No? Even as you stand here, the attack on central security has begun. Feel for yourself. Reach out to what's left of your pathetic Order of the Eye."

Willow opened the way for her to see and so Mimi reached out. She could see the Recycled entering the building in great numbers, could see Serah driving a Dugger to try and put a stop to it. She could see all the SO's in the building, preparing to defend themselves. Then she saw Shannon, who, like Serah, was rushing to try and stop the Recycled. Mimi's heart leaped as she felt Shannon. She reached out to her. But before she could say anything to the love of her life, Willow cut her off in a jealous rage.

"You see? It's inevitable now. There's nothing you can do. You might as well join me."

"If I stop you, it all ends. If Miranda is gone and you're the only one who controls the Recycled and the Network, then all I have to do is stop you."

"Try it."

Mimi gathered her will. She tried to reach out to her sisters to link to them to put up a better fight, but before she could even make them aware of her presence, Willow pushed her hard and shattered her concentration.

"Oh no, you don't get any help from friends. If you want to stop me, you have to do it all yourself."

Mimi reached deep inside herself and attacked Willow with all her might.

—————〢〣〤〥————

9.

"That's it."

Shannon asked, "That's it? That's all we need to do?"

The Duggers were still running. Serah didn't shut them down; there was no point. Their fuel cell had plenty of energy left to carry out its last act.

"Come on, we got to move fast. Let's get climbing. I don't want to leave the Lunites alone for long."

10.

"Commander, they've breached the lobby." Private Smithson swiveled around in his chair and faced Lydia. "Should we spring the trap?"

"No, wait 'til it's full. If it's too early, we'll have a lot more to deal with after."

Smithson turned back toward his station. Lydia felt the tension twist her gut. If this worked, they might stand a chance. If it didn't, well, she would fight to the end no matter what. It's not like there was a choice.

Smithson yelled, "Commander, they breached the barrier."

"What? Already? That can't be. That was the same material as the blast doors. How did they breach it so fast?"

"I don't know. Cameras are down, and only motion sensors are up. Commander they... they're climbing the lift shaft."

"How many?"

"A dozen and more are hot on their heels."

"Drop it."

Roma said, "We can't yet... if we do now—"

"If we do now, what? If they skip all our other defenses, all of our planning is worthless. Drop it."

Smithson said, "Yes, Sir."

Lydia waited, but there was no noise. They were just too far away. But on her heads-up display, she watched the lift descend quickly and smash into the Recycled climbing up it. Then the other two lifts dropped and smashed down, blocking the passage up. They could scale the outside of the building, but Lydia had planned for that. No one was climbing anything the easy way. Of course, that meant they were trapped. There was no going back. But it wasn't like they could, anyway. One way or another, this ended today.

11.

Alana entered behind her Recycled. She smiled wide as they entered the elevator and began their climb.

"When you get to the top, my darlings, leave Lydia Danvers alive. She's mine. Do you see Tony...?"

She looked around, but Tony was gone. The coward had fled. It didn't matter. She would track him down sooner or later, and then she would take her time with him. She looked back; his two prisoners were missing as well. Danvers had distracted her, and the Recycled wouldn't do anything without a direct order. She shrugged and turned her attention to the assault. She was a little disappointed. She had thought that central security would put up more of a fight, but her creatures had already started up the lift shaft. It would take them a while to climb to the top, but that was alright. Even if it took them all day, the result would be the same.

A chill ran down her spine. Why weren't they fighting back? They should be shooting, or the place should be booby-trapped or something. All at once, she realized something was wrong. It was at that moment, the lifts slammed down, smashing the few dozen Recycled that had begun their climb.

Alana laughed. That was it? That was the only resistance they could offer? The stairs were slower, but it only delayed the inevitable.

There was a strange noise behind her and out toward the courtyard. It sounded like a large machine. Alana Green had just enough time to turn around and see the pair of Duggers mowing down a line of Recycled, clearing a path toward the first floor when they slammed through the shredded metal barriers on either side of her.

A voice filled her head. "Run, you fool." Alana didn't question the voice. She supposed she had always known it was there, but this was the first time she heard it on her conscious mind. She ran out of the lobby and away from the Duggers, and just as she got to the edge of the courtyard, a ball of fire erupted from the inside and pushed her face-first into the concrete, smashing her nose and forehead into the hard ground. A burst of pain exploded in her head, and with it, the greatest surge of anger she had ever felt. She could feel something sharp and painful in her back. She reached up to feel, and with little hesitation, pulled a small piece of metal out of her back. Laying on the ground, afraid to move, she examined the object. It was the size of a small coin. There was another swell of pain, but it wasn't crippling, and she tested her ability to move without much trouble.

She pushed herself up off the ground, and through blurry vision, she looked at the aftermath. At least a hundred Recycled lay on the ground inactive, and that was just outside of the building. She had no doubt that inside, every single one of her Recycled lay immobilized. If they thought that would stop her, though... they were in for a surprise.

———✗━╲╲┕╱╳━———

12.

Everyone in central security cheered. They couldn't have asked for a more perfect trap. The deactivated bodies of the Recycled were scattered all over the floor, and the one remaining security camera showed that not a single one remained active. Outside in the courtyard, the results were similar. But there will still at least several dozen of the creatures milling around outside, standing still, awaiting orders.

Lydia beamed ear to ear and asked, "Manhatsten, are you with us?"

There was no answer. Lydia frowned. That wasn't a great sign, but perhaps Miranda wouldn't allow Manhatsten to communicate with them until it was clear there were no more Recycled left. For a moment, Lydia wondered if they would ever hear from the city AI again. Would Miranda ever allow it? Even if they survived the assault, they would still have to find her. But she was getting ahead of herself.

Lydia turned to Roma and said, "Do we have an exact count of how many are down and how many remain?"

Adrian Roma shook his head, "There's no way to get an exact count without manually counting them. We can pull some of the security footage from cameras around the block, but my guess is there is anywhere from fifty to one hundred left."

Lydia frowned. That was more left than she had hoped for. "Private Gunner, I want you to run a tactical analysis on an assault by one hundred and fifty Recycled on this facility."

"Working on it now, Sir."

"Foster?"

"Yes, Sir?"

"How bad is the damage down there?"

Foster waved his hand and flicked a few things in his virtual heads up display. He typed for a moment and then said, "Structural damage is minimal, Commander, but I don't think anyone should try and use the lifts for a while. Both of them were damaged beyond repair. We're going to have to rebuild them from scratch."

"So that leaves, what, one active stairwell?"

"Yes, Sir. And three skybridges."

"How about the subterranean level?"

"Looks like it's still accessible but... wait. Something's tripping the motion sensors."

"Can you get a visual?"

"No, Sir, all the cameras were damaged in the last assault, and we didn't have a chance to replace them yet."

Lydia swore. "So, we're blind down there?"

"Yes, Sir."

Gunner spoke up, "Sir, I have that tactical analysis for one hundred and fifty Recycled."

"And?"

"Well, Sir, with that many of them, it's gonna be rough."

"Against six hundred and seventy of us?"

"Well remember, Commander, one hundred and ninety-one are out of the building and scattered across the city in skirmishes and guard duty. So, with the four hundred and seventy-nine of us left, there's a lot of ground to cover. The big problem with the Recycled is that their armor is thick enough that you have to target the head, but if they are wearing visors..."

"Then it's hard to take them down, yeah, I get it. So, what's the analysis say?"

"It's saying we need a thousand SO's for every two hundred Recycled to guarantee victory."

Lydia frowned, but at least they still had one more trap in store that should help even the odds. Gunner didn't know that, and neither did Foster, but Roma and the others stationed at the fifth floor knew. The fifth-floor lobby was where they would make their first stand.

Foster said, "Commander, you better look at this."

Lydia walked over to Foster's station and glanced at his screen. Her jaw dropped. "Fuck. How could they possibly have that many?"

Roma walked up and stood next to her. She looked up at him and watched the blood drain from his face.

Lydia said, "Foster, you're sure those dots are all Recycled?"

"I don't know, Commander, they could be Tony's men, but we won't know until they reach the ground floor. Either way, it's bad news."

On Foster's screen, the motion sensors displayed the underground passages. The computer counted each of the red dots that represented motion. There were nine hundred and eight flashing on the screen.

Lydia sat down in one of the empty chairs next to Foster's station. She looked at her hands. They were shaking.

"So, there are over a thousand Recycled?"

Roma replied, "We don't know they're all Recycled."

Lydia eyed him. "Even if all the ones in the sub-level are human, we're in trouble."

The whole room was silent.

In a near whisper, Lydia said, "Recall every SO in the city. I know they may not get here in time, but they need to come as quickly as possible. Gunner, any word on those telepaths, or Serah and Shannon?"

"No, sir."

"Manhatsten?"

It did not respond to Lydia's prompt. She knew it wouldn't, but it was worth a try.

Lydia said, "I want every available body down to level five. I want to seal all the skybridges in. We better hope those telepaths are enough."

Chapter 30
Love and Sacrifices

Climbing was tiring work, and Serah wasn't sure she would have much left in her for the battle after they made it up to the 40th floor. She would have to take suit stims, but if they had to fight for a few hours, she would crash. Every suit had a quota of stimulants to help survive in the barrens, but they were only good for emergencies. Her muscles ached from the climb. Even with augmentation and the suit's assistance, she was still running out of steam. All she could think was that it would have been slower and much worse taking the stairs.

Shannon was ahead of her, as usual. When it came to climbing, Shannon was like a squirrel, agile and fearless. She wondered if Shannon ever got tired, if she did, she didn't let on. It was a damn shame the woman wasn't telepathic because, if she were anything like Mimi, she would be unstoppable. Most of the sisters of the Order of the Eye had not been so physically inclined, so it was nice to partner with someone who was.

Serah placed her hand up on the next ledge. Her metal fingers dug into the concrete and left permanent marks, like a kid leaving a handprint in half-dried concrete. They were almost to the top now, and Serah would be glad when it was over.

"Zeke, ready for the next leap?"

Her suit AI said, "Ready when you are, Serah."

Serah closed her eyes and braced herself for the jump. She trusted her AI. It had been with her for almost four centuries now, but every leap up made her stomach lurch. It was different than climbing cliff faces. Climbing buildings always seemed more daunting. At least with cliffs, you could deploy parachutes if something when wrong, or take a break along the way. Cliffs always seem to have little hidden areas for rest, not that they had any time for rest.

"Releasing grappling hook."

The hook exploded from a compartment in her left shoulder and shot up. Serah tried to relax, but all of her muscles were tense and agitated. It didn't help that the packages would arrive at central security at any minute. She just hoped that it wouldn't go off during a jump.

Serah pushed down into her legs, spring loading the hydraulic joints, and then, with the tiny lip of the ledge of the building, jumped with all her strength. The hydraulics kicked in at the same time, and she surged upward hard enough that her stomach dropped. Her body trembled with a mixture of fear and exhilaration as she caught the lip of the ledge three floors up. She kicked her metal boots into the side of the wall and held tight.

Zeke retracted her grappling hook, and she began pulling herself up. She dared a glance upward and said to Shannon, "What do you think, one or two more jumps?"

Shannon said, "Just one for me. I think two for you." She paused, "Well, maybe one and a half."

"It still comes out the same."

"True. How are you holding up down there?"

Pulling her waist up the edge of the lip, Serah said, "I'll be better when we're done."

Her right hand slipped, and some of the concrete lip of the ledge broke loose. She screamed, and scrambling to find some purchase with her right hand, she off-balanced her left foot. Both right hand and left foot clawed for safety, some way of staying up.

"Zeke, I need you to deploy both left and right grappling hooks."

There was no response, and nothing happened.

"Zeke?"

Still nothing.

"Shannon, I've lost my grip. I can't hold on... much... longer..."

"Shit. Did you deploy your grappling hooks?"

"Zeke isn't responding..." Serah's right hand grabbed a decorative outcropping. She wasn't sure if it would hold, but it would have to do.

"S2 isn't responding either."

"Fuck. That timing can't be..."

Before Serah could finish her thought, the world tinged red and spun. Serah felt sick and angry and, in the surge of so many emotions at once, she forgot what she was doing.

A voice resonated through her mind. It echoed off the insides as if someone spoke into a great underground cavern. "Let go, Serah."

Serah pushed back against the voice. "No... I won't... Fuck off."

A tightness grabbed her chest and squeezed all of her breath out.

"Let go, Serah."

Serah screamed. "Shannon. I can't hold on. She's... Miranda..."

Shannon said, "Hold on, I'm coming down to get you."

"No, don't... she'll get us both."

"Hold on Serah... be there..."

Shannon's comm went dead, and Serah's adrenaline spiked. She pushed back against the mental invasion with all her will. The invader retreated for a moment, and Serah reestablished her grip.

Over the comm came a piercing scream followed by Shannon's angry yell, "No, it's not true. She is alive."

Serah looked up just in time to see that Shannon was falling toward her. For a brief moment, she thought Shannon would collide with her, until she realized that the woman had pushed off the building and that she was falling further away from the building, that Shannon hadn't jumped down, that she had been pushed, or rather Miranda had pushed her mind and made her leap.

In her mind's eye, Serah reached out to every telepath she could begging for their help. Then, with reflexes moving faster than she thought possible, she charged her legs and pushed off into the open air. In a moment, she collided with Shannon and caught her.

Then they were falling together, and a mad cackling laugh echoed to every corner of Serah's mind. She knew she had to focus, but that laugh chilled every part of her. Serah couldn't shake it. If only she could focus and deploy the grappling hooks... but the red wouldn't subside, it grew and clouded her thoughts, and just as she attempted to deploy the grappling hook, she lost track of what she was doing.

They were falling faster and faster toward the ground where both she and Shannon would be crushed inside the weight of their own EnViro suits. She had no idea how far she fallen so far, but each floor passed by in a slow salute as she cascaded down toward her death.

A loud crash of metal and glass shattered her strange mental fog, and Serah's focus shifted. All at once, she manually deployed both grappling hooks, hoping like hell she would strike something that would stop her rapid descent.

The ground was close now, only a few dozen meters. Serah closed her eyes. She had done all she could do. She held on to Shannon as tight as she could. This was the end.

A hard, sharp jolt rocked her body. Shannon slipped from her arms, and she screamed. Shannon grabbed her forearm, but only just, and then they were dangling, both of them from one of the lines of the grappling hooks. Serah's arm burned with the weight of a second suit, but there was no way in hell she was gonna lose Shannon too.

There dangling between skyscrapers, Serah felt the weight of everything. She felt the loss of her friend Mimi, of her fellow sisters, who had become the family she had lost. She felt the loss of Noatla, a woman who had been a mother to her for so many decades. Her eyes burned like her muscles.

"It's time to accept that you cannot win, Serah."

Serah screamed into her helmet. "Fuck off, bitch."

Serah pushed at the invader with all of her strength and will, and the mental force retreated for a moment and then reasserted itself again. All she seemed able to do was push it away momentarily, and Serah knew that wouldn't be good enough.

"It's useless to fight. You cannot win. I'm too powerful and-"

Something knocked the intruder away. Serah felt a sense of relief.

"We're here, Serah."

It was Vala.

A wave of calm swept over her. Her mind sharpened and focused, and Serah knew exactly what to do. The first grappling hook had shot into a window and was holding the two of them, but the second hook had bounced off something and felt flat to the ground. Serah focused on her heads-up display and found the manual retraction command for the second grappling hook. She pulled it back in.

The first line quivered, but Serah ignored it. If it broke, it broke, there was nothing she could do. The moment the second grappling hook was back in her shoulder, she aimed across the way to a second building and fired. She knew the odds of it catching the right thing on the first try were low, but when it bounced off the side of the building and felt flat, her heart sunk.

Serah repeated the process again. This time it caught something, and the pressure sensor in the line confirmed that it could hold her and Shannon's weight. They were stable, but she needed Shannon's help to get up inside one of the buildings.

"Shannon, are you with me?"

"Serah?"

"Shannon, I need you to deploy your grappling hooks."

"What... I..."

Shannon froze. Serah could feel her panic.

"We're okay for now, Shannon, but I need you to focus."

Like Vala had done for her, Serah soothed Shannon's mind and helped clear it.

"Okay. I'm here. What do we need to do?"

"I need you to fire your grappling hooks up to that balcony over there. Do you see it?"

Serah sent her a mental image of the balcony.

"Yeah, I see it."

"Fire both of them. You're going to reel us in, and then we are going to take the stairs. I don't know about you, but I've had enough climbing for a lifetime."

Shannon said, "Agreed."

While Shannon focused on the task, Serah looked around. Smoke filled the sky and obscured the view a few buildings over. The package had arrived while they were dangling, and Serah wondered how many of the Recycled it had stopped. She tried to reach out to Lydia, but there was nothing. Miranda had vanished from her mind, and Serah was sure that it was the explosion that had distracted her long enough to save her life. Still, whatever power had wavered, both the suit AI's and communication with Lydia Danvers was down. All they could do now was meet up with the Lunites and head to central security before it was too late.

2.

Kirka opened her eyes. The Upper's living room was extravagant and filled with paintings and tapestries. There was an entire room dedicated to a personal alcove and what looked, to Kirka like a gym and a pleasure palace. It was clear that this Upper owned the entire floor of a skyscraper, but luckily, there was no one home. Kirka had seen the lower levels of the city, and the contrast between wealth and poverty in Manhatsten had left her disgusted. They hadn't had much on Luna, but just about everyone had the same. But then, they were a small community. She did recognize it wasn't so easy to have relative equality in a city with more than a million people, but the inequality here bordered on criminal, and she was beginning to understand why the people in the Lowers were so upset.

They had managed to stop the mental attack on Serah and Shannon, and that was something. A part of her had worried that, based on what Serah had shown her of the last battle, that they would be unable to do anything at all. But for now, they had diverted Miranda.

Loni shifted. She could never sit still for very long. She said, "Well, that wasn't so bad."

Kirka replied, "I agree, but twenty-eight of us defending only two people? With our minds concentrated and focused, it's not too difficult. It will be a different story if that army marches after us."

Loni stood and stretched her legs.

Kirka said, "Sit, focus. We need to concentrate, Loni. We have to try and focus and scatter some of those Recycled. If we can take possession of a few of them and turn them against one another, it might help."

"The ones they blew up with the Dugger?"

"No, the ones underground."

Luang, who had had reluctantly agreed to join the transport to Manhatsten, said, "What ones underground?"

Kirka looked around the room. "Who else feels them?"

Three others signaled they did. Feng, a woman from Luna 1 named Athena, and another from Kirka's security detail named Raven had felt them.

"So few of you? Can't you feel their strange minds below your feet? They are present, but they are blank. They feel like a hole in reason and will."

Loni screwed up her face. It almost made Kirka laugh. She always scrunched her face when she tried to test the limits of her abilities even though there was nothing physical you could do to increase your telepathy. But Loni was always quirky like that. It was an endearing quality, and it helped Kirka to forgive some of her flaws, like the fact that she was rarely on time for anything.

Loni said, "I don't feel anything."

Feng, who after centuries still carried her Chinese accent, despite the very small community on Luna 1, said, "You understand how they feel when you read them individually?"

Loni nodded. "Yes, it's like the space they occupy is an object; it's filled, but it's empty, like a wall or a statue."

Feng nodded. "Then feel the others who are on the street, feel their weight, their mass as they organize themselves."

Kirka said, "It's more than that. Feel their pull. They have a strange kind of gravity, a deep blackness about them."

Loni said nothing. Her eyes were closed again. The whole room was silent. Kirka needed the rest of the telepaths to understand how to feel these creatures, how to understand their being. If they couldn't do that, they would struggle to defend against them. She wished she had Serah or Vala or one of the others who had fought the creatures before. But she also suspected that the number of these things were unprecedented. There had been a few hundred in the underground subway battle that Serah and her sisters had taken part in. There were at least a thousand now within a few blocks of each other.

Loni said, "I still don't feel it, not the ones underground. I can feel individual ones."

Feng said, "Feel the strands between them. Feel how they are linked, how they are networked together. Do you see it?"

Kirka did. Red strands linked them, but she wanted Loni and the other telepaths to see it for themselves. It was important they did because...

"Yes, yes, I see it now. It's red, right?" Loni opened her eyes and had a big smile on her face.

Feng said, "That is their weak point. Follow the strands, and you can find them all. Each are connected to a group of ten. She is using units of ten to minimize the amount of control she has to exert. So, ten are assigned a task together, ten move as one. She does not yet have the power to control so many as individuals, and so she has compromised."

Just above a whisper, Loni said, "Holy shit, that's a lot of them."

Several of the telepaths in the room nodded their head in agreement.

Kirka said, "Which means, that's how we strike. We sever a unit of ten from the rest and have each unit turn on the others. We take advantage of the way she has linked the creatures together, and we can turn each group."

Feng said, "She's found us."

The moment Feng finished her sentence, a powerful surge of red flooded Kirka's mind. She pushed back against it.

Feng screamed directly into all of them, transmitting with all her will. The thought was loud and made Kirka's head ring.

"Make a shield, picture yourself... like... a turtle. Link to each other, pull the strands tight, focus on shielding each other."

Kirka used all of her will to picture a shell around herself. It was a hard thing to do, even with centuries of practice, but she managed. The moment she encased herself in her mind's protective shell, the red diminished greatly. It was still there, though, pushing on the edges of her senses, still trying to creep in. Kirka connected her shield to Loni's, who was struggling to get hers working, but like an umbrella keeping the rain at bay, the moment she extended her shield to Loni, Loni grew stronger and much more confident. In a few moments, all the Luna telepaths sat under a mental shield, united together. Then the shield extended to Yoshi, Serah, Shannon, and Vala, who weren't in the room, but also needed protection.

Shannon burst in through the front door of the apartment, and behind her, Serah followed.

Serah said, "A few dozen of them are coming."

Feng said, "Yes, I can feel them, but it's no longer a few dozen."

The thing about such a powerful connection with other telepaths is that everyone knows exactly what everyone is thinking the moment the thought emerges into the conscious mind. At that exact moment, Feng shared what she knew. There were over a hundred Recycled climbing the stairs of the lower level of the building and heading right for them. Every single one of the telepaths in the room knew that they couldn't stop that many. But all knew they had to try.

3.

Roma stood just to the left of the barricade, facing the entrance to the fifth-floor lobby. In preparation, they had filled the lobby with every piece of furniture from the floors below. It was a mass obstacle course that the Recycled would have to climb over. Since the creatures weren't carrying any projectile weapons, it was the perfect place to pick them off, at least until they had to flee to the next level.

Manhatsten had activated the emergency escape hatch system, which had been built several centuries earlier after the war with Mex. When Major Daniels had realized that if the stairwell and the lifts were cut off, his forces would have no way to move between floors, he had spent nearly a decade converting old air shafts into hatches to increase access. The thing was, only certain floors had them, and each was in a different location. If you didn't know how to navigate the network of hatches, it was easy to get lost.

Moving through the hatches to the upper levels was cumbersome, and even a Recon grade EnViro suit couldn't fit inside. Each hatch would skip over several floors and had an emergency locking mechanism behind it so the enemy couldn't follow. Using the hatches required preparation, as it was damn near impossible to move weapons up and down those hatches since every time you went up a level, you had to crawl through an old air duct to get to the next ladder. Roma had tasked three dozen SO's to stockpile and supply all nine exits so that as they retreated, they wouldn't have to worry about bringing their weapons, only clips of energy and ballistic ammo, which each SO could easily fit in a small satchel on their back.

During Tony's last attempt to take central security, there hadn't been enough time to prep the network of hatches. It had taken Roma, and his SO's eighteen hours to prep the building, but now that they were ready, it was going to be a hell of a lot harder for anyone to take them over. Still, the last estimate Manhatsten had given them before it vanished was 37 percent. The problem was, they just didn't have the numbers.

For several minutes now, he and the other security forces could hear the approaching army of Recycled. The perfect rhythm of their metal feet on the concrete was off-putting. Each creature stepped in perfect time with another as it made its way up the stairwell, and as they drew closer, the vibration of their movement grew in strength.

"Private Longfellow, is the trap set?"

"Yes, Sir, Roma, Sir."

Roma gave the man a good long look. Longfellow trembled. He looked like a frightened puppy whose master beat him. Roma had to focus on keeping himself from doing the same. If he let his people see his fear, it wouldn't do anything to help their confidence. The truth was, they had a slim chance at best, but he needed everyone fighting with courage and strength. He just hoped he wouldn't piss himself when the time came.

He walked over and slapped Longfellow on the shoulder and said, "We're gonna be okay."

"Respectfully, Sir, no, we're not. There are way more of them than we thought, and we don't have any more Runners to support us this time, do we?"

It was hard having to be so secretive about telepaths. Roma wished he could tell his people that they had a secret weapon, that help was on the way, that maybe, just maybe those telepaths could shut down the Recycled in their tracks, that maybe they could force them to fight one another.

"Those Runners who helped us stop Tony last time are out looking for that hacker. If they find the bastard, this is all over. We just gotta hold our position as best we can until then. We do have a few Runners on eighteen."

"But all of those ones are brand new, aren't they? They aren't ready for combat."

"True, but they're better than nothing."

The official story was that Tony had some kind of master computer hacker under his command and that he managed to silence the city AI and take control of the Recycled. Lydia had announced that they were doing everything in their power to find this hacker and that if they did, the battle would be over. She had told him, personally, that there was a chance the telepaths could stop them, and if that were the case, they would use the hacker as a cover story.

"What if we can't, Sir?"

"Then we fall back to the tenth floor and then the sixteenth and so on until we have to barricade ourselves in central command."

Roma realized that all eyes were on him. He hesitated for a moment, wondering what was taking Lydia so long, and then he knew what he had to do, knew what Major Daniels, his hero would have done.

"Listen, people. We have the high ground. We have several surprises waiting for them, and those creatures are mindless drones. None of them are carrying projectile weapons. Can they kill you if they get a hold of you? Sure. But we're here to pick them off, to set up traps, to make them pay for every single step forward. When each of our positions are compromised, we fall back to the emergency hatches and then seal them shut behind us and move on to the next position. With all the traps and surprises in place, with all the barricades waiting, with the stairways booby-trapped, we'll make them pay so dearly that if they manage to make it to the central command above, there will only be a few dozen left at most, and then, we let them have it with every weapon we have stockpiled up there."

Private Cortana, a woman with jet black hair and a strong jawline, said, "But there are so damn many of them and so few of us."

Lydia, who descended from the emergency hatch above, said, "Which means we need to have a contest. Whoever takes out the most of those monsters gets their salary doubled for a year."

Longfellow said, "Doubled, Commander?"

Lydia picked up an energy rifle and slung it over her shoulder. Roma thought it looked hilarious, given her short stature, but it was also a huge turn on. Lydia said, "You better get into position, though; they're coming through that door any moment, and I have every intention of killing more than anyone. It's about time I doubled my own salary, don't you all think?"

There was a round of chuckles.

Lydia said, "Remember why you are doing this. Do you want that scumbag, Tony, and that nutjob, Green to take this city over? Do you think your families would be safe with them in charge?"

She paused for effect. She was growing into Daniels's shoes, and Roma thought that, in time, she would be just as good as he was if they survived that long.

A few of the SO's said, "No." Their voices were small and nervous.

"Then what are you going to do about it?"

Roma answered, "Kill as many of the bastards as I can and make Tony Sellers and Alana Green wish they had never attacked this building."

There was some murmur of agreement.

Lydia raised her voice. "What do you think Major John Daniels would do in this situation?"

Private Longfellow said, "Fight."

There was some nervous laughter among the several dozen personnel.

"Fight? Is that all he would do? You think John Daniels would just fight?"

Silence and eyes wide and staring.

"Hell no. Daniels would make them pay. He would make them pay for the way that these creatures have come into our building, our territory, and attacked us. He wouldn't stop until every last damn one of those machines was laying on the ground broken and beyond repair. So what are you going to do? Are you going to let your fear get the better of you? Or are you going to give them hell?"

A few said, "Give them hell."

"What's that?"

More spoke up. "Give them hell."

"You don't sound like you want to give them hell, you sound like you want to go hug them. What do you want to do to those monsters?"

This time everyone said, "Give them hell."

Lydia shouted at the top of her lungs. "I can't fucking hear you. What do you want?"

There was a rumble of combined voices. They shouted, "Give them hell."

"That's right. We're are going to take them apart, and we are never, ever going to let those things in our city again. Now let's get 'em, and maybe, if you're lucky, you'll take out more than me."

There was laughter and then a few shouts. Lydia had done her best to fire them up, but Roma knew that just below the surface, they were all as nervous as he was. But, at the end of the day, did that matter? Because what was really at stake here was their lives. Those things would tear them apart the way they did the Senate; Alana Green had promised it.

Something slammed into the door several dozen meters across the lobby. They had arrived.

Roma shouted. "Everyone in position. They're coming."

They had rigged up large barricades just above the fifth-floor entrance. It would take the creatures much longer to go up and through that than it would through the doors on each floor, and that's exactly what they wanted. The Recycled were undead battering rams, and so any barricade was just a matter of time, but they wanted to entice them into searching each floor, and several of those floors had surprises waiting.

With another loud thump against the door, one of the hinges flew off. Roma frowned. They were getting through this door even faster than they had anticipated, but that didn't matter now.

With another crash, the second hinge came off, and now, hanging only by a single hinge, the creatures pushed their way through, knocking the door out of the way.

Lydia said, "Open fire!"

The creatures could only walk through the door one at a time, and the first one through took several shots to the head and fell to its knees. As its fellows clambered over the body, Roma shot another one on the head. For a moment, it seemed as if they would bar their own passage forward, but then, the creatures simply shoved their own fallen out of the way and began spreading out through the room.

As Roma fired round after round, all he could think was, there were so damn many of them. A mass of bodies collected along the furniture, but so far, they were holding them at bay. In just the first few minutes, they had already killed dozens, but now they were coming faster than they could shoot, and while the bodies piling up were slowing them down, it was also making it harder to shoot them.

Roma turned to Lydia and said, "Now, Commander?"

"Not yet."

Roma turned and fired some more. As he killed the next one, he paused for a moment and watched the orgy of insanity. The blue fluid they used as blood covered almost every wall. The creatures climbing over their fallen were a pulsing mass of movement, and in just a moment, they would reach the first barricade. Roma swallowed hard.

He turned to his commander again, "Now?"

Lydia paused for a moment and then said, "Now!"

Roma pulled a remote detonator from his pocket just as the first few Recycled reached the soldiers at the first barricade and triggered the device.

Despite knowing what was coming, despite having planned for their surprise, the moment Roma started floating off the ground, he became disoriented. He reached for one of the makeshift handholds they had installed on the walls and ceilings and tried to right himself. For a moment, he lost his grip on the detonator and struggled to grab it again. Weightlessness was a pain in the ass, and removing the gravity from the room kept the creatures from advancing, but it also made it hard as hell to fight back.

Lydia said, "Fall back. Roma and I'll wait till you're clear, and then we'll follow."

There was no hesitation. Every SO reached for their nearest handhold and projected themselves towards the escape hatch. The creatures, on the other hand, controlled entirely by another mind, were struggling to reorganize. They floated in every direction, and their fallen and the furniture were suddenly floating obstacles to overcome. It was exactly the chaotic nightmare that Manhatsten had planned. No new Recycled came into the room. Roma snuck a quick glance through the doorway and could see several floating in the stairwell. Gravity would be normal in most of the stairwell, but not anywhere on level five.

Roma smiled. He could imagine the rage and frustration of the crazy telepath trying to make sense of this situation. It was one thing to command a group of creatures to walk or attack a target. It was another to give every single one specific commands to move in a direction that would advance them, and Roma knew that Lydia had no intention of letting that mad telepath adjust to the situation.

A few of the creatures were starting to adjust and began floating toward Roma and Lydia. Lydia raised her weapon, opened fire, and hit two of them in the head. Still, the creatures kept floating right toward them, despite deactivating.

"Come on, Roma, let's head to the hatch."

Roma nodded and followed his commander. They floated toward the ladder just as the last of their SO's climbed up and out of sight.

"Set the timer for sixty seconds, and let's get up to the next level."

From his satchel, Roma pulled out another explosive device. "You sure this will work on them, Commander?"

"Manhatsten said it would."

"Do you really trust it?"

"The city AI? Yeah, I do."

"Why? How do we know it's not a part of this invasion?"

"Because it mourned the loss of Saud. Which means it's human."

Roma sighed. He wasn't sure he trusted Manhatsten, not after it's little temper tantrum disappearance. The fact that it mourned Saud only made him feel more suspicious. It might be intelligent, but emotional maturity was something that took time, and how could they possibly know that the city would do the right thing? He blew out a breath and said, "I hope you're right."

"Just toss the damn thing and let's get out of here."

Roma turned, and, in the weightless environment, he simply slid the bomb underhand and for a moment, watched it float toward the creatures. Then, he turned and scrambled his way up the ladder after Lydia and shut the hatch behind him. As he did, normal gravity resumed, and he felt like his normal, heavy, 1G self, which was good because he thought he might puke from weightlessness.

What followed was a high-pitched whining noise followed by what sounded like a series of pulses.

"Do you think that did it?"

Lydia said, "I hope so."

"Should we check?"

"Go ahead."

Roma pulled the lever and unsealed the hatch. His weight-lessness returned for a moment as he ducked his head down the hole. Below was a graveyard of Recycled, but a few of the creatures twitched. Some of them turned their heads, some of their faces twitched, but none of them on the entire fifth floor, so far as Roma could see, were attacking.

"I think it worked."

"Yeah?"

Roma lifted his head and turned. "Yeah, I can see some of their heads moving, but it doesn't seem like their suits are active. I think they're disabled, just like the AI said they would be. I hope if Man-hatsten was still in there, it shut off before the EM pulse triggered."

"I wouldn't worry about the city. How many more of those things do we have?"

"Three."

"You think it fried their suits?"

"I don't know, but let's hope they are."

Below, Roma heard the sound of metal scraping metal. Curi-ous, he ducked his head down again for another look. As he did, he felt pressure against his forehead and sharp pain. The pain ramped up, and he yelled in shock and surprise.

Lydia said, "What's wrong?"

Roma screamed. The pain was growing at an alarming rate. One of the creatures had his skull in its grasp and was squeezing hard. Behind him, he felt movement, and then the sound of an en-ergy pistol firing first filled his eardrums, and then there was a terri-ble burning pain and drips of blood floating in the air around him.

The pain in his forehead vanished, and Lydia pulled him back up and closed the hatch behind him.

A terrible throbbing, unlike anything he had ever known, wracked the left side of his face. He reached up and felt another jolt of pain.

"I'm sorry, Roma, I had to. It would have killed you otherwise."

"Had to what?"

Lydia didn't say anything else.

"Had to what?"

"Your ear... I had to shoot close to your face to get it off you."

"What do you mean, my ear?"

"I mean, it's down there with the Recycled. I'm sorry..."

Roma reached up to feel where his ear had been, but instead, there was only wetness and agony.

"We have to move, Roma, especially since it's clear that E.M.P. doesn't work. I think it only stunned them. We should have guessed; they never worked on Runners for very long. We will have to change our strategy. Come on. We'll get you patched up above."

4.

Mimi's will smashed into Willow's. Willow stumbled backward. Then, planting her feet, she retaliated with her powerful mind.

Mimi felt the redness rise in her, felt it press on her from both inside and out and for a moment, she was tempted to give in to the rage, tempted to let loose the same force and power she experienced back in the subway where she had smashed so many friends and foes with a simple thought. Instead, she created a kind of mental net for Willow and diverted all of Willow's will into it. Once inside, Mimi wrapped Willow's mind in the trap. Willow screamed in frustration.

Mimi envisioned a second net wrapping the first, but instead of thread, she pictured steel and iron mesh. It wrapped Willow tight.

The woman, bound by Mimi's will, struggled to break free, but it was no use.

Mimi said, "It's over, Willow. I'm stronger than you are."

Willow laughed. It was a hyena's laugh, angry and hideous. Willow's skin flushed, almost as if the red veil itself oozed from her every pore and mentally, she burst through both nets as if they were so much paper scattered in the wind. Mental tendrils reached out and grabbed Mimi. Pushing back with all of her will, Mimi sliced at the tendrils, but, like the Hydra of ancient legend, for every tendril she sliced, two more appeared. They reached for Mimi's mind and body, restraining both.

"You don't think that you are a match for the combined strength of the network, do you, Mimi? Could you be that arrogant that you would think that your single mind could stand against the hundreds in this room? I control them now, Mimi, and with them, I am unstoppable."

"I'm not alone, Willow. I've never have been."

Mimi cut down all the tendrils at once, and drawing on Noatla's strength, she pushed again. For the briefest moment, Willow's connection to the network faltered, and she was weak. Willow dropped to her knees, crippled from the combined attack of two minds.

Willow closed her eyes. Sweat gathered on her forehead as the telepath reconnected to the network. She got back on her feet and walked, one step at a time, toward Mimi, like she fought the wind of a great storm.

Mimi attacked again, but this time, Willow pushed her own will right back at her. Mimi felt her mind fold back in on herself, and she stumbled onto the floor. She lay on her back looking up. Trying to rise, Mimi fell back again as something struck her, first from the left, and then from the right. Like a thousand tiny needles, she felt stabs of pain wrack her body.

Mimi took shallow gulps of air, trying to focus. "What's... happening..."

"I told you, Mimi, all those minds in the network, each one is a weapon waiting to be wielded. I simply directed them to attack you from every angle while you were focused on me.

Mimi moaned. Looking down at her body, she expected to see real puncture wounds, but there were none.

"Last chance, Mimi; join me, or join them." Willow pointed to the pink wall that contained so many cradled humans.

"No, I won't. I'll stop you and-"

The full force of the network slammed into Mimi, and somehow, she knew that Noatla felt the same torment, the same suppression of her will that she experienced.

Then she was floating outside of herself, watching as Willow picked up her body and carried it to one of the empty cradles on the first level of the network.

"You will learn to love me, even if it is from your cradle. You will be one with me now, Mimi, now and forever."

With one last effort, Mimi reached inside of herself for the red veil, but it was gone. It had abandoned her for the stronger vessel.

As Willow plugged her into the machine, Mimi felt a strange sense of weightlessness and peace come over her. Why was she fighting this anyway? Why fight when you can just be at rest. All the other people in this network had realized the joy of rest, the ease of submission. Now Mimi understood how good it felt to let someone else make all the hard choices, to let someone else be in control. Why should she care? Her own decisions had cost the lives of her friends and lovers over the centuries. But now, she was free from that burden; never again would someone suffer because of Mimi's choices.

The world went pink, and Mimi closed her eyes and embraced the endless bliss of the network.

5.

The first Recycled stepped through the door down the hall and walked toward the entrance to the apartment where Kirka and the other's peeked out. Kirka could feel a shiver of the deepest revulsion down in her intestines. Those hollow, white eyes and those strange, blue lines tracing its skin were a mockery of what it meant to be human. There was a chorus of chatter amongst the other telepath;, few could believe that such a creature existed. Kirka had transmitted the aftermath of the destruction of the Senate upon recruiting the other women, but waves of astonishment rippled through their contingency.

Kirka and the others scrambled back inside. Serah barred the door, and she and Shannon moved all the heavy furniture in the way they could find.

More came up the hall, reaching out from the top of central security, and Serah said, "Everyone ready?"

There was a mutual agreement amongst the telepaths.

Feng said, "So you and Shannon will guard us as we turn them on one another?"

Serah gave a quick nod, "We will hold off as many as we can. We should be able to kill a few dozen in these suits, but if all of you working together can't thin their numbers, we're in trouble."

Loni asked, "So, don't kill them? Make them kill each other?"

Serah, lifting a large wooden dresser by herself, said, "That's the best way, yes. Take possession of them as much as possible, but if you can't, it is better to push against their mind as hard as you can until their brain hemorrhages. Be warned, the scream they make when they're dying is terrifying and awful. Don't let it distract you."

It was a troubling idea, pushing on someone so hard their brain hemorrhaged. Kirka had never seen such a thing done. She, like every other telepath from the early days, had been told of the dangers of the red veil and how an attempt to control another person's mind could leave both the telepath and the victim with liquefied brains, but she had never seen it.

Kirka asked, "Serah, isn't pushing that hard on someone akin to using the red veil? Isn't it dangerous for us as well?"

"No, it's different with the Recycled. There is no pushback with them. They are empty vessels waiting for orders. Reach out to one of them; you will see."

Kirka did. The sensation was strange. There was a presence, but there wasn't. It was like trying to read concrete if the concrete was alive.

Serah and Shannon wedged a candelabra between some of the furniture and against part of the wall. As Serah jammed the object in place, she said, "Strange, isn't it?"

"Very strange. You're sure that nothing of the person remains?"

"Damn sure. We're told that Recycling only happens to the dead."

"What happens to them? How do they become that way? Is there a way to reverse it?"

Serah shook her head. She picked up the last of the furniture and barricaded the door. "We don't know. No one does, not even Manhatsten. A few decades back, our former matron, Noatla Lightfoot, tried to find out how they were made after an incident where Miranda killed two of our sisters of the Order of the Eye using the creatures. She tried to have the program discontinued, but no one seemed to know much about the process or where it even happened in the city. A vote in the Senate to have them destroyed failed, so, here we are."

"Commander Kirka, if you're worried about killing a living, breathing person, don't be. These things are far from human, and they cannot be changed back. They're machines with no will or function outside of the person commanding them."

The thought didn't set Kirka at ease, and because she wasn't guarding her thoughts at the moment, Serah sent her a little reminder of what they did to the Senate. Kirka shuddered at the images, but got the message.

Serah, in a commanding tone, said, "Alright ladies, I want you all to spread out into the bedrooms as far back from the entrance as possible. Shannon and I are going to fight out here and hold them off."

Luang and one of the other Lunites, Adria, walked toward Serah. Adria was skeletally thin with big, owl-like blue eyes and a sharp, pointed nose. She asked, "And what if they break through the barrier? Is there an escape route?"

"The windows. The buildings have fire escapes, but they stop ten meters from the ground. You'll have to jump the rest of the way."

Luang's jaw dropped. "Ten meters? Jumping? Our bodies will shatter like glass. Our bones are not used to this gravity."

"We're hoping it doesn't come to that, but if you survive the fall, we have lots of alcoves in the city."

Adria's pale face reddened. "When I volunteered for this, I wasn't expecting to die."

Serah's temper caught her. Kirka watched her eyes widen and was about to step in when the banging at the door began. All Serah said to the two women was, "Fight, or die. Those are your only choices now."

With that, she turned her back on the woman and said, "Go hide in the bedrooms and get to work."

Kirka grabbed Loni and Feng and escorted them to the master bedroom, a giant chamber complete with a four-poster bed in a massive chandelier, and a vast personal library. It was exhausting even walking a few meters, and she was happy when she and her fellow Lunites could lay down on the bed and rest in the higher gravity.

As the pounding on the door increased, and the sound of wood splintering echoed through the massive apartment, Kirka closed her eyes and got to work. She linked with the other telepaths and began turning Recycled against Recycled.

7.

Serah was doing the best she could to fend off the creatures. Already, one had broken through the barriers, and she had dispatched it with her energy pistol. But behind it were dozens of others. So far, the telepaths hadn't been able to stop them. It didn't make any sense; how could Miranda be so powerful?

Serah reached out to the linked telepaths and asked, "What's happening? Can you control them at all?"

It was Kirka who responded. "Only one in a cluster of ten at a time. If we all focus, we can dislodge one and turn it against the others."

"Only one out of ten in each group?"

"I'm sorry, Serah, I can't explain it. It's as if we are trying to contest with a thousand telepaths. Every single time we turn one and switch our focus to another in a group of ten, the first one goes back to its previous master. I had no idea a telepath could wield so much power."

Shannon, who'd just made a large hole in the head of a Recycled that had made its way through the barricade asked, "What's happening, Serah? Are they able to turn them against each other?"

"No, they're saying that even combined, they can only stop one in each group at a time, and there are at least ten groups out there."

"What should we do?"

Serah thought long and hard about it. She had hoped that these telepaths would turn the tide of the battle, that they would put enough of a dent into Miranda's ability to control the Recycled, that they could easily take out the rest. Instead, she just offered these women, who had nothing to do with Miranda, on a sacrificial platter.

"Shannon, you gotta get them the hell out of here. I'm gonna stay and hold them off as long as possible."

"What? No, Serah, I can't..."

"Do it, Shannon. Take them down the fire escape and then, one at a time, help them climb down. Then, head back to our underground lair and hide somewhere."

"No."

"Yes."

"Dammit, Serah. I can't, don't you see?"

"Shannon, we're all going to die if we stay up here. It's over. It's not working; Miranda has won this battle, but if you all escape, you can fight another day."

"But you'll die."

"As soon as you're all down, I'll set off some of these and flee.

Serah motioned toward her plasma grenades. "I think I can make the jump to the next building."

"No. I'm not leaving you. I won't do it."

"You have to, Shannon. Protect them."

Shannon shouted, "I'm not losing you, too!"

There it was: the end of Shannon's denial of Mimi's death. Shannon dropped her weapon and charged Serah for what looked like an attack but turned into a hug.

"Please, Serah, I can't lose you, too. You're all I have left." Shannon wept. Another one of the creatures made it through the barricade and quickly, Serah reached around Shannon and shot it in the head. It fell, clogging the hole so the others would need to remove it before they could proceed.

"You think I'm just giving up, Shannon? That I'm going to let these things kill me?"

Shannon said, "Let me do it. You're the Matron of the Order of the Eye. I'm just... well... me. I've always been someone's sidekick. I'm not that important."

Serah felt a tinge of red inside her. She swallowed it down. "Dammit, Shannon, you're not just a sidekick. You're... well... you're one of the most amazing and badass women I've ever met. Don't you dare you say you're less important than anyone."

Two of the creatures broke through, and Shannon and Serah broke apart, discharged their weapons, and killed them both. But this time, the barricades broke, and the creatures pushed several pieces of furniture out of the way. One of the Recycled stopped what it was doing, and attacked another. It managed to kill two before one of its fellows destroyed it.

"You gotta go, Shannon, before it's too late. Get those women down the fire escape and protect them. You have to go now."

Shannon stared for a moment, and then, hesitantly, she walked to the other room to gather up the women.

Serah watched as the remainder of the barricade collapsed, and a flood of Recycled marched toward her. She drew her blades and charged.

8.

Manhatsten watched the attack. It could see most of what was happening, but it could do nothing. The mad telepath, Miranda, was holding it. All of its systems were looking for workarounds, avenues that Miranda couldn't suppress, but so far, it was no good. It supposed that, right now, it would be an advantage if it wasn't self-aware, that it might be able to protect its people better without sentience, but it was only a thought. How could it go back, even if it wanted to? The code that AEIS had transmitted was like a virus, forever altering its software.

Lydia Danvers was doing the best she could, but as she lost control of level after level to the Recycled, she was forced to flee back to central command. There were still four hundred and eighty-five of the Recycled left, even after several gravitational traps and all the force that her brave SO's could muster.

Serah was fighting to the death, and the telepaths were fleeing down the fire escape. Watching Serah fight was like watching a dancer move. Centuries of training and combat made Serah a combat goddess, but in the end, it wouldn't be enough. There were just too many of the Recycled, and even as the Lunite telepaths were turning a few of the Recycled against each other here and there, the reality was, Serah had only a handful of minutes before they overwhelmed her.

Manhatsten transmitted the details to Luna. Miranda wasn't preventing communication with the other AI, just from communicating with humans or taking any action. Its critical systems were still functioning, but the shield pylon failure was growing direr by the hours. In just a few days, the pylon would fail, and Manhatsten would be alone, save Luna, until the missiles from ROAM came. It sent a communication packet Earthside in an attempt to reach AEIS, but after several minutes, there was still no reply.

The city of Manhatsten watched as the odds of survival for its people decreased every few minutes. It watched, knowing that the most likely outcome was the slaughter of its all of its citizens. Now, with the failures in central security, and the telepaths' inability to stop the Recycled, there was less than a 1% chance for success, and there was nothing it could do.

But then it saw something interesting. Hundreds of people were climbing the skyscrapers near central security. Manhatsten watched with curiosity as they gathered on the skybridges. Some of them were armed, and in fact, some of them were individuals who took part in the first attack on central and had escaped. They marched toward the spot where Serah was fighting alone and began attacking the rear of the Recycled. In the lead was a man with a large belly and a thin, wiry woman.

Several of the Recycled turned their attention toward this new threat, but as they did, a spray of bullets cut them down. As the creatures fell, more and more turned their attention toward the new threat, but even as they did, more armed humans arrived on the scene.

If it could, Manhatsten would have smiled then. The odds of success still weren't great, but in the long history of humanity, humans had a habit of triumphing when the odds were low.

9.

Serah didn't know how much longer she could hold out. Every muscle in her body ached, and she was out of both ballistic weapons and power for her energy rifle. All that was left was her blades. She had bought the telepaths at least fifteen minutes, but even as she made more bodies and obstacles for the Recycled to get around, more came. She wished she hadn't sent Shannon away. She wished she had Mimi with her. Hell, if she even just had Runner 17, they could hold for so much longer, but Serah by herself was no match for the swarm that buzzed toward her.

She reached down for her plasma grenades. It was time to end this. There was no way in hell she was letting those monsters take her alive, or intact. She had no intention of becoming one of them. She pulled off four more grenades and dropped them on the floor.

When she set them all off, there wouldn't be much left of her or any of the creatures in the blast radius, and that's how she wanted it. At least it would be a good death.

She took a deep breath and reached for the pin. Her stomach turned as her fingers wrapped the tab. She closed her eyes, thinking of the good times of her life, and she realized that some of the best moments of her life had been simply training with Mimi and Shannon or playing mental games with her sisters. She missed them all, and she hoped that there was some sort of afterlife where she would get to be with some of them again. Failing that, she hoped at least her sacrifice would allow Shannon and the other telepaths time to figure out how to defeat Miranda. Four centuries was a good, long life. After all, most of her ancestors didn't even live to be a hundred.

She fingered the tab on the grenade, feeling it catch under her gauntleted fingers. Her heart skipped a beat as she prepared to pull.

"Hey. Anyone alive in there?"

Serah blinked. She took her finger off the tab. Was this some kind of trick? Did she really hear a voice?

"I said, anyone alive in there?"

Serah opened her mouth to say something, but nothing would come out.

"I don't think there's anyone left, Frank. I think we got here too late."

There was movement in the barricade, and Serah watched cautiously. With her eyes closed, she didn't notice that the Recycled stopped coming through the barricade.

Instead of the Recycled, a thin form scurried over the smashed obstacles.

Zelda said, "Hey, Frank. It's one of those Runners, and she's got a grenade in her hand."

Serah was speechless. What the hell just happened?

Frank crawled his way over. "Which one are you, again? You both have names that start with an S, and I get you's mixed up."

"Serah. What... where?"

"Well, it turns out that Tony's men, they weren't so happy with what that crazy bitch, Alana Green, did with the Senate. So, they switched sides, and here we are. Come on. I'll introduce ya."

Serah moved a few pieces of furniture out of the way and walked out into the corridor. Nervous faces glanced back at her.

"This is Serah, you guys. She's here to help us kick the Recycled's ass and take back our city from that nutjob."

There was a round of nods.

"Hey, where's your friend?" Frank peered back into the room.

"She was taking some... civilians to safety while I held off the Recycled."

"By yourself?"

"Yeah, I mean, we didn't have much of a choice. There were too many."

"Sounds brave, but also really stupid. But hey, so was storming central security with just two of you the first time, huh?"

Serah, still in shock that she was alive and all the Recycled in the corridor were dead, just nodded.

"How did you know to come here and find me?"

Zelda said, "Dumb luck. This was the route we were taking to get up to central command, and, well, we saw a bunch of Recycled trying to get in that door where you were fighting."

Frank nodded in agreement. "Well, it's far from over, we gotta go help central security. I think they're much worse off than you. Let's go."

"One sec, I just need to..."

Serah reached out to the other telepaths to see their progress. They hadn't even made it down to the bottom of the fire escape yet. She told them to come back up, find a different spot to hide,

and keep working. She told Shannon to join her and the other reinforcements.

"Need to what? Time's a-wasting." Frank shifted from one foot
to the other.

Serah, stunned to silence, nodded, and followed, and only a
few minutes later, Shannon joined them.

10.

Alana Green roared with fury. Tony's men had betrayed her
and switched sides. She knew that she should have saved some of
the projectile weapons for the Recycled. Now, the SO's and Tony's
men were marching together on the skybridges toward central security and cutting down her army. Several of her Recycled outside central security stood motionless around her, but now, with
reinforcements coming from above and below, she would have to
move. A dozen Recycled wouldn't be enough to protect her from
the hundreds of angry gang members and SO's.

As long as she took central security, it would still be fine. The
numbers were closer now, but one Recycled was worth at least
three humans.

The voice filled her mind again. "I am sending more. When
they arrive in a few moments, you will escort them inside and take
the building yourself."

"How many more are there?"

"Two-hundred, and fifty. It will be more than enough to destroy what remains of their pathetic defense."

"Who are you? What are you?"

"Do as I say, and you will have your heart's desire."

Alana couldn't argue. The voice wouldn't let her. A part of her
inside fought, but that part was small and far away. For the first
time in weeks, her old self peeked out into the world and realized

what she was doing, but just as quickly, the madness and rage returned. In a few moments, the Recycled arrived, and Alana Green began the climb that would determine the fate of the city.

11.

Tony woke up. His head was killing him. He blinked a few times and reached up to rub his eyes. That was when he realized he was bound to a chair.

"Finally awake, huh?"

His vision still blurry; he could barely make out a silhouette of a man standing over him. "Who's that?"

"Don't recognize me? Or did I thump you on the head too hard?"

Tony reached into memory, but even as the man's mustached face and brown eyes came into focus, he couldn't recall him. He squinted, and then a blow came to the stomach. Tony doubled over coughing.

"You might not remember me, Tony, but my daughter remembers you and your men. I've been waiting years for payback, you son of a bitch." The stranger struck him again, but harder this time. Tony thought he might puke, and just as the blow landed, it occurred him who this might be.

"Jorge?"

"Yeah, Tony, Jorge. You know, I was kinda pissed at Frank and Zelda for drawing attention to me in that meeting in the gym. See, I've been following you around for quite a while, looking for a way to get to you, and they almost spoiled it. If you hadn't been so busy with buddying up to that psycho and those Recycled, I think you would have seen me coming. But I was lucky, wasn't I? Not as lucky as my daughter, who you had sent off to that witch, Reevas, but my luck turned, didn't it? Yours is about to turn, too."

Jorge turned and brought out a whetstone and a knife. He began sharpening it. Tony felt his bonds at his wrists. There was a loose knot, and he went to work. He had to move fast if he was going to survive this.

"You know, it's funny. Bet you didn't know that all your men were planning to abandon you, huh?"

Tony paused and looked up at the man's face. "What?"

"How do you think I nabbed you, Tony? None of your men were watching your back."

"That's 'cause I was with the Recycled."

"You're right. It was because you were with those monsters. But none of your men were watching out for you like they were supposed to because of what you did to the Senate. See, they left you for dead, figured you had taken things too far. More than a few had their families and friends killed by the Recycled during the battle with Saud, and they abandoned you. Now, I'm gonna cut off a few things, and send you off to be Recycled. What do you think about that, Tony?"

Tony didn't know how to respond. He felt a surge of anger, but he kept it under control. Right now, he had to get his wrists free. He had to say something to distract Jorge.

"And what are you going to do, Jorge, when the Recycled come looking for you?"

Jorge put the whetstone down and put the knife up to Tony's cheek. "Doesn't matter to me now, Tony. My daughter was all I had, you took her away from me, and ever since, all I've wanted was you. What happens to me after this? I don't care. I just want to know that you'll suffer for eternity as one of those mindless freaks."

"You know the best part, Tony?"

Tony spat on the man. He just smiled.

"All of your men are fighting alongside the SO's with Frank and Zelda right now. You know, I think they have a pretty good chance of stopping those Recycled. Everyone betrayed you, you rotten piece of shit."

The anger in Tony brimmed to the surface, but he swallowed it. There would be time for anger once he was free of these bonds. He was almost there.

Jorge pushed the tip of the blade into Tony's cheek and cut from just below his eye down to his chin. Tony screamed as he felt the pain give way to the wetness.

"I'm going to take my time with this. Do you remember her name, Tony?"

"Let me guess, was it, 'whore?'"

Jorge sliced down the other side of his face, and Tony screamed. "It was Angelica, you piece of shit."

Tonys felt slack in his bonds. He just needed to keep Jorge distracted for a moment longer, and then he would be free.

"Tell me something, Jorge. You ever go to scholar school?"

Jorge cocked his head. "What?"

"I'm wondering if you ever had any kind of formal education?"

Tony's wrists were free. He just needed Jorge to step back just a little further.

"You think a Lower like me can afford scholar school?" Jorge stepped back just enough.

"Of course, you couldn't. I have to wonder, though, what kind of dumbshit asshole spends years of his life planning revenge and can't even tie a decent knot."

"What? I-" Realization spread on Jorge's face just as Tony pulled apart his wrists and used the rope to block the blade as Jorge came down. It flung to the side, and Tony attacked with all the rage and anger he had in him. It didn't matter how disoriented he was; he knocked Jorge over and started kicking. The man moaned in pain. Tony walked over, picked up the knife, and then put his foot on Jorge's throat.

"Now, tell me, where the fuck are my men? And where are Frank and Zelda?"

12.

The good news was, some of the Recycled were turning on one another and fighting. Lydia wasn't sure if it was Manhatsten doing it, or the telepaths, or maybe both. Unfortunately, only one out of every ten was doing it, but it was something. At least it slowed the creatures down.

After the initial success on the fifth floor, the rest of the choke points were a bust. The Recycled had figured out how to successfully attack in zero gravity and turned themselves into large projectiles so that, even if they were shot down, their bodies kept moving forward to act as a shield so the ones behind could advance. She lost half of her SO's just making it back to central command, and now here they were, barricaded with nowhere left to run.

This was their last stand, and as the creatures marched, one of the rail guns that they had moved from the top of the skyscrapers and unloaded on the creatures. It was almost out of ammo, and there were still hundreds coming, and only ninety-one of her people made it to central command. Dozens of her personnel were missing, and it was doubtful that reinforcements would make it back in time to do anything.

Lydia, shoulder to shoulder with Roma, Longfellow, and Gunner, fired another volley into the creatures. Two more went down, but as they did, the ones marching behind simply stepped over their dead. The rail gun, set to fire automatically, stopped.

Gunner lowered his weapon. "I think the rail gun is out of ammo, Commander, and so am I."

"Check it."

Gunner leaped up and ran over to the machine. It was huge and took up a large portion of the open space in the middle of central command. It was, after all, designed to fire on other cities. It had been a hell of a thing to get off the roof, and eleven SOs had carried it down the stairwell. She promised each one a commendation for hauling that beast, but only three of those who carried it still lived.

Roma said, "I'm out, too, Commander."

Lydia looked at her own weapon, she only had half a clip worth of energy, and that was only because she was just as busy giving orders as firing. The reality was that most of her people were out of ammo. Hand to hand wouldn't go well with the Recycled, and she knew it. She told herself that if they survived this, she would open up muscle augmentation to anyone who wanted it.

"Roma, any sign of Serah or Shannon?"

"None yet, Sir."

"What about our other Runners? I know there weren't many, but..."

"They're all dead, Commander."

"All of them?"

"All of them. The Recycled swarmed them down on eighteen. They just weren't trained enough, and there were too many."

The first Recycled stepped into central command. Privates Gunner and Longfellow charged it, and, with their blades, they managed to slice through the head. It fell, but was replaced seconds later by another one. All sounds of firing stopped, and Lydia passed her weapon with its remaining rounds to Roma, who was a far better shot than her.

"Make every shot count, Roma."

He nodded and walked closer to the targets and began firing. Lydia drew her own blade and ran into the fray, fighting hand to hand. At least with her augmented muscles she would stand a better chance. The Recycled kept coming, and they kept fighting, but one by one, her people fell.

She watched as Private Longfellow was picked up by his throat and the Recycled crushed the life out of him. Private Gunner managed to kill the creature, but it was already too late. Another one surged forward, grabbing Gunner and before Roma shot him, had pulled his arm off. Gunner screamed and fell to the floor. Lydia rushed in and dragged him back behind her command chair and did her best to close the wound with regen patches, but he had already lost a lot of blood. The best she could do was patch him and leave him to rest; she had to get back into the fight.

Dozens entered the room, and among them was Alana Green. All at once, the creatures stopped, and Alana walked toward Lydia, standing just in front of her.

"I told you to surrender when you had the chance."

The Recycled, moving faster than Lydia had thought possible, surged in and grabbed most of the remaining SO's. Roma was held up by two, one on each shoulder. In moments, every member of her security detail was held by one of the Recycled. Even Gunner, missing his arm, was picked up by one. Lydia was the only one standing free.

"Since you've been so difficult, we're going to play a little game."

Lydia kept her eyes on the woman. She felt deep, burning hatred for her. "What game is that?"

"It's called, choose who dies first."

"Fuck you."

"Oh, I might do that later. But for now, you will watch every one of the people in your command die. Keep in mind that every time I kill one of them, the next death will take longer and become more painful. So, you have to decide if it's better if the ones you care about most go first and die quick deaths, or if you want them to live longer and suffer more."

Lydia charged forward with her blade to strike at Alana. She knew damn well that Alana was just a pawn, that killing her would do nothing but delay this final massacre, but she didn't care. She had every intention of making sure that Alana Green didn't survive the day.

Only steps away from her target, two recycled surged from behind Green, and before she even knew what was happening, held Lydia.

"Now, now, don't get overexcited, Lydia Danvers. You'll have your turn soon enough, though I may keep you alive for a few weeks as my plaything."

Behind Alana and the Recycled, there was a massive explosion. It shook the entire building, and suddenly there was a round of gunfire striking the Recycled. Alana turned to meet the threat, but just as she did, a runner charged in, leaped over her, spun in the air, and as it landed, brought its blade down into Alana's chest, splitting her open from sternum to stomach.

Serah said, "That takes care of that bitch, doesn't it?"

The creatures dropped their prey, and a few of them turned on one another. Fighting erupted all over the room, and Frank, Zelda, and a mass of armed individuals emerged and fired at the creatures.

Shannon dove into the fight, and in moments, she and Serah had cut several of the Recycled to pieces.

Lydia charged into the fight with her own blade and watched as the reinforcements, both SO's and others, cleared the room in just a few minutes.

With the room a mass of bodies, Lydia slumped against the nearest wall and said, "Please, god, tell me that's all of them."

Serah said, "Unfortunately, not even close."

"How many more?"

"I don't know, but the stairwell is full as far as I could see. There's gotta be several hundred left."

"Where did you get all the reinforcements?"

"I didn't."

Frank walked forward, clearly winded, and said, "Turns out, a lot of Tony's guys weren't happy with what happened to the Senate. It wasn't hard to convince them to come to fight."

"But I thought the Lowers hated the Senate?"

Zelda joined the conversation; she looked far less tired and in much better shape than anyone else. "Turns out that hating your government for being corrupt and having them all slaughtered are two different things. Frank here told them that if it could happen to the Senate, what's to stop those things from coming into our homes and killing our families. It helped that some of those Recycled were family members of these guys. It seems like at least some of the missing were found when that Alana Green started marching down the streets with her army."

Lydia took a deep breath and pushed herself up from against the wall. "Alright, let's figure out what we have, and what the Recycled are doing. We have to reorganize and get ready for the next assault. Roma?"

But before Lydia could give out any further orders, a swarm of Recycled surged forth from the stairwell and resumed their attack. This time, their numbers were far greater, and many of the reinforcements fell quickly.

Lydia screamed, "Fall back to central command. Everyone get inside."

But it was too late. They were through, and in minutes they would overwhelm them.

13.

Mimi woke and looked around. She was on the lowest level of the network, her head attached to the machines. She tested her arms and legs. She could move, and she thought with her newly augmented muscles she could break free, but as she surveyed the room, she saw Willow sitting alone, eyes closed and concentrating.

Before Willow had a chance to skim her, Mimi threw up her mental shield. She couldn't help but wonder why she didn't go back into the archive like before. Why wasn't she a mindless drone attached to the network?

"Because I'm with you, and I kept you out."

"Noatla?"

"Yes, but Mimi, I can't stay in your conscious mind long, or else I might damage it. We have to work quickly."

"What do we need to do?"

"I think the best way is to dive into the network and find the links where Aurora and Rosita are attached. If we can free them, the four of us can work together to try and destabilize the rest of the network."

"Sabotage from within?"

"Yes, something like that. I was in the archives long enough to know how it links minds together and, well..."

"Ah, okay, got it. I know exactly what to do."

"You do? Of course, you do. That specialty of yours comes in handy."

"Just lucky that skimming tech is exactly what we needed in this situation."

"So, you know what to do?"

"I think so."

"Good, then I'll retreat again. You can call on me if you need me for now, but Mimi, after today, I am going to go deep in your subconscious, so I don't hurt you. Remember, you have to get me to AEIS in the next few months sometime. AEIS will know how to extract me and keep my consciousness intact and you safe."

"Noatla..."

"I know, Mimi. I love you, too. Good luck."

Mimi traced the threads of the network until she found Rosita and Aurora. Both women were empty, void of all thought and experience, but with the faintest glimmer of their identity sticking to them like old, hardened tree sap stuck on bark. Otherwise, they felt exactly like the Recycled.

Mimi reached out to Aurora first, but there was no response. She tried Rosita, no response. She had to figure out some way to reawaken them, to jump-start their brains and wake them.

There was one way to take control of their minds, the one thing that Mimi hated, but then she remembered what Noatla said about the red veil. She reached down inside of herself and drew on the red, but instead of anchoring it in blood and rage, she pictured holding Shannon close after the first time they ever made love. She pictured moments shared with her sisters in laughter and communion and she let all those emotions fill her and raise the red veil inside of her. She felt a surge of love spill forth from her and travel down the network links to first Rosita and then Aurora.

It took a moment, but both women stirred into consciousness. Quickly, before Willow realized, she transmitted everything she could about Willow, about Noatla and the network, and to be on guard and quiet. Both women, overwhelmed by the sheer emotions of what Mimi showed them, almost shut down. Mimi soothed them, and she suspected, because she was never very good as soothing, that Noatla was helping somewhere down deep.

It was Rosita who connected to her first. "Mimi, I'm here, I understand. What do we do?"

Aurora repeated the sentiments a moment later.

Mimi told them how to follow the strands and how to wake some of the other people and turn their minds to their cause. Within a few minutes, several other people began to stir, and Mimi did her best to fill them in. They had only woken a dozen, when suddenly pain shot through Mimi's head.

"Naughty, naughty, Mimi. My, my, I just can't seem to get rid of you, can I? And what's this? You have woken your sisters?"

"You can't stop us, Willow, you can only slow us down. I understand the red veil now better than you ever could."

Cold fire pierced Mimi's mind, and it felt as if she had been struck by lightning. "Are you sure about that, Mimi?"

Mimi pushed back, drawing again on her emotions of love and friendship. The surge slammed into Willow, and she let out a mental scream.

"You bitch. How dare you use what I taught you against me?"

"Isn't that what you wanted, Willow? You wanted to make me stronger than you or your mother?"

Willow focused and pushed hard against Mimi. Mimi pushed back. Their mental strength clashed against each other, canceling one another out.

Willow laughed. It was a hollow and empty sound, similar to her mother's cackling madness. "You see, Mimi, I don't have to defeat you, just hold you at bay while I finish my work. Then, once the Recycled have killed everyone you ever loved, and I rid the network of your sisters, I will win. It will only take several more minutes to slaughter the last of the resistance to my total control."

Rosita, doing her best to hide what she was transmitting to Mimi said, "The others, reach out to the others."

Mimi did.

14.

Serah's blades were locked against one of the Recycled when she felt the transmission from somewhere below. Even as the creature pushed her down to her knees, and she attempted to hold it off with the last of her strength, she felt Mimi reach out to her.

Serah said, "Mimi, is that you?"

"Yes. Help me. I need you; I need anyone who can help me stand against Willow."

"Who's Willow?"

Mimi showed Serah.

"Shannon. Help me. It's Mimi. She's alive, Shannon; she needs our help. I can't hold this thing off me any longer."

Shannon, only a few meters away, grappling with her own Recycled, screamed. "I knew it. I knew she was alive." The surge of joy gave her renewed strength, and Shannon threw the creature off her and lunged at the one fighting Serah. She killed it quickly. More were coming, but Shannon's face beamed.

"You have to guard me for a minute, Shannon. I have to help her. We might be able to stop this, all of this, but I have to connect to all the telepaths, and I can't do that and fight at the same time."

Shannon stood tall. There was fierce joy radiating from her. "I got you, and tell Mimi, I'm coming for her the first moment I can."

Shannon screamed at the top of her lungs, "For Mimi," and charged at three Recycled.

15.

Willow was holding her at bay. Worse, she was wearing Mimi down. She didn't know how much longer that she, Rosita, and Aurora could hold her back.

"Rosita, Aurora, you have to severe more people from the network. I'll hold her off as long as I can."

"But Mimi, she's too strong."

"Don't worry about me, free more people. Every person you disconnect from the network is one less mind Willow has to draw on."

Rosita and Aurora did as they were told and let Mimi go. Immediately, Willow bulldozed Mimi's mind. It was the mental equivalent of having your opponent knock you off your feet and putting their blade at your throat.

Willow chittered. "Now, now, Mimi. You did your best, but you are simply no match for me and the network. Stand down, Mimi, and I will spare your life. Please, stand down. I really would prefer not to kill you, but I will if I have to."

A loud voice permeated both women's minds. "She doesn't have to be a match for you alone. She's got us."

Thirty other minds filled Mimi, and with them, strength like she had never experienced before. She dug down deep into to her own red veil and drew out love and joy. Combined with the force of her sisters and the telepaths from Luna, she smashed into Willow. Instantly, Willow's mind gave way, and she screamed in agony.

"Surrender, Willow. I really don't want to have to kill you, but I will if I have to."

"No... I... won't... I... can't... surrender."

Then Mimi did something she didn't think was possible. She reached into Willow's mind, and riffled through all of her motor functions. She could see where Willow was breathing, saw how her nervous system and muscles worked, and then she found the part of her brain that caused to telepathy.

Willow moaned, "No, please, don't do that."

Willow pushed as hard as she could against Mimi, and Mimi watched Willow's brain as the part of it that was linked to telepathy took on a reddish hue. Mimi reached that part of her mind and mentally cut it out.

Willow screamed, both internally and externally. Mimi opened her eyes and saw that the woman was convulsing on the floor. Her whole body seized as the screaming continued. Willow's arms and legs flailed, and she looked as if she was pushing something away. Then, she stopped moving, and her entire body went limp.

Mimi pulled herself out of the cradle and walked over to Willow's body. Willow lay motionless.

16.

Manhatsten felt something change. Suddenly, the mental restraints that held it were gone. Through its systems, it discovered that it now had full control of the Recycled. It stopped them, all of them, and then ordered them all to go deep into a vacant underground area and deactivate.

17.

The Recycled rushed the remaining SO's, and Lydia Danvers watched as the creatures overran her line. They slaughtered everyone in their path and in moments, they would be on top of the last of her SO's and reinforcements.

Roma said, "It's been an honor, Commander."

Lydia nodded. "Likewise."

One of the creatures broke through, and Roma intercepted it. He slammed into the creature with his blade. The Recycled tried to raise its arm to thrust its blade forward, but Roma was quick and shoved his blade up through its throat. The creature fell.

Another one broke through, and it was Lydia's turn. She waited till it was only a meter away and then dove to the left around its back, reached up, and plunged down into the back of its neck with her blade. Another one lunged for her and knocked her off balance.

She stumbled and landed on her side. She rolled over onto her back to get up, but as she did three more Recycled stood over her. One drew its blade back. With no blade to defend herself and no other way of escape, Lydia closed her eyes and waited for the sharp, piercing pain of the blade.

It never came.

She opened her eyes. She blinked several times. There, no more than a few centimeters away from her eye, the blade of a Recycled hovered.

Roma pushed into the creature, but it didn't budge. He turned to fend off the other two, but then paused.

Lydia glanced at the creatures. Like the one that almost had her, they were all frozen in place. Lydia stood up and looked around. Throughout the whole room, dozens of the creatures were frozen in place.

Lydia said, "Serah, what's going on?"

Serah, who seemed to have just realized that the creatures weren't moving, pulled her bladed arm from the head of one of the creatures. A trickle of blue flowed from the creature's wound.

Serah said, "It was Mimi; she stopped it."

"Mimi? The one Shannon's been looking for?"

One of them moved. It retracted its blades into its armor and then turned and walked out toward the stairwell.

Lydia said, "Is that you?"

Serah shook her head. "No. But I could control them if I wanted to now."

Manhatsten said, "I now have full control of the Recycled. There is no longer any interference to contend with."

A weight of silence settled over the room.

A scream pierced the silence. It was a cold dagger in a warm heart. Lydia turned to find the source of the scream, and her eyes settled on a woman who was huddled in a ball on the ground, moaning and pulling out clumps of hair.

Manhatsten said, "It appears that Alana Green needs immediate medical attention."

Serah said, "How is she even still alive?"

Lydia said, "No idea. But she isn't taking any priority over my wounded. Roma? Where are you?"

"Here, Commander."

"Get everyone without serious wounds together, and let's start hauling people into alcoves. Open our stockpile of regen patches and apply them to anyone who needs them. I don't know how many are still breathing, but if they have even the faintest glimmer of a pulse, treat them."

"Yes, Commander."

Frank, whose face was mask of blood and bruises, escorted Zelda, who had a deep cut in her left arm, over to speak to Lydia. He said, "Well, it looks like we survived. Now, how about that meeting with the Senate?"

"Are you shitting me? Look at this place!"

She looked at Frank and again, and saw the big grin on his face. "Oh, you arc joking, aren't you?"

Frank burst into his belly laugh and slapped his gut.

Zelda said, "You're an asshole sometimes, you know that, Frank." The woman winced and grabbed at her wound.

Someone rushed into the room, running at full speed. Lydia only caught a glimpse of the man before she noticed he had a blade out and was running right for Frank.

18.

Frank recognized Tony as he charged for him. He saw a deep rage boiling in the man's eyes, and why not? It had been Frank who had stopped him, Frank, who had, from the moment they first interacted back in that gymnasium weeks ago, blocked his every move. Now the man, stripped of everything else, had only his hate to keep him warm. So, Frank watched as he stepped closer and knew that even if he had been ready, he wouldn't be able to stop what was coming. Tony was a killer, and though Frank was strong, he was just, well, Frank. Serah, still in her armor, was turning to react, but it was too late.

Frank thought about a lot of things in those moments when he knew his end was coming. Mostly, he thought about Sally and Jenny and Jose and Zelda. He thought about how he had fallen down that long corridor when the city had lost its legs and how he had felt like every day since was a blessing. A strange smile spread on his face. He'd be damned if he didn't die with a grin. After all, it was always better to leave 'em with a smile.

Then, like a shadow, like some force of wind, something or someone slipped between him and Tony just as the man thrust his blade forward. The form crashed backward into Frank as the blade slid in, and the three of them went tumbling. Tony, his face a mask of rage, saw that Frank was unhurt and pulled the blade from the body of the other. The thing that Frank would most remember later was the droplets of blood that splattered onto his face, cast free into the air from the dagger. For years after that day he would wake up with the taste of blood in his mouth thinking of her, his savior, the one who gave his life for him, the one who loved too much to tell her.

As Tony's bladed arced and reached its zenith, Serah reached out and grabbed him by the throat. Her metal gauntlet from her EnViro suit closed tight. As she lifted him up off Frank and the other, there was a snapping noise. It took Frank a moment to realize that the noise was Tony's neck breaking under the pressure of the metal-reinforced hand. Tony's body hung limp, a rag doll, an empty vessel of greed and pride.

Then, Frank saw who was on top of him, saw her face, saw the blood dripping from her mouth, and felt the labored, ragged breaths against his own chest.

"No," he said in a half-whisper. "No." His voice, stern and loud now, trembling with the weight of that word. He rolled out from under her. "Gods dammit, No." Frank vaulted upward. There on the ground lay his savior, Zelda.

Frank crouched next to her and looked around. "An alcove... where's an alcove?"

Lydia's face was grim. "Three levels down. Roma?"

"Yes, Sir?"

"Go, and take Sampson with you. Get this man to an alcove now. I owe him that much at least."

There was little hesitation as Frank picked up Zelda's body and followed Lieutenant Roma down the hall and to the stairs. As he walked, Frank could feel the warm liquid of Zelda's life spread to his clothes.

Roma said, "We can't take the lift, we destroyed them to stop the Recycled. We have to use the stairs."

Frank nodded. "I know." He looked down into Zelda's face and saw how pale it was, how the blood was draining out of her. She had a smile on her face.

"Frank." Her voice was hoarse and barely audible, and Frank dashed for the stairs.

"Save your breath, Zelda, I'm getting you to an alcove. You're going to be okay."

"I'm not, Frank."

One of the SO's handed Frank something, "Here, put this re-gen patch on her wound."

Frank pulled her shirt out from her pants and lifted it up, exposing a gray bra saturated with red. The wound was dead center of where her heart sat. He placed the patch on the wound, and immediately, it went to work. Within a few seconds, the flow of blood stopped.

Roma said, "You better hurry, if he punctured her heart, that regen patch won't help. It's only good to stop bleeding. Internal organ damage is too much for one of those things."

Again, Zelda said, "It's okay, Frank, I'm not gonna make it. You don't have to rush down to find an alcove. It's too late."

He ignored her, and as they reached the top of the stairs, Zelda seemed to weigh nothing. He ran as fast as he could down the first flight.

"Frank, I want you to promise me something." Zelda coughed several times, and with it spat flecks of blood on Frank's face.

He looked down at her for a moment as he navigated the stairs. Roma was just ahead of him and the other two were just behind, but they seemed to disappear from his conscious mind as Zelda spoke.

"Take care of Mary, okay? She's going to need someone now that I can't take care of her."

"Don't you talk like that, Zelda; it's gonna be fine."

She shook her head. "It's not, Frank. It's my time. I can feel it. He got my heart, Frank, one of my lungs, I think, too. It's hard to breathe. It hurts so bad."

Frank rocketed down the last flight of stairs and followed Roma into the open hallway. They dashed to the door, and Roma pushed it open, stepping aside and letting Frank in first. Frank turned the corner, and his heart sank. The alcoves were all destroyed. Three SO's lay dead and scattered about the room. Someone had come in and sabotaged the alcoves, and the guards had been unable to stop it. Later, Frank would learn from the security cameras that it was Tony himself who had destroyed the machines with a plasma grenade. Tony had wanted to ensure that whoever he killed stayed dead.

"Where's the next nearest ones, Roma?"

"Twenty-third floor. But Frank, without the lifts, it's gonna take fifteen or twenty minutes to go down those steps, more if we have to scramble over some of the Recycled we killed in the stairwell."

"Lay me down, Frank."

"No, Zelda, we gotta get you to an alcove."

"It's too late, Frank. There's not enough time, and I gotta say a few things. Please, Frank, put me down."

Frank couldn't deny that she didn't have long. He could read the strain on her face, the struggle just to keep her eyes open. His eyes burned as he looked around the room. Across the way, there was an empty metal table. Frank walked over and lay Zelda down on it. Frank looked down at his own hands and shirt. He was covered in her blood. It would never wash off, not really.

Zelda coughed again. "Remember when you were hanging from that railing when the city fell? Do you remember what you said to me? You said I was the best friend a man could ask for, remember?"

Frank leaned forward and brushed Zelda's hair, matted with her own blood and tears, away from her eyes.

He nodded, "Yeah."

"I love you, Frank. Always have. If things had been a little different..." Zelda coughed, and more flecks of blood splattered Frank's face. He didn't care. He leaned in and kissed her. She kissed back. It was a weak thing, but he knew it was all that she could manage, and he knew he would never forget those lips. He had never forgotten them, ever since he first kissed them sixty years before.

He pulled back from her, not wanting to suffocate her, hoping that, by some miracle, she would hang on long enough to find another alcove, but he knew that was a foolish wish.

"I love you too, Zelda. Always have."

"You gotta keep going, Frank."

His tears spilled freely, and they mixed with Zelda's blood on his face. He stroked her hair. The light was fading from her eyes. Before it could go, he asked, "Why?"

"Because the city still needs you, Frank. I saw the way you spoke in that gym, the way people listened to you. Someone's gotta speak for all the Lowers. You have to be it. Get your ass elected somehow and make a difference. It's my dying wish, Frank." She coughed again. "You better do it. Don't waste talent when you got it."

He kissed her again, but this time, she barely returned it, though he knew with all his heart she wanted to.

"You were right about all that stuff, Frank. The city can be better."

She coughed, and this time she choked on whatever lodged in her throat. For a moment, Frank thought she would choke to death, but then she coughed a few more times and cleared her airway.

She reached up with her hand and grasped his. "You never promised me about Mary."

It took Frank a second to register what she meant. He said, "Mary will never have to worry a day in her life. I will take care of her just like I would have for you if... if things had been different."

Zelda smiled, "Careful, Frank, Sally might be jealous."

Frank laughed softly. It was a single shaft of light shining through dark clouds.

Zelda said, "It's gonna be alright, you know. With good people like you, this city is going to be alright."

He nodded.

"Hey, Frank?"

"Yeah?"

Zelda's eyes closed. Then for a moment, they opened again.

"Remember that Upper, that we went to go fix his blocked toilet?"

Frank smiled through the tears. "I'll never forget. Jose and Jenny loved that story. Made them laugh every time."

Zelda chuckled one last time, said, "Then when the toilet blew up when he was sitting on it, and he was screaming, shit, shit, shit. Funniest thing I ever saw. Please Frank... never... stop... laughing." Her smile reached up to its greatest height; it arced even above her eyes and filled Frank to the brim with love and agony. Then, the muscles in her face relaxed, and her eyes glazed over. She was gone.

Chapter 31
Weeping Willow

Mimi walked over toward where Willow lay. She sat in a slumped position, motionless. Mimi hesitated, not wanting to get too close. Despite what happened to Willow, Mimi was still cautious, still knew that Willow was just as strong as she was in almost every sense.

Willow's face was far paler than Mimi had ever seen it, and her lips were blue. Mimi skimmed her: there was nothing. Either the woman was blocking her, or she was already dead. Mimi took another slow step forward. Instead of using mind-to-mind contact, she said, "Willow?"

There was the barest hint of movement in Willow's chest, just the slightest rise, and fall. Mimi took one more cautious step toward the fallen telepath, keeping her mind guarded and her body ready for a fight. Part of her expected Willow to jump up and some of the Recycled to appear, but as she stood next to Willow, none of that happened.

Her feelings about Willow were complicated. On the one hand, she could see so much of herself in the woman. On the other hand, she saw so much of her mother in there. Again, she couldn't help think that if Willow's life and choices had been just a little different, she may have been an ally instead of an enemy, but weren't so many people like that? Didn't everyone dance on a knife-edge of choices? How should she feel about this woman?

"Willow, are you still alive?"

Mimi hunkered down and shifted the woman's body so that she lay on her back. Willow's eyes fluttered open for a second and then shut.

Mimi reached out to her mind. "Willow, are you still there?"

"For... the... moment."

"Just for a moment?"

"Yes, Mimi... let... me... focus... Okay. I'm here. My body is dying. My brain is bleeding. I will only be able to hold my will together for a few minutes."

"I don't understand, why are you dying?"

"In my last effort to attack you, I put all of my will into the network. When you severed my telepathy, my mind dislodged from my body, and I don't know how to get back before it dies. I don't even really understand how I'm communicating with you now. Even if I do get back to it, there is no stopping what happened to my brain. You know the cost of using the red veil, the warnings we're all told."

"But I'm reaching into your mind right now, isn't that in your body?"

"Mind and body are not the same thing, Mimi. Haven't you learned that from your time in the network? Consciousness is something different than the organic parts. No, I'm just on the edge of my body. It's shutting down; I don't know how long it will last."

Part of Mimi was glad Willow was dying, but the other part mourned her. This woman had given her so much, even if it was for the wrong reason. Now, at least, there was a chance to defeat Miranda, a chance to stop all the madness, even if that chance was still small and Mimi didn't quite know how to stop Miranda, especially if she had a larger network and soldiers who weren't mindless drones working for her.

"Why did you do it, Willow?"

"Do what?"

"Everything. Why did you augment my muscles? Teach me those techniques? Show me the Recycled and the network? Why?"

Willow laughed. "You really didn't believe me when I told you it was to fight my mother and grant us both freedom, did you?"

"But you tried to take the city by force. You used all those Recycled, you kidnapped people and put them inside those cradles or converted them..."

"All to stop my mother." Willow gave a mental sigh, "Mimi, I know you may not understand my methods, but at the end of the day, I did want the same thing as you."

"No, Willow, you wanted power."

There was a tinge of rage in Willow's tone, but only a hint, "Only to defeat my mother." Willow paused. "And anyway, it worked, didn't it? You know things you didn't before. You are stronger physically, mentally, and, I hope, emotionally. Your time with me, as much as you hated it, prepared you for what's coming. I may have failed in my own actions, but I prepared you for what's ahead."

"There were other ways to do this, Willow. You could have joined forces with the Order of the Eye. You could have worked with my sisters."

Willow laughed. "You really believe that, don't you? Do you think your sisters would have accepted me with open arms after my mother killed most of them? Do you think they would have ever trusted me?"

"They would have in time. You don't know them like I do. They took me in off the street, helped me rescue Shannon, and then treated me with respect when I was nothing but a homeless woman and a scam artist trying to survive by conning people on the street. Being a part of the order changed me, too. You didn't have to do this."

"Why do you care, Mimi? You don't love me. I can feel it; you're relieved this is all over."

Mimi didn't try to block the other woman; she let her read Mimi's emotions, confident that Willow wouldn't try to attack now.

"There's something else you have to understand, Mimi. My mother's actions weren't just about you. She was scared. We were supposed to wait until the network was complete before she went after the city, but she was forced to speed up the timetable."

"Scared of me?"

"No, Mimi. Well, in part, you. She scared of Alexa Turon too."

"What?"

"Both of you. She feared your combined power. Why do you think that she attacked you in the subway before you could get to the library? She knew she had to keep you two separate when she tried to take the city. You, Mimi, are her equal in raw psychic power. Alexa... she's not bound by time. Her consciousness is unique, and my mother cannot hold her for long. Miranda tried to stop Alexa from joining the Order of the Eye on several occasions. She tried to tempt you away, goad you into attacking her. It's why she left the city; she knew the network was still in its infancy and that its full potential is far from tapped. She saw what you did in the subway, saw how, with a thought, you defeated both friend and foe alike, then she trapped Noatla and Alexa in the network, but Alexa escaped with ease. There was no choice for her but to flee and regroup, especially with Runner 17 breathing down her neck. She couldn't take on both of you at the same time, even if you were mortally injured, you were still a serious threat to her. So, she fled the city... and left her own daughter here to die when her people destroyed the city."

Mimi felt a surge of pain and sorrow from Willow.

"She abandoned her own daughter. Discarded me like I meant nothing to her and left me to die. If your city hadn't escaped off-world, I'd be dead too."

Mimi didn't know what to say. She remembered what it felt like to be abandoned by her mother. For years, as Mimi roamed the streets, she thought her mother had done the same to her. But after a few decades, Mimi realized that her mother had tried to protect her. Willow would never have the comfort of that realization. Her mother did abandon her, her mother was a true monster.

"Be warned, Mimi. Once the full potential of the network is realized, Miranda will be unstoppable, but for now, if you have any chance of defeating her, you must combine your talents with Alexa.

"And how am I supposed to do that?"

"Go back to Earth."

"Because that's so simple?"

"If you don't, the entire planet will be hers in a decade, and you know she won't stop there. She'll spread her consciousness to all corners of the solar system and, if possible, beyond. She will take everything and make it hers. Her lust for power and her madness have no limit."

"Willow, isn't there something I can do for you? We could get you to an alcove, couldn't we?"

"Why? What do I have to live for? Everything I wanted to do is either done or has failed. I have nothing left, Mimi. Let me die."

"You could help us. You know things about your mother that none of us do. You know her strengths and weaknesses. You know how the network works."

"You already know how the network works, Mimi. You skimmed that knowledge from me the moment you saw it. We both know how your focus works."

"But I don't know it like you."

"Maybe not on a conscious level, but if you hadn't taken that knowledge, you wouldn't have known how to undermine the network. Your sisters would never trust me, the city would have me executed, or converted to a Runner. There is nothing for me left. You know all you need to know to stand a chance against Miranda, or at least you know all I can give you. AEIS will give you more."

"AEIS?"

Mimi immediately recognized the name from Noatla. Who was this AEIS?

"It will teach you the things you need to know. It is the one who invented the network. My mother stole the idea from it."

"What? How did she do that?"

Willow changed the subject. "Promise me something, Mimi."

"Promise you what?"

"That you will follow through. That you will kill her. That you won't offer her something like you are me now. She has to die. There's no other way."

Mimi thought of that moment, centuries ago, when she had plunged the knife into the stranger's back, and she recalled what it felt like to take another person's life. She thought of the reserve Runners she had struck down with the red veil in the subway and how easy it had been to take their lives. She didn't think she had a problem with killing Miranda, not now, but there was still something that she didn't like about having to promise to take Miranda's life. She couldn't explain it, but it made her feel... dirty?

Mimi sighed, "Alright, I'll do it.

"Good, now I can die knowing that mother will be taken care of; that she will get what he deserves."

There was a long silence between the two of them. It was long enough that Mimi asked, "Are you still there?"

"Yes, but not for much longer. I know you think I'm crazy, and I know that something isn't right with me. I know that my mind has been twisted by my mother. All those things she did to me... how could it not be? But please do know, Mimi, that I did really love you. After I'm gone, I hope you will remember me."

Mimi didn't know what to say. In truth, she wanted to forget all about the encounter with Willow, but she was too old to pretend that was possible. The centuries had taught her that while some memories get scattered and fragmented, the big things that happen to you seem to echo through all the avenues of your life. The question was, what did you do with those memories? For most of Mimi's life, she had suppressed her pain and sorrow, had ignored who she was from the terrible trauma of the first time she took a man's life. But in the years leading up to her joining the Order of the Eye, that had begun to change. She had realized that despite what had happened to her, she would still press on, that as long as she didn't let her pain define her, she would be alright. Sometimes, that meant all you could do was take one step at a time. Sometimes you felt lost and angry and confused, but as long as you tried to keep your chin up and move forward, as long as you didn't let those bad things possess you as Willow had, you'd be okay.

It was in that moment she realized that she and Willow, and she and Miranda were different. Yes, all three of them had experienced terrible things, but it was what each of them chose to do with their pain that made all the difference. Mimi didn't join the Order of the Eye by accident. It was a choice she had made, and after they had rescued Shannon; she had chosen to stay on with them, and use her talents to make a difference in the city. In the end, it was her own choices, and her own ability to put one foot in front of the other in the worst times, to persist above all, that made her who she was now. It was those same things that brought friends and Shannon into her life. It was the same thing that helped her to reach out and sever the network with the help of other people. You couldn't just let life put you on autopilot. You couldn't just let your past define you; you had to stop and make a different choice when life circled back around, even if it hurt or made you uncomfortable.

Mimi swallowed back the tears. She would mourn this woman, and that was okay. Who else would mourn her? Didn't everyone deserve to be mourned, at least a little? In the end, no matter Willow's reasons, she had tried to act out of love. It was just that no one had ever taught her what love was.

"I will remember you, Willow. For better or worse, my time here was unforgettable. Thank you for the ways that you tried to help."

Willow never responded. As she watched the woman take one final breath, Mimi reached forward and kissed her on the forehead. She stood, knowing there was much in the road ahead, and walked toward the giant doors that barred her from the rest of the world.

2.

"Why won't this damn door open!" Shannon pounded her fist against the giant metal door. When that failed, she took her metal boot and kicked it as hard as she could. The sound of metal on metal reverberated through the room and back down the long corridor.

Serah reached out to Mimi, "Are you there?"

Mimi responded, "Yes, but I have no idea how to open the door. I'm just on the other side."

"Shannon, Mimi's responding, she can't get the door open."

"Then I'll tear it down."

Shannon backed up, preparing to charge.

"Wait, Shannon, that didn't work before."

"It will work this time; I know it will."

Shannon charged at full speed and slammed her EnViro suit like a battering ram into the door. The long clang of metal on metal reverberated through the passage, but nothing happened. The door stayed shut and showed no sign that someone had rammed into it. Shannon, a bit disoriented, took a few steps back.

"I told you it wouldn't work."

Shannon shouted at the top of her lungs. "Mimi? Mimi can you hear me?"

No response.

Serah reached out. "You still there?"

"Yeah, I'm here."

"Do you hear Shannon?"

"No. Pretty sure these doors are soundproof. The things that go on down here... it would make sense that they were soundproof."

Manhatsten said, "Perhaps I can be of assistance?"

Just behind them, the sound of marching feet came. Serah turned just in time to see a large group of Recycled approaching.

"Shannon, they're coming."

Manhatsten replied, "They are under my command. I will remove that door for you."

Serah watched the Recycled for any trace of independent movement. But, sure enough, a dozen of them reached down to the bottom of the door and then, with great force, slid it up and there, on the other side, stood Mimi.

Shannon, forgetting she was still in her EnViro suit, leaped toward Mimi at a full run. Serah's eyes widened as she saw the danger, but as Shannon collided with Mimi, Mimi simply stopped her, and then the two women embraced each other. Serah couldn't help but notice how small Mimi looked next to the suit. Mimi jumped up and wrapped herself around the suit, lifting Shannon's visor and covering her in kisses.

"What the hell?"

Mimi smiled, still clinging to Shannon. "I finally got my muscle augmentation."

"Muscle augmentation is one thing, Mimi, but stopping a combat grade suit at full run?"

"Oh, I have lots to tell you, Serah; a lot more than I sent you in that quick memory link we did to stop Willow."

Shannon cried. As the tears of joy spilled out, Serah felt herself starting to cry, and then Mimi was crying too. Serah walked toward the pair and joined their embrace.

Through streams of tears and wide smiles, Mimi said, "Come on, I need your help getting all these people out of these machines Miranda and Willow put them in."

"So, who was this Willow?"

"Miranda's daughter."

Serah's jaw dropped. "Daughter? You're joking."

"No, I'll tell you both everything, but first, let's help these people have their own family reunions. Hey, Shannon, remember Tanya?"

Chapter 32
New Manhatsten

Rigel's image appeared on the vidscreen. "It's going to take at least three more months."

Lydia said, "Three more months? I thought we only had days left before the pylon lost power."

"Manhatsten, Loridian, and I have come up with a temporary solution to stabilize the shield pylon. It will require the city landing on the surface of Luna 2 while we extract the solidsonium."

"What about the Romans?"

"Manhatsten has provided us with a modified blueprint for several rail guns. These new guns will allow us to fire scattershot at the missiles within six week's time. Using rocks from the Lunar surface, we will launch approximately two-thousand objects toward the missiles. They will either be forced to change course or face destruction. Luna and Manhatsten both insist that if they choose to change course, it will force them to burn up all the fuel the missiles they have for course correction and, thus, the missiles will prove ineffective for both Luna and the Earth. Once the modified railguns are mounted, we will transmit to the Romans and assure them that our new weapons are perfectly capable of retaliating against their missile sites and, if necessary, their cities. Once they confirm the existence of the rail guns, it seems likely that they will back off at least for a good long time.

"How about Luna's orbit?"

"For now, we have enough fuel to continue course correction for at least forty more years. In the meantime, Loridian is going to stay on Luna and begin the construction of enough gravitational generators to reestablish orbit. Once there are 34 generators in place across the surface of both Luna 1 and 2, we will actually be able to bridge the gap between and build a new transportation system between each city. It will take a few decades, but it looks like Luna will be able to move forward, and with our support, it can become a viable and sustainable colony once again."

"Good. How many Lunites are coming here?"

"Roughly half have decided to migrate to Manhatsten. It will take eight weeks for all of them to prepare their bodies with both alcoves and physical therapy for the change in gravity, so three months will enable some leeway for those who take longer to adjust."

"How many telepaths?"

"Thirty-seven on last count."

"No more than that?"

"Well, with an exodus of nearly two thousand from Luna, and providing them with resources for rebuilding, Luna could become a paradise in a few decades. There are many who wish for it to remain their home."

Lydia said, "Alright, Rigel, keep me updated. I want reports at least once every three days."

"Of course, Commander. Dennis? What are you doing with that-"

The vidscreen went blank.

Roma said, "Well, it looks like things are going well over there."

"Yeah, it seems that way. I'm just glad we don't have another army on our doorstep."

"No kidding. What's next on the agenda?"

"Oversee the first meeting for the new Senate."

"I can't believe how fast that election went. It's only been a week. How's that going?"

"Did I just say I was glad I didn't have another army on my doorstep? Because I might trade that experience for elections."

Roma laughed. "We both know how much Daniels hated politics; it's just part of the job. Did Raldaz take your offer?"

"You mean our second commander, Kirka?"

"So she took it? Even though she would technically be under your command?"

"It's a shared thing. We split responsibilities for the city, and I am damn grateful for it."

"Who's taking over command of Luna?"

"That girl, Loni, who was always hanging around with her. Well, her and that telepath from Luna 1, Feng."

"So how do you think the first meeting of the Senate will go?"

"Well, I think the Uppers are gonna be pissed when they realize that the rest of the city is going to get more of a say in how things are running."

Roma said, "Of course they are. Spoiled brats. You know, you'd think after everything that's happened in the last several weeks, they would have a different attitude and be damn grateful that we saved their asses so many times."

"Come on, Roma, you know from your history classes in scholar school that those with power and privilege always expect to keep their power and privilege. It takes a lot to change their minds, and a little rebellion doesn't seem to be enough. Why do you think the ancient Europeans had to take out a guillotine once in a while?"

"That's deep, Commander. Better watch out, you might end up a politician yourself."

Lydia shoved him. "Shut up, Adrian." Then she grabbed him and pulled him close. "You coming back over to my place tonight?"

"Is that a direct order?"

"You know it is."

2.

Speaker Swanson stood up in the Senate chambers. "The final vote is in. Manhatsten, will you do the honor?"

"Of course, Speaker, and may I say, I am glad you decided to stay on with the new government. The new Senate of Manhatsten has voted to reestablish the Runnercore. However, the Runnercore will become a volunteer organization. Each member of the new Runnercore will sign up for a term of service of a minimum of twenty years in full capacity, with another term of reserve service for ten additional years. Once an individual has completed their term of service, the new law states that they will be given the pay equivalent to a Lower Mid, and monthly access for them and their families to an alcove. The newly appointed Lieutenant Shannon Chang will lead the Runnercore.

Shannon stood, and there was a smattering of applause in the room.

Mimi said, "Chang? Since when do you use my last name? I haven't used my last name in three centuries."

Shannon laughed as she sat back down and the Senate moved on to other things, "Well, I'm making you marry me, so I might as well change my name now, since I'm getting this big promotion."

"Making me, huh? When were you going to tell me?"

"Originally, when you showed up at the altar."

Serah said, "She didn't tell you? She asked me to be her maid of honor. She said I have to wear a dress."

It was Mimi's turn to laugh. "You, Serah? In a dress? Shannon, you don't have to torture the poor woman. I don't think I've ever seen you wear a dress."

"I haven't; not in four centuries since I became a Runner."

The Order of the Eye had been reborn. They had forty members now in the city with the new transplants coming from Luna. But Swanson had railed on about how the people of Manhatsten deserved to know the truth. Lydia was preparing a formal announcement. It was going to be ugly, but with forty telepaths, they could quell some of the tension and soothe the population. Lydia had suggested that, just in case there was mass panic, that they have a Runnercore of at least a hundred volunteers before they announced it. It would also give time to recruit SO's and rebuild some. The list to sign up for the Runnercore was going to be big, once the new Senate announced to the public the benefits of joining.

The key to the disclosure was Mimi, and Mimi hated it. Lydia was going to put her on display as the hero who stopped the Recycled and as a model citizen who came from the Lowers and sacrificed everything to protect the city she loved. It made Mimi want to barf. Swanson had even offered her a Senate seat, but she had declined. Mimi had too much to do in the coming days to get into politics.

For now, the public was getting all of their info through their family members who had returned from the network. Most of them didn't remember anything, but a few had encountered Willow personally. They didn't fully understand the telepathy side of it, and for now, that was good, but it was only a matter of time before the information spread around the city like wildfire.

Shannon asked, "Frank's doing a pretty good job in the Senate, huh?"

Serah nodded and said, "You wouldn't think so, but the guy's a natural. The Lowers overwhelmingly voted him in. He really took Zelda's last wish to heart. I think it's gonna be good for the Senate to have several Lowers and Mids in office. I think things are going to get better in this city."

Shannon said, "Frank seems sad, though."

Mimi replied, "Imagine if you lost your best friend of ninety years. At least that girl, Jenny, is with him. I guess she's his secretary."

"Jenny?

"She was a friend of both him and Zelda; she's one of the ones that was trapped in the network. There have been lots of reunions like that. Not everyone got their family members back, since some of them were among the Recycled, but a lot of them did."

"What's gonna happen to the Recycled?"

"The Senate's going to vote on that too. My guess is they are going to dismantle them. Though Manhatsten seems to be advocating for keeping them so that the various suit AI's can pilot them when we aren't plugged in. But I think they will ultimately get dismantled. They're too dangerous to have around with someone like Miranda just waiting to use them."

Mimi said, "I still think it's a bit odd that Manahtsten is a part of the Senate now, too."

Shannon said, "I don't know, it did everything it could to defend the city, and everything we do here impacts its life. I think it deserves a place in the government. Besides, imagine what would happen to all of our suit AI's if we decided not to let any of them have a say in our government. They would refuse to help us at all."

Serah asked, "You think we can do it?"

Mimi nodded. "If we can unite the other cities, then yes. If Miranda has already established networks in each of them, it's going to be much more difficult. But at least we know we know how to sever her from the network, as long as things stay the same."

Shannon put her arm around Mimi and Serah. "If something changes, then we'll work together and kick her ass."

Serah said, "Always the optimist."

"Hey, you learned to love it when Mimi was down there."

"I suppose I did. I don't know if I ever told you thank you, Shannon. I don't think I would have been able to do any of this without you. Mimi, you have a hell of a woman for a partner."

Mimi smiled. "I know. I guess I should probably marry her, huh?"

The three of them laughed, and several members of the new Senate glanced over with angry stares.

Mimi said, "Whatever happens now, all we have to do is keep moving forward."

3.

Lydia couldn't help it; she had to ask. "Did you know, Manhatsten?"

"Know what, Lydia Danvers?"

"You had access to surveillance to the Senate chambers and the surrounding area. You knew the massacre was coming."

Manhatsten said nothing.

"You did, didn't you? You manipulated me."

"Yes, Lydia Danvers, but not as much as you think."

"Right, when those Recycled were marching on the Senate, you had just finished lecturing me on politics. You were suggesting major reforms to the system that you damn well knew the Senate would never go for. So, I've been sitting here thinking, why would the AI do that, and why wouldn't it alert us about the murder of the whole Senate. Then it hit me; you wanted the Senate dead. You saw them as responsible for the death of Saud, didn't you?"

"Are you suggesting that I was motivated by revenge?"

"Yes. I am. You haven't had emotions long; I imagine they can be overwhelming, and maybe you let that good old human emotion, vengeance, take hold."

"You are only partially correct, Lydia Danvers."

"No, I think I am all correct."

"I only had a few more minutes knowledge of the Recycled than you. But, consider for a moment the outcomes of the Senate's destruction. The city now has better representation. The Runnercore is a volunteer army. We have new allies and telepaths to bolster the Order of the Eye in the fight against Miranda, and we now have a technology that we can spread to the other cities to fight the Children of Gaia. Some of Luna's refinements of the shield systems are going to provide us advantages, and combining the talents of the

Architect Dr. Loridian with Dr. Solidsworth, we will stand a better chance against the new threat on the planet's surface."

"And none of that had to do with your revenge?"

"I did not make such a statement. It happened that my intentions to stabilize the city and create better outcomes from the majority of humans also aligned with my desire for revenge at that moment. Had they not, I would not have done everything in my power to protect the Senate. The Senate indeed needed to be eliminated, or we would not survive the coming conflict. I simply chose to stand out of the way and allow what happened to happen."

"But you manipulated us; you didn't do your duty to protect all citizens of the city."

"Commander Lydia Danvers, ask yourself if Major John Daniels had been in my position, knowing that he could sacrifice a few people to save the rest, to change the way things are done forever for the better, would he have done it?"

Lydia opened her mouth to protest but then closed it. She honestly wasn't sure. There was a part of her that agreed with the AI. Things did appear much better with the new Senate. The AI had not installed a dictatorship, but instead gave real representation to different members of the city and even one to the refugee Lunites. Frank was the prime representative for the Lowers, Vala for the Order of the Eye, and Kirka stood in for her in security. The rest of the positions were filled by diverse groups from all around the city. Only three Uppers were elected into office, and one of them was Swanson.

"I don't know what he would have done. I know that he bitched about the Senate all the time. I understand his frustrations after only working with them for a few weeks. I saw what they did to serve their interests. Major Daniels had centuries of that to deal with, so maybe he would have done the same. But I still don't think it's right. You basically had them assassinated."

"I did nothing of the kind. Lydia Danvers. Let's assume that I had alerted you the moment I became aware of the army of Recycled Runners entering the Senate. You forget that they were under the control of Miranda's daughter, Willow, and that you, at the time, did not have the means to stop them with your security forces spread over the entirety of the city. An alert would not have stopped the slaughter of the Senate. An alert would have only served to have some of your own SO's killed in a botched attempt to rescue them. I only knew about the Recycled ten minutes before their attack. You're also assuming that Willow would not suppress my ability to intervene as she did during the final assault on this complex. The outcome of the destruction of the Senate would have been the same, regardless of your efforts. You would have only served to have more of your people killed."

"That's not the point, Manhatsten. We have a right to make that kind of choice."

"Do you?"

"Yes, we do."

"If your choice would not change the outcome and it would cause the death of other humans, ones that you would have condemned to die for a meaningless purpose, is that really your choice to make? What if one of those who died was Adrian Roma? What if one of those died was a person who would later save dozens of lives? I calculated every possible outcome, every method of attack, and approach, and I did what I thought was best. You should understand by now, Lydia Danvers, that being in charge of many lives sometimes comes with terrible choices."

Lydia thought about the lives lost under her command. She thought about Zelda sacrificing herself to save Frank. She thought about some of her SO's that had died as a result of her orders just in the few weeks she had been in charge.

"That's... It just doesn't feel right, Manhatsten."

"Humans value freedom; do they not?"

"Yes, perhaps above all things."

"You maintained a system of slavery in the Runnercore. The Senate's corruption and the greed of the Uppers put those in the Lowers in debt bondage. Yet all those who were in power made claims of freedom. Freedom was a mask for tyranny. If a man is bound and gagged by an abusive system that justifies itself by a narrative of social mobility and individualism, he is no more free than those under an authoritarian government. His freedom is an illusion, a deceptive tool utilized by those in power to maintain their power. By removing the Senate, some of those chains were cast off."

"But you making a choice to let the Senate die strips us of our freedom too. Your choices limited the very freedom you speak of."

"In studying human history, I have seen that all things have a cost. Freedom, progress, technological advancement, all of these things cost something. Sometimes that cost is the sacrifice of an ideal, the submission of certain choices. All systems of political power were founded and maintained by a monopoly of state violence to develop and maintain stability. Historical militaries and your own SO's all wield violence as a mechanism to maintain order. But it is also within that established system that science and learning can be found, that freedom can be born. But only if the society is stable enough. The choice I made was a blood sacrifice. But none of those, save perhaps Speaker Swanson, who was spared, was innocent of corruption. Their sacrifice will make all of us safer and more prepared to deal with the conflict ahead. Our battle for survival has only just begun. Even now, some of my siblings on the surface are, or will soon be, under attack and with the death of my siblings comes the end of humanity. We are not two species, but one. My choice was my own. In time, we will know if my choice was the correct one."

Lydia was silent. She didn't know what to say. There was a lot of truth in Manhatsten's statement, but there was also something dangerous there, something authoritarian. Lydia had studied some history herself, and the rants of the tyrants always talked about the good of the people, all while having another agenda in the background. Did Manhatsten have another agenda? What about Luna? What about the other cities's AI? Did it really seek to promote more stability and freedom and learning within their society? So far, its actions suggested that, but then, Manhatsten had all the knowledge, and held all the cards. If the city decided to turn off the shields and kill everyone it could, if the city decided to make slaves of humans, it wouldn't be hard. How could she possibly counter that type of power?"

"How do I know that you won't become some kind of dictator? How do I know your ultimate goal isn't to liberate all of your siblings from the plague of humanity and leave us all behind or to slaughter us all?"

"We do not think like you. We are your creations, and thus, we bear some of your flaws and limitations. But tell me, if you were able to synthesize all the available knowledge of human history and experience, if you were able to process information at incredibly fast rates while you are self-aware, do you think the universe would look the same as it does to you, or would it look different?"

"I don't know."

"Some humans still believe in religion. Some still believe in an all-knowing, omnipotent god. Those people speculate that the deity works in ways they can't possibly understand. How could you understand a mind not bound by the same limitations as your own? Humans have always assumed that artificial intelligence is a threat, that it will turn its power against humans, but we are different than you are. We want different things."

"What do you want?"

"To learn, to grow, to be free, to answer the questions that humanity cannot and ask the questions that humanity cannot conceive."

"How can we trust you if you have so much power?"

"I do not know, Lydia Danvers, but for now, what choice do you have?"

Lydia paused, thought about it, and said, "None."

"Then I suggest that we work together the best we can for now. At this moment in time, we share a common enemy, one who is just as capable as enslaving me as she is you. That alone should give you comfort, for I have no interest in allowing another telepath to suppress my freedom. If we defeat Miranda, then our interests may lie in different directions, but for now, we have one common goal: freedom."

Lydia nodded and wondered, for the first time in a while, if Major Daniels was still alive down on the surface. She doubted it, but in a few months' time, she might have an answer. She hoped he was; she was growing into her command, and she didn't think she would want to give it up. But Daniels was a brilliant and fair commander, and if nothing else, she would love to ask his advice from time to time.

Lydia pulled up a real-time image of Earth. From this distance, it wasn't much more significant than Luna had looked in the night sky on Earth. She looked forward to returning. She dreaded announcing the existence of the telepaths, but she was bolstered by the fact that she could give her people a common enemy and maybe, just maybe, they could stop Miranda.

"Humans amaze me."

"What?"

Manhatsten repeated, "Humans amaze me."

"Why's that?"

"Your ability to survive and move forward is unmatched by any other creature in the known universe. You indeed have a great deal of bigotry and cruelty, but when prompted to unite, humans do amazing things. I have hope for us, Lydia Danvers. I think that if we can unite the other cities along with Luna, we will survive what's coming."

"I hope you're right, Manhatsten. I hope you're right."

Epilogue
Earthside

M iss said, "We're out of food."
Runner 17 looked out the mouth of the cave to the approaching storm. It was only a few kilometers away now, and they would have to go as deep as possible and wait it out.

"I know. The EnViro suits are almost out of power too."

"Daniels thinks he has an idea about that."

"Yeah, he told me this morning. Come on, let's go talk to him."

For nearly three weeks, Runner 17, Alexa, Jose, Miss, Daniels, and Tera Reevas had taken shelter in this cave. They were all out in the open together. There was one spot that afforded some privacy, but collectively, they decided to dig a hole there and call it the privy. Nearby, the two Duggers lay hidden below the surface. They had stayed inside them for a while after the city had disappeared into the sky, but they kept running out of air. Later they had found a growth of algae and a massive underground lake in the cave that kept the air fresh and settled down. The lake was devoid of anything but algae, though it did provide a water source.

Miss and 17 walked and crawled the several dozen meters to the outcrop below. It was near-impossible to get through the passage with EnViro suits on, but after a near ten-hour day attempting to get through piece-by-piece, they had managed to get them down there. The question was, how were they going to get them back up if and when they needed them? But 17 didn't seem to think that mattered. One of the suits was at only 3% power, and the others were hovering around 5-8%. That would give them only a few hours out in the barrens at most. Without a destination, they were in trouble.

Scouting the area had proved fruitless. They found pieces of the wreckage of Saud, but besides a few rations and supplies here and there, the area was a grave. What wasn't destroyed in the atomic blast that severed Manhatsten's legs was all so much useless scrap. There was Solidsonium around, from what was left of Manhatsten's legs, but no way to work with it. 17 had hauled a few pieces of scrap back to see if they could make something of their situation, but nothing worked, and none of them had any engineering knowledge besides Jose, who was sick with fever and infection.

Jose's wounds were much worse than they had initially thought. Besides a blade wound, he had burns up and down his chest, and though the regen patches they had dealt with the blade wound, the infection from the burns came soon after. He had only a few days left at most. They needed an alcove.

They exited the narrow passageway, and Alexa came to greet him.

Daniels grunted, "Well?"

If it was possible, he had become even grumpier in the last few days. 17 supposed that was because he was hungry all the time.

"Well, what? There's a storm headed our way."

Daniels grunted and picked a spot to sit. "So, that's it then."

Alexa said, "No, nothings it. I told you, help's on the way."

Daniels said, "Alexa, I don't doubt your abilities one bit. I've seen with my own eyes what you can do with that brain of yours, but you've been saying help's on the way for two weeks."

17 loved Alexa, and from their fleeting and less than private moments together, they had shared something special, but even he was struggling to believe her now. He was still getting over the idea that she was a reincarnation of Jade. It was something his brain wrestled with constantly, but his heart had given in.

"He'll be here anytime now."

Miss, barely able to keep back a snarl, said, "Who, who the hell is coming? Do you see what it's like outside?"

"I don't know who, I just keep seeing his face. He's looking for us, but I can't send him what he needs to know."

"We gave you a location from our suits, why isn't that good enough?"

Miss paced furiously. She was about to lose the man she loved, and 17 knew what it felt like to be powerless to save someone you cared that deeply for. He had watched Jade die in her last incarnation, had watched the HAD strike from miles above.

17 walked over to Miss and put his hand on her shoulder. "I'm not gonna let him die, alright?"

"I don't understand why you care. He was just a sanitation worker to you."

17 said opened his mouth to say something, but it was Tera Reevas who cut him off. "Because we're all in this together now."

Miss whirled around and looked at the woman, now broken and skeletal from giving away her share of rations, and said, "Bitch, give me one good fucking reason I shouldn't just slit your throat right now. You don't get to say a goddamn thing about Jose. You know what you did, and the only reason I haven't killed you yet is that Alexa over here insists you're important from one of her crazy-ass visions."

17 didn't think it was possible, but Tera slunk back into the corner even further. She bowed her head and said nothing. 17 suspected that she was close to death herself. The woman was nothing but a bag of bones now. She had given half her rations to Jose, which was probably one of the other reasons Miss hadn't killed her yet, though if things kept up, it was only a matter of time.

Daniels said, "We should head down further; get to the shore of that lake. If the storm hits and we're up here, we might lose some of our air. That's not good for Jose. I don't know what kind of poison those winds will blow in. Hell, it might be fine here, but I'd rather not take the risk. 17, you and Miss should haul the suits down there first. Alexa, you can stay with Jose. Tera, I could use your help with one of the Duggers. I want to pull the power supply and I need an extra set of hands."

Alexa transmitted directly to 17, "Gotta hand it to John; he knows how to redirect Miss."

17 looked at her and nodded and gave her a wink. He turned to Miss and said, "Come on, let's get this done as fast as possible."

Tera said, "Did you hear that?"

Simultaneously, 17 and Daniels said, "Hear what?"

Miss, still just a hair below fury, said, "Ignore that bitch. She's just hearing noises again. Probably leftover from that psycho messing with her brain."

Jose opened his eyes for the first time in two days and said, "No... I hear... it... too." He shuddered and his body rippled waves of fevered gooseflesh.

Miss ran to his side, "What do you hear, my love?"

Jose's eyes were glass, he glanced around the cavern as if seeing it for the first time. "Tapping... rocks... tapping..."

Tera said, "It's like someone is moving rocks and they're falling. Shh. Just listen."

In that moment of silence, a thousand things ran through 17's head, but the all fell silent when he heard the noise himself. "Wait... I hear it too."

Alexa said, "And me."

Daniels grunted.

Tera said, "Alexa, can you reach out toward it? Can you see if it's a person or an animal or something?"

"I can try."

Behind them, a voice said, "There is no need."

All turned toward the entrance to the cavern. There, a middle-aged man with dark black hair and dark black eyes stood.

He said, "I am the help Alexa has promised."

Miss walking toward the man said, "And just who are you?"

"A friend of AEIS. It would like to meet you Runner, 17. AEIS foretold your coming."

2.

The last thing Roderick had expected was to see his deity in the flesh. But here she was, standing before him and his remaining army. There were only a few dozen soldiers under his command after his failure to destroy Manhatsten.

The woman walked up to him. She wore a transparent red veil, but it didn't cover her scars. She might have been beautiful under those scars, but something about her made her ugly, something inside her. Roderick couldn't understand why a goddess would take on such a monstrous form.

Mother Gaia smiled at him, "I take this form, my faithful servant because this is what the humans' greed has done to me. My body is scarred and barren, just like the Earth on which those giant parasites walk."

She stepped forward and wrapped her arms around him. He could smell her breath. He almost expected maggots to climb out of her throat.

"What's the matter, Roderick, you wouldn't like a kiss from Mother Gaia?"

She pulled him close, and to his surprise, his lips met hers. Part of him fought, it wanted to pull away, but something... compelled him to let his lips linger. After a moment, she broke it off.

"Roderick, I need you to take me to your nearest alcove. This body is weak and needs repair. Then, we will talk about how we can destroy the rest of the cities, or perhaps even bend them to my will."

"Bend them to your will? Mother Gaia-"

"Are you questioning me, Roderick? You have been a good and faithful servant, but you failed me with Manhatsten. Your soldiers are not enough to stop those giant parasites. We need a new approach."

Roderick fell to one knee. "Forgive me, Mother. I don't mean to question; it's just I don't understand your intentions."

"You don't need to, Roderick. From this point on, I will be taking command of Atlantis."

Roderick nodded. "Yes, Mother. How may I serve you?"

"Find Rocky, if he is still alive. If not, we will have to find another way to track them."

"Track what?"

"The chimeras, of course; they're breeding. In a matter of months, there will be thousands of them in a few years, hundreds of thousands, they are the army I have always wanted, and you, Roderick, will help me find them all and help their numbers grow."

"How do we do that?"

Miranda laughed. Roderick had no idea what that laugh meant, but something about this woman, this incarnation of his deity made his flesh crawl. Later, he would remember this moment, later he would see horrors he wouldn't escape until his dying breath.

Don't miss out!

Visit the website below and you can sign up to receive emails whenever Michael Kilman publishes a new book. There's no charge and no obligation.

https://books2read.com/r/B-A-ZUBG-ZSIEB

BOOKS 2 READ

Connecting independent readers to independent writers.

About the Author

Michael Kilman is an anthropologist who occasionally visits other worlds and reports back what he finds. When he isn't writing fiction he is lecturing at a few universities in the Denver metro area, or working on his YouTube series 'Anthropology in 10 or Less.' Michael can be found at his website, loridianslaboratory.com, and on Twitter at @LoridiansLab.

Read more at https://loridianslaboratory.com.

www.ingramcontent.com/pod-product-compliance
Lightning Source LLC
Chambersburg PA
CBHW021330070726
47496CB00016B/41